THE SECRET OF CRUTCHER'S CABIN: A WESTERN TRIO

THE SECRET OF CRUTCHER'S CABIN: A WESTERN TRIO

Walt Coburn

GUNSMOKE

First published 1999 in the US by Five Star

This hardback edition 2012
by AudioGO Ltd
by arrangement with
Golden West Literary Agency

ISBN 978 1 445 88147 8

British Library Cataloguing in Publication Data available.

Printed and bound in Great Britain by
MPG Books Group Limited

TABLE OF CONTENTS

Don of the Black Serape

This short novel first appeared under this same title in *North-West Stories* (3/27) and proved to be one of Walt Coburn's most popular stories. It was subsequently reprinted by Fiction House as "The Maverick Legion" in *Walt Coburn's Action Stories*, a single-issue pulp magazine published in 1931. Fiction House later reprinted the story a third time under the title "Gringo Guns" in *Action Stories* (12/41). This marks its first appearance in book form. It was a story obviously very much inspired by Walt Coburn's experiences as a young man while in Mexico and a member of Pancho Villa's so-called *gringo* battalion.

Part One

Beginning the story as related by
Captain Pançhito de la Vega

I
"El Lobo"

Who are they, you ask?

Ah, *señor,* you are not the first stranger in Dos Palmas to voice that question. Unlike the others, you shall have your answer.

A man to look at twice, eh, that tall one with his beak of

a nose and red coals of eyes, deep set under the silver-crusted sombrero? His erect carriage of a soldier of many years, arms folded under his black serape, he makes a picture. Know you why he holds his arms thus? The reasons number two — two reasons that make the flesh of one creep, I tell you.

The right arm under that serape is a withered and shrunken thing, horrible to the sight. That, *señor*, is one reason.

The other arm, also concealed by the black serape, is strong as woven steel. Its hand grips always a long-bladed knife, whetted to a needle point. And that is the second reason.

His companion, *señor?* Ah, when one speaks the name of the beautiful *Señorita* Magdalena Álvarez, it is as if one breathed a prayer to the *Virgen María*. She is a saint, *señor*, and no less. To see those dark eyes of hers so clouded always with a terrible sorrow, yet no word of reproach or complaint passing from her soft lips, to see her walk across the plaza, as you now see her, her hand touching the withered arm under that black serape, one can scarcely keep from crying out, no?

Eh? *Sí, señor,* he is her father. That skinny old buzzard who walks beside the dove is none other than Don Diego Álvarez — the don of the black serape, the villagers call him. The good people of Dos Palmas offer their prayers toward the fulfillment of two things: one, the death of Don Diego; the other, the happy marriage of *Señorita* Magdalena Álvarez.

A story behind their prayers? *Por Dios, señor,* it is the tale of the most terrible tragedy Dos Palmas has ever witnessed — a story of love and hate, and spilled blood and black vengeance. *Caramba,* how that Álvarez can hate! And the

Señorita Magdalena, an angel held in bondage, must bear the bitterness of him whose heart is black and shriveled.

Dios willing, *señor,* I, Panchito de la Vega, shall some day be given the honor to slit the skinny gullet of that turkey buzzard. He is the most dangerous knife man in all Mexico, that black don, despite the fact that he is blind like the bat in the sunlight. And yet, it is not fear of him that stays my hand. Rather, *señor,* it is because I do not wish to bring further sorrow into the life of the *Señorita* Magdalena.

Perhaps you have heard of an *americano,* by name Major Stephano Doyle? Ha, so I thought — for who in Mexico has not heard of that *yanqui?* It is none other than he who lends assistance, although no one — Don Diego least of all — suspects his presence in the state of Sonora. *Caramba,* how that Diego hates a *yanqui!* For it was another countryman of yours who crossed his iron will, twenty years ago.

They called him El Lobo, here in Mexico — El Lobo, which, in your language means The Wolf. He was well named, that hard-riding, hard-fighting *yanqui.* But more than that, *señor,* he was a man. May his soul rest in peace!

Although it has been twenty years, I recall El Lobo clearly. A tall, straight-backed young man he was who sat his horse with enviable grace. Handsome, too, in a bold, gray-eyed way. They said he had been two years in your West Point when he was expelled for insubordination. I can well believe it, too, for his was a reckless boldness that would gall quickly under discipline.

From bad to more bad went this El Lobo, until, when he rode up to the Álvarez *hacienda,* he was no more than a border renegade who lived from sunrise till sundown nearby the grave of the devil and by virtue of his skill with gun or knife. *Diablo,* what a fellow! And mark you, *señor,* he had the grace and manner of a son of the dons, too. He came from an excellent family, no doubt.

That day, to Don Diego Álvarez, El Lobo and his rag-tag following of border ruffians came as if sent by the *Señor Dios*. Or, at least it so seemed to Don Diego then. Later he swore it was none less than *el diablo* himself who had sent the *yanqui*.

Here in Mexico, *señor,* one has one's enemies. The Álvarez family was beset by many such, for theirs was an arrogance that stung like a whiplash all those beneath their station in life. There on their great *hacienda, señor,* ruled not the laws of Mexico but the supreme monarchy of Álvarez. Inside the thick walls of Don Diego's private prison were devices of torture as cruel and inhuman as those of the Inquisition. He had his own army, well-equipped, trained by his own iron hand. He and his few friends gathered there on Sunday to watch the bullfight.

Don Diego himself acted as matador, and Spain could not produce his equal. He killed his bulls with the same graceful ease that he played his guitar. A don he was and a son of the dons — a *caballero* to quicken the heartbeat of any *señorita* who passed his way. *Diablo,* what a man!

Brave, handsome, cruel — the proudest man in all of Mexico, the most powerful and most feared one, too — that was Don Diego Álvarez. His enemies were as many as the spines on yonder cactus. *Yanquis,* Mexicans, even the Spanish who held big land grants beyond the Álvarez border feared and hated Don Diego. Most of them carried a knife they hoped to sheath in his breast. Those few less bloodthirsty paid for Masses that the *Señor Dios* might work a miracle and remove the devil's curse of the don of the black serape as he was sometimes known.

But always Don Diego killed those who faced him with a

naked blade. Of priests and prayers and such, he would have none about him. And yet, as years went on, knives were still sharpened and prayers were still muttered before the statue of Our Lady of Sorrows at the mission.

Things still stood thus when El Lobo rode boldly through the gate of the *Hacienda* Álvarez, his men following him with fear in their hearts. The great gate clanged behind them, and this El Lobo sat his horse with a smile on his lips and little sparks of excitement dancing in his gray eyes.

I was there and saw.

I saw Don Diego, fresh from his *siesta,* come to the long verandah. I was sitting there, enjoying the cool shade of the late afternoon with a *cigarro* of the brand Don Diego had sent to him direct from Havana. He was, as was his custom, wearing a thin-bladed dress sword — a vanity of Don Diego's who always played at being soldier. He stood stiffly there, scowling from under his black brows at this ragged group of men and their bold leader. I thought I heard him mutter a curse under his breath. Perhaps he feared his enemies had at last come to kill him. *¿Quién sabe? Sabe Dios.*

Then we saw this straight-backed leader whip a blade into the last rays of the sun, swinging it up smartly in a perfect salute.

"*¡Caramba!* A soldier!" I heard Don Diego mutter. "Panchito, thou clown, art thou blind? On thy legs, stupid one!" And out came Don Diego's blade in answering salute.

I wore no sword, albeit I had been fetched from Madrid to teach Don Diego fencing. I still held my old rank of captain of cavalry with pay that was fabulous. I was on my feet by now, *señor,* as became a soldier, and stood beside my master, watching him with inward feelings that were a mingling of respect and amusement, this bit of make-believe — a byplay, *señor,* of silly vanity. Yet half an idiot must see that both these men were brave past the point of valor.

I tell you now that more than twenty years have not dimmed the memory of that moment when this El Lobo faced Don Diego Álvarez. And I had been a military man since I was of age, fought against the *yanquis* in the Spanish-American War, and had seen much of the melodrama of soldiering. I still see those blades, shining like streaks of silver light, reflecting their naked gleam in the eyes of those two men. And, mind you, I did not know as yet the identity of this man with the gray eyes.

"You will do me the honor, *señor,*" I heard Don Diego then call out after the custom of our people, "to alight. My house is yours. I am your servant."

And because he was a don and the son of a don, one felt, when he voiced that bit of formal greeting, he really meant it. Yet, I knew that the man who spoke owned a heart as black as the wing of a buzzard. That was the way of this Don Diego Álvarez.

Caramba, those days and nights that followed! Wine and food and buttoned foils flashing like live things there in the armory. And between these fencing bouts, and talks of war and soldiers from the time of blowguns and broadswords, I learned to know this man whom Mexico called El Lobo. We none of us ever knew him by any other name.

It was not from what this El Lobo said with his lips, *señor,* that I came to know him, for he talked less than a little of himself. But in the evenings, there in the patio, when the music softened and became *muy dulce,* it was my habit to study his face.

It was a sensitive face, *señor* — ever changing with the moods of this outcast who had once been a gentleman and was seeking, among strangers, to forget. What it was he hoped to forget, I never learned, for, as I have told you, the man talked not of himself. But whatever those things were that he sought to drown with wine and danger, they came to haunt him then in the evenings when the guitars throbbed like broken hearts and even Don Diego became quiet and thoughtful.

As a scholar studies a book, *señor,* I studied the face of this El Lobo. And in the end I was given the pitiful satisfaction of knowing that I had not misread what I saw written there in his gray eyes. *Hola,* did it not almost cost me my life in the end?

For there came an end, after many months, months during which El Lobo drew pay as the head of Don Diego's army. May the *Señor Dios* forgive me for my part in what followed! Sometimes I think I became as mad as El Lobo and Don Diego, but to this day I cannot recall the exact cause of that period of utter madness. Youth? The wine? The love of make-believe? The combination of them all. *Sabe Dios.*

To El Lobo it was an opiate to deaden the pain of past regrets. To Don Diego it was the wild dream of a man drunk with the love of power. To me — a man who in a moment of quick temper had shed royal blood at the point of my sword one night in Castile, thus exiling myself from the country I loved — it was excitement. I was a soldier. I could never be anything but a soldier.

And in a way, Don Diego's plan was not an impossible one. Since that day an illiterate *vaquero* has sat on Mexico's throne, and even at that early date we saw the vanishing of the Díaz regime and Mexico's need of a new ruler. But not, *señor,* such a ruler as Don Diego Álvarez would have made. I still believe, *señor,* that another man, given Don Diego's wealth and power, might have slashed his path to the City of Mexico and the dictatorship. Or, had it not been for El Lobo, an Álvarez might have ruled Mexico.

"God has sent you!" Don Diego told this *yanqui* more than a few times when many empty wine bottles stood about, and he became extravagant in his terms of praise of the man who headed his army. "It is no less than the *Señor Dios* who sent you to me."

"Perhaps," said El Lobo one night. "Perhaps you are right."

And not knowing then what lay in his mind, I wondered at the odd look on his face.

That was a week before I came upon the Doña María Álvarez and this *yanqui* in the deep shadow of the garden. Because we saw so little of the wife and household of Don Diego, and because until now the Doña María had not entered into my life, I avoided the mention of her in my telling of this tale. She was sobbing, *señor,* and the arms of the *yanqui* were about her. I tell you, I was startled — startled and hurt, as if stabbed. It is an ugly thing to know of a woman — that she has broken her holy vows of marriage. But I had no time just then to waste in idle thoughts. The voice of the *americano* cut through the velvet of the night like a rapier.

"You are armed, Captain de la Vega?" he asked, putting her gently from him.

"No," I replied, trying to meet his calm with dignity. The thing was distasteful, I assure you. I would have said more, but he cut me short.

"You are a gentleman, Captain de la Vega. I shall trust to your honor as a gentleman to speak to no one about what you have seen, during the moments it will take you to go to the armory and return with two rapiers. After your return I shall assume the responsibility of your silence. I shall kill you, my eavesdropping friend."

Whatever effects I may have had from the wine I had

drunk during the evening were wiped away by the sting of his open hand against my cheek. The Doña María gave a startled little cry and ran in between us.

"By the respect and love that you bear me, *señor,* you must not fight."

"This man has seen too much," said El Lobo stiffly. "He will no doubt judge us wrongly, for his is but a little knowledge and dangerous. There is no other way out of it. He must die."

And he bowed me away before I could hear her frantic plea for my life — providing, of course, that he was the better swordsman, which I then doubted. The slap had been a stiff one, and, as I hastened toward the armory, I was filled with rage. I have told you my temper is one easily fired, no?

I passed Don Diego's room, pausing for a moment on the pretext of borrowing a match from the man who always stood guard there. I was gratified to hear the sound of Don Diego's drunken snoring. It would take a fusillade of cannon to awake him. I lit my cigarette, noting with a certain grim satisfaction that my hands were steady, and went on in quest of the rapiers.

Returning, I found El Lobo waiting in the garden. He was stripped to the waist and wore his riding breeches and boots. I handed him both blades without a word and jerked off my shirt and undershirt. I thought I caught the faint sound of a sighing sob back in the shrubbery, but I had no way of making sure that the Doña María still lingered in the garden. I still recall the heavy odor of a thousand blossoms that filled the soft darkness. It reminded me of Spain and what I had left behind in another such garden. For a moment I almost wished this El Lobo *yanqui* might run me through at the first thrust.

But, *por Dios,* when it came, *señor,* I was at him like a tiger. I had been raised with a blade in my hand. And when our blades met and slithered there in the moonlight, my ears caught the sharp, startled gasp of a woman. I knew now that the Doña María was near, and I tell you, *señor,* I felt sick inside with the wretched business. You see, I had grown fond of that *yanqui* who, even as I, had once been a gentleman. As for the Doña María — well, she was married to an evil man, and all of Sonora loved her as they hated Don Diego. Always, during the three brief years — not brief to her, *Dios* knows — since Don Diego had brought her home as his wife, she had done all in her power to atone for her husband's wickedness. The poor knew her as one knows a saint, *señor.* Moreover, in her sweet, saintly way, she had been kind to me.

Sí, señor, I was sick at heart as El Lobo's point darted at me like the flicking tongue of a snake. In and out, in and out, pressing me against the high adobe wall of the garden until I felt the leaves of a vine that grew against the adobe crush under the bare flesh of my shoulder. That *yanqui* was fighting like ten devils wrapped in one, his face white and set, his gray eyes like slits of naked steel.

Once I thought I heard Doña María praying aloud. For me, for the *yanqui,* for us both, perhaps. *Sabe Dios.* If those words she sobbed formed a prayer, *señor,* then the *Señor Dios* heard, and answered it. El Lobo, lunging like a madman now, tripped on a vine and stumbled forward. I felt the burn of his point against my side, searing the rib like a hot iron. And then his rapier struck the vine-covered wall, snapping the slender blade near the hilt.

From beyond the bushes came the sound of footsteps and the voice of Don Diego. *Caramba,* what a moment! There stood that Spaniard, a statue in the moonlight. Behind him was the telltale lout who had heard the slash of our rapiers and awakened his master. I saw now that Don Diego held a sword in his hand, a cavalry saber. His face was white as parchment, and his eyes were red coals against the pale skin.

I tell you, *señor,* death hung in the blossom-scented air of that garden. The Spanish are a jealous race. This Álvarez, with his black heart and red eyes, was no less than *diablo* himself as he loomed there.

El Lobo, breathing quickly, that broken rapier still in his hand, looked from Don Diego to me. He was cool now, cool and ready and dangerous, for all that he was unarmed. His left fist was clenched, and he had dropped into the position of the boxer. A foe to be reckoned with was that El Lobo.

Still, what chance has one unarmed against two men with steel in their hands? Less than none, *señor,* and the *yanqui* knew it. Yet, he smiled, and waited.

"Don Diego," I said, trying to appear nonchalant, "you are a moment late. The *Señor* El Lobo and I have been deciding a wager."

"With such weapons?" Don Diego spat the words from between bared teeth. He referred, of course, to the rapiers. Wagers are decided with buttoned foils.

"We are soldiers, El Lobo and I," I continued, putting a touch of your *yanqui* swagger into my voice. "Soldiers, not school boys. No game has flavor when it lacks the spice of danger."

"Men fight with such weapons," snarled Don Diego, "for one of two reasons. *Love,* Captain de la Vega, or *honor.*"

He took a step forward, his upper lip curling in a snarl.

"Since neither of you blackguards has a shred of honor left you, I take it that you fought for love. On guard, thou jackal! When I've crucified you against yonder wall, I'll split the *gringo.*"

And he came at me like one insane. From the Doña María, hidden among the heavy-scented blossoms, there came not a sound. Later I learned that she had fainted when she saw her husband.

Santa María, señor, what a situation! For the second time since moonrise I became angry. True, I was a fugitive from my home, an outcast, but I had yet to place a stain upon the name of de la Vega which, though fallen into bad financial straits these past few decades, is a proud and honorable one. This murderer had defiled it, and I vowed to exact payment. I congratulated myself at that moment that I had not taught all of my tricks to Álvarez.

¡Diantre! He was mad to the point of sheer insanity. His saber sliced about my ears, slashing at my blade. He sought to cut me down like a reed. But I had lived too long in cavalry barracks to be slaughtered thus. Besides, I stood in the shadow and my longer blade kept him in the patch of moonlight. Each time I thrust, a red spot appeared on his white flesh. Poof! I could have killed the man a dozen times over. But I had vowed to myself that in my own way I should make Álvarez taste well the steel of de la Vega.

And when I slid from beneath his rushing, paying him each time with a fresh wound, Don Diego had his first taste from the goblet of fear. Ha! Though I should die the next instant, I had avenged the insult to my name and honor. I saw that bodyguard of Don Diego's lunge at El Lobo. From the tail of my eye I perceived the *yanqui* trip the coward, then throttle his thick neck.

Strange as it seems, *señor,* one has one's own reflections at such times — swift thoughts, like rapier thrusts through the brain. I saw our dreams of conquest shattered in bits there on the worn red tiles of the garden walk. Don Diego had been our *patrón*. Now he was our bitterest enemy. The lives of El Lobo, *yanqui* adventurer, and Captain Panchito de la Vega hung by the most slender of threads. Yet, *señor,* I cannot say I was sorry.

I knew not what I fought for, except that the honor of Doña María lay in my sword hand. When the time should come, I would die like a gentleman and a soldier. I was younger, then, *señor,* and the perfume of flowers hung heavily there in the garden. It recalled another garden, another night, and still another such man, arrogant and merciless, who I had killed to shield the honor of the fairest red rose in all Spain.

¡Válgame Dios! I meant to kill Don Diego Álvarez then and there. There are times when I have most bitterly regretted the omission. But even as I was ready to puncture that throat of his, the prayer of a woman stopped the blade.

"Not that, *señor!*" cried the pitiful voice of the Doña María. "For the love that you bear your mother, *el señor capitán,* do not kill him!"

¡Diantre! Is that not the way of the woman, always, *señor?* But recall you the fact that I have told you this Doña María was more saint than human. So I made the grave mistake of sparing the life of the don of the black serape. It was at that moment I was so foolish as to forget the nature of the man I fought. I lowered my point.

You see this scar that runs like a red welt from temple to chin? That is where his saber caught me. *Santa María,* I thought for the moment that I was beheaded. Only that the blow was a glancing one, I assure you, such would have been the case. With one last thrust, *señor,* I put an end to that duel. A bitter end to it!

The right arm of Don Diego lay exposed from shoulder

to wrist. As a surgeon knows where to make the incision for a delicate operation, so did I know where to slit the flesh. When my blade ripped free, I knew that never again would Don Diego Álvarez hold a sword. No surgeon alive could ever splice those severed tendons. Time would shrivel that muscled arm and make of it a shrunken, loathsome thing. I had wiped away the insult to the de la Vegas. I was content.

And it was pleasant, too, to see him grovel before me.

But then, when the battle should have ended, it was scarce begun, *señor.* Don Diego bellowed out, calling his guards. From the barracks came the quick notes of the bugle.

Stupidly I stood there, my left hand pressing together the lips of that saber cut. My only thought then was to go on fighting when the soldiers came.

Not so, El Lobo. He had made his plans, *señor,* and what had occurred there in the garden had been but an interruption of the business of his night — his and Doña María's. His fist knocked Don Diego senseless.

"Quick, Panchito," he whispered, taking my arm. "You are into it now, my brave friend. *Pronto,* man!"

And the three of us, El Lobo dragging one with each hand, stumbled from the garden. I looked across my shoulder and caught a last glimpse of Don Diego lying in a heap, the blood from his arm spilling across the red tiles to soak into the ground where grew the Doña María's favorite white rose bush.

Outside were the followers of El Lobo, waiting with saddled horses. I made out the old Mexican woman who was nurse and governess to the tiny Magdalena, daughter of Don Diego and Doña María, an infant of two years or thereabouts. And before I was aware of what was to come, I was lifted into a saddle, and the crowd of us were racing at breakneck speed across the desert.

I knew we were heading south. They told me that, even when I had fainted from loss of blood, I still held fast to my rapier.

II
"The Passage of Doom"

I have told you, *señor,* how I had come to know El Lobo. During the days that followed, I knew for a fact all that I had read in his eyes before. One may live with other men during an entire lifetime of prosperity and still never get a glimpse into his heart, no? But in times of adversity, when all the emotions of a lifetime are crowded into a few brief hours, men's souls are laid out naked that all may see the heroism or the cowardice written there. That, my friend, is the manner in which I knew that exiled *yanqui.*

Whatever he may have done back in your country, whatever mistakes he had made, what crimes he had committed, I know not, for he never spoke of home. But this much I do know, *señor.* That one whom Mexico called El Lobo — The Wolf — was a man. He and the Doña María loved one another. Both told me that. But by the holy laws of her faith she was bound to Don Diego Álvarez, and, so long as he lived, there could be nothing but a handclasp between them.

Now mark you, *señor,* the *yanqui* was not of her faith. Yet never once did he reproach her or plead with her to break her vows. Rather, he gave his strength to carry on during moments when love must seem greater than ten thousand vows. I tell you, *señor,* there lived a man. I salute his memory.

Our goal was the City of Mexico where the Doña María and her child would be safe among the friends of her dead father. Consider, then, the hopes, the dreams, the future of that man whom we knew as El Lobo. For him, beyond the deliverance of the woman he loved into safe hands, there remained nothing. How many men, *señor,* knowing that, would have gone on as that *yanqui* did, robbed of every dream of happiness that a man holds highest in his heart?

"Panchito," he spoke one evening when only he and I remained beside the dead coals of the campfire, "it is given to few men what God has entrusted into my care. It is as if I were in love with one of His angels. I wonder, my good friend, that He should put such a trust into hands so soiled as mine."

That was the way he looked at it, *señor.* And yet, he once told me, he had no religion.

From Dos Palmas, *señor,* to the City of Mexico is a long journey even in times of peace. Consider, then, such a trip with the army of that devil of a Don Diego at our heels. *¡Caramba!* I saw those men of El Lobo's, men from all stations of life, face those terrible odds, and, wherever one of them fired his last shot, there died a hero. El Lobo was their only god. They gave him the only thing they had left to forfeit — their lives. Of them all, *señor,* not one died the death of a coward.

I saw a *yanqui* Indian, one that civil law branded as a thief, go without water that he might give what splashed in his canteen to the baby Magdalena. I saw men reared amid thievery and crime, men of violence, *señor,* sit about like children at the feet of Doña María, whom they called their "Lady of Sorrows." We knew heat and chill and hunger and thirst. And always, like angry hornets swarming, the soldiers came with Don Diego cursing them on.

The wound in my cheek healed slowly for we had no surgeon with us. No man but suffered in his own way during those endless days. Yet, I cannot recall hearing one word of complaint. And in the mountain pass called Sangre de Christo — which in your language means "Blood of Christ" — where white water boils down cascades of mist and slips out onto the desert to be sucked into the dry sands, we witnessed the passing of the man called El Lobo.

The Sangre de Christo marked the line past which no Álvarez dared set foot. Once through the pass, we were safe. Already we had come upon the federal outpost, and the guard had ridden back to summon the troops from the fort. I cannot forget that morning, *señor,* though I live forever. It stays in my memory like a beautiful picture. I see the trees, their tall tips touched by the first light of sunrise. The waterfalls, with the sun coloring the mist with rainbow tints. Yucca blossoms, tall and straight and white, like nature's flowers set by His hand on an altar of His own making, draped with vestments of ferns and white mist, holy in their unaltered simplicity.

Those are not my words, *señor,* but those of Doña María, for it was she who likened the place to God's altar. Sometimes I wonder if she guessed what was to come. It was there, *señor,* that for the first time her lips touched those of the man she loved.

Don Diego, knowing that he could not cross beyond this place, chose to make one last, desperate attempt to wipe us out. *Dios* knows, he almost succeeded, for he came by a way unknown to us. Out of that peaceful scene he and his men were on us.

"Like rats caught in a trap," whispered El Lobo, "we are thus caught, my good friend."

We crouched in the pitiful shelter of the rocks, our

bodies shielding Doña María and her child. As my rifle barrel grew hot, I prayed to the *Señor Dios*.

"Panchito, my friend," spoke that *yanqui* — and he was smiling, *señor* — "it is to you that I trust the life of the one I love. Take two of the best horses and make a run for it. Do not leave her side, *amigo,* until you have delivered her and her baby into the keeping of the good sisters at the convent in Mexico City."

"It is you, *señor,*" — I did my utmost to protest — "who should escort the Doña María and her child."

"Captain de la Vega," he said, a trifle stiffly, perhaps, to hide what lay like a leaden weight in his heart, "does even a jackal outlaw desert his men at such a time? Besides, they would fight under no other leader, and Don Diego would win in his hellish purpose. The life and honor of Doña María are at stake. I know of no other man to whom I would rather entrust her." And he found my hand and gripped it.

I did as he commanded. There was no other way, *señor.* And while I made ready the horses, I gave them their last moments with one another.

He was holding her in his arms when I returned. She was very brave as she kissed his lips for the last time. Then I placed her and the child on a horse, and we rode away across the chanting waters of the Sangre de Christo. I knew that we should never again see that brave soldier whom we knew as El Lobo.

I looked back once toward the pile of rocks where those men fought to hold the pass. I saw the figure of a man in boots and breeches and white shirt, and the sunlight caught the shining blade in his hand, sending to us the mute farewell of a gentleman of courage.

Señor, perhaps it is better that we never knew his name,

eh? It is well to remember that nameless *americano* as El Lobo, the one who gave his life for the honor and love of a woman. No braver soldier, no truer *caballero* ever lived. I salute his memory.

And so it was I, Captain Panchito de la Vega, who delivered the woman and child into the excellent keeping of the nuns there at the convent. Well do I remember her smile that held the sorrow of all the world in it, as she took my hand in farewell. Her words of thanks still linger in my heart to lighten the burden of a dishonored soldier's existence. Even when the long arm of Don Diego Álvarez reached out and fastened its talons, and I paid heavily for my folly, her words and her smile were as a ray of bright sunshine in my prison cell.

I never saw her again, *señor.* One does not escape from that prison at the Álvarez *hacienda.* But while I paced the stone floor of that sunless cell and fought to keep my health and reason during the interminable months of darkness, I knew she prayed for me, there in her convent of peace and quiet. And after many months of solitary darkness — when the only familiar face I saw was the evil one of Don Diego's as they stretched me out on the rack — I was given my freedom. Ragged, my body covered with the filth of that dungeon, I was thrust out into the glaring sunlight without a word of explanation.

I tremble to think of it.

Blinking, shambling, my beard and hair grown snowy white, I was let loose. I had lost track of the months that had become years, *señor.* I had gone behind those gray walls a strong young *caballero.* I shambled forth a broken wreck of an old man. That was my punishment for crossing the will of the don of the black serape. But, *válgame Dios, señor!* That was but the least of that black-hearted one's revenge.

How was I, a thing scarcely human in my utter misery, to know of that barter in flesh made by that thrice-cursed Álvarez whose existence stains the honor of Spain and Mexico!

An old friend risked his neck to take me into his house and care for me. And only after many weeks had gone by, and I was able to doze in the sunlight of his patio without waking from my sleep screaming at the rats, did anyone talk to me of the terrible thing Don Diego Álvarez had done.

¡Dios! I can scarcely speak of it without losing my senses, *señor.* I wish to be at his skinny throat, ripping the black heart from his carcass and casting it to the buzzards. For, by the blood of my patron saint, *señor,* that Álvarez had prevailed upon those authorities in Mexico to return to him his daughter. Doña María they could not deliver back into his foul hands, for she had long since taken her place among God's angels. To the daughter, almost a woman grown and the living image of her mother in body and soul, Don Diego talked. For all his devilish cruelty, that Álvarez has the smooth tongue of an orator. He told her that her mother had deserted him, that he was old and lonely and needed the love and companionship of his daughter. And finally, as the trump card, he told her of that Captain de la Vega in prison and swore to release me if she would return.

¡Virgen María Santisima! Consider such a barter in human flesh — the life of a young and beautiful girl, *señor,* in exchange for a sack full of vermin-fouled bones such as I! Do you wonder I went mad as a lunatic? With my bare hands I was at that buzzard, right here in the plaza, while yonder band was playing. And he cackled in my face as he cut me free with his knife and kicked me into the dust like a man kicks aside some mangy cur that snaps at his heels. And when the madonna of a daughter knelt beside me, her

tears wetting my torn face, I wept like a child. I had not yet recovered from those years in Don Diego's prison.

Caramba, what a situation, no? And when friends had carried me away, sobbing like a weak fool, I knew that I must wait until a further day to wring that buzzard's neck. It was then that they told me Don Diego had gone blind — blind, *señor,* as the stones.

My sword had withered his right arm. The *Señor Dios* had taken from him the gift of sight. In a measure, justice had overtaken the don of the black serape. To some extent his followers had deserted him since his blindness, but his power remained sinister enough, even so. Only through the eyes of his daughter can he see a world grown black as if he lived in one of his own dungeons. Magdalena Álvarez is a saint, no less.

There is a tale that one day, shortly before her birth, Don Diego came upon the child's mother, Doña María, innocently chatting with some *caballero* of Dos Palmas. Once, some years before, Diego and this Mexican had been rivals for the fickle smile of some dance-hall girl. Of this former soiled page of the black don's life, the Doña María knew less than nothing. Her chat with this Mexican was meaningless and harmless.

Yet, mark you, the blackness of soul of this Diego Álvarez, *señor.* When the baby is born, Don Diego has the child christened Magdalena, after the woman of sin who washed the feet of Christ! Do you not wonder that the *Señor Dios* does not strike such a terrible man dead as he walks across the plaza?

I tell you, *señor,* Magdalena Álvarez is a saint, no less, even as her mother was a saint before her. All of Mexico, including that black don himself, knows that for the truth. And mind you this, *señor,* but for that saint of a daughter of his, Don Diego Álvarez would never see another sunrise.

¡Caramba! Who among men can fathom the reasoning of a woman? That *Señorita* Álvarez vows to take care of her blind father to the end of his days. I tell you, it is no less than madness. The man who can change that order of things shall reap his reward, *señor,* as surely as the *Señor Dios* makes the sun shine. The *Señor Dios* and the town of Dos Palmas will surely reward him who frees yonder dove from the talons of the don of the black serape!

Part Two

Being the continuation of the story now as related by Captain Richard Clarke

I
"Steve Doyle"

"The *Señor Dios* and the town of Dos Palmas will surely reward him who frees yonder dove from the talons of the don of the black serape!"

My eyes were under the spell of the white-haired Spaniard's black ones. This Captain Panchito de la Vega, who twice had staked honor and life for the name of a good woman, was once again about to risk his all for the sake of a third lady. Aye, and I knew he was making a bold play for my assistance in the matter.

I suppose I was flattered. Well, and why not? Understand, this Captain de la Vega was not a man to make quick friends. Moreover, his name was one that conjured up some picturesque doings south of the border. Captain Panchito de la Vega, Spanish gentleman and cavalry officer, picked up and laid down in old Mexico where a fighting man can always get a meal ticket and more than likely face a firing squad in the end. The name was a familiar one along the border. Lately, the rumor had linked Captain de la Vega with one Steve Doyle, Yankee filibuster and soldier of fortune.

There was no doubting the truth of de la Vega's story, for he was not of the lying type. Under those freshly laundered white drill clothes was a lean, muscular body that had been ripped and broken and mended again. His face, hard-bitten by deep lines, was stamped with tragedy. The opaque blackness of his eyes hid a background of heroism and bitter sorrow. The hand that toyed with his wine glass was the lean, sinewy hand of a swordsman, its corded wrist hard as woven steel. The face itself was handsome, dark-featured, with a snowy mustache. No man with half a brain could ever mistake his calling.

I recall a famous canvas of some Spanish cavalier that once hung in the Chicago Art Institute. Panchito de la Vega might have been the model for the artist who had done it.

Of Steve Doyle, I knew quite a bit. I choose the word *knew* advisedly, for there was — and still is — a wealth of rumor regarding Doyle. Around El Paso, where one rubs elbows with Mexican exiles, gunrunners, promoters of revolutions, federal spies, and notorious outlaws, I had heard Steve Doyle discussed more or less freely. It would seem that this swashbuckler had fought under every leader in Mexico.

He had fought for Madero under Pascual Orozco, down in Chihuahua, and attained the rank of lieutenant at Cuidad

Juaréz in 1910. When Madero on that memorable May day refused to carry out the custom of shooting his prisoners, the Yankee was there to take his bow along with the Mexican leader.

When Porfirio Díaz tendered his resignation as dictator of Mexico, Doyle was one of the picturesque soldiers under Huerta who acted as bodyguard for the aged ex-ruler on his protected flight to Vera Cruz. Doyle wore a captain's uniform when he accompanied the triumphant Madero into the City of Mexico. Like Madero, the young Stephen Doyle was a true patriot and was riding with his head in the stars, full of boyish dreams. No doubt he had visions of some day being the head of Mexico's army.

So much for Captain Doyle and his dreams. Madero's rule snapped like a weak bit of steel. With the rebel chief Zapata looming like a black cloud on the horizon, Madero by his well-meaning attempts at policy incurred the displeasure of his followers, and they under Victoriano Huerta turned on him like a wolf pack.

When Madero was made prisoner in his own palace, that courageous young Yankee, Doyle, met the treacherous invaders with a grin on his lips and a single-action .45 in his brown hand. It took five lead slugs and a machete to knock him down. He awoke in prison and was informed that Huerta was dictator of Mexico and that, when his wounds had become healed, he would be shot with his back to an adobe wall. Unlike the kindly Madero, this new dictator did not believe in the sparing of prisoners.

From his prison cell, where he lay swathed in blood-soaked bandages, Doyle witnessed the murder of Madero who in the young American's eyes was the ideal ruler of a harassed country. Huerta's bullets, when they snuffed out the life of Madero, murdered the dreams of the young soldier of fortune.

Six weeks later, when he made his escape, Doyle was a different man. The smile had gone from his unshaven lips, and his eyes were hard as frozen steel. Ragged, a scarecrow of a man, he was picked up by one of Carranza's rebel leaders. Carranza, a Madero man, was now openly in the field against the butcher, Huerta. This rebel chief of Carranza's was none other than Mexico's Robin Hood, the notorious Pancho Villa. Villa, for all his faults, was a general and a judge of human nature. He saw past the rags and filth that covered Doyle. He saw the cold light in the Yankee's gray eyes, the devil-may-care twist to the bearded lips.

"You are for Huerta, *Señor Gringo?*" asked Villa, toying with a .45 as he smiled at the prisoner.

"If I was, I'd deserve shooting. Damn Huerta! If you're one of his bloody followers, pull the trigger!"

Pancho Villa beckoned to an orderly.

Doyle, expecting the adobe wall and a squad of bad-shooting peons, laughed mirthlessly into Villa's face. It was a bold gesture. "What is your name?" came the quick inquiry. "And if you give me a toad-stabber, I'll whip you and your whole damned army!"

"Perhaps," smiled Pancho Villa who possessed a sense of humor — albeit that humor had a habit of assuming a grisly garb. "What rank did you hold under Madero?"

"Captain."

Pancho Villa turned to his orderly.

"*Hombre,* show *Major* Stephano Doyle to a bath and a uniform and a meal. Report for orders in the morning, Major Doyle."

That was how Steve Doyle joined Villa and followed that able general into the battles at Juaréz, Ojinaga, and Torreón. Doyle's cavalry outfit was a motley gathering of every known nationality, but they were fighters, every man of them. College men, cowpunchers, ex-convicts, patriots, and Major Steve Doyle was their fit leader. This was in 1914.

Remember the Tampico trouble when the United States sailors and Marines took over that port? When our gobs and leathernecks gave the natives a sample of Yankee fighting? Back in April, 1914? We lost sixteen men and seventy more were wounded. One hundred and twenty-six Mexicans were killed and over three hundred more wounded after three days of street fighting.

Doyle and two of his Yankee lieutenants were hiding there at the time. Doyle had picked up a wound some days before, and his companions had slipped him into town to smuggle him out to a doctor's care on the first boat. The three of them accounted for all of the Mexicans who tried to break into their hiding place. A Marine sergeant and a squad of his land sailors had to drag away the pile of dead Mexicans to get into the hut where the three men, out of ammunition, waited for the coming of more Mexicans.

"You, inside there!" barked the Marine sergeant. "Hit the deck with your mitts in the air. Come outta that!"

"Come an' get us!" came the challenge from inside.

Then followed a string of good, colorful Yankee profanity that caused the Marines to gasp and lower their guns. Then they grinned at the red-necked sergeant in charge.

"Hey!" bawled the sergeant, "who the hell are you, in there?"

"Right back at you, son," called Doyle weakly from the darkness of the hut. "Who's giving this lead party, anyhow?"

"Uncle Sam," snapped the sergeant. "And a couple nephews."

"Wipe your feet and come in, Uncle," invited Doyle.

And that's how it happened that a Navy doctor fished the bullet from Doyle's thigh at Tampico. In taking the town, they undoubtedly saved the life of that follower of Pancho Villa who would help put Carranza in power some weeks later.

Here, there, and everywhere in Mexico Doyle and his troop popped up and vanished once more to reappear two hundred miles away. Rumor hung some ugly stories on them. One Stephen Doyle was no longer welcome north of the borderline dividing Mexico and the United States. They claimed that Doyle was with Pancho Villa when the Mexican chief slipped into United States territory and attacked Columbus, New Mexico, on the 9th of March, 1916. Villa, a bad enemy but a loyal friend, publicly denied the accusation made against his Yankee major, but who would believe him? Surely not the United States, for Pancho Villa was now an outlaw.

A week after the battle at Columbus, when Pershing himself led his expedition into Mexico after the elusive Villa, that wily rebel who was by now safely hidden in the fastness of his mountains ordered Major Doyle to report to him.

"The time has come, my friend, for us to part," he told Doyle. "You have been a good friend to Pancho Villa . . . who never forgets an insult or a favor. Your Americans are here in Mexico, and *Dios* knows what may happen. Rather than see you desert me because you will not fight your countrymen, I release you. Ask anything of me you wish. If I cannot grant it now, it shall be yours when Pancho Villa is dictator of Mexico."

Pancho Villa had his own dreams. Had he been less handicapped by lack of education and circumstances, those dreams might well have come true, and Major Steve Doyle,

American, might have become head of Mexico's army. But fate, in cheating Villa, burst another bubble for Doyle.

"*Señor* General," Doyle told him that day, "I accept your tendered proposition. When you are dictator of Mexico, I'll ask my reward. Until then, *adiós*. I've had a bellyful of fighting, anyhow. *Adiós,* until we meet again."

They shook hands. Together with the mere handful of men who chose to go with him, Major Doyle rode away that night and, so far as one can learn, vanished utterly. In due time he was reported dead.

Mexico offers no reward for the bleached bones of a dead man. The name of Major Steve Doyle became but a memory smothered in the rush of revolutions, counter-revolutions, and the big news that the United States had declared war on Germany. Steve Doyle, so far as the United States or Mexico was concerned, was dead and forgotten. Perhaps, to make a random shot of a guess, Pancho Villa, who never forgot a friend or an enemy, helped bury the name of Doyle in order that his Yankee friend might be given his chance. Perhaps. Who knows?

I have given you, as nearly as possible, the true history of Steve Doyle up until the time my trail crossed his. Perhaps some of it is wrong. Because of my friendship for the man, I have not set down a black mark against him. I could not and be faithful to a man who once saved my life.

If there was a drop of the craven in Steve Doyle, I never saw it, and I knew him under conditions when a man becomes either one of two things: a hero — or a damned coward. This much I am ready to swear to. The man I knew could not be guilty of the crimes chalked up against Major Stephano Doyle.

It's a queer old world, eh? And through the drab little incidents of a man's existence, the little, monotonous days and nights that are trivial and soon forgotten, there runs the steel thread of fate. On it are hung the big incidents of a man's span of life, one by one, like pepper pods hung on a line to dry. Here and there one, more brilliantly red than the others, stands out. My friend Panchito de la Vega calls it his *Señor Dios*. Steve labels it "fool luck." I call it fate.

How was I to know that night in Dos Palmas, when Captain Panchito de la Vega, a chance acquaintance at the *Cantina* Madrid, unfolded his tale of the don of the black serape — how was I to know what was to come of it?

In the telling of his tale, he had made bare mention of Steve Doyle, the name of a ghost. Nobody in Mexico believed for a minute that Major Steve Doyle, who had been with Villa, had really come back. Those who stood high in border affairs laughed off the name and put the newcomer down as some impostor seeking sensation.

This new Steve Doyle was as tangible as a mirage. No man, when pinned down to cold common sense, could tell you he had seen this newcomer, this ghost of the notorious Major Stephano Doyle, as Villa called him. Rumor runs riot along the border anyhow. Some petty rebel is always trying to press-agent this or that, and those who are wise shrug away such yarns with an air of boredom.

Of late months that rumor of Captain Panchito de la Vega and Steve Doyle had become shopworn and threadbare. Border officials called de la Vega a white-headed old dreamer gone loco. The mention of Doyle was met with an incredulous grin.

Now this soft summer night, when the band played *muy dulce* waltzes, I sat at the same table with Captain de la Vega and heard him mention Steve Doyle. And I believed in the old Spaniard and his story. If there was a deception in this mention of Doyle, I knew it was not on the part of the

Spanish swordsman. The lie was passed automatically to the American.

"Señor," came de la Vega's voice through the dusk that was made yellow by the candles in the *cantina, "salud."* His glass touched mine.

When we had set down our empty glasses, I voiced the question uppermost in my mind.

"Where is this Stephano Doyle?"

But only his faint, enigmatic smile and the opaque blackness of his eyes gave me answer.

I thought of Magdalena Álvarez. In passing, our glances had met and lingered and been torn apart reluctantly. I'd seen some beautiful women, women of every class and several countries, but the face of Magdalena Álvarez was the most beautiful one I had ever seen. It angered me beyond all reason that such a girl should be in any way connected with Major Steve Doyle whose reputation was tainted with black scandal and spattered red with blood.

Understand this much. I had never to my knowledge seen Doyle. I knew him only by reputation, and his reputation was bad. How was I to know that he was the man I'd laid beside in a shell hole over on the Belgian front? I'd known that man by another name. Besides, that night in Dos Palmas I'd come directly from El Paso where they said Major Stephano Doyle was dead. I was naturally of the opinion that this man who called himself Steve Doyle was an impostor, seeking cheap notoriety.

To think of that girl being perhaps in love with a four-flushing, border fortune-hunter was sickening. I suppose I was jealous. Well, why not? I'd lived thirty-four years without losing my head over any woman. Here was one whom I hadn't even spoken to, and I was ready to make a fool of myself over her. And she was in love with a man who was either a blackleg outlaw or the cheap imitation of one.

Those were my thoughts that evening as I sat there with Captain de la Vega. I came to the point bluntly. I've never been a man to quibble.

"You have a purpose in telling me the story of the don of the black serape, Captain," I said a bit sharply. "You seek my aid. Well, you have it, on one condition. If I can win the *Señorita* Álvarez away from this Doyle fellow, I'm going to do it."

I felt my ears go red as I said it. Had my companion been an American, he would have taken this opportunity to haze me a little. This white-haired old Spaniard only smiled as a father might smile at his son. I tell you, de la Vega was a gentleman, and I inwardly thanked him for his thoughtfulness.

With his own hand he refilled our glasses. He was smiling, and his eyes had grown soft as a woman's as our glasses touched. "My son," he said gently, "I am an old man who has seen more than his portion of life. But a short hour ago I saw your eyes meet the eyes of Magdalena Álvarez. It was given to me to behold the beautiful miracle of the birth of love. May the *Señor Dios* bless you both with happiness."

When we had drunk, he leaned across the little table toward me.

"Señor," he said earnestly, "because I perceived that miracle, I told you her story. Otherwise, you should never have heard it from my lips. It is not I or the *Señor* Doyle who seek your aid in this matter. It is that girl who is bound by a foolish vow to the side of her thrice-cursed father."

"She loves Doyle?" I persisted.

"Love? *Señor,* her love is a sleeping thing, unawakened. Her lips have never touched those of any man. She has seen our Stephano only in my company in the shadow of night, and but three times, all told."

He would have said more, and I would have listened with both ears to every word, but an interruption came. Again fate dealt the cards. Fate dealing, and death paying off the bets. It happened quickly enough.

Four Mexicans, feigning drunkenness, careened into our table. It was my first glimpse of the sinister power of the don of the black serape. A few short, explosive words, an upturned table and spilled wine, raw steel flicking like streaks of silver light. I caught a swift glimpse of Captain Panchito as he hurled his chair into the face of the leader, then his knife swept up from his waist, and the man went down. Something hot burned my shoulder, and I swung at a tense, brown jaw. I had to kick the second one, he came so abruptly. I'd have given a lot for a gun just then.

Somewhere a whistle shrilled swift discord above the band music. A moment and the wide plaza swarmed with running men.

Captain Panchito's voice rasped in my ear: "*¡Pronto, señor!*"

We hurried toward some tethered horses, and he shoved bridle reins into my hands. The next moment we were mounted and tearing at a reckless gait into the star-filled night. Other men, perhaps half a dozen, rode with us. The feel of a horse between my legs, the rush of wind in my face, felt strangely invigorating. My shoulder burned, and I felt a bit light-headed. I did not know until later that the Mexican's knife had bitten to the bone.

We were riding a broad trail that permitted three abreast. Captain Panchito rode on my right, another Mexican on the left. Vaguely I saw them bend low at times to miss the raking branches of mesquite and catclaw bushes. Well, I was into the mess and no mistake. I thought of Magdalena

Álvarez and must have laughed for Captain Panchito asked why I was so happy.

Then the trail ahead became suddenly choked with horsemen, and the Mexican on my left shoved a Colt into my hand. "Bend low across your horse, *sènor,*" he called.

I needed no such warning. Crimson streaks spat at us from the blot ahead as we charged them at a run.

It was each man for himself, there in the dark. I thanked God for my good horse and the gun, although I held my fire. I might need the six cartridges later. Meanwhile, it served as an excellent club.

My training at the Army school of equitation was serving me well now. Wrestling on barebacked horses trains a man for such mêlées. I unseated three before I had use for my clubbed gun. It cracked the skull of my fourth enemy just as he tried to knife me.

Then I found myself in the midst of a swarm of knife-swinging riders, and began jerking the trigger of my gun. Still they came, closer every split second. I think I shot three times. There must have been a dozen men trying to get at me. Kicking my feet from the stirrups, I slid to the ground. One hand gripping the saddle horn, I crouched against the side of my rearing, plunging horse. Another horse crushed toward me, but I hung on doggedly, letting my own horse drag me along.

"At 'em, *hombrecitos!*" I heard a voice shout somewhere at the fringe of the mob. "Eat 'em up, troopers! Give 'em hell, babies!"

When that voice grew colorful with good, unvarnished United States cuss words, I bet myself a new hat that I had been wrong and the profane gent was one Steve Doyle. That voice had a familiar ring, too, although at the time I laid it to my excitement.

"Atta babies!" he barked, and the sound of his voice was closer now. "Give 'em hell. Warm your mitts on this, greasers!" A hand grenade exploded in their midst.

Something struck my head, and I went down like a man drowning. The Yankee's voice lulled me into black, humming slumber.

The splash of water in my face awoke me. I thought I was delirious, when I saw the face that bent over me — the face of Sergeant Jim Brophy, the fightingest top kicker in the A. E. F.

"Easy, skipper, take it easy," he was telling me. "You got a biff on the conk. And one of the Black-and-Tans shoved a pig sticker into your off wing."

I tried to roll over. Jim's voice it was and no mistake. I was lying on some blankets spread alongside a fire. Still I was uncertain until his hands gripped my shoulders and forced me back.

"Tell him I'm not goofy, Brophy," I begged him.

"Goofy? Listen, skipper, I was thinkin' the same thing, see? When Panchito and me picks you up for croaked back on the trail, and I struck a match to see if you was one of us or one of Álvarez's crows, I like to passed out. My old skipper down here in this flea-bit country! Strike me deef, dumb, and paralyzed, if I didn't think I was nuts."

He laughed shortly.

"It is well, *señor,* that you are not dead," said Captain Panchito de la Vega, lifting my head and shoving a bottle of tequila against my teeth. "Otherwise, I assure you, Major Stephano Doyle would have killed every Álvarez man in Sonora."

"Major Stephano Doyle?" I choked over the fiery Mexican liquor that went down my throat.

"Meanin' me, Captain Clarke," grinned my former sergeant, Brophy. "I went into your outfit under a phony name. Had to, see? Steve Doyle wasn't liked much in the States."

This time, when I struggled to sit up, he did not shove me back on the blankets.

"You mean you're the Major Steve Doyle who fought with Villa?" I asked. "Doyle of Juaréz, Parral, Ojinaga, and Vera Cruz?"

"I'm the blackguard, skipper. Doyle, the crook that was at Columbus."

"That last is a damn' lie!" I blurted.

"Thanks, skipper."

The bitter twist to his mouth was gone again. He was the easy-smiling, devil-may-care sergeant who had, at the risk of his own life, saved mine at the Argonne push.

II
"Knives in the Night"

Scarlet days stud a man's life, and each one, though separate from the rest, is linked by the steel thread of fate. Those lesser days in between are but an interlude. Captain Panchito de la Vega calls it *Señor Dios*. Steve Doyle says it was fool luck that brought me into Sonora. *¿Quién sabe? Sabe Dios.*

At any rate, there I was, growing a set of hog-bristle whiskers as I soaked beneath the shade of a pepper tree and impatiently waited for the wound in my shoulder to heal. Old Captain Panchito de la Vega and Steve Doyle stayed with me there. Sometimes a silence hung over us like a gray cloud. Each of us had a burden of memories that at times grew heavy. Those are times when it is well to have companions who understand the golden value of silence.

Other times we talked for hours beside the campfire with the stars winking at us from the sky that seemed almost within arm's reach. Our talk was of this and that and everything that three men might talk of under the spell of a Sonora night. Men whose lives lie for the most part on the knees of the gods, men who have, to quote Steve Doyle, pulled the devil's nose and got away with it, are joined by a bond of comradeship that is fraternal in its simplicity and strength. Captain de la Vega, perhaps prompted by the guitar of some Mexican follower as he played and sang for his companions, told us of Spain, intimate little things that he knew Steve and I would bury deep in our treasure chest of memories.

It is a good thing to unburden one's soul to men who listen well and forget when the next morning's sun comes to drag us back to reality. Aye, such friends are rare. Few, indeed, are those to whom one can, in some moment of confidence, lay bare the secrets of his life and in the morning keep that one's friendship. How often do we draw away from someone to whom we have talked too much the night before?

But because the three of us faced a common danger, with odds piled high against us, because our *mañana* might bring death to any or all of us, we talked and forgot — and the next night we talked once more. And when silence came over us and the spark of our cigarettes glowed in the fading firelight, we were content.

But one thing marred the perfection of those evenings for me. That one thing was the girl, Magdalena Álvarez.

Mentally, I compared myself to Steve Doyle. He was a man to quicken the heartbeat of any woman. Tall, splendidly made, his thick, somewhat curly black hair graying at the temples, he was a handsome figure of a man. His boots and breeches were of English make and, though shabby and somewhat soiled, still bore the unmistakable stamp of perfect workmanship. Two heavy cartridge belts sagged about his waist, holsters tied to each thigh. His guns were single-action Colt .45s, white-handled and short-barreled. He wore them well and with the hint of a swagger that was fascinating. His skill with those two guns was little short of miraculous.

Steve was the ideal soldier-lover and no mistake about it. His wit and quick smile and native gallantry offset his lack of education and polish. Somehow his careless speech had a charm about it, too. I could see why Magdalena Álvarez might easily love him, and, damn it all, it made me sick inside.

You see, I'd known Steve when he was Sergeant Jim Brophy of the A. E. F. and his motto was "love 'em and leave 'em." From Camp Lewis to Paris, and back again, my top sergeant had blazed his trail with careless kisses. He and a French colonel had fought a duel in Paris over some dancer. I'd yanked him out of a jam with a British aviator over some London barmaid. I'd seen him shed his chevrons and whip the toughest buck in the outfit, then walk off with a bleached blonde hasher in Hoboken, using her handkerchief to dab at his bleeding nose. All with the same grinning, don't-give-a-damn attitude. I never saw him twice with the same girl.

Compared to Steve, I wasn't much to cause a second look from any woman. I never think of clever things to say until I'm alone in my tent or room. Crowds strike me dumb, and women awe me, as a rule. I'm always conscious of putting my worst foot forward, if you know what I mean. I'm more or less of a wet blanket at a party. My timidity used to be the joke of the officers' mess.

Well, I weighed my chances against Steve's, and it took the heart out of me. Still, before I'd let him play fast and loose with Magdalena Álvarez, I knew I'd make some sort of damn' fool of myself. I used to lie awake, staring at the stars, framing some sort of direct-from-the-shoulder talk to hand him. But never once during the days and nights of my convalescence did he give me the opportunity to bring up the subject. Save in the most matter-of-fact way, the girl's name was never mentioned. I didn't know, of course, that Captain Panchito de la Vega and Steve had discussed her and her father and the situation.

I sensed the fact that Steve did not care to discuss her, and I took his reticence as a certain sign that he was planning another conquest. It was the one thing we should have gone into and didn't. An almost fatal mistake, so it turned out later.

I told myself more than many times that I'd cut in and spoil his game, even at the cost of our friendship. It was not mere jealousy, understand. It was simply the decent thing to do.

Magdalena Álvarez was not a French dancer, a British barmaid, or a Hoboken blonde. My love for her was a matter quite aside and something to be considered later, if the gods were kind. If not, I held it as something too sacred to mention to anyone, even Captain de la Vega. He knew of my love for her. He was well-bred enough not to bring up the subject even by the barest hint. For that I was grateful. You see, I had not yet learned the extent of his understanding, or the loyalty of Major Steve Doyle.

On the twelfth evening after our fight in the plaza at Dos Palmas, Captain de la Vega asked me if I felt fit enough for a night's ride. "It seems, *señor,*" he said, smiling, "that spies have located our hiding place, and that Don Diego's men plan an attack before daybreak. It is the move for which I have been waiting. He does not know, of course, that his spies are also in my employ, and it was my suggestion that they tell the don of the black serape where we are camped."

"When his men attack our camp, we ride to the *Hacienda* Álvarez?" I guessed.

Captain de la Vega nodded. "There will be soldiers there, do not worry. We shall have our midnight meal of fighting, *señor,* against odds, too. *¡Hola!*" He laughed softly at the thought.

"The *Señorita* Álvarez?" I questioned, my voice a bit shaky in spite of my effort to control it. "She will be there?"

"She will be in the garden, *señor,* keeping her first love tryst, if it may be called such."

It was a feeling akin to nausea that came over me. My hands felt clammy, and I went hot and cold by turns. The power of speech seemed to have gone from me, and I turned away without a word. In turning, I saw Captain de la Vega's smile wiped swiftly from his lips. He was hurt or angry, or both. Well, he had nothing on me. I was sick to the toes of my boots. Sick and mad. The thought of her in the garden with Steve Doyle while the rest of us fought for her freedom sent cold shivers of jealousy all over me.

As I sat on my bed, shoving cartridges into my belt loops, I saw the captain and Steve Doyle talking by the horse corral. I was in the shadow, and they did not notice me. Broken bits of words came to me, there in the dusk, and without meaning to eavesdrop I picked them up to add to my bitterness of heart.

"But *señor,*" — it was Captain de la Vega's voice — ". . . unfair to Captain Clarke . . . besides the *Señorita* Magdalena may not. . . ."

Doyle's infectious laugh cut him short. "Leave the skipper to me, see? Him and the little lady. A guy is always grouchy when he's got a wound that's healin' . . . and I've seen love make a guy as touchy as hell . . . when it comes to the handlin' of a frail, little Stevie don't need to study no books."

I'd heard enough — more than enough to make me sick and hurt and fighting mad. I got it that the captain had told Steve of my love for Magdalena Álvarez, and the breach of confidence, together with Steve's attitude, was like the twisting of a dull blade in a man's side. A wave of savage anger swept over me, and I found myself with a gun in my hand.

For the moment I forgot I owed my life to Steve Doyle, that we had gone through hell together, and that he was my friend. I had the feeling that I was being used. A man hates the rôle of a fool, and, besides, I was tortured with jealousy. Love does queer things to a man.

I took a step forward, determined to call for an explanation. I wanted a showdown and was willing to fight, if need be, against all of Mexico to get it. I aimed to declare my hand and back it up with a gun. I'd long since passed the limit of common sense where Magdalena Álvarez was concerned.

But the *Señor Dios,* or fool luck, or fate, or what you will, stepped between me and my two comrades and took the issue out of my hasty hands.

I have said that I stood in the shadow. In the dusk that was half twilight, half night, with piles of pack litter throwing misshapen blots of black shadow on the ground, I suppose I blended nicely into the background. Not so the figure that seemed to rise from the bowels of the earth almost within arm's reach, between me and the horse corral.

It loomed up in the same lantern glow that threw Steve and Panchito clear as cameos against the yellow screen beyond.

Startled by the appearance of this new figure, I halted. I still held my Colts. I saw the man's right arm come slowly back. I caught the glitter of a naked knife held poised for its throw. The sight of it jolted me back to normal, and my brain clicked with that swift mechanism made perfect by months of training. There come many times in the life of a soldier when his very life hangs on his ability to act before he thinks.

In split seconds I grasped the situation: Steve and Panchito silhouetted against the lantern light — the poised blade as it hung ready for its swift flight. I shot from the hip and was given the satisfaction that my ability to use a six-shooter was still as good as ever. My bullet smashed the Mexican's wrist. Before he could run, I brought him down.

I was choking him into submission when Steve and Panchito came up on the run.

Steve pulled a match across his boot and shoved the flame into our faces.

"Knock me purple if it ain't the skipper!" he grunted. "And look who he's holdin', Panchito!"

"*¡Válgame Dios!* Ortega, no?" Panchito said.

"Ortega himself, the don's pet knife-slinger. You copped Diego's right-hand bower, skipper. How come?"

I explained briefly and choked a sputtering corroboration from the man on whose belly I sat. Steve found a flashlight and held it close to the man's writhing face.

"He's all hopped up on marijuana, Panchito. Skipper, you've knocked over Don Diego's chief of staff, pet murderer, and the slickest one of the Álvarez thugs. Likewise, *amigo,* you've saved my life. This baby has had a knife named for me for many years. He and I met when Ortega was Huerta's main gaffer."

We were surrounded by a circle of brown faces now. Steve took charge of Ortega who was mouthing vile curses and trying to spit in Doyle's face. Steve, cold and indifferent under the abuse, snapped a quick order to his men, who dragged away the cursing Ortega.

"About time we rattled our dewclaws, eh, Panchito?" he said, consulting his watch. Panchito nodded.

"Are you all heeled, skipper?" he asked me. "Better pack an extra gat. It'll be all close quarters stuff, see?"

A quick order brought horses. I was astonished at the orderly way they swung into a column of fours out of that seemingly slipshod, undisciplined camp.

"Not such a bad outfit for a bunch of greasers," said Steve, as if reading my thoughts as we rode along at the head of the column, our stirrups touching.

"With all credit to Major Stephano," came from Panchito, who rode on my left.

The short rattle of carbines in volley fire brought me up stiffly, my hand gripping a gun butt. But the cupped flame that lighted Steve's cigarette showed his face indifferently passive.

"Our friend, *Señor* Ortega," he said, pinching out the flame, "will throw no more knives."

It dawned on me that our prisoner had gone down before a firing squad. The shooting of prisoners, as I knew, was customary in Mexico. These fly-by-night armies are not equipped to handle captives. Still, even though the doomed man was a murderer, the thought of a firing squad was unsavory to me. Also it was distasteful to think that an American could become so callused toward such methods of warfare.

Steve's attitude toward me was an odd combination of our old relationship and the present status we now held. I had been his superior officer in France. Here he outranked me in every way. Though he did his best to conceal it, I knew he looked upon me as a rookie. And he was quite right. This guerrilla warfare was a new dish, and I nibbled at it hesitatingly. Steve simply ate it up without bothering to masticate the hard lumps.

I began to understand some things about the man that had puzzled me not a little overseas. At times he had been insubordinate to a marked degree. A one-eyed man could see he was a born leader and only the handicap of his lack of education had kept him from being commissioned. Also he had the annoying habit of breaking every Army regulation with a disregard that was appalling.

I began to understand now. He had been Major Stephano, Villa's pet officer. No wonder he had fretted under our discipline. Recalling some of the dressing-downs I had given him, I marveled that he had not shot me on the spot. But he had taken it at attention, albeit his eyes could not keep from winking. I had wondered at the time and had always entertained the bothersome idea that he was laughing at me inwardly.

Again I thought of Magdalena Álvarez and her love for this man who, if I may coin the phrase, had out-Villaed Villa. I ground my teeth till my jaws ached.

One thought came to comfort me as we rode along into the night. I had saved Steve Doyle's life, even as he had once saved mine. Our score was even. Each man for himself and the best man win.

He was to meet Magdalena in the garden, eh? Well, I'd be somewhere in that garden myself. I occupied my fevered brain with the composition of the love speech I'd make to that girl who had won my heart, head, and gun with one lingering glance.

Riding there on my left, Captain de la Vega hummed softly to himself. Some Spanish song, a love song, so I judged. No doubt, his memories were in it; no doubt, he had spanned a score or more years, and an ocean to boot, and was once more riding as rides the cavalier.

Steve had fallen silent. He rode, so I perceived in the half light of a rising moon, with his head lowered in thought. Hardly the attitude of a lover who soon is to meet the woman of his dreams. Still, a man who has often loved and ridden away must, after a time, become a bit weary of the game. Anyhow, love doesn't work the same way with every man. As in this Mexican war game, I was a rank greenhorn in comparison to Major Doyle when it came to making love. How could such a rookie as I interpret the signs of love in another man?

Oh, well, it was a lover's night, anyhow. I had my plans and was set to brave hell, high water, and gunfire to win the woman I loved. I'd do it fairly, too, damn it all.

Steve dropped a little behind to pass back some order. A long catclaw limb raked me painfully across the face, and I swore softly. The sound brought Captain de la Vega back from his land of rapiers and serenades.

"You are ill, *señor?*" came his anxious inquiry.

"Ill?" I chuckled. "Man, I feel like a million dollars."

"That is good, *señor.* One needs to feel like that million dollars when one passes beyond the gateway of the don of the black serape," he added dryly.

A horseman loomed suddenly on the trail ahead. Captain de la Vega called a quiet command. "Who comes?"

The horseman halted. "Enrique!" he answered the challenge.

"Advance, Enrique, and give the password." I knew Captain de la Vega's gun was covering him.

"María," the horseman called softly. That was the countersign of the night.

Major Doyle questioned him with swift efficiency. A few quick commands passed down the column, then we swung from the main trail, and like some trick of magic our cavalry, like so many quail, was hidden in the brush.

With Steve and Panchito I rode for a few minutes, then dismounted.

"Take care your horse doesn't nicker, skipper," said Steve in a whisper. "We're lettin' the don's outfit slip past, see."

We must have stayed there an hour. Unaccustomed to the ways of the desert, I heard no sound of their passing. Steve and Panchito, however, by some uncanny sense timed the passing of the Álvarez column. They gave them ample time to ride on past earshot, allowed for a band of straggling rear guards, then swung once more into the saddle. Like the covey of quail, gathered by a low-pitched whistle, we once more filled the broad trail, the column moving with a surprising lack of noise.

Again Panchito hummed softly. Once more Steve rode with lowered head buried in thought.

But even lovers' dreams must end. The crash of a carbine ripped the night. Then, like Roman candles on the Fourth of July, crimson streaks flashed across the trail. A man screamed in agony.

"That damned Enrique!" I heard Steve bark, "double-crossed us."

Then he wheeled his horse and bellowed sharp orders. I was alongside him. Behind me came Panchito, swearing or praying, I knew not which.

The men were in a panic, and Steve was doing his best to calm them. That carbine fire from the brush that flanked the trail was mowing them down fast.

"Into the brush, then!" bellowed Steve. "Hand pick 'em and get 'em! I'll kill the first man that runs. Ah! Enrique!" He jerked a man from his saddle. "Look, *hombrecitos!*" In his arms he held aloft the kicking figure of the man. "Look you! The traitor, men!"

With splendid disregard for the flying bullets, Steve held the man aloft with the ease of a strong man in a vaudeville act.

"Like this," he cried, when they looked in spite of their fright, "like this does Major Stephano treat such dogs!"

With a swift downward movement, he dropped the man across his saddle horn. The sickening snap of the poor devil's back and a scream pierced through the crack of guns. Doyle flung the broken, senseless body under the feet of the rearing horses.

Sick with horror, I shut my eyes. I'd been within a few feet of Doyle when he did the thing and got the full jolt of the shock.

"¡Pronto, señor!"

Dimly, as a voice calling through some horrible nightmare, I heard Panchito and felt the pull of his hand.

"Por Dios, señor," he croaked at me, "while there is a way ahead, come! It is for her! For Magdalena! *Dios,* make haste!"

And when I sat stupidly, he jerked the reins from my hand and dragged my horse after him. I lost sight of Doyle as he spurred his horse for the brush.

"For Magdalena! For Magdalena!" Old Panchito kept telling me that as a man might talk when arousing someone from an anesthetic. I suppose I must have made a stupid picture with each hand filled with a gun, yet not firing a shot. That god who looks out for children, drunken men, and fools was riding with me, although the lead droned like a swarm of hornets above our heads as Panchito led the way along the ambushed trail.

"Hold on!" I called. "We can't quit like this."

Even if Steve Doyle was a barbarian fighter, I wasn't going to leave him. We'd been buddies, and we still were bound by the ties of comradeship. When I jerked the bridle reins from the old Spaniard and swung my horse back into the thick of it, I heard him groan out something about loco *yanquis.* But the old rascal, nevertheless, charged with me, stirrup to stirrup, as we shot ourselves a path through the mob that crouched there, firing at us in desperation.

I knew their breed. They'd stand their ground till their carbine magazines were pumped dry, but they lacked the morale and nerve to take the gaff while they reloaded. Steve was counting on that, too. I could hear him calling out orders, shouting derision at Don Diego's jackals, laughing, even singing. And his men, rallying from that first shock of withering gunfire, were likewise yelling. Steve knew his stuff and no mistake.

Panchito, swinging a heavy cavalry saber, fought like he loved it. He had lost his hat, and his silver hair looked like snow in the moonlight. Steve appeared from somewhere, coolly shoving fresh shells into his .45.

"Hey, skipper!"

He was looking about for me with that grim desperation of a mother who owns a child that is forever getting out of sight. He'd been like that in France.

"Hey, skipper!" he bawled, taking a snapshot at a running Mexican. "Where the hell's the skipper?" He'd located Panchito. "Thought you guys was in the clear?"

"*Dios,* Stephano, the man would not run!"

I heard Steve chuckle. Then I called out and shoved my horse toward them. The firing had dwindled to a half-hearted, random exchange of shots. The thud of running horses could be heard. Brush cracked. A bugle warbled liquidly.

"Hurt, Cap?" called Steve anxiously.

"No," I told him. Confound the man for his solicitude. I was over age and able to handle myself. But he just chuckled at the shortness of my reply.

"How you fixed, Panchito?" he asked.

"*'Stá bueno,*" smiled the Spaniard, cleaning his saber on the mane of his dancing horse.

"You darned old butcher," chided Steve. "Well, let's get outta here. The boys are already on the way. We gotta shake our legs, too. These babies may flank us when they've got their second wind. They'll snap at our heels all the way. Ten miles to go, see, and maybe another gang of highbinders layin' for us along the trail. Damn that Enrique for a double-crossin' dog."

He cursed the luckless Enrique till my blood ran cold.

"It is bad luck, *señor,*" put in Panchito gravely, "so to curse a dead man."

"Dead man!" snorted Steve. "Enrique's no more dead than we are. That was one of Diego's lieutenants I busted."

"I don't get you," I cut in. "The thing was brutal enough, even if the man had been Enrique, the traitor." I made no effort to keep the disgust from my voice. Memory of that poor devil's passing sickened me.

Steve did not make an answer for some minutes. We had swung past a score of trotting horsemen and once more rode, he and I and Panchito, slightly in advance of the column.

"Captain Clarke," he said finally, and, when I looked at him, I saw that his face was more deeply lined than I ever before had noticed, "it is by such inhuman stunts as you saw that a man survives in this country. You ain't a bit sicker than me, comin' down to cases. This Enrique bird has a lot of friends in my outfit, see. Guys that might quit me cold and follow Enrique to the other side. I seen 'em mass up for a double-quick retreat, and I knew I had to act fast.

"I see this greaser of Don Diego's comin' at me with a pig sticker a foot long. I glaums him and busts him like you seen, makin' them *hombres* think that I'd killed the traitor, Enrique. So, instead of quittin' me like a pack of coyotes, they stuck and fought it out. The result is that me and you and Panchito live to fight another night."

"It is by such tactics, *señor*," nodded Panchito, "that one survives here. When in Mexico, one must use the methods of other leaders. I grant you it was an ugly thing to witness, but Stephano speaks no less than the truth when he says our lives hung on the moment."

"I'm sure learning things," I said. "Enrique got away?"

"I'm afraid he did, skipper. He's a slick number. Part white and went to school at Yuma. I tell you that black don has a drag in this section and no gettin' away from it. For all our connivin', he's wise to our plans, Panchito. He'll be ready to glad hand us with a mess of hot lead."

"Then why not postpone the attack?" I suggested.

Steve and Panchito exchanged a mirthless grin.

"No can do, skipper. Like them Romans or Russians or whoever them trick soldiers was, we burnt our bridges behind us, see? Diego's men has copped our wagons, mules, chuck, and all heavy equipment except spare mounts and ammunition. It ain't like the fightin' we done acrost the pond. Down here we shove a sack of jerky in our pockets, make our little old fight, then scatter like rabbits.

"We'll take a crack at old Diego Álvarez, then hightail it

for the hills," he continued. "You and me and Panchito will make a run for the American border with the *señorita*. With old Don Diego dead, it won't be so tough a break for us, see? Them babies of his ain't carryin' on for no stiff. They'll *viva* to beat hell for him while he's alive to pass out *pesos*, but, once he's a corpse, they'll lay down and roll over while we ride out the gate."

"It is the *Señorita* Magdalena," said Panchito, frowning, "who so stands between us and her cursed father. Let us hope that she will be in that garden to keep her tryst."

"Don't worry, Panchito," chuckled Steve, "she'll be there."

I clamped my jaws to keep back the words that choked my throat.

III
"The Jest of the Jackal"

Captain de la Vega no longer hummed his Spanish tunes. Steve Doyle now rode with his head held high, peering into the shadows along the trail. Ahead of us a dozen scouts explored the trail and kept in constant touch with us. To a man these scouts — Yaquis trained by a lifetime spent in the saddle and on foot in the desert — displayed an eagerness to please that was almost pathetic. I began to get the idea now, of that grisly Enrique incident. Fear of Major Stephano, deeply implanted in their peon minds, would keep them from turning in any false reports.

Strangely enough, mile after mile was traversed without mishap. We might have been alone on that desert, so far as the sign read. The men were allowed to smoke once more and talk in subdued tones. Now and then the sound of a laugh came up to us.

"They've been issued a few shots of tequila," explained Steve. "Boosts the morale. That and the marijuana will fill 'em with fightin' stuff, to make up for their lack of natural guts. They'll need all they got before many hours."

"So far, so good," I ventured.

"It is when the don of the black serape keeps his talons hidden," said Panchito solemnly, "that he is most to be feared. Me, I do not like the looks of it."

"Nor me," grinned Steve uneasily. "He's got some ace up his sleeve. Ha! Told you, skipper."

Three of the Yaquis came out of the night, their horses at a stiff trot.

"*¿Por que?*" challenged Steve sharply as they drew rein.

"Don Diego's men . . . perhaps one hundred . . . they come, *señor,* to surrender, singing as they ride. Drunk, perhaps, and they say that Don Diego is dead. They have his head stuck on a spear."

"There was one," said Steve in the Mexican tongue as he toyed with his Colt, "whose name was Enrique. He lied to Major Stephano. You saw what became of Enrique, no?"

"*¡Sí, sí, sí!*" they chorused. "But we speak the truth."

"You saw the head on the spear...the head of Diego Álvarez? Careful how you speak, *hombre*."

"It was too dark to make out the features," admitted the Yaqui who acted as spokesman for the trio. "But they were cursing Álvarez and shouting *vivas* for you, *señor*."

"Hmm. Another trap, eh, Panchito?"

"Most likely."

A few staccato orders and the trail held not so much as a mule. In ambush, we lay along each side of the trail. It was thirty minutes by Steve's watch when our patience was rewarded by the clatter of horsemen approaching.

The clink of a chain mingled with the muffled thud of hoofs in the dust, a babble of voices in discordant shouts and snatches of songs that were tainted with lewd profanity. This much my haphazard knowledge of the language told me. The songs damned Don Diego and praised Steve and Panchito.

We let them come into the pocket of bristling steel. Then Steve himself barked the challenge that halted the ragged column of riders.

"Who goes?" he roared above their obviously drunken babble.

"*¡Amigos! ¡Amigos!* Friends!" This prompt answer came from a dozen mouths.

"*¡Viva* Major Stephano! *¡Viva* Panchito de la Vega!" roared others.

"Halt. Sit your saddles, *hombres,* or you die like the trapped rats! Drop your guns on the ground."

And when a lull of hesitation followed, Steve gave orders to his men.

"*Hombrecitos,* pick you each a man. When I give the command, shoot him dead. Ready! Take aim!"

"No, no, no!" came from the column. Their guns clattered noisily from their saddle boots to the ground. Empty hands waved high in the air.

"*¡Amigos! ¡Amigos!*" they called.

"Whose head sticks on that spear?" called Steve.

The gruesome thing bobbed horribly above their heads, ghastly enough there in the white moonlight.

"The head of a traitor!" came the reply. "The head of Enrique! See for yourself, *señor!*"

A hemp torch lifted alongside the grimacing head of the man who had been traitor to Steve Doyle.

"He tells the truth," whispered Panchito.

"He sure does," agreed Steve. Then he called to them

again in a loud tone. "Who leads you, *hombres?*"

"I, Pasqual Peranteau."

"The half-breed Frenchman," grunted Steve. Then he whispered softly: "I tell you, Panchito, it's a damn' trap. Watch out."

"That Peranteau," replied Panchito softly, "is a clever one."

"Sí," agreed Steve quickly.

I was surprised to see him get to his feet and stride boldly into the clearing where this Peranteau and his men sat their horses. A bold move and no mistake. Again I learned a lesson in the psychology of warfare in Mexico where many a crisis is turned by the spectacular.

Steve reached up and took the spear and its grisly burden from the man who held it. He tossed it aside as a man discards some useless trifle. Then he swung to face this Pasqual Peranteau.

"It is said, *Señor* Peranteau," said Steve, mockery in his voice, "that you are quite the devil of a fellow among the women, eh? Was it not you who fought a duel with another of Diego's lieutenants over that daughter of his?"

"I had that honor, *señor.*"

From our shelter we could see that trimly uniformed officer stiffen smartly in his saddle. I wondered if he had missed the insult of Steve's smile.

"What is your favorite weapon, *Señor* Lieutenant?"

I felt the startled grip of Panchito's fingers on my arm.

"A long blade of steel, *señor,*" came the swaggering reply, "is the weapon of a gentleman."

"Such as this, eh, *amigo?*" And Steve saluted with a saber he had picked out of the motley stack of weapons that lay on the ground.

This Peranteau fellow must have smelled a rat. He began

backing his horse on its haunches, looking about for some opening. But Steve reached up and jerked the man from his saddle. No sooner had his feet touched the ground than Steve picked up a second saber — shoved it into Peranteau's hand.

"¡Hombrecitos!" called Steve to his men, "keep these Don Diego *espurios* covered! I'm going to slice off the ears of this butter-tongued son of a she-goat. On guard, you lyin' rat!"

He pricked the man with his sword.

"Por Dios, señor," protested Peranteau, "I tell you we come to. . . ."

"To slip one over on us, you half-witted monkey!" snarled Steve. "Well, you ain't outsmartin' nobody, see? How's that for a starter?"

Steve's blade slashed. Peranteau clapped a hand to the side of his head.

"Your ear's on the ground, if that's what you want," taunted Steve. "I'm gonna collect the mate to it."

Peranteau, with a shrill yell, came at him, saber slashing like white lightning. I saw Steve give ground, his blade meeting the swift one of the half-breed's and sending showers of yellow sparks as the two met and slid away. It was my first taste of desperate sword play, and it held thrills crammed into each second as the two went at one another like demons. From my untutored viewpoint, they seemed evenly matched.

But Captain de la Vega, who loved a good blade as a horseman loves a Thoroughbred or a violinist loves a Stradivarius violin, swore with husky vehemence into his white mustache.

"¡Caramba! That devil Peranteau! Stephano cannot last long. Not against such a one as that Frenchman." Then, when Steve's blade slashed an ornate chevron from the

shoulder of Peranteau, the old Spaniard drew a quick breath of satisfaction. "Ha! You saw that one, *señor?* Splendid, no? *¡Ojalá . . . !*"

Peranteau had lunged forward. Steve, in defending himself, tripped, faltered, and, before he reclaimed his balance, the other man was at him, slashing like one possessed. Steve, on one knee now, ducked and parried. Captain de la Vega, with an oath, leaped forward to put an end to the cowardly attack. But Steve either saw him or sensed the movement.

"Back, Panchito!" he panted. "My fight! How's this . . . you lady's boy?" And with a quick, sidewise movement he was out from under that swishing saber and hurling taunts at the Álvarez lieutenant.

"The Major Stephano," said Captain de la Vega, once more at my side in the brush, "is in need of no aid from me. Such a one, *señor!* Eh! His bag is full of tricks."

It wasn't real swordsmanship on Steve's part. Even I, unlearned as I was, knew that. It was simply his superb strength and agility. In and out, his footwork fast and smooth, he baffled the panting Peranteau. From all sides he was at him. More than once he slipped in behind, and the flat of his blade spatted smartly as he spanked the half-breed.

Peranteau's rage was that of one gone mad. He cursed and sobbed and his saber made wild swipes that found an echo in Steve's taunts. The humor in horseplay is strong in the peon. Men on both sides now saw that Steve was making a clown of this Peranteau. Their jibes ran like foxfire from mouth to mouth. Tragedy was becoming comedy, and Major Stephano was, by his clowning, winning over men who had come to partake in some bit of treachery. Captain de la Vega relaxed to the extent of a cigarette. I followed his example.

Slash. Crash. Shower after shower of orange sparks as the sobbing Peranteau warded off the terrific blows of Steve's saber. No man's wrist could stand it long.

I heard Steve's taunting laugh. I saw Peranteau's sword go spinning through the air. The American, with a quick leap, was on the man's back, and a smart blow sent Peranteau's drawn Luger after his lost saber. Peranteau was knocked to his knees. Steve, astride him, slapped him with the flat of his saber.

"Walk! Trot! Canter! Giddap, mule!"

And he did not quit his clowning until the man between his muscular legs lay sobbing with his face in the yellow dust. Steve held the man's ear between thumb and forefinger, saber poised in his other hand.

"Now, you louse," he said hotly, "come clean with the inside dope on your game or off goes your other ear. Squeal, you damned pig, squeal!"

Peranteau, his words coming jerkily, blurted out his plan of treachery. Don Diego was not dead. Enrique had failed and paid the extreme penalty for his botchery. Diego had sent out Peranteau and his men who, under the guise of deserters, should mingle with Doyle's men and, when the proper time arrived, attack at close quarters with the knives and pistols hidden under their shirts.

Steve, still seated on the man, went through his pockets with swift thoroughness. A long knife and a package of cigarettes were the results. Steve appropriated one of the latter and lit it.

"Marijuana," he spat disgustedly and threw it aside. "Got the makin's of a white man's smoke, skipper?"

Captain de la Vega and I had, upon Panchito's suggestion, left our position to stand near Steve and his victim. I handed Steve my half-smoked cigarette. I noted with no little relief that Peranteau had lost only the tip of one of his ears. Steve, perceiving my scrutiny, chuckled.

"A few words to these men, Stephano," suggested Panchito in an undertone, "and they will follow you to the death."

"You said it," agreed Steve, and faced the men who had ridden here to fight for Don Diego.

"Hombrecitos," he told them, in their own tongue, standing with widespread legs, cigarette in one hand, naked saber in the other, "the man you followed here is a braggart and a coward. In the army of Pancho Villa, Pasqual Peranteau would be following behind with his yellow tail curved between his legs, making tortillas with the women. You see how he acts when he faces a real man, no? Poof! He is too harmless a thing to waste a bullet on. You men are too brave to follow such a leader. Instead of taking his head on a spear back to that Don Diego Álvarez, I take him back alive. Before the sunrise, Álvarez will be dead. You have my word for it, and Major Stephano Doyle has never lied to friend or enemy. With Diego dead and rotting in his grave, what becomes of you, eh? Poof! You'll be worse than dead, for Sonora will spit on those who killed their good men at the bidding of the black don.

"How many of you are married?" he asked. "All men with a wife step forward."

They came, their brown faces solemn with uncertainty. They made up a large majority of Peranteau's following.

Steve halted them. "You are brave men, but foolish ones. This business of fighting is for men who leave no wives and children when a bullet or knife finishes them. No one man under my command is married. Throw away your guns, *hombres*. Go back to your homes where your wives pray and your children cry for you. Tell them to pray to the *Señor*

Dios that Magdalena Álvarez may find her happiness. Go, *hombrecitos,* with the friendship of Major Stephano to remember during your evenings of peace when you sit and smoke and listen to the laughter of your children. *Señores, buenas noches*. We part in peace."

Well, it was an odd bit of sermonizing to come from a man like Steve Doyle. Even though I felt that perhaps this swashbuckling rascal had a selfish purpose behind his words, I could not stand there unmoved. If ever a man seemed the embodiment of deep sincerity, Steve Doyle did as he stood there, his handsome head held high. There were tear stains on the dusty cheeks of a lot of the men who shook his hand awkwardly, then rode away, one by one, into the night.

When all that remained of them was the pile of small arms at Steve's feet, he faced those of Peranteau's men who remained.

"Those of you who wish, may join my men. Those who choose to go to their homes will not be cowards, but men who think of mothers and perhaps a sweetheart waiting somewhere in the moonlight. Your choice, *caballeros,* must be your own, not mine."

Some of them rode off in the wake of the older men. Others stayed. Steve booted Peranteau to his feet and shoved him into an empty saddle under double guard. Then we rode on.

Again I had learned a lesson, and I understood now why the Mexicans worshipped their Major Stephano. He was a born leader who played on the emotions of men as a musician thrums the strings of a harp. It was like him to try to shatter it with flippancy. I'll always think that Steve felt ashamed for revealing his softer side, although God knows it had done a lot to wipe out the memory of his cruelty.

"Married guys in a Mex army, skipper," he told me as we got under way, "are a damn' nuisance. Their wives and kids trail along. They're the K. P.s of the Mexican army. I got used to a lot down here, but I can't digest no rear guard of weepin' dames an' squawlin' kids. Got a match handy?"

IV
"Shadowed in Scarlet"

Pepper pods, strung one by one on a line with, here and there, one more vivid scarlet than the others — of all the nights in my life, this one stands forth, in retrospect, as the reddest of them all. Hatred and love, the bitter and the sweet, the chill of silvery steel and the warmth of crimson silk are woven into the fabric of that memorable night. The low-pitched laughter of a woman who greets love, the death rattle of a man dying with a red blade in his stiffening grip. The heavy perfume of roses still reminds me of spilled blood.

Peaceful looking enough — there in the moonlight — were those white walls and the red-tiled roofing of the *Hacienda* Álvarez. Long, low buildings, they were sprinkled with feathery blots of shadow from the giant palms that grew inside the huge patio. A high wall shut in the patio and garden beyond. One must pass through a heavy, solid oak double gate to enter.

We had halted on the rim of a short mesa that looked down on the home of the don of the black serape. Through powerful night glasses we studied the place, for we must wait, so Steve told me, before we swept down on the place.

Horses, grouped in fours, one man holding the bridle reins, pawed restlessly and shook themselves to the accompaniment of rattling equipment. Like a myriad of fireflies, cigarettes glowed under huge sombreros. White teeth flashed against dark brown faces. Low-toned words droned or crackled according to the mood of the speaker. The business at hand subdued the voices of the Mexicans in spite of the potency of their marijuana."What a night, no?" said Captain de la Vega. "One could choose no better one on which to fight for the honor of a woman. I have known two others, such as this. My one regret is that the *yanqui,* El Lobo, cannot be here to help us enjoy it. To love, to fight . . . and later, *señores,* to meet in some quiet spot where the wine is excellent. What more can one ask of life, eh?"

"A home," I suggested a little bitterly, perhaps, for the future just then looked black with uncertainty. I could not feel that carefree something that seemed to fill Panchito and Steve. "A home and kids."

"May the *Señor Dios* grant your wish, *señor,*" said Panchito gravely. "As for me, I ask for nothing but that, when the time comes for me to say *adiós,* I shall die like a soldier."

He stood there in the moonlight, a trim, white figure, chin lifted proudly, his thick hair silver-white against the lean darkness of his handsome face. Yet, in his gay smile with which he faced his fate there was something terribly pathetic. For him, tomorrow could hold nothing. It takes a brave man to stand as Captain Panchito de la Vega stood at that moment, and smile.

"All I've got to say" — Steve's careless voice cut into my musing — "is that I'm gonna make it tough pickin's for the baby that has a bullet with my name on it. A wife and kids is all right for you, skipper. You got a rosy little future loomin' up like a red sunrise, see? No border gover'ment guy is gonna pick you up and stake you to a two-by-two room in some hoosegow when you step north. But for a guy that's gotta stick in this flea-bitten country, a wife and family are just somethin' to worry about. Love 'em and leave 'em. A kiss in the dark is as close as I'm ever gonna come to a weddin' ceremony."

"By God, Doyle, you lie!" I croaked. I was on my feet, shaking like a man with a chill. My voice was like a crow's, and I stood over Steve who still squatted squaw fashion on the ground. "I can't hit a man that's sitting," I told him hotly. "Get on your legs and take it. I'm going to thrash you within an inch of your life. Get up!"

He got to his feet slowly, and I saw his jaw muscles bulge and quiver. He'd gone white under my words. Slowly his hands unbuckled his two gun belts and dropped them with their white-handled guns to the ground.

"We've been closer than brothers," I told him, "but, before I let you soil that girl's lips with your damned kisses, I'll kill you. Put up your hands and fight!"

He stood there, white as paper, trying to grin. There was no anger in his eyes. Just a hurt look that a dog might have when his master is going to strike him for something he is innocent of doing. I was too crazy with anger to read the meaning of that look, and I swung at his face.

The blow never landed. A pair of steel arms gripped and held me helpless. Panchito's voice, trembling with emotion, filled my ears.

"*¡Por Dios, señor!* Have you gone loco? You know not what you are doing. Get hold of yourself, *señor.*" Then he called across my straining shoulders: "Go, Stephano! *¡Pronto!* In half an hour, return!" And in spite of my struggling he held me.

Steve stooped and picked up his gun belts. He walked away with them dangling from his hand. His steps dragged sluggishly, and his head was lowered. When he had gone,

Captain de la Vega let me go. With a face like carved stone, he waved me to a boulder.

"You might have run him through with a dull sword, *señor,*" he said sternly, "and hurt him less. Tell me, my son, what prompted you to act so like a man gone mad?"

Well, I told him. In short, blurting sentences, hot as the fever that ran in my veins, I told him of my love for Magdalena, of Steve Doyle's manner toward women, of my plan to fight for love. And as I talked, I noticed with indifference that his face softened. He was smiling when I had finished, but there was a shadow of pain in his eyes. I had left nothing unsaid.

"My son," he said, laying a hand on my shoulder when the last word had left my lips, and I sat, silently and defiantly, there on the rock, "I am more than ever convinced that none other than the *Señor Dios* sent you here. I can know now that in passing the heart and soul of Magdalena Álvarez into your keeping, I have done a little to balance the black marks on my book. But you have greatly wronged a man who loves you better than he loves life."

"You said she loved him," I burst out. "You told me yourself that she was to meet him alone in the garden."

"Eh? What is that you say, *señor? Caramba,* man, it is you, not Stephano, who meets Magdalena in the garden. True enough. Stephano made so bold as to arrange the meeting by messages sent secretly to her. There was a time, *señor,* before you came to Dos Palmas, when he and I had planned that he make love to her and free her from Don Diego. We planned that they . . . Stephano and the girl . . . flee southward to a seaport where a boat would be waiting . . . from there to South America where, through friends of mine, Stephano should find a position.

"Your coming altered our plans. You loved her. Though

she may not be aware of it, she already loves you. The United States is a better place for her than South America. You, a gentleman of family and education, can do for her the little things that so please a woman of her breeding. The best blood of Spain runs in her veins, *Señor* Clarke. Even Don Diego, for all his faults, is from a line of glorious women and brave *caballeros*. Hatred and bitterness have merely shriveled his heart. Even Stephano knew that she was not meant for him. He told me so many times. It was with the utmost reluctance that he consented to our earlier plan. That, despite the fact that Stephano Doyle loves Magdalena Álvarez with all his heart, as cleanly and bravely and understandingly as ever man loved woman, his sense of unworthiness . . . nothing else . . . made him unwilling to declare his love."

I waited for no more. Half blind with shame, I stumbled away to find Steve. Panchito, smiling understandingly, let me go.

From group to group, I passed, searching for him, but in vain.

"Well, you double damned son of a mule collar" — came a soft chuckle from the shadows behind me — "are you still rarin' to tear my can off, or do we shoot it out with shotguns?"

I found his hand in the dark shadows and hung to it. But when I tried to talk, he jabbed me playfully and none too gently under the ribs.

"I getcha, skipper, I getcha," he said. "When one of you slow workers does fall, he falls all the way. No more sense than a loco horse. Got a match?"

Well, I'd seen Captain de la Vega face his tomorrow with a smile and a soldier's courage. I knew that Steve Doyle's careless, don't-give-a-damn flippancy hid a heartache. I compared myself to these two and to that other American, El Lobo. The comparison made me feel darn small and petty — even when Steve threw an arm around my shoulder and led me back to the spot where Panchito waited.

He was standing bareheaded, talking to someone — a slim youth wrapped in a gay serape, face hidden under a huge sombrero crusted with silver.

"Captain Clarke," said Panchito, "I have the honor of presenting *Señorita* Magdalena Álvarez."

I stood there, gasping like a fish thrown on dry land. My eyes were fixed on the dark oval of her face under the shadow of the huge sombrero. The girl made a marvelous picture in her velvet jacket and black, flaring, Mexican breeches, showing crimson above the polish of her high-heeled boots.

I must have made a sorry figure for my clothes were torn by brush and none too clean. I had shaved that morning, but a catclaw limb had slit my cheek, and the dried blood stained my jaw.

Her greeting was the graceful courtesy of the Spanish. She followed its formality with a slender hand thrust toward me.

"Captain de la Vega," she said, as I clumsily held her hand, "has told me of you." Our glances met and lingered as they had one other time.

Then she turned to greet Steve.

"Swell night for a canoe ride, no?" grinned Steve, taking her hand in that easy way of his. "All we need is water and the boat and mebby an oar. Would you mind dustin' me off and tellin' me how come you're here?"

"Don Diego Álvarez," said Captain de la Vega grimly, "sent the *señorita* with an escort to us. He bids us to come . . . you and Captain Clarke and I . . . to the *Hacienda* Álvarez to be his guests at a midnight banquet."

"Strike me bowlegged, Panchito! You're kiddin'!"

"It is his wish," insisted Panchito, "that we three come alone."

"Do tell," grinned Steve, hitching up his gun belts. "When giraffes grow pink wings, when elephants root in. . . ."

Something in Captain de la Vega's eyes silenced Steve. Behind the girl's back, the old Spaniard was making frantic signals to me.

"When do we start?" Steve caught his cue nicely.

"Shortly, my Stephano." Panchito was again calm and smiling. "Captain Clarke, will you be so kind as to entertain the *Señorita* Álvarez while Stephano and I attend to some important matters that need our care before we ride to sup with Don Diego?"

"It will be the most pleasurable moment of my life." I took advantage of Spain's language and ultra politeness to voice my real feelings. I was glad I'd studied the language.

"You speak our language skillfully," smiled Magdalena with a sidelong glance that quickened my pulse.

I heard Steve chuckle as he and Panchito moved off into the shadows.

Alone with her, I felt awkward and tongue-tied. All my nicely rehearsed speeches now seemed silly and wholly uncalled for. I tried to find a place to put my hands which seemed too large for my pockets. It was an agonizing silence that fell over us as we two stood within touching distance there in the moonlight. It was Magdalena who broke that silence in an odd manner.

Her face was partly turned from me, the features hidden in the shadow of her hat. "May God, in His mercy" — her words came with low clarity in English — "forgive that man who is my father."

I saw her slender shoulders quiver under the bright-hued serape. I knew that she was weeping. In an instant I was at her side, my arms about her, holding her close as she buried her face against my shoulder. For some moments we stood thus. Then she became quiet and struggled feebly for release. But my arms held her.

"I love you," I whispered huskily in an unsteady voice. "I want to take you away. My sister and mother are in San Francisco. Their home will be yours. When you have learned to know me and trust me, perhaps love will come, and I will ask you to be my wife. If love does not come, it makes no difference in. . . ."

But her arms reached up and about my neck. I read what lay in her eyes, and our lips met. I was the happiest man alive.

Once over my stage fright, I talked enough. We both talked on and on, and our talk was no doubt filled with the delicious inanity of lovers the world over. Nonsensical as it sounds to others, it is terribly important to the two who, by endless repetition, pledge one another in that great love that maroons them on an island of dreams while the rest of the world with its noise and worry and sorrow is as the sea hidden beneath a dense fog.

I forgot Panchito and Steve and the oddity of Magdalena's presence here. The don of the black serape and his sinister power were forgotten. It was Steve's voice that dissipated that fog and brought us back to earth.

"No hittin' in the breakaway, folks. Me 'n' Panchito have been whistlin' and coughin' to bring you two outta your trance. I was gonna call the bugler."

I knew what it cost Steve to lose the love of Magdalena. Yet, there was nothing but sincerity in the grip of his hand.

"You each drew a prize," he grinned. "No whiter man

than the skipper ever walked. No finer woman ever breathed. I'm wishin' you both the best of everything."

And I knew he meant it.

Captain Panchito embraced us both. His dark eyes were misty with emotion. The gravity of a *padre* and the reckless gaiety of a *caballero* blended perfectly in his blessing.

"And now," he said presently, a gay smile on his lips, "we go to receive the blessing of Don Diego. We'll turn his midnight banquet into a wedding feast, eh, my children?"

I saw Magdalena's face go white as chalk. Her shoulders trembled in the embrace of my arm. I knew that she was gripped with mortal terror. Because I had not yet glimpsed the terrible cruelty of the don of the black serape, because my love gave me the confidence that scoffed lightly at defeat, I laughed away her tears.

"Though your father and I are enemies of long standing, my child," smiled Captain de la Vega, "he has respect for my judgment. Let the handling of Don Diego rest with me."

"But I know my father," protested the girl vehemently. "He has some terrible purpose behind his invitation."

"You say he is alone at the barricade."

"Save for the two soldiers who guard the gate. I myself heard him dismiss all save those two. A messenger rode in with some strange news that upset him. He drove me from the room when the man came in."

"That man was Pasqual Peranteau?" questioned Captain de la Vega, smiling oddly. I could see his dark eyes glowing like red sparks.

Magdalena nodded.

"It was I who sent Peranteau to him, child, with word that the terrible power of Don Diego Álvarez was broken and trampled in the dust."

"I do not understand," she said faintly.

"No, I'm afraid you do not, and the time is too short for the explaining of it. You must trust me."

Her hand found mine and clung there. I reassured her with my touch that she could depend on me till death.

I was doing some fast thinking. Peranteau, then, had been allowed to escape that he might bear the evil tidings of his disaster to the black don, even as Enrique had done. I wondered what had been the penalty of Peranteau's returning.

"Stephano and I," said Captain de la Vega, "have been wondering how Don Diego would accept defeat. Evidently with good grace, by the looks of things. I give you my word, *señorita,* if there is a drop of mercy or a measure of justice in the body of Don Diego Álvarez, I shall bring it forth this night. I once vowed to kill him. I now renounce that vow. Where steel has failed, perhaps sympathy shall win our purpose."

"If not . . . ?" questioned Magdalena with strange quietness in her tone.

"It is for the great *Señor Dios* to decide. Judgment will have passed beyond our hands. By the love I bore your mother, child, I swear to let the decision rest with Him."

"I could ask nothing beyond that, *señor.*" And she left me to take Panchito's two hands in hers.

Steve brought our horses, and we mounted. He and Panchito rode ahead of us, side by side. Now and then a faint snatch of Steve's laughter floated back to us. Once I caught the words of a gay song that Panchito sang in a rich, low-toned voice.

Behind them, our horses kicking up puffs of sluggish yellow dust, the girl I loved rode side by side with me, our stirrups touching, our hands clasped. Perhaps, after all, it is just as well we did not suspect the peril that lay ahead of us.

V
"Banquet of Doom"

The challenge of two villainous-looking guards halted us at the great wooden gate.

"Who goes?"

Captain de la Vega gave answer to the challenge, and there was a note of reckless joy in that old Spaniard's voice. "Captain Clarke of the United States Cavalry! Major Stephano Doyle! Captain Panchito de la Vega! With us rides the daughter of Don Diego Álvarez! One side, thou gaping clown, or I'll warm my blade in your scrawny neck!"

We rode into the moonlit courtyard where the century-old palm stood. The shod hoofs of our horses clattered on the sun-baked tiles. I caught the odor of orange blossoms. A door opened, and an old woman servant stood against the yellow-lighted room beyond. We stood in the strip of light that came from the house, and I heard the old servant sob — "Praise God." — when she saw Magdalena. "It is the wish of Don Diego that the company enter," she told us in a cracked old voice. "He awaits you in the dining hall."

"Like a damned black spider in his web," chuckled Steve in my ear. "Keep your mouth shut and your eyes peeled, skipper. Be ready for anything and keep your guns handy."

Through a long hallway lit by occasional candles stuck in niches along the wall, then through a doorway into a long room that was like an old-world setting, we passed. The walls were hung with tapestries, bits of armor, and rare paintings. A long, low table of massive oak was set with glittering silver and glass and exquisite bits of linen worked by the Mexican women into delicate drawn-work designs. Beyond was a fireplace wide enough to spit a steer. A fire burned there, despite the fact that the night carried but a bare hint of chill.

Before the fire was a huge, high-backed chair covered with red leather, studded with shining brass nails. Against the scarlet background of that chair was outlined the stiff figure of a man — Don Diego Álvarez.

Black velvet, white linen, not a shred of color to relieve the severity of his garb, the black don sat there. He looked more lean and terrible than ever. His sightless eyes looked squarely at us, unblinking. He rose and bowed, his mouth twisting in a one-sided smile.

"A pleasure, gentlemen." I heard his voice for the first time and was startled at the very lifelessness of its tone. "An honor to have as guests such an illustrious trio."

After the custom of her people, Magdalena had vanished. The black don waved a lean hand toward chairs.

"Be seated, *caballeros*." He dropped into his chair. With uncanny accuracy his sightless eyes, like burned-out coals set in sallow wax, singled out Panchito.

"Long years, eh, my friend, since you and I drank together in this room?"

"Long years, aye," smiled Captain de la Vega who, apparently, was enjoying the situation.

"You and I and our mutual friend, the *yanqui*. That nameless one, El Lobo."

Vanity hid his shriveled arm under the graceful fold of his black serape. His other hand picked up a gold box filled with cigarettes and held it toward us. Panchito and I each accepted one.

"I roll mine," came carelessly from Steve who looked about the room like some grinning school kid.

"My Pasqual Peranteau informs me," said Don Diego, when a silent-footed servant brought wine, the color of liquid gold, "that my men are beaten and scattered into the hills like stray goats. I congratulate you, my dear Panchito, and wish to show you how Don Diego Álvarez accepts defeat."

With a steady hand he lifted his wine glass. From somewhere beyond the room I thought I heard the sound of muffled sobbing, but I could not be sure.

"Gentlemen, a toast!" said Don Diego. "Drink you, *caballeros,* to the fairest lily in all Mexico. To Magdalena Álvarez!"

We drank. Then we waited for the next move of the black don. Even Panchito, I could tell, was startled when it came.

"I am told, *señores,* that she loves a *yanqui. Señor* Clarke, no?"

"You are well informed," said Panchito.

"Better informed than you think, *amigo.*" Undoubtedly those sightless eyes shifted to the chair where I sat.

"*Señor* Clarke," he said, "I am informed that you are from an excellent family and your record in peace and in war is a clean one. That is well. It is said that you are a brave man." His thin mouth twitched queerly, as he paused a moment, then went on. "By intercepting certain messages, I learn that you and my daughter have an appointment. You were to meet by the white rose bush at the far end of the garden. The hour of meeting was to be midnight. It still lacks five minutes till yonder clock chimes the twelve strokes. You may consider yourself at liberty to meet her there in the garden, *Señor* Clarke."

I caught the look of warning in Steve's eyes. My guns were loaded and within easy reach.

"I shall keep the appointment, Señor Álvarez," I said stiffly.

"*Señor* Doyle!" The black don turned his blind eyes toward Steve now. "You seem to have proven yourself an able matchmaker. It would be cruel, indeed, to deprive you of the pleasure of seeing the fulfillment of your efforts in that direction. You shall be repaid, *señor.* We shall give the lovers ten minutes, *señor,* then you shall follow *Señor* Clarke into the garden. There you shall be entertained as befits a gentleman of your chivalrous nature."

I saw Steve's jaw muscles tense and quiver, and he grinned at the blind don.

"I call the bet, Don Diego," he said grimly. "I give you fair warning. . . ."

Panchito cut off Steve's words with a sharp look. Don Diego, however, ignored Steve's unfinished sentence and now turned to Panchito.

"My friend," he said in that flat voice, holding no inflection, "I have waited long for this night. While the *yanqui*s enjoy the pleasure of the garden, you and I shall entertain one another, eh?" His teeth bared in a lipless grimace. "Just you and I, my Panchito, shall play a delightful little game which I myself have thought up for your benefit. My blindness has limited my pastimes, these late years. Our old sport with the foils is no longer possible for one who lives always in the black shadows of night. So, I have perfected a substitute whereby a soldier may indulge in his passion for excellent steel. That you may share my blindness, I have had made a hood of black velvet which you shall wear. The room will also be in total darkness. Does it sound tasty to your palate, friend Panchito?"

"I am already impatient to play this game of blackness," came promptly from Panchito. His eyes danced with tiny lights of excitement.

"Señores," said Don Diego, when the servant appeared once more and filled our glasses with that excellent wine,

"love is, with one exception, the most powerful emotion in life." He lifted his glass. "Let us drink to that exception. *Caballeros,* to that thing which breaks the weak and mends the strong. To that which is the master of fools but the slave of one grown bitter in wisdom. *¡Caballeros!* To *hate!*"

He stood, glass held high, then drank. Panchito drank with him. Steve and I set down our glasses untouched.

Awed into silence we saw these two white-haired descendants of the dons drain their glasses, then smash the bits of glass on the red-tiled hearth. They had sealed their pledge of hate. Later, death would sit in judgment while these two fought.

Don Diego's sightless eyes now fixed themselves on a heavy, exquisitely carved table some ten feet away. On that table lay a black silk neckscarf and two daggers in a case of red leather.

"The bit of silk," said Don Diego, "is, I believe, well chosen, my Panchito. It once belonged to Doña María. You no doubt are aware of its use in connection with the knives?"

"We each hold an end of the scarf in our teeth?" smiled Panchito.

Don Diego nodded. "Until one of us shall, perforce, let go," he added.

I'd heard of this Mexican fighting game. Each contestant holds an end of a neckscarf in his teeth. Armed with long-bladed knives, they literally rip one another to pieces. Bad enough to fight thus with one's eyes open — but blindfolded!

I could not keep from shuddering. I have all Americans' fear of a knife. I'd rather face a machine gun than a knife in the hand of a Mexican who understands its use. But Captain de la Vega looked as pleased as a chess master who is about to match wits with his equal at the game.

The booming of the huge clock startled me. *Bong! Bong! Bong!* Deep-toned as a distant bell, it was like a death knell, the strokes of the midnight hour coming with long intervals between. In spite of myself, I counted them as I sat there, rigid. And that old, skinny devil of a don with his yellow skin and his cruel mouth stared intently at me, his eyes unwinking.

"The hour when lovers meet," he said in that dead voice of his, as the twelfth stroke fell like a blow on the silence of the room. "*Señor* Clárke, I shall not try your lover's impatience any longer. Later, when each of us has had his entertainment, we shall again meet here and partake of supper."

He rose and bowed formally. His hand pointed to a small door at the side of the room. I had already surmised that this door led into the garden.

In a way, I understood why Panchito and Steve had deliberately ridden into what seemed to be a trap. Though the followers of this don of the black serape were momentarily scattered, his power still stained Mexico. So long as Don Diego lived, Magdalena's happiness was in jeopardy. All our lives were in danger of a murderer's knife until Don Diego's life and his sinister power had been stamped out. Panchito, Steve, and I must face our separate dangers, fight our fight, and win.

Panchito had told Magdalena that he would try to find kindness and justice in the heart of Don Diego. Because he wished her to enjoy the first brief hour of her newborn love, he had lied. As well seek justice and softness in some poisonous snake. They had counted on me to understand without being told.

So, when I stepped through the door into the garden beyond, I sought not love, but lurking death. Gripping the butt of my Colt, I stood with my back against the door I had closed behind me. I saw the dark outlines of various flowering bushes, clear cut against the sky beyond the high wall. They were trees, rather than bushes, loaded with pink blossoms. Their branches sent splashes of shadow across the wide, tiled wall some fifty feet away. Motionless, tense, I waited for my eyes to become accustomed to the dark shadows.

I expected a shot or a thrown knife. But neither form of death came to threaten me. What came to relieve the silence of the night was the low-pitched laugh of a woman. It came from the far end of the garden, close under the shadow of the wall. Only a woman who is held in the arms of her lover laughs in that low-pitched, throaty tone. Magdalena in the arms of another? I went icy cold, then hot with swift fever at the thought. Then I heard the murmur of two voices, a man's and a woman's closely blended as if their lips were touching. Hot with a terrible rage, sick with fear of what my eyes should see, I stepped from the shadow of the doorway and strode with swift steps along the shadow-splashed walk.

I forgot that those flanking bushes might hide a man in ambush. I forgot even to glance to either side of me. My eyes were glued on that wall, straining to pierce the shadows that hid the woman who had laughed into the eyes of some lover. Jealousy had disarmed me and lowered my guard. Steve, in his wisdom, would, no doubt, have grown more cautious. I, like some blundering dolt, stumbled recklessly on.

Well, my eyes found what they sought. I pulled up short, shaking and sick. I still maintain that God, who understood what horrible torture seared my heart, willed that I should halt in the black shadow of a huge rosebush.

I saw two heads pressed closely together, lips clinging.

The woman's arms held the man's head down to her face. I caught the hint of oval face under a lace *mantilla*. Her back was toward me. It was, beyond all doubt, the most horrible moment of my life.

Some sort of hoarse cry came through my clenched teeth. With a swift movement the man pushed the girl back into the black shadows against the wall. Dimly I caught the sound of her startled gasp. Then she blended into the shadows, shrinking back against the adobe wall with its covering of vines.

"Ah, *Señor Gringo*," the man's voice taunted me.

Though I had seen him but once before, I recognized Pasqual Peranteau. He had bathed and put on fresh clothes, and apparently no worse for the rough treatment he had gotten from Steve now faced me with all the assurance of a man who is quickly about to dispose of an inferior enemy.

For a long moment I stood there speechless, unable to move. The scene I had just witnessed stupefied me. Then something hot stung the muscle above my collarbone. Someone hidden along the path behind me had thrown a knife at my back, but the shadow that partially hid me had saved my life. The blade that ripped the flesh and fell in the foliage beyond served a purpose remote from the calculations of its thrower. It sent my fighting blood pounding through my body. But as I swung my .45 up to shoot, Peranteau, with a swift leap, was at me with a sword. The flat of its blade sent my gun spinning, and the sharp point pricked with warning pressure against my chest. Instinctively I recoiled a step, Peranteau's taunting laugh following me.

"Ramón, thou donkey of inbred ancestry," he called in a low tone, "fetch the *gringo*'s rapier that he might be given the honor of dying like a gentleman." He grinned nastily into my face. "You will pardon the over-zealous actions of my Ramón. Poor devil, he is cursed with the feeble brain of a half-wit. His obsession is the throwing of knives in the dark. It is the first time I knew him to miss his mark."

A misshapen human being with a horribly twisted spine sidled with beast-like gait along the walk, holding a rapier in his hand. His head twisted to lift a distorted face toward mine as he handed me the weapon. Making tongueless sounds, he hitched himself back out of sight. Peranteau and I stood alone in the blotched moonlight, facing one another.

Save for a haphazard schooling in the use of a cavalry saber, a sword of any description was a useless weapon to me. Recalling Panchito's anxiety for Steve when he faced this half-caste Frenchman, I knew the folly of facing such an able antagonist. But I had no intention of letting this half-breed think I was afraid of him. Under my right armpit the hulk of a big caliber Colt still threw the odds in my favor. The gun was hidden by the leather jumper I wore. My left hand was free, and I'd put in some long hours at left-handed gun play. Yet, I was loath to use the advantage of my gun. I wanted, more than anything else just then, to humble this damned gamecock and made him eat dust.

He stood there with lowered point, rolling the sleeve of his shirt back from his sword arm. His left hand thus engaged, the point of his weapon lowered, he held my eyes with an unwavering stare, a mocking, insulting smile on his mouth. A muffled little cry from the vine-covered side of the wall was like the sting of a rawhide lash.

With a backhand slash that carried every ounce of strength in my right arm, I whipped my blade across the unprotected face of the man. The dull back of the sword caught him across the eyes. As he staggered back, blinded for the moment, I swung with all my might at his sword arm. My blade caught him across the back of his hand, and his weapon slipped to the red tiles. With a quick movement I picked it up. The next instant both those pig stickers were broken and thrown in the brush.

The bushes moved behind me. I whirled and was on top of the hunchback just as he was poised with another of his knives for a clean throw at my back. My gun barrel cracked his ugly skull, and he went down in a misshapen heap.

"Now, my love-making *amigo*," I told Peranteau as I blocked his path, "I'm going to knock your block off in good old honest United States fashion. You got a licking coming, and I'm the gent to do it."

He was still half blind from that blow across his eyes. I waited for him to recover, not forgetting for a moment that he'd try some Mexican trick. I could be fairly certain that he packed a knife somewhere about his person. He'd have a gun, too. I wondered which he'd try for first. I'd shoved my gun back in its holster, out of sight. I was sure he hadn't seen what method I'd used to put the hunchback out of the picture. He probably would figure I had lost my one and only gun.

My guess was correct. I saw the beginning of the movement that meant gun play. I stepped in, and my right swing clipped him just as his Lugar slipped free of the scabbard in his waistband. As he staggered backward, off balance, I kicked the gun from his hand and then stepped back. From the tail of my eye I caught some sort of movement in the shadow of the wall. It gave me no little satisfaction just then. Well, she'd see a lot more before long.

He came at me with his fists this time. Almost every man knows a little of rough-and-tumble fighting, and Pasqual Peranteau, in his travels, had picked up considerably more than the rudiments of that game. He covered fairly well and didn't make the mistake of rushing blindly. I was glad of that. It would make the fighting more interesting. I blocked a left swing and took the defensive just to test his style.

We were fairly well matched for build. I figured I gave him less than fifteen pounds the best of it, and he had it on me for reach. We sparred for a moment, swinging, blocking, side-stepping. He had the advantage of knowing what sort of footing lay in the patches of shadow. The uneven tiles made steps uncertain.

His face was my target. I concentrated my efforts on the marking up of his features. I wanted to slit his lips, smash his nice, even nose into a flat pulp. To do that, I'd take whatever punishment he was man enough to hand me. In landing a nice right cross that would close an eye for him, I let him step inside my guard. I realized the folly of my mistake the second he closed with me in a clinch. Close fighting gave him the chance to use the knife he had hidden somewhere on him.

He hung on with both arms. We strained in locked grips, legs set, backs twisting, wrestling now. He dared not let go long enough to reach for his knife. My left arm held his right one against his side. I figured his knife would be where his right, rather than left, hand could reach it. He held my right wrist in a vise-like grip. Perhaps he thought I, too, had a knife, or perhaps past encounters with knife wielders like himself gave him the idea.

Odds even, anyhow, I grinned to myself.

But my grin became a stifled curse as his teeth sank deeply into my left shoulder. He hung on like some bulldog, trying to loosen the grip that pinioned his knife arm. The pain maddened me. He sank his teeth deeper into my muscle. I'd have to chance the knife. Suddenly dropping my left arm, I spun backwards and shot my left fist in an uppercut as we came apart. The blow caught him on the cheek as he reached for his knife.

I followed it with a right swing that brought a yelp of pain from him. Blood spurted from his nose. As his knife slid into view, I landed a second smash on that nose, and I knew I'd ruined its straightness for all time. He stumbled backward, slashing at me blindly with his knife. The blade slithered within bare inches of my face. Once it ripped my leather jacket and the shirt beneath, the keen point tickling my ribs.

I forgot my fear of a knife. I dimly heard the startled, frightened woman's scream, thin as a knife point, somewhere behind me. I was fighting mad with a recklessness I still cannot understand. My only excuse is that my world of rose-petal dreams had crashed with a sickening thud about my ears, and I meant to maim the man who had thus robbed me of that one sweet, splendid love that God had given me.

That knife was here, there, everywhere about my face and shoulders, darting at me from every angle as I smashed blow after blow into that distorted face. Now and then I felt the bite of the knife point, and, each time I tasted steel, I paid Peranteau in good American punches. I could have disarmed the man fifty times, but I wanted to give him odds and beat him to his knees. My rage had passed all limits of reason.

He cursed and sobbed while blood smeared his face and clothes, and I knocked him down a dozen times. He knew how to take punishment, that man. His nose was broken, his eyes bruised and swollen, his mouth split and puffed, but he came back at me, time after time, hunting my heart with his knife that was red to the hilt with my blood. Each time I knocked him down, he stayed a little longer.

On his hands and knees, blood dripping from his battered face, he rose slowly. A black shadow darted from the rose bushes, rushing me from behind. Sharp steel ripped at my back, and I whirled to face this new danger. My distorted nostrils caught the heavy scent of perfume. The rustle of silk told me that my fresh antagonist was the girl. In an instant this new attack, this sample of Spanish love, took the fight out of me. My unclenched hands hanging like leaden weights by my side, I stood unguarded there as a small bundle of silken fury came at me with one of those broken swords. Lucky for me that broken blade was dull of point, and there was enough left of my leather jacket to cushion the blow that drove that broken rapier squarely at my chest.

Instinct flung my arms around her. Her head writhed back from my blood-soaked clothes, and I looked down into a face white as ivory save for two eyes that glowed with hatred. I laughed. Laughed like a crazy loon, for it was not the face of Magdalena Álvarez.

Still cackling that crazy laugh, I took the broken sword from her and held her arms. Peranteau, his face terrible in its fury, made a last rush, his ugly knife swinging for my throat. Still holding the girl in the crook of my right arm, I landed a left swing that sent him down to stay.

I gasped for breath while trickles of sweat half blinded me.

As in a dream I heard the patter of running feet, the muffled thud of blows, a woman's voice calling my name from somewhere in the darkness. Inanely I still clung to the girl in the black silk dress while she beat clenched fists into my face in cat-like fury.

Then violent hands jerked me off my feet. Half unconscious, I made one last dizzy effort to go out fighting. I jerked my gun free and shoved the muzzle against the man. It was a single-action .45, and my thumb pulled back the hammer. I pulled the trigger, wondering stupidly why the weapon did not discharge.

"My God!" grunted the man's voice close by my ear as I sank into unconsciousness, "it's the skipper."

Later, I learned that Steve had jammed his thumb under the hammer of my gun and saved me from unwittingly killing my best friend.

VI
"Daughter of Sorrow"

Water splashed in my face. Fiery tequila trickled down my throat, half choking me. Coughing, sputtering, I struggled to sit up.

"He will not die?" It was Magdalena's voice, torn with grief.

"Die? From a few dozen scratches? Lady, the skipper's knife-proof. In his younger days he must've been a sword swallower, see? Dead? Say, give him another man-size shot of this firewater, and he'll be doin' a highland fling. Atta boy, skipper, drink hearty."

When the blinding ache in my eyes had cleared a little, I saw that I was in a small, bare room. Candles burned. Steve and Magdalena talked in low voices, as if afraid of being overheard. One of them on each side of a wide bench on which I lay, they worked with white bandages and some sort of antiseptic that burned excruciatingly when applied to my raw wounds.

"Quit grinnin', you gosh-darned mule," complained Steve, "and lay quiet while I swab some more of these vaccination marks. You must've fell into a mess of barbed wire. You're a mess, skipper. And don't try to tell me that carbolic acid hurts when it hits a knife cut, buddy."

He dabbed at a new place on my shoulder, and I set my teeth to keep back a grunt of pain.

"We ain't got much time." Steve turned to Magdalena, who clung to my hand in pitiful silence. Her lips moved in some prayer. "The skipper's settin' pretty. Quick as I get this bandage on, I'll let him up. You slip off now and meet us where I told you."

"But my father, *señor?*"

"Don't fret about him. Him and Panchito are holdin' a pow-wow behind closed doors. I peeked in a few minutes ago, and they shooed me out with dirty looks. Panchito's talkin' turkey to that old son-of-a-gun . . . what I mean is . . . they're in conference, see? You leave your dad to Panchito. Pick a clean spot on the skipper's map and kiss him good bye. You won't see him for fifteen minutes, mebby twenty. 'At's a gal. Now run along and pack your warsack for a long trip. You're gonna see the United States *muy pronto.*"

And when Magdalena had gone, Steve forced another big drink down me.

"Where's Panchito?" I asked.

Steve had dropped his mask of jocularity now. He jerked a thumb in the direction of a closed door.

"In a little room beyond that door, skipper . . . him and that damned Diego. Door's a foot thick and bolted on the inside. Walls too thick to hear anything. How d'you feel, old timer?"

"Not so bad," I lied.

"Some little old garden party, eh? Thank me for jarrin' you loose from that broad you was rasslin' with. Your old lady wasn't more'n two lengths behind me, see? If she'd seen you muggin' that baby, you'd've put in the first year of your married life explainin' away that touchin' scene."

He was grinning again. Kidding me along, I knew, to help pull me together.

"Go to hell, you bonehead." I swung my legs to the floor.

"Now you're percolatin' on all six cylinders, skipper. Say, you sure spoiled Pasqual for parlor work. Only that I hate to poke a lady in the jaw, I'd have busted that dame so hard she'd sleep a week. Her and that Pasqual guy pulls this Romeo stuff to get your goat, see? Her dolled up in your miss's Sunday-go-to-church rags, lollygaggin' around with this bullfighter bird, makin' chili love under the shelterin' palms. But I bet they don't try to pull no badger game on the next *gringo*."

Both of us stared at that heavy oak door, waiting for it to move, wondering what lay beyond. It was a foot thick, criss-crossed by bands of wrought iron, studded with huge nails, a massive thing, set on great band-forged hinges. I would never have guessed how much drama could be contained behind something so inanimate.

Life-and-death drama. Together we stared at it, Steve and I, helpless to aid the man who was somewhere beyond that barrier. Seconds dragged past with horrible slowness. Whose hand would it be that should swing open that door?

I forgot the sting of my wounds, the dizziness in my head, as I waited. Steve's face was set in grim lines, his eyes slits of hard glass. Should it be the black don whose hand moved back the bolts — may God pity him, for he'd get no mercy at our hands. It was a grim vigil and no mistake. Steve's voice, startling in its very careless calm, made me jump. I'd been tense as a tightly wound steel spring.

"This Diego bum," he was saying, "is a nervy son-of-a-gun, skipper. After you stepped into the garden, he sat there with them damned eyes of his glarin' at me, lickin' his lips while the clock ticked off the ten minutes before I'm due to follow you. Like some hard-boiled colonel that's got a guy up on the carpet for bein' drunk or A. W. O. L., see? It gets my goat. 'I bet ten smackers,' says I, spittin' on his floor to show him I ain't at attention, 'that the skipper picks up the marbles out there in the garden.' And strike me tongue-tied, if the old buzzard rooster don't call my bet. Now it'll be my luck to have Panchito croak the old goat, and there won't be so much as a plugged nickel in his pockets."

He shook his head sadly. I noticed for the first time that around his throat ran an ugly red welt. His neck was bruised and swollen. Steve grinned and stroked his throat gingerly.

"I got it as I stepped into the garden, when my ten minutes were up. Some guy sittin' in a tree dropped a rope over my head and yanked me off my feet. Greaser necktie party the don's givin' for me special. And I'd still be swingin' from the limb of that pepper tree only I'm packin' a Bowie knife and cut myself down. Then I shinnied up the tree after this hangman party. When I departed from the tree, he was fillin' a noose in his own rope."

Again silence fell over us. Even Steve could not talk for long with that door in front of us. Then a thought struck me like a blow in the face. I was on my feet. My action startled Steve.

"Hear somethin', skipper?" he whispered huskily.

"No. Listen, Steve, and see if you can figure this. If Don Diego is blind, how in hell could he tell it was five minutes to twelve when he told me to wait till midnight, then go into the garden? How did he know when your ten minutes were up?"

Steve, too, was on his feet now. Odd that we hadn't noticed the flaw in Diego's actions before.

"If Diego ain't blind, skipper," said Steve thoughtfully, "he's the champeen actor of the world. It takes a smart guy to fool all the people for as many years as he's bin blind. Still, how could he tell time without seein'?"

"Hanged if I know," I told him.

I looked about quickly. My eyes finally rested on the bench where I had lain. Not much of a battering ram, but I wasn't going to look any longer at that infernal door. Steve nodded and grabbed one side. We crashed the thick bench endwise against the door.

The hinges creaked ever so faintly. The door swung slowly open. It had not been barred. We rushed into the room.

A candle burned on a table. On the floor lay a knife, red with blood that was still sticky in its freshness. Beyond that, the room was empty. Moreover, we had come through the only door that entered into the room.

We stood there, stunned into stupidity, trying to grasp the significance of that empty room. A puddle of blood on the floor told of a struggle. There lay one of the knives that had formerly been in the red-leather case.

"They left while you were in the garden, Steve," I said.

"Not a chance, skipper," he shook his head. "I ain't so dumb as all that. When the lady and I brung you in here, the first thing I done was to try that door and try it hard, see? It was sure bolted hard and fast on the inside. It's bin unbolted since we brung you in. Once, when we were bringin' you outta it, I thought I heard the door squeak. But when I looked around, it was still shut tight. I was too busy seein' if you were dyin' to pay any more attention to it. I bet my left eye somebody opened the door, looked us over, then shut it."

"But how did Panchito and the black don get out? There's just the one door and no window."

I took the candle and examined the wall near the spot of blood. I found what I sought — a small door, perhaps three feet high, hidden behind a cob-webbed portrait of some ancient Álvarez. But to save my neck, I could not find the hidden spring that opened it. Nor could Steve.

"Unless I'm all twisted," said Steve, "the dinin' room is on the other side of the wall. Let's have a look in there."

At double-quick time we retreated through the little room where I had lain on the bench, along the dimly lit hallway, then through a doorway into the dining room where the four of us had sat by the fireplace. All the candles save those on the mantelpiece had been snuffed out. The table, with its shining array of sparkling glass and shining silver, mocked us as we slowed our pace and stepped into the room.

The ticking of the clock came, the sound of our own pounding hearts, beyond that a tomb-like silence. The coals of the mesquite fire sent a dull red glow from the fireplace. I saw Steve, a pace ahead of me, halt and drop into the crouching pose of a man about to leap. As I looked past his bulk, I saw what sent a chill along my spine and deadened the hope in my heart.

For, erect in that high-backed chair, black and white against the scarlet leather, sat the don of the black serape. Silent, terrible, that black-and-white image of everlasting hate sat motionless. His shriveled arm lay hidden beneath the folds of his black serape, while the lean, talon-like fingers of his other hand, resting on the wide arm of the chair, held a half-emptied wine glass. The uneven candlelight sent weird shadows across the mask-like, parchment-hued face of the terrible old man. His mouth was twisted cruelly, his eyes, burned-out coals, seemed more deeply set than ever.

Steve slipped a gun into my hand. His other six-shooter dangling in careless readiness, he stepped toward Don Diego.

"No, no, my friends!" It was Panchito's voice, calm, steady, coming from the doorway behind us. I thanked God aloud as I whirled about.

There stood Panchito. Even in the shadow, I saw his white teeth flash a smile. Beside him, his arm about her shoulder, stood Magdalena.

"Don Diego and I," he announced in that formal manner he could so readily assume, "have declared a truce. It is his one wish that we leave his house immediately and in silence. I have given my word that we shall respect that wish. In return for the sparing of his life, he releases Magdalena."

I noticed that Panchito looked old and tired as he stood there, with Magdalena clinging to him, her eyes wide with sorrow. She would have gone across the room to her father but for the Spaniard's restraining arm.

"His feeling toward you, my child, has been not one of love but of hatred. It is his last wish that you leave him without a word or caress of parting. Come, my friends, before Don Diego regrets this one generous deed of his wicked life and blocks our way."

I needed no further urging to leave that room. I was at Magdalena's side and none too soon, for she wilted like some delicate flower crushed by a heavy hand. We carried her out into the courtyard where horses pawed impatiently.

Steve, who had lingered in the dining hall a moment, now joined us. Riding four abreast, Panchito and I holding Magdalena in her saddle as she revived slowly from her swoon, we passed through the unguarded gateway.

I saw Steve, as he rode along beside me, examining an

exquisitely etched dagger, set in precious stones. I had noticed the thing where it hung on the wall among the other relics of old Spain that belonged to the house of Álvarez. He met my questioning glance with a grin.

"Told you it'd be my luck, skipper," he said in a barely audible tone. "There wasn't so much as a thin dime on the old geezer."

When I stared stupidly, his grin widened.

"Then let me 'n' your miss ride on ahead, see? From where I'm settin', Panchito looks like he needs a pick-up."

In that easy manner of his, he appointed himself escort for Magdalena. Chatting in a carefree manner, as if we journeyed on some picnic, he was making light of past sorrows and dangers, painting for her bright-colored pictures of the United States. I was not surprised to catch the sound of her timid laugh as he made some remark. In his own way, Steve Doyle was a diplomat.

Panchito drank from Steve's bottle of liquid fire.

"You are hurt?" I whispered.

He shrugged, smiling.

"A scratch, no more. But for the kindness of the *Señor Dios,* I should now be dead by the treacherous hand of the black don. Even to the very last, *señor,* that Diego Álvarez feared me and resorted to cunning in his attempt to kill me. You listened to his proposal, no? That I should wear a black hood and share his blindness? *Señor,* it was the plan of a cold-blooded murderer, for Don Diego Álvarez was *not* blind. Some skilled surgeon, but a month ago, removed the cause of blindness and restored the black don's eyesight. So clever was that human devil, *señor,* that no member of his household, save one, knew of the operation. His diabolical cleverness at acting deceived even Magdalena.

"So, *señor,* when I, hooded with that black velvet cap that fastened about my neck, stepped into the darkened room to play life's final game with Don Diego, I alone was blind."

I saw him cross himself before he continued.

"It was none less than the *Señor Dios* who so decreed that the only one of Don Diego's household who saw through his deception was a person who hated Don Diego with all the hatred of a Mexican woman who has seen her son murdered to further the plans of the black don. The woman was Don Diego's seamstress. Her son was that unfortunate Enrique, whose head Don Diego had stuck on a spear that Peranteau might work his trick by which they hoped to snare us.

"It was she who fashioned that black hood. It was she who laced it on me and, following Don Diego into his darkened room, led me by the hand. In fastening the lacing, *señor,* that old woman whispered words into my ear. Words that chilled me to the very marrow of my bones. I, blindfolded, was facing one of the most skillful knife men in all of Mexico. Like a trussed pig, I was at the mercy of a man who has long forgotten the meaning of such a word. So it would seem, eh?

"But quite the contrary, *señor.* The terrible sight of Enrique's head on the spear had turned the woman's blood to acid, and she now felt only bitter hatred for the man who had killed her son. Her skill with her tools that had long served Don Diego now became her means of revenge. For that hood that covered my face, since Diego had inspected the diabolical thing, had been pierced by a myriad of tiny slashes. The nature of the fabric and her skill as a worker of cloth concealed these openings.

" 'The prayers of a heartbroken mother will give strength to your arm, *señor,*' she whispered in my ear as she made a pretext of a last examination of the hood. Then she closed the door, and I was left alone with the man who set about to murder me.

"Mind you, *señor,* that Don Diego, even with such an advantage, despite his skill with a knife, feared me, for, *por Dios,* he knew I was unafraid. He could have told me then that he was not blind, and, while I ripped off that hood, he could have killed me ten times over.

"But no, *señor.* Fear or pride, or perhaps both, kept him silent. I could have laughed aloud when he spoke for the first time. *¡Caramba, señor!* Either from eagerness or guilt, that buzzard's voice shook.

" 'My dear Panchito,' he croaked at me, 'some maudlin *padre* left one of his holy candles hereabouts. That your *Dios* may have aid to witness your death struggles, I now light it.'

"Consider the sacrilege, *señor!* Cloaking his own devilish designs with such words. Poof! He did not guess that the light of that candle should guide my blade, not his, to his flesh.

"I saw the match sputter as he lit the candlewick. I saw his grinning lips writhe, his eyes glitter with anticipation of his act. For a moment he stood there in the flickering light, with his knife and the scarf that had once been worn by Doña María.

" 'Speak up, my dear Panchito' . . . he carried his shamming blindness to the very end . . . 'sound your voice that I may hand you your end of the scarf. The scarf to which still clings the faint perfume used by Doña María. You thought I did not read your love for her in your eyes, years ago, eh? You with your prayers and rosaries! Is there not a commandment that deals with a man who makes love to the wife of another? Speak up, my dear Panchito, that I may let you touch with your mouth that scarf which belonged to her.'

"I spoke then, *señor.* The hood hid the paleness of my face and the trembling of my lips. *Caramba,* I was beside myself with rage. But it was a rage that was tempered with judgment. I vowed to make him pay in his last moments for his insult to the *Señor Dios* and the name of a pure woman.

" 'Listen, thou unclean thing of an evil brain,' I told him. 'Witness thou a miracle of Him whom thou blaspheme.'

"With that dagger held in the palm of my hand, I stepped to the candle and touched its point to the wick that burned. Then, with him watching, I stooped and picked from the floor the discarded match he had thrown there. Picked up that bit of burned match with my dagger point. Never, *señor,* have I seen such a look on any man's face.

" 'You see!' he croaked in a hoarse whisper. 'You see through the hood!'

" 'Thanks to my *Señor Dios,*' I told him. 'Tell me, my Diego, by what occult powers can a blind man see another pick up a match with a dagger, eh?'

"With a cry of rage he was at me. The scarf discarded, he slid his knife at my chest. Those slits in the hood were none too useful for quick work, and he missed my heart by a skin's breadth, his blade sliding around my rib. I took swift advantage of my opening. My blade went to the hilt in his black heart. Panchito de la Vega had kept his vow.

"When I had checked the flow of his blood, I carried his body into the dining hall by a secret passage in the wall. That the *Señorita* Magdalena might never know the manner of his passing, I arranged him in his chair, covering his wound with his black serape. May the *Señor Dios,* in His understanding, forgive the lie of that deception."

He pressed something soft and black to his lips. I knew without asking that it was the scarf of Doña María that he kissed, then carefully placed under his jacket next to his heart. We spurred forward to join Magdalena and Steve.

Again I rode alongside the woman of my heart. Once more Steve and Panchito, my comrades who had made possible my greatest happiness, rode side by side into the dawn of another day.

For Magdalena and me it was to be the sunrise of love. For those two ahead, it would be but another tomorrow. In spite of the great love God and my two friends had given me, I could not keep the ache from my heart, not even when the frivolous words of Steve's song drifted back to us.

It was when we halted for breakfast prepared by riders, who appeared apparently from nowhere, that Steve sprang his surprise.

"If we won't cramp your style too much, skipper, me and Panchito will go on across the border with you."

He chuckled at my startled look.

"If you got any drag with them border bulls, skipper," he went on, "you might do some good. Get the idea?"

When we left that little camp, I rode with lighter heart for between us we managed to map out a plan whereby Steve could pass unmolested into his own country. Panchito, who had done no wrong in the eyes of the United States, was free to cross as he willed.

My plan was simple enough. Steve still carried his Army discharge made out under the name of Sergeant James Brophy. Nine-tenths of Mexico believed Steve Doyle of Villa's army to be dead. The remaining tenth, all border officials and men of sound judgment, would be open to conviction under certain conditions. For instance, if one Jim Brophy, a World War hero, could be induced to accept a position with that hard-riding, fast-shooting little troop that guard our international border, they would be more than willing forever to bury one Major Stephano Doyle. Simple enough.

So it was that Steve Doyle died down there in Sonora, and Jim Brophy found a commission waiting his signature in El Paso. I could have found something of the sort for Panchito in due time, only fate stepped in.

The bank in El Paso had mail for Panchito — impressive-looking envelopes of thick linen paper spattered with red seals. Among the long envelopes was sandwiched one of pale lavender, faintly scented and crested with an impressive coat of arms. I saw the old Spaniard's hands shake as he opened this one, ignoring the others, much to the bank president's annoyance. There were tears in his eyes when he very gently placed the letter inside his coat.

"Ah, *señor,*" he smiled at me, "the *Señor Dios* is kind." He said no more, but we knew that the exile of Francisco de la Vega had come to a happy ending.

We parted that night in El Paso — El Paso, which, in the language of the Mexicans, means The Pass. Fit name for this place of our last meeting. For each one of us it was the passing into a new life and the beginning of better things.

What better spot could we have chosen than this Baghdad of the border, where the lobby of an ultra-modern hotel is thronged with all manner of men and women bent on strange missions; where well-groomed men and women in evening clothes converse in low tones with booted, hard-eyed men who come from the moonlit desert; where many a dress coat of New York tailoring conceals the blue steel of a .45. There are found sleek foreigners whose idle loitering hides a mission of dangerous intrigue; swarthy Mexicans with fat wives and beautiful, expensively gowned daughters; remittance men, usually a little drunk, chat easily with the exiles from across the border; a sprinkling of secret service men and a few officers from the fort; race-track men; a white-haired *padre;* a notorious gun-runner, the latter in close conference with a bellhop. Above all is soft music and the sparkle of diamonds . . . El Paso, the gateway to the north.

Through it passed Panchito on his way to his lavender-scented love. Magdalena and I, never to return to that country of her birth where she had known only sorrow, passed on. Only Steve remained, Steve in his beloved uniform, gay, flippant, handsome, his eyes alight with the thrill of fresh adventure.

As our train pulled slowly away from the station, we saw him standing there, erect and smiling. He threw me a last salute. There was a fascinating hint of swagger in that salute, a don't-give-a-damn touch that was splendid. He would be a popular officer. I can't explain exactly why, but, when I returned that salute, I was thinking of El Lobo, who lay at rest in an unmarked grave, down there in Mexico.

We stood there on the observation platform, Magdalena and I, until the last little light of El Paso winked at us and was no more . . . El Paso, the gateway to the north . . . for us, it was the gateway to happiness.

Señor Satán

In his autobiography — published posthumously as WALT COBURN: WESTERN WORD WRANGLER (Northland Press, 1973) — Coburn confessed that "my plots came from the stars. I might awaken in the middle of the night with some idea which would keep me awake. Perhaps it was nothing more than a single character, or a catch phrase I had heard, or a horse which reminded me of one I once knew, and the man who rode that forgotten horse. Dreams took shape; the plots just came from nowhere." Much of *"Señor Satán"* has about it the quality of a dream, even to the island's sinking into the sea once the characters leave it. *"Señor Satán,"* set during the era of the Volstead Act in the United States, was first published in Fiction House's *Action Stories* (6/30). It was subsequently reprinted in *Action Stories* (4/42) under the title "The Gun-Brand *Gringo*." This marks its first appearance in book form.

I
"Buried Gold"

"Gold?" cackled the crazy hermit of the Sangre de Cristo, pointing with a skinny finger toward the notched skyline beyond the strip of desert. "Aye, gold aplenty there. But I tell you, young feller, as I've told other fools that's stopped here at my cabin, it's gold that belongs to the dead. There's blood on that buried gold, and the way to it is marked by the white bones of fools that's gone across that desert in the hopes of fetchin' it back. Aye, I've warned 'em. But they laugh in my face and tell me I'm cracked. Which I am, but so would you be, if you'd bin where I bin and back. To hell and back, no less."

"You've been across the desert and back, old man?" asked Jim Driscoll, cautiously leading up to that dread question he feared to ask because he already guessed the answer that would come from this cackling, crazy-brained old hermit.

"Aye, across 'er and back. Leavin' the best part of me there where the damn' gold shines in the sun till it fair blinds a man. Leavin' my strength and my guts and my brain there where the skeleton hands of dead men are filled with raw gold. Fools! Fools!

"Man! Wasn't I one of 'em? Straight and strong and handsome as yourself, lad. With a taste for adventure and the gold fever a-drivin' me on. Laughin' at God, darin' the devil. Aye, and a-crawlin' back on my hands and knees, with a broken body and a cracked mind, and my tongue swollen and black from thirst."

The voice of the old hermit broke into a thin wail, then died into silence. He stood there in front of his cabin, staring with unwinking, glittering eyes across the miles of waterless wasteland that separated the Sangre de Cristo peaks from the San Angelo Mountains.

Jim Driscoll watched the white-bearded, white-maned, ragged, old wreck of a man. In spite of the twisted spine and the bent legs, there was a terrible sort of strength in that broken body. A crazy, desperate sort of strength. His gnarled hands were strong as steel claws, and those long, sinewy arms — Jim Driscoll had seen them lift great rocks in the building of a wall around his hut that was made of genuine boulders.

For a long moment the hermit stood there, staring with terrible eyes across the desert, which was shadowed now in the coming dusk. What horrible visions the old man was conjuring up, only his cracked mind could know.

"You spoke of other men who have tried to cross the desert." Jim Driscoll gave voice to that dread question that he had been waiting long hours to ask. "Has there been any man in the past six months who set out for the San Angelo Mountains?"

"Aye, one man. He's dead."

"Dead? How do you know, old man?"

"They're all dead, all the fools who would not listen to me. No man can live out there. Nothing is alive there." Now he whirled, eyes glittering strangely, staring with maniac suspicion at the younger man. "Why do you ask about a man who passed this way? What was that man to you?"

Jim Driscoll thought the twisted, crouching old hermit was going to leap on him. One of those gnarled, black-nailed hands had slid inside the greasy flannel shirt, and Jim saw the tip of the wooden handle of a butcher knife. Then the knife slid back into its makeshift scabbard under the shirt. And the hermit's bearded lips twisted into a cackling laugh.

"Skeered yuh, did I? Aye." He tapped his forehead with a grimy forefinger. "Cracked. Queer notions git into my head. And if you'd bin to hell and back, you'd git notions, too. . . . There's them as thinks I've got gold cached here. There's some as 'ud kill fer gold."

Jim Driscoll's hand came away from his six-shooter. He wondered if it wasn't the big Colt .45 that had checked the hermit's impulse to use the butcher knife. What a sweet companion this old devil would be in case a man was forced to stay overnight. And why had he so quickly flared into a killing mood at Jim's question?

Behind the hermit's erratic actions lay a shrewdness that made Jim Driscoll do some thinking. How much of this babbling about dead men's gold was real? How much was clever acting?

In Jim's mind was the warning given him by a Mexican goatherd back across the slopes of the Sangre de Cristo: "Beware, *señor,* of that old *hombre*. He alone guards the secret of the Sangre de Cristo. Never turn your back to him."

No amount of money would tempt a Mexican or Indian to cross over the divide to the southern slope of the mountains where the hermit dwelt alone. Yet some of those Mexicans were brave men, and the Yaquis who lived in the hills were said to be fierce warriors, unafraid of death. And what was the secret of the Sangre de Cristo? Gold? Hidden treasure?

In the early morning, before the heat waves distorted vision, a man could stand on this peak where the hermit dwelt and without binoculars see the white sand of the beach where the blue sea lapped. And musty tradition had it that this cove had, in days gone by, sheltered the booty-laden pirate ships that cruised the southern seas. Later it had been used by whalers. Sailor folk claimed that it was here that the old whales came to die. The beach, for two miles, was covered with the huge, bleached bones of whales. Back behind the dunes was water fit to drink.

Down there in Mexico were any number of strange tales of buried treasure. In the little seaport towns crafty rascals netted a living from the fake maps they sold to adventurers lured there by yarns dealing with pirate gold. More than a few of those unfortunate adventurers had died in their vain search. Others managed to get back to the villages, forever cured of treasure hunting. Yet, there were always some who would still come to be taken in by the map-makers, for until the end of time that bait of buried treasure will lure men into danger and hardships and sometimes death.

It was not pirate gold that took Jim Driscoll across mountains and desert to the Sangre de Cristo. He wondered how much was guessed about the presence of a man in cowpuncher garb, riding a stout horse, and leading a second horse with a light pack of grub. No cattle grazed on the south slope of the mountains, where there was little water and scant food. Nothing to tempt a cowpuncher. What decent excuse could a cowboy give for being here, for wanting to cross that strip of desert to the San Angelo Mountains beyond? The San Angelos — where only a handful of Indians and Mexicans and a scattering of white-skinned renegades hid out between raids.

As the crow flies, the San Angelo Mountains were about two hundred miles below the international border between the United States and Mexico. There was a circuitous trail there that followed around the end of the Sangre de Cristo peaks and avoided the desert save for a fifteen-mile strip easily crossed on a stout horse. It lengthened the distance by perhaps seventy-five miles, but its way was not barren, and there were water holes within an easy day's ride of one another. Now and then the Mexican rebel troops, hard pressed by the *Federales,* took that trail to the San Angelo Mountains. They could hide there or escape by boat to a safer port.

The port of San Angelo, thirty miles down the coast from the Whalebone Cove of pirate legend, was notorious as a tough town. Renegades of every description lived there — Mexican bandits, American smugglers and outlaws, aliens deported from the United States seeking to return via the smuggling route, handlers of opium and other drugs bartered there with the smuggling gangs.

There were ugly ruffian hangouts, opium dives, squalid saloons. Blatant music, stabbings, plots, and counterplots. Burros and parakeets and fleas and white dust. Naked children and razor-backed hogs. Gold money changed hands. Gay serapes and women all in black. Wrinkled old men sitting in the shade, waiting to die. Life was priced cheaply there. Men defied the laws of nations and sneered at God's commandments. Such was the port of San Angelo, just below the old Whalebone Cove.

Between the San Angelo Mountains and the Sangre de Cristo peaks there stretched that grim desert with its heat and thirst and bleached skeletons, its hundred-and-one weird tales of buried gold and violence. There the terrible sandstorms buried and uncovered both men and the gold they sought. The wind dug pits and built mountains of sand, sometimes laying bare the hidden secrets of its grim vastness.

Few men had ever found the treasures so ruthlessly guarded by the desert. The Mexicans and Yaquis told vague tales of strange happenings — murders, robberies. And it was their belief that the old hermit of the Sangre de Cristo held the secret of the hills and desert in his cracked brain.

"What secret?" Jim Driscoll had asked many times as his trail led southward toward the Sangre de Cristo. "What secret does the old man hide?"

"*¿Quién sabe, señor?* Who knows? It is a secret that concerns only the men who start across the desert to find gold. They never return. Nor do they ever get to the port of San Angelo. They die."

"It is a long journey," Jim Driscoll would say. "The heat is terrible. There is no water. They die of thirst. There is no secret to that."

"You do not understand, *señor.* It is not always the thirst and heat that causes them to die."

"What, then, kills them?" Jim Driscoll had inquired, a little impatient with these superstitious peons.

"*Dios* knows, *señor.* Ask no more questions. You will bring down the curse of the Sangre de Cristo. There you may learn that which you seek to know. But, *por Dios,* it will mean your death. Turn back from your journey before it is too late."

"I am not searching for gold, *hombres.* I seek a man. A tall, blond-haired man with a scar across his forehead. He came this way within the past six months. You say he passed along this trail. He went on toward the Sangre de Cristo. I am not after gold, *amigos.* I seek a man."

"That man must be a great friend or a bitter enemy, *señor,* that you would follow him to the Sangre de Cristo."

"A great friend, *sí, señores.* Perhaps a bitter enemy. That is something that I shall be able to learn when I find the man. It is the answer to that question in my heart I hope to learn from that man."

"That man went on, *señor,* to the Sangre de Cristo. By now, he will be dead. Turn back, *señor,* before it is too late. That which you wish to know lies hidden in the same grave that holds that man."

"He would be a hard man to kill," Jim Driscoll had persisted. "He is big and strong and can crack a man's bones with his two hands. He travels well-armed and well-mounted. He fears nothing on earth or in hell. Something tells me that he is alive."

"He is dead, *señor.*" The Mexicans spoke with a discouraging finality. "This man, who is your friend or your enemy, is dead. Turn back, *señor,* in the name of God."

But Jim Driscoll was not of the breed that turns back. He

had kept on. On across the slopes of the Sangre de Cristo peaks and on to the stone cabin of this old hermit.

Now the hermit of the Sangre de Cristo leered crazily at Jim Driscoll and ran his long, black-nailed fingers through his tangled mat of greasy, white beard.

"The man you ask about is dead. As dead as you'll be, young fool, if you pick up his trail."

"You can't scare me, old man, with your crazy tales. And you can't make me think that the man I am hunting is dead. I'm starting across the desert now. It'll be cool all night. My horses are stout. I've cut down my grub supply and loaded on enough cans of water to take me and my horses across your desert. There'll be a full moon, and I've got my bearings before I start. I've got a six-gun and a carbine and plenty of shells. And before I set out, I'll slip you this hunk of news. I'll kill any man that skylights himself. That goes for you, and it goes for your damned friends. You're not half as loco as you let on. Any more than I'm the drifting cowpuncher that I might seem to the peons. I reckon you get my drift."

The hermit's face twisted with fury. Again his hand slid inside the bosom of the greasy, blue-flannel shirt.

"Better not try it, old man. Because it wouldn't bother my conscience a bit to kill you."

Jim Driscoll's six-shooter was in his hand now. And his strong white teeth showed in a grin that held no humor.

"Ye'll die for this, ye fool!" screamed the old hermit in his rusty, cracked voice. "Aye, ye'll die slow and in the agonies o' hell. Staked out naked in the sun with yore tongue as black as a crow's wing, beggin' fer the water that'll be within sight. Aye, by the mark o' Judas, ye'll die. With clear water within the sight o' yer eyes, and with gold a-shinin' there in the sun. Gold that's had its washin' in the blood o' fools that went mad and killed one another fer the yellow coins stacked there in chests. Gold, by the devil that spawned them as come there, gold enough to buy the souls o' honest men and women. Gold enough to break the back of men as tried to carry it away."

Jim Driscoll's blood chilled at the sight of this croaking old man whose eyes glittered from under bushy white brows. Half sane, half mad, with the eyes and hands of a murderer, the hermit of the Sangre de Cristo fouled the air with his cursing and raving.

Jim Driscoll listened, forcing a derisive grin. Perhaps, so he thought, if the old hermit reached the point where his maniacal anger got the better of his discretion, he would blurt out something of the black secret he guarded. But Jim Driscoll was doomed to disappointment, because with a final outburst of profane insults the old man whirled and ran crabwise on his misshapen legs back into the stone hut.

Jim Driscoll leaped for the shelter of some rocks. And just in time, for a shower of buckshot rattled against the granite boulders. Again and again the hermit blazed away with a shotgun from a small porthole fashioned in the wall of the hut.

Anyhow, decided Jim Driscoll, *I've got the old hellion's number, and it doesn't take much imagination to guess what's become of more than one of the gents who landed here.*

Jim Driscoll slipped away through the boulders and brush to a little cañon where he had left his horses. It was already dusk when he swung into the saddle and, leading his pack horse, rode down the trail and toward the first level of the desert that lay ahead of him. From up on the slope still came the boom of the hermit's shotgun. The old devil was continuing to spatter the rocks with buckshot.

II
"Gunrunners' Trail"

Jim rode until night dropped its black shroud across the desert. Then he pulled up and unslung a pair of night glasses. For almost an hour he scanned the black slopes of the Sangre de Cristo. And finally his night vigil was rewarded by the crimson-yellow stab of a signal fire against the blackness.

"That," he told his horse, "spells what we want to know. And we know that somewhere ahead somebody is a-watchin' that signal. There, it's gone. The relay station has picked it up. And we'll be on the lap of the gods until further orders. On the lap of. . . ."

Jim Driscoll broke off in his voiced musing. His ears had caught the sound of horses coming. Horses carrying riders that jabbered in the Mexican tongue. And through the jargon of peon Spanish words, there cut another voice, speaking English.

". . . and that goes, Hamlin, just as it lays. You'll double the pay, or we quit. And if I say the word right now, you'll never see the States again. Get the slant?"

"You've got me over a barrel, Quick, and you know it. But don't get the idea that you're pulling something smart. Because you're not. In fact, Quick, you're putting across the dumb play I've been betting myself you'd try. What I'm getting at, Quick, is this. . . ."

The muffled crack of a gun. A man's stifled curse that ended in a moan. Then the voice of the man called Hamlin.

"Just leave his damned carcass there where the buzzards can get to it, Pancho. And learn a little lesson from the passing of the late Raymond Quick. What I'm getting at, Pancho, is the simple fact that it takes a hell of a smart *hombre* to slip anything over on the *Señor* Harley Hamlin.

Do you follow me, Pancho?"

"Weeth perfect pleasure, *Señor* Hamlin," came the low-toned, musical voice of Pancho.

"Want to say a little prayer, Pancho, over the late, lamented Raymond Quick?"

"No prayer, *señor.* My prayers go to bless the fortunes of Pancho Gómez."

"You'll need 'em, my *amigo,* when you kick off. And ride ahead of me, my dear Pancho, not alongside. I'd love to trust you, *compadre,* but it seems that the milk of human kindness and tolerance and so on is about dried up in the good old system, if you get me. . . . I said . . . ride ahead, you mongrel, crossbred son of . . . then take it where it'll do you the most good, you half-breed rat!"

Again the flat spat of a gun, pumping hot lead, followed by the dull crash of a body hitting the ground. Hamlin's voice rasped into a snarl as his gun ripped apart the silence.

"And now, you dirty greaser, you'll know who's boss!"

Suddenly it was like bedlam breaking loose. Pack mules and saddle horses tearing past. Bullets crashing. Groans and curses. The rasping laugh of this Harley Hamlin as he taunted the Mexicans.

"Come and get it, you yellow-bellied sons! I have enough hot lead to go around."

"Whoever," gritted Jim Driscoll, gripping his Winchester, "and whatever you might be, Mister Hamlin, you sure ain't a coward. One against a dozen. Well, here's lessening the odds by one."

With a wild cowboy yell, Jim Driscoll jumped his horse into the open. His gun threw spurts of flame as he rode up alongside the tall white man who, a six-shooter in each hand, was charging here and there among the confused Mexicans whose guns cracked with wild disorder.

Side by side, Hamlin and Driscoll charged the disconcerted Mexicans.

"Many thanks, old lad," cried Hamlin. "You got here in the nick of time. Damned decent thing to do."

"Keep the change," Jim Driscoll flung back as he rode down a pair of murderous-looking Mexicans who yelled for mercy.

A few minutes of fast, desperate fighting, then Hamlin's voice, calm, deadly cold, dangerous, called to the Mexicans to lay down their guns.

Jim Driscoll had time now to size up this white man. There was that about his manner of speech which hinted of England, rather than the United States. Jim saw a tall, finely proportioned man in worn but well-cut cavalry breeches and boots, a white shirt stained with blood at the shoulder. A high-crowned Stetson at a rakish slant on a head of close-cropped, sand-colored hair. A clipped mustache that gave a dignity to the clean-cut bronzed face. Strong white teeth flashed Jim Driscoll a quick smile.

Then Hamlin went on with the brisk business of disarming the Mexicans and sending them to round up the frightened pack mules. When this was attended to, he turned to Jim Driscoll.

"You know, old man, you probably saved my life. The name is Harley Hamlin. Yours?"

"Driscoll. Jim Driscoll."

"It is a pleasure, Jim Driscoll, to meet a gentleman of such generosity and courage. You're alone?"

"Yes. Alone."

"Traveling toward San Angelo Mountains, perhaps, or Whalebone Cove? I'm asking the impertinent question in the hope of returning the recent favor. Because, if you don't already know, it's a damned dangerous trek. Fact is, I know of no surer way of committing suicide. If you met the genial hermit of the Sangre de Cristo, you may have some intimation of the dangers that lie along your trail ahead. And since you've put me so in your debt, it's my duty, as a former gentleman of honor, to dissuade you from your purpose."

"But I won't be dissuaded," grinned Jim Driscoll. "I'm goin' on."

"Madness, old man, sheer madness. It's a two-plus-two-makes-four proposition. Cut and dried, y'understand. The beggars will snuff out your bally old light. You'll be snuffed out, Driscoll."

"Better that, Hamlin, than to be a damned coward."

"I don't quite take in the idea, of course, but this matter of a man's courage or cowardice is a bit overdrawn. It's plain suicide. There's a bit of difference, y'know, between courage and foolhardiness."

Jim Driscoll smiled. "It wasn't so many minutes ago that you took a long chance yourself."

The tall Englishman shrugged his wide shoulders. "A forced issue, Driscoll. My recent business associate, the late Raymond Quick, had arranged with his old chum, Pancho Gómez, to put me out of the way. I anticipated their moment for the dark deed and rather took them by surprise, y'might say. It was a sportin' proposition from the start. High stakes and winner take all. The loser's end is death.

"I should have informed you, perhaps, that the business with which I am connected is not exactly legal or quite honorable. And among such chaps as Quick and the suave but sinister Pancho, one finds but little honor. The result is, old man, that I'm now alone in the game, with an unsavory following of tanned-hided blighters who would slit their own grandmother's throat for the price of a jug of pulque. I don't even speak their silly language. If I weren't afraid of insulting you, Driscoll, I'd offer you a partnership in the business."

"Is it that bad, Hamlin?" asked Jim Driscoll.

"Quite. But there's the good old tang of danger in it. And it's remunerative. Though I like to give the beastly business a sort of dignity by calling it import and export trade, frankly speaking, I deal in gunrunning and whiskey smuggling. Importing guns for the silly rebels, exporting liquor for the thirsty Americans. Disgraceful sort of thing and all that, but I'm too stupid to hold down a decent job, and I can't possibly get along on the few pounds that come quarterly from home. And I chucked the only decent chance I had to marry money. I'm chatting quite openly, old man, what?"

There was a sensitive and disarming frankness about the big Britisher. Jim Driscoll chuckled.

"You're heading for the Sangre de Cristo peaks?" he asked Hamlin.

"Should be at the spot by daylight, if these bally idiots don't mutiny. Then I'll trek back to Whalebone Cove for another supply."

"But you told me it meant sure and sudden death to cross the desert?" said Jim Driscoll.

"For you alone, yes. I pay toll to the beggars at both ends. To the odorous and untrimmed hermit of the Sangre de Cristo, and to the more frequently bathed and barbered Peter Tovich at San Angelo port. I am one of the accepted blacklegs, y'know. Dyed with the same stinkin' brush and so on. Lolling in the same mucky hog sty with the entertaining hermit, the genial Tovich, the lately departed Raymond Quick, and a score of other blackguards of evil tastes and putrid pasts. One of their damned fraternity. A sordid mucker, Driscoll."

"If I throw in with you, Hamlin, then I'd be able to go with you, under protection, to Whalebone Cove and Port San Angelo?"

"You'd have protection, such as it is, to be sure. But if it's gold at Whalebone or San Angelo that you're after, I'll frankly discourage you, old chap."

"I'm not after gold. I'm looking for a man."

"Ah! Jove, that complicates things. Rather. The men who dwell in these parts are not apt to extend the dear old welcome in the manner of the famed Western hospitality. I can't call to mind any of the inner circle, the chosen ones of the blackleg lodge, as it were, who would appreciate guests. I'm a bit inclined to share their attitude. If you could do so, friend Driscoll, it might simplify matters if you'd further enlighten me as to the nature of this seeking of a chap who dwells among us derelicts tossed by the tide of decency upon the forgotten sands of Whalebone Cove. In fact, old man, if we're to become at all friendly, I'd have to insist upon something of the sort.

"I've numerous enemies here in this earthly purgatory of the damned, but there are, among the flotsam and jetsam, a few good old chaps who would go through hell to do me a favor. I feel much the same toward them. And should it so be that you are searching for one of them and your motives are not of the chummy nature, then I'll have to let you go alone along your jolly path to oblivion. Perhaps you follow me?"

"Sure. I get your idea, Hamlin. We'll each go our own way. I'll take my chances on getting across the desert, the same as you'll take your chances getting along with these Mexicans. Ships that pass in the night, Hamlin. No hard feelings. I'll even plant your friend Quick and his pardner, Pancho Gómez. By the way, if it isn't asking a personal question, is this fellow, Quick, the same gent that once run a gambling house at Juárez?"

"Right." Hamlin's tone was crisp.

"And Pancho Gómez, mebbeso, is the same Pancho Gómez who once double-crossed Pancho Villa?"

"Same chap, Driscoll."

"Then I'll take the great pleasure of plantin' those two *hombres* under the sand. And before we part, Hamlin, let me congratulate you. You beat a tough combination when you out-foxed those two *hombres*."

In rapid Spanish Jim Driscoll asked the sullen Mexicans some questions. They gave reply in a sort of pathetic eagerness. One of them produced a shovel and handed it to the American. Hamlin took this all in with a sort of astounded attitude of silence.

"These chaps show you a devil of a lot of respect, Driscoll."

"I was raised among their kind, Hamlin. My daddy was an old Texas cowman. We run cattle in the old Palomas country, down in Chihuahua."

"But you don't speak like a cowboy."

"Ever hear of Stanford University, Hamlin? Well, till the cattle market dropped into the bog hole, I attended that university. Three years, Hamlin, and a few months in my senior year."

"I see."

Jim Driscoll shoved out his hand. "So long, Hamlin! Good luck. Better watch your step with these boys, because from the way I see things they thought more of Pancho Gómez than they think of you."

Hamlin smiled grimly. He took Jim Driscoll's proffered hand. Their hands came apart.

"So long, Hamlin!" Driscoll's left hand gripped the

shovel that a Mexican had handed him.

"Good luck, Driscoll."

They parted there. Hamlin, with a gun in his hand, herding his band of sullen Mexicans, Jim Driscoll to perform the grisly burial rites.

The night separated them. The round, white moon pushed its way across the star-filled sky. Ships that pass in the night. Trails that meet and pass their opposite ways.

Jim Driscoll found the dead body of Raymond Quick, smuggler and renegade, outlawed from the country of his birth. Quick lay there in the moonlight, a bullet hole through his heart.

"Señor," called a hushed voice, "*por Dios, señor,* water. I am dying."

Jim Driscoll, his six-shooter ready, followed the sound of the pain-racked voice to find a tight-lipped, bloodstained man hidden in the mesquite brush. He bent over the dying Mexican, holding a filled canteen to the stiffening lips of Pancho Gómez, who was about to bid farewell to his life of many crimes.

"The *Señor* Driscoll," breathed the dying Mexican. "I remember, *Tejano.* I have stolen many of your cattle. Yet, when I am suffering, you share with the miserable Pancho your canteen . . . let me warn you against that *Señor* Harley Hamlin. He is a very damn' dangerous man. Almost as dangerous, my friend, as that man whose trail you follow."

"You know why I'm here, Pancho?"

"There is even now, in my pocket, money paid into my hand . . . the right hand that was to put a knife or a bullet in your back. Do you not remember, *Señor* Driscoll, that I worked for that big, blue-eyed son of sin there on his Hachita Rancho? I saw him no later than last week. His spies had brought news of your coming. He has friends here. Harley Hamlin is, perhaps, one of them. I cannot be sure of that, because Hamlin makes but few friends. More water, *señor,* in God's name . . . *gracias, amigo.*"

"Where is that man I am trailing?" asked Jim Driscoll. "Where will I find him?"

"At the port of San Angelo, perhaps, or Whalebone Cove. Perhaps somewhere in the peaks of the Sangre de Cristo. *¿Quién sabe?* He stays never longer than a day or a night in one place. He knows that death follows him closely. He has made enemies, that *hombre*. I have even heard him say that he would rather have many enemies than many friends. That there was no real friend to any man. A wicked man, that one."

"What is he doing here?" Jim Driscoll pressed his questions ruthlessly.

"He is the dictator of San Angelo. To him Peter Tovich and all the smugglers, such as Quick and Hamlin, pay money. When he sends out an order, it is obeyed. He is king here. When a man refuses to obey him, that big son of sin will break him with his hands. He has cracked more than one spine. His pistols have shot down many who stood against the adobe wall. He is dictator, that big one."

"What name does he use down here?"

"He is called Don *Diablo* and *Señor Satán*. He claims to have been born there at Whalebone Cove. It is his boast that his father was a British pirate and slave dealer who sailed the Mexican waters, that his mother was a woman of title in Spain whom that pirate captured and forced into marriage. That he was born at Whalebone Cove when the pirates came ashore to bury their gold. He knows the sea well, that Don *Diablo.* If ever you live to see Whalebone Cove, you will find there a grave marked by a beautiful monument of Italian marble. Don *Diablo* put it there to mark his mother's grave, so it is said. And not a stone's throw from there stands an old gallows where the pirate and his crew were hung by the British. Or perhaps it was the Spanish. I was always too drunk to remember when Don *Diablo* told me the yarn."

Jim Driscoll fetched a flask of brandy. But even as he held the bottle to Pancho's lips, the wounded man quivered, lay quiet, the faint rattle of death in his throat.

Jim Driscoll closed the staring eyes and dug a single grave to hold both Quick and Pancho Gómez. Before he buried them, he searched their pockets, seeking some clue that would aid him in his dangerous hunt for the man who called himself Don *Diablo.* Quick's pockets revealed little. Save for some crumpled greenbacks, nothing of value came from Pancho's overalls. But as Jim Driscoll was laying the Mexican in the grave, he discovered a trinket that at first he took to be a religious medal. It was a gold disc fastened by a buckskin thong about the fellow's throat.

Jim Driscoll lighted a match. For a long moment he studied the gold slug. It bore the coat of arms of Spain and the date 1750. Pancho, or some man before Pancho, had drilled a tiny hole in the old coin and run a buckskin string through it, to wear it as a luck piece.

Well, it didn't bring Pancho much luck, Driscoll thought, *and I'm some superstitious myself concerning charms and such, but it isn't every day in the week a man runs onto pieces of eight, or doubloons, or whatever the old boys called their dough. And, so, I'll just separate you from it,* amigo. *There may be something to that story of pirate gold. And this story of Don* Diablo, *who used to be named Captain Wylie Hackett when he owned the Hachita Rancho . . . this story of his being a pirate's son . . . may be something in that. I've heard tell of ships that cruised the Mexican coast long after the Civil War, raiding the little towns, stealing girls and gold that the Indians dug for the* padres, *smuggling stuff into the U.S. ports along the Texas and Louisiana coast. No doubt, there could be truth in Hackett's yarn.* Dios *knows he had gold from somewhere. Said it was from Pancho Villa's big cache. Mebbeso. Most mebby not so. Now I wonder . . . did Wylie Hackett, alias Don* Diablo *of San Angelo port, really pay Pancho any money to get me? Somehow, I sort of think Pancho was lying, although a dying man is supposed always to come clean with the straight and honest. So, if he lied, he had reason to lie. Keep a-thinking along that line, Jimmy old boy, and you may stumble onto something. You might just be lucky enough to stumble. . . .*

Jim Driscoll broke off in his musing. He shoved the gold piece in his pocket and with a swift, smooth motion whirled, his six-shooter in his hand.

III
"One Slick *Caballero*"

A low-pitched, musical laugh came from the far side of a clump of brush. The strumming of a guitar. A hauntingly plaintive tenor voice, singing:

Ees a long, long trail a-winding,
Eento thees land from my dreams
Where thees nighteengale ees singeeng.

"Riley!" called Jim Driscoll. "Riley Rodriguez! You old son-of-a-bitch!"

"Son-of-the-beetch, right back at you, *Señor* Jeem Driscoll."

Still strumming the guitar, a small, beautifully garbed

Mexican *caballero* in black suede leather jacket and trousers trimmed with silver braid, huge silver spurs chiming, white teeth gleaming in the shadow of an enormous silver-crusted sombrero — there swaggered Riley Rodriguez, self-labeled the best-dressed *caballero* in all Mexico. With him came the strong odor of perfume.

"You 'ave the most damn' remarkable ears to hear me where I am hide, Jeem. *Santa María,* I 'ave tie thee spurs een flannel cloth. I made not a sound of a creeping mouse. Yet, son-of-a-beetch, you hear me."

"Heard, hell. I smelled you, you damned fashion plate of what the well-dressed *vaquero* wears when he goes a-courting."

"Hah!" smiled Don Riley Rodriguez, as he embraced the grinning American. "You like thees new perfume, no? I get you a quart."

"Not if I see you comin' with it, *caballero.* Lordy, but you're a plumb welcome sight for tired eyes, Riley. If ever a man was in need of a guiding word of wisdom, it's your friend, Jim Driscoll."

Don Riley Rodriguez smiled and indicated the two dead men. "I come too late to see thees fight. I hear thee shots and come *muy pronto.* I find, eenstead of per'aps thee *Señor* Hamlin, you, my frien', weeth two dead steefs who I recognize as one *muy malo hombre* of a *gringo* name' Raymond Queeck. And also, very moch dead, that evil one, Pancho Gómez. But the *Señor* Hamlin ees gone on, no? Weeth hees pack train loaded weeth gons and bullets. And you, my frien', here alone. You are not hurt som' place?"

"Not yet, Riley."

"*¡Caramba!* So queeck as I learn that no other than my ol' *compadre* of thee beeg war, my ol' *amigo,* thee Sergeant Jim Driscoll, ees comeeng thees way, I start for thee Sangre de Cristo. I step up on thee best damn' horse een Méjico.

"I say to my men . . . '*Hombrecitos,* thees revolution of wheech we are belong against, thees monkey business of the highjack stuff, weel have to wait. My *amigo,* my brother een thee arms of thee war weeth thee *gringos* and thee Heinees, he ees a damn' fool and thee fighting son of thee sea cookies, an', eef I don' bust thee ol' galluses to get there, somebody ees going to get een to thee 'ell of a sweet ruckus, and my ol' boddy of the beeg war ees going per'aps to keel off thees smuggler, Don *Diablo.* And then wot thee 'ell we do for gons and bullets that we highjack?

" 'Anyhow, besides, thees *Señor* Jeem Driscoll weel get heemself kill' so dead as a last month's corpse eef I don't get there to take heem into my 'ands. So, *hombrecitos,* you seet tight een thee saddle. Wait for me unteel I return back weeth you. And een thee case that I do not come back, ride after that *muy maldito,* thrice-cursed son of a peeg, Hamlin, and keel heem slow and weeth moch pain. Because you weel know that he has bomp' off your magneefeecent Don Riley Rodriguez, whose oncle ees thee war deepartment of Méjico besides being the beeg cheese een thee United States of George Washington and Teddy Roosevelt. Salute, *hombrecitos,* thee memory of those *presidentes* and *soldados.*

" 'And do not forget the *viva* for Don Diego Vicente y Buenaventura María de la Vaca. And a cople of cheers and a snappy salute now for your own very magneefeecent Don Riley Rodriguez, who was weeth thee *americanos* een the bigges' damn' war that was ever pull' off een any place. Powder Reever! Thee mile-wide and thee foots-deep! Let 'er bock! *Adiós* . . . do not forget to cut off thee ears of that Don *Diablo* and send theem, or per'aps the whole damn' 'ead, to my beloved and *muy grande* oncle.' "

Jim Driscoll, smiling widely, watched Riley Rodriguez go

through his grand gestures. The salutes, the gestures of magnificence, the cheers. Don Riley left nothing undone in the manner of acting out his touching farewell to his troop of ragged followers somewhere back in the hills. Don Riley again embraced his friend.

"And now, Jeem, we 'ad better shake thee old foots. Not so damn' far be'ind me are come that miserable Toveech, whose nose I shall som' day cut off from hees face and shove down hees neck. I would 'ave brought weeth me my armee, but some sleeck son-of-thee-beetch steals half the 'orses. And some of thee gons. And my new boots made een the City of Méjico by thee bootmaker who 'as made my boots since I was a small boy. They were ver' swell, magneefeecent boots, though thee old rascal should be cut off at thee ears for mak' theem so beeg. *Santa María,* one would think that Don Riley Rodriguez 'ad thee foots of a paddle-footed peon. Hah! I'll geeve that old one a beeg hunk off my mind when I step eento that shop and say to heem . . . '*Hombre,* look at thee boots on thees foots. What thee 'ell, Beel, you theenk you celebrate, no? The birthday from Santa Claus? Or the Eighteen Amendments?' "

"You were saying something about bein' followed?" Jim Driscoll asked to get him off the subject of the bootmaker.

"*Santa María, sí.* I get so warm' up about thee meeting you, my frien' of thee beeg war that makes thee last revolution down here look like notheeng less than thee sauce of thee apples. We go! Say, how do you like thees suit?"

"It smells like the swellest one I ever caught you wearing."

Jim began shoveling dirt into the wide grave. Don Riley rolled and lit a husk cigarette and watched the quick burial.

As they mounted and rode away together, Don Riley Rodriguez played softly on his guitar. He had brought it along, so he took pains to explain, on the chance that he might get time on the way back to stop at some *hacienda* where dwelt a most beautiful *señorita*. It was the intention of Don Riley to stand beneath her window and sing some love songs.

"You haven't asked me what fetched me down here, Riley."

"No. That ees your own very moch personal affair. What I know ees that orders 'ave gone out to breeng you . . . alive eef possible . . . or eef not possible, to breeng you dead . . . to Don *Diablo* at thees place he calls hees home near to Port San Angelo. Thees place ees a small island, ten miles from thee shore. All rock, and thees house where he leeve ees like thee castle. Machine gons and a tough crew to handle thee gons are guard there always. There ees only one small cove where a skiff can land, and only when thee tide ees just so."

"So I've heard. And I'm going to see the inside of that castle of his or die trying. And I'm going to break up this smuggling racket. I've taken it up with the officials in Mexico City."

From his pocket Jim Driscoll took a gold badge. For a moment it lay in the palm of his hand.

Don Riley Rodriguez smiled, but something of the gay comradeship was gone from his black eyes as he said softly: "Ees a 'ell of a swell, magneefeecent badge, my frien'."

"I've been in the government service since I got back from France, Riley. Almost had this gent who calls himself Don *Diablo,* two or three times. But he always slipped through the trap. There's been three of my men killed by him or his gang. Two other boys I've let come down here have disappeared. Another one . . . so I've good reason to think . . . sold out to this Don *Diablo* who, during the war, was listed as Captain Wylie Hackett. His war record was one that any man could be proud to claim. I'm to get assistance from the government of Mexico while I'm here. I talked with the officials there at Mexico City."

"Per'aps you meet thees *muy grande* oncle of mine?" asked Don Riley. "He ees some kind of thee war department. A *general. General* Diego Vicente y Buenaventura María de la Vaca."

"He was gone on some military business."

Don Riley Rodriguez smiled. His nimble fingers picked his guitar. "He ees a *muy* magneefeecent *general.* A snorter with beeg *mustachios* and thee fat belly."

"If I'd known he was your uncle, Riley, I'd have put in a request that he have you detailed to help me."

"And what thee 'ell of a swell joke that would turn out to become. Not later than las' week, there at San Angelo, do I not see a placard post' offering thee reward for my head and weeth thee signature of my very fat-'eaded oncle wrote on thee end of thee paper? Only that he ees thee brother of my dead mother, and that he ees old, I would get on thee best damn' horse een Méjico . . . wheech you see me now rideeng . . . and ride eento hees office and poll hees *mustachios* unteel he howled like thee wolf. And all because I do not agree weeth that oncle on some ver' small poleetical questions."

"But it doesn't seem reasonable, Riley, that he'd get so violent about it and want you killed."

"You do not know thee ol' roareeng bulldog, my frien'. He start to tell me somethееng about thee military. What thee 'ell he know about thees military theeng? I show heem thee medal I breeng home . . . thees *Croix de Guerre* weeth two palm leaf, thee Victoreea Cross, the Italian and the Belgium Cross. Likewise thees Iron Cross of the Sauerkrauts. I am all dress' up een thee new uniform I get made. I pin on thee medals, but I say no word to nobody how I buy theem out of the New York three-ball hock shop. I buckle on thee sword wheech I buy off a member of a swell, elegant lodge een Los Angeles. I click thee heels to attention. I pull out thee sword and salute that oncle. I show heem thees medal. And I say to that old goat . . . 'Behold, *Señor General,* a true, magneefeecent example of the military.' "

Don Riley smiled and shrugged his trim shoulders.

"How thee 'ell am I to know that thees old billygoat ees just get thee news from Guadalajara that I eshoot hees favorite *commandante* of thee military at Vera Cruz because that peeg of a peeg makes thee insulting crack about thee perfume on me?"

"But you're his own nephew. He wouldn't have you shot for that."

"Ees a ver' 'arsh man, that oncle," sighed Riley, "about thee matter of moneys. He ees likewise at thee same time angry because I lose some money on a rooster fight and thees miserable *hombre* who takes my you-owe-me for thees money takes thee paper to thees angry oncle. And when thees oncle ees geeve me thee beeg bawl-out, and thees silly Captain López, who ees thee grand military aide, snickers behind hees hand, then I, Don Riley Rodriguez, lose my temper. I flash out thee magneefeecent lodge sword and stick eet through thee legs of that snickering fool.

"Believe eet from me, my frien', only that he ees hid' behin' the chair, I should have push thees grand lodge sword through hees belly. But only hees legs show . . . and get eet directly straight from me, Jeem, I puncture both legs. He squeals like thee peeg. Everybody ron to see what thee 'ell, Bill. And my oncle ees bellow like ten bullocks. I leave thee place ver' angry. I swing thee leg across thee silver saddle that rests on thee back of the best damn' horse een all Méjico . . . wheech I now ride . . . and I ride out of that confusion. So I resign from my rank as lieutenant of cavalry.

And when I get to Port San Angelo, I get thee word back to my *hombrecitos* who likewise resign that night and ride to join their magneefeecent Don Riley.

"So here I am, Jeem. And you can believe eet direct from me, my frien', before long I will lead thee best damn' army in Méjico. And at thee 'ead of them I shall ride straight down thee street to thee palace of Chapultepec and offer my sword to *el presidente*. Hah! Can you not see thee balconies filled with thee most beautiful *señoritas,* tossing roses wheech I weel catch een my sombrero, thus! I 'ave already made thee arrangement to hire thee music. The band weel . . . *válgame Dios!*"

Don Riley's voice dropped to a whisper. He pointed ahead. There, coming over the rim of a tall sand dune, rode a troop of horsemen, at a jog trot, deployed formation.

"Toveech," hissed Don Riley. "Toveech, thee black butcher weeth hees *gringo* murderers! Shake thee foot, Jeem. Follow me!"

Don Riley — Jim Driscoll riding close behind and leading his pack horse — quit the main trail and rode off at an angle. But the noise of their movements was picked up by one of the enemy, who fired off his gun.

"Straight at thee peegs!" snarled Don Riley.

He flung aside his beloved guitar and jerked the two Luger pistols he carried.

IV
"Hot Lead — Cold Steel"

"Powder Reever!" cried Don Riley, standing in his stirrups. "Let 'er bock! Charge!"

"Let 'er buck!" cheered Jim Driscoll, his six-shooter ripping slits of fire in the moonlight.

The line of horsemen up ahead was jumbled into confusion as the two men rode straight for them. It was unheard of for two men so boldly to charge twenty or thirty armed fighters.

"It's a trap!" called a voice. "Look out, you boys. There's more of 'em."

Don Riley was yelling swift commands in Spanish to an imaginary following. Jim Driscoll grinned as the line of horsemen scattered to the brush. Bullets whistled and droned. Jim and Don Riley were riding at breakneck speed down the other slope of the sand dune. Through the broken, confused line luck was with them and on into the shelter of the mesquite thickets beyond.

Jim Driscoll had caught a glimpse of a squatty, black-bearded man on a huge black horse. This man was swearing in a broken jargon of English, Spanish, and some foreign tongue that was Polish or Russian. The black-bearded man was rallying the men who had scattered in panic. Now, with his men following, the black-bearded rider was giving chase.

Plainly Don Riley's beautiful mount could outrun the pursuers with ridiculous ease. But Jim's two horses were hard put to keep any sort of lead during a hard mile of this desperate race.

"They're gaining, Riley. You push on. I'll slide off and into the brush and take my chances."

"What you try to pull off, Jeem?" smiled Don Riley, "the bed-time stories? We are not lick' yet. Not by thee long shot, boddy. I 'ave . . . what you call heem? . . . thee joker up thee coat sleeve. That *hombre* that you hear say to theem others that eet ees thee trap. The *hombre* that says to those bums that there ees more of us? Well, that *hombre* ees my frien'. And when he learn that Toveech ees make thee march thees way to follow Hamlin and Raymond Queek and per'aps kill off thee *Señor* Jeem Driscoll of the U.S. government patrol, then that friend gets thee word to thee Mexican soldiers at the *cuartel,* and they follow behind thees Toveech bunch of bums. Almost any time now, Jeem, we meet theem federal cavalry. Sent from thee City of Méjico to work weeth you. Hah!"

"*¿Quién es?*" barked a sharp command.

"*¡Amigos!*" called Don Riley. "Pass thee *Señor* Jeem Driscoll of *los Estados Unidos y Tejas* to boot. And get ready to shoot, because behin' us comes Peter Toveech and hees *gringos.* And snap up thee slick salute, *hombre,* to Don Riley Rodriguez, thee most magneefeecent! Hah, *Capitán* López! How are thee legs, *Señor Capitán?* And do not get gay, *Señor Capitán.* Because, eef I become once more angry, I weel shoot you een thee belly and every *soldado* under your command weel follow their magneefeecent Don Riley eento thee hills. *¡Hombrecitos! ¡Soldados! ¡Vivas* for your own Don Riley Rodriguez!"

"*¡Viva! ¡Viva! ¡Viva* Don Riley!"

"Now, *Señor Capitán* López," smiled Don Riley, "pull een thee ears, or I shall cut theem off and mak' you eat theem weethout thee salt. You get me eento thee 'ell of a sour place een thee affections of my oncle. But, what does that old bullock do but send you out to San Angelo. He ees like thee little joke, that *general.* And so do not snicker no more, *Capitán.* Because thee chair of my oncle ees not so handy no more to hide behin'. *Por Dios,* here comes that bunch of bums! *Señor Capitán* López, thees ees my good frien', *Señor* Jeem Driscoll. Let anything happen, and I weel bit off your nose and feed thee nose to thee peegs. We shall meet again, *Señor Capitán,* and I weel ask you once more to snicker behind thee hand."

Don Riley held out his hand to Jim Driscoll.

"I must go, my frien'. I return to get that gueetar I leave behin'. Then to join my men. Thees *Capitán* López ees, for all hees snickers, thee 'ell of a brave man. Stay weeth heem. Soon we meet again. Always I weel see that no 'arm comes to you. *Capitán* López weel tell you, eef you 'ave not already guess, why I mus' go now. *Adiós,* my boddy. Go weeth God!"

Their hands gripped. Don Riley whirled his magnificent horse and was gone in the night. Just then, the renegades under Tovich clashed with the federal cavalry. Already Captain López was among his men, riding here and there in the hail of bullets, an upright, gamecock-tailored officer. Urging his fighting men to greater recklessness, his sword was flashing and his voice challenging Tovich to personal combat.

Jim Driscoll found himself caught in this whirlpool of desperate hand-to-hand fighting, there in the moonlight. Now Tovich, finding the odds against him, was calling to his men to retreat. And they were losing no time in obeying.

For these military police under López were of that tough fiber that had once made the Mexican *Rurales* as fine a mounted police organization as ever rode in the tracks of crime. They took no prisoners, and so, because they knew they could expect no quarter in turn, they fought with a desperate fury that was putting to rout the mongrel crew of white renegades under the butcher, Tovich. Some of those renegades were dying hard. Their gritted taunts could be heard among the spatter of carbines.

Jim Driscoll was trying to fight his way through the mêlée to where the black-bearded Tovich, surrounded by a knot of unshaven, hard-bitten followers, was trying to organize a retreat. But ahead of Jim Driscoll rode the dapper Captain López, a handful of his men behind him.

Now a burly, leering, cursing, white renegade came at

Jim Driscoll. Jim's gun hammer fell on an empty shell. He charged at the man with his carbine as a club. A bullet ripped through Jim's hat. Then the carbine knocked the burly outlaw from his saddle, just as a diminutive Mexican soldier shot the fellow through the head.

A clubbed rifle now grazed Jim's shoulder. A gun blazed behind him. He rode at a man whose face showed whitely in the moonlight. As Jim Driscoll fought to get to that man, he called out a name.

"Schwartz! Dutch Schwartz! Stand and fight, you damned skunk! Fight, you traitor!"

But the mêlée was too thick to let Jim through. He caught a last glimpse of the man who had once been one of his border patrol and now was a smuggler under Tovich and Don *Diablo.* Dutch Schwartz's round face was white as chalk, his blue eyes shining in the blaze of guns and the white moonlight that made it almost daylight. A last, tense grimace and Dutch Schwartz turned tail.

Now a fierce struggle was going on up ahead. Captain López had fought his way to where Tovich and his men were making a last, desperate stand. López and the black-bearded Tovich were within arm's reach of one another, slashing at each other with cavalry sabers. Then the Mexican's horse went down.

Jim Driscoll shoved a cartridge into his carbine and took quick aim. Tovich was half hidden by his men, his arm lifted as the saber in his hand swung upward. His white teeth were snarling behind his curly, black beard. Jim Driscoll pulled the trigger. The bullet, missing by the fraction of an inch, furrowed the black-bearded jaw. Tovich shook his head like a wounded, shaggy bear.

Now a horse leaped into that crowd. There was a gleam of silver, black, and scarlet. A knife, like a shaft of light, slithered through the air. Its thin, gleaming blade struck Tovich in the arm, just below the shoulder. With a howling curse, he let go the red-bladed saber.

Before he had hardly been seen that dashing figure in black and scarlet and silver was gone as swiftly as he had come. Only his knife, buried to the hilt in the thick arm of Peter Tovich, was there to mark his sudden visitation. Now, as Jim Driscoll crowded his way through to the fallen Captain López, Tovich and his men fled in a wedge that plowed through to freedom.

Jim Driscoll lifted Captain López up behind him. The Mexican officer was cursing hotly at the fate that had denied him the life of the black-bearded renegade.

"But thanks to you, *Señor* Driscoll, my life, at least, is spared me for another attempt. You acted swiftly, *señor*."

"It wasn't me that put Tovich out of the running."

"Who, then?" asked Captain López as they rode about, gathering the Mexican troopers into shape and attending to the wounded.

"It was Don Riley Rodriguez. He came like a streak. His knife looked almost like a flash of white lightning. Then he was gone again. Listen!"

From somewhere out there on the desert, like the tinkle of a silver bell, came the song of a rider who spurred for the safety of his hills and the comradeship of his faithful followers. With a Mexican love song, the song of a *vaquero* who rides to meet love under the stars, so Don Riley Rodriguez rode away into the dawn. Alone, singing his *vaquero*'s song to the vanishing stars.

"Some day," said Captain López, a little sadly, "Don Riley will die with his back to an adobe wall. It may be my duty, *señor*, to give the command to the squad of soldiers to fire. And so Mexico will lose a brave soldier and a gallant *caballero*."

V
"Bloodstained Gold"

Back in the rough hills that led from the desert to the peaks of the Sangre de Cristo, Harley Hamlin rode behind his pack train, on up a twisting trail to the rock hut of the hermit. A light burned in this hut, and against its yellow background showed the bent, twisted, white-bearded old hermit of the Sangre de Cristo. His powerful hands gripped a shotgun, and from under shaggy brows his glittering eyes blinked suspiciously.

"Pipe up and sing out yer name!" he snarled. "Who be ye?"

"Hamlin. Harley Hamlin, old topper. Put away the ghastly weapon."

"Is Quick with ye, Hamlin? Why don't he sing out?"

"Raymond Quick is dead. So is Pancho Gómez."

"Aye, and 'twas that damned spy askin' fer the boss as done the dirty job, I'll lay to that."

"Wrong, old chap. And I've a notion you were a party to the plot. The two of 'em planned to blot me out of the picture. I left them behind for the buzzards. So, my jolly old bit of hard tack, if you've any like notions, stow 'em away in your ruddy old sea chest."

"The cap'n will have ye strung up fer this night's work. But mebby he'll not be so hard on ye when he finds out that ye killed this spy, Driscoll."

"But I didn't kill the Driscoll fellow. He was quite hale and hearty when we parted. And I'll jolly well tell you, or the captain, or whoever else is interested, that I've no intention of killing Driscoll. I like the chap. Now, throw one of your bally old fits and die in it."

The old hermit shook like a man with palsy, cursing

thickly into his matted beard. Hamlin laughed mirthlessly. And the old hermit stomped back into the hut, cursing Harley Hamlin for a fool.

"*Buenas noches, Señor* Hamlin," called the soft voice of Don Riley Rodriguez as that gentleman stepped from the boulders nearby.

"Cheerio, Riley. Gad, you've the most annoyin' damned habit of popping out of nowhere. I thought you were at San Angelo. How the devil did you get here?"

"On thee best damn' horse een Méjico, my frien'. I 'ave been here half an hour. Poof! . . . you put thee ol' graybeard in thee bad humor, no? Take care, *señor.* That ol' one ees not so 'armless. You breeng thee many gons on thee mules?"

"That, old chap, is a subject we won't go into."

Don Riley smiled. "Per'aps not. Per'aps yes. Ees like thees, *señor.* I 'ave thee best damn' army een all of Méjico. But thees *soldados* of mine, thees brave *hombrecitos* 'ave not thee gons. So, when I hear that thee *Señor* Hamlin and thee *Señor* Queeck and that *muy maldito* Pancho Gómez ees on the way from Whalebone Cove to deliver thee load of gons to that Don *Diablo,* who weel sell them to *General* Manuel Herrera at thee Sangre de Cristo, then I theenk weeth my head. I say to my *hombrecitos* . . . meet your magneefeecent Don Riley at thee cabin of thee hermit of thee unbathed beard at one hour not much later than midnight. And we weel pull off thee highjacks. Shoot to keel these Raymond Queeck, because I do not like heem. Likewise, also bomp off that *muy maldito* Pancho Gómez, who ees thee lousy bom. But geeve thee *Señor* Harley Hamlin thee chance to talk turkeys."

"Sweet of you, old dad." Hamlin's voice had became brittle. "And I'm to understand that I'm now bein' highjacked?"

"I believe, *Señor* Hamlin, that ees thee absolute correct word. Only keep thee shirt on, *señor* . . . and thee 'and off thee gon, please. Because be'ind every rock and every bush ees one of my *soldados* weeth thee gon pointed at you. Also likewise these *hombres* under your command are my ver' swell good frien's. Shall we now talk turkeys?"

"You have all the advantage, old highjacker. Speak your ruddy piece."

"Theese Raymond Queeck ees thee damn' good *amigo* to Don *Diablo,* no? And Don *Diablo* ees going to raise 'ell when he hears that *hombre,* Queeck, ees die. Jus' like thee *General* Manuel Herrera ees feel bad about losing Pancho Gómez, who ees one of hees best men. And so thee *Señor* Harley Hamlin stands not so hot. Thees ol' hermit ees now listen weeth both ears there een thee cabin. He don' like you so moch. You get thee ideas?"

"Meanin', old burglar, that I'm in bad around this section of the dear old wide open spaces? Go on, Don Riley."

"At thee port of San Angelo, where you 'ave thee many friends, *señor,* you weel be fairly safe so long as you do not take thee chances. Ees that correctly right?"

"Right," snapped Harley Hamlin.

"But eet ees not so easy to get back een safety to San Angelo. Between here and there ees Peter Toveech. Toveech and thee dead *Señor* Queeck were thee good *amigos* together. Not so hot, no?"

"Rather, old bean, not so bally hot. Go on, brother Riley, you're beginning to interest me. I'm beginnin' to see the ruddy old light."

"Een thee pocket of my saddle ees gold," said Don Riley. "Enough gold to pay you for your share of thees gons which I am highjack off from you. I geeve you that gold. But thee *Señor* Queeck and thee *muy maldito* Pancho Gómez needs no gold where they are. So we charges that to thee ledger on thee profits and lose eet. You, *señor,* receive your share and thee safe escort back along thee trail to Port San Angelo. I get thee gons for my *hombrecitos*. The *General* Manuel and Don *Diablo* gets thee headaches. That, *Señor* Hamlin, ees w'at I call talking thee turkeys."

"I quite agree with you, old chap. It's all very jolly and all that, but Don *Diablo* . . . Captain Wylie Hackett . . . self-styled soldier of fortune and promoter of revolutions is going to be a bit peeved with you when he learns you've gotten hold of these guns that were to be delivered to him and his old chum, General Manual Herrera. Aren't you getting in rather wrong with the dear captain?"

Don Riley shrugged and lit a cigarette. "Ees jost one of theem theengs, *señor*. Too bad, bot can't be help' none whatever. Here, *señor,* ees thee gold."

"How about that escort back to Port San Angelo?"

"The same *hombres* who come weeth you here. I shall tell theem to land safe at San Angelo. And there you weel meet my good frien', Jeem Driscoll, who ees thee salts of thee earth."

"You know the Driscoll chap?" asked the Britisher, surprised.

"Was he not my sergeant een that cavalry which never saw thee horse een France? Was he not thee best top kicker that ever called squads East? Was he not that same hard-boil' son-of-a-gon that put me on latrine duty for talking een rank? Did he not slough me een thee guardhouse for fighting? And did he not crawl on hees belly through thee mud and thee barb wires and thee machine gonfire and thee shell holes, out eento thee nobody's damned land to breeng me back when I 'ave thee bullet een me? You can say all you damn' please, *señor,* about thee beeg *generales,* but thee bes' damn' soldier een that *gringo* war ees Sergeant Jeem Driscoll of the Ninety-First Division. And what I mean, I don't mean mebby perhaps. Let 'er bock!"

"I didn't know, Riley, that you'd been in that dashed old bit of a brawl with the Hun."

"I've 'ope to spit een your mees kit, I was there. You, too?"

"Four years of it, old top. And damned little blighty between shifts. Over there? Rather." There was a twist to the Britisher's lips that hinted of bitterness.

Don Riley saluted him gravely. "And now, *Señor* Hamlin," smiled the Mexican, "I shake thee 'and good bye. I 'ave here a letter I write about you to my frien', Jeem Driscoll, wheech you geeve to heem. *Adiós, señor.*"

There was a military brusqueness about that *adiós.* Don Riley gave some staccato orders in Spanish. The Mexicans left their pack mules to fall in behind Hamlin as the Britisher returned Don Riley's salute and rode away.

The pack mules with their loads had gone to grazing. It was nearing sunrise now. There was no sign of any of the soldiers of whom Don Riley had spoken to Hamlin. Humming softly to himself, Don Riley rode over to the open door of the hermit's cabin.

"Come out, ol' man, or I trow thees gold money away, and you weel crawl on thee 'ands and thee knees like thee dog trying to find thees gold that Don Riley Rodriguez breengs from that place where only you and the dead 'ave been. Come, old mate. Eight bells and all ees well. And there ees blood on thee gold that comes from Whalebone Cove, no? Hah!"

Crabwise on his bent legs, babbling incoherently, his

eyes glittering with greed, the hermit of the Sangre de Cristo sidled out into the first slanting rays of the morning sun. With him he dragged a sack made of soft, tanned leather.

Don Riley Rodriguez stepped off his horse. From one of the saddle pockets he took a handful of tarnished, discolored, old coins. By the manner in which his wrist tensed, those coins were heavy gold.

"Aha, *Señor* Hermit, ahoy *Señor* Pirate, no? You and I, old man, we know that secret. Jus' now, like I tol' you, I pull thee *muy grande* bloff on thee *Señor* Hamlin. I 'ave no *soldados* here. Only me, Don Riley Rodriguez, thee *caballero.* Those *méjicanos* weeth thee *Señor* Hamlin, they planned to get thees gons. They are evil men. But, *por Dios,* they are ver' damn' moch afraid of Don Riley Rodriguez, who say he has thee *soldados* een thee rocks and thee bushes. You hear me talk that bloff, old pirate? You see theem turn from *muy bravo* bandits eento thee same number of sheeps? Did I not say to you, old sailorman, that I would show you how thee one brave man weeth thee brains ees better than one hondred *soldados* weeth gons. You behold me now, old one who counts hees gold, a man who keeps hees word, no?"

"Aye, lad," replied the hermit. "Scuttle me, if ye wouldn't 'ave made a fit mate fer the blackest ship as ever dropped hook at Whalebone Cove with 'er decks runnin' red."

Don Riley brought forth a black bottle. The gnarled hands of the hermit grabbed it.

"Rum?" he croaked.

"Rom, *sí*. From thee barrel that was buried there where thee dead guard thee gold. Ees damn' strong stoff, I tell you."

"Ye seen nothin' o' the bird, matey?"

"I do not see thees parrot, no."

"Ye looked keerful, lad?"

"*Sí*. But there ees a parrot bird een Port San Angelo that talks beautiful, swearing een three languages."

"Damn yer parrot o' Port San Angelo! 'Tis my own bird as was stole from me that I want."

"Ees damn' long time since you lose your bird, old sailor. Twenty-five years?"

"Fifty. But he'll be livin' somewhere, lay to that. Fifty years, aye, and more, since I was left ashore at Whalebone Cove with a dent in my skull and my spine warped. Left to die there in the sun. With my tongue black from thirst and the stink o' dead men in my nostrils. Gold red with blood and piled waist high in a heap. And me a-dyin' with the shine o' the gold fair blindin' me.

"I'd gone down a-fightin' with a cutlass in each hand. Back to back with Bloody Jack Hackett himself, fightin' a drunken, rum-soaked, mutinous crew gone clean mad at the sight o' so much gold. Back to back, Cap'n Hackett and me fought 'em back till the dead 'uns piled like cordwood, and the sand was puddled with blood and slit entrails. Billy Bones, the parrot, a-screechin' and cussin' fit to make yer hair curl. Till the first mate and the ship's carpenter, Mister Chips, and a handful o' them as hadn't bin in on the mutiny got back to shore from inland where they'd bin fillin' the water kegs. Aye, lad, that was a fight, there at old Whalebone Cove. And cracked in the brain as I am, mind ye, old Handy Hands kin recall it to the last damned corpse that lay there rottin' in the sun. And me so bad off I can't crawl to windward. Left there to die like a dog by the bloody, black-hearted skipper o' the blackest ship as ever come up the coast with her hold packed with stinkin' black men.

"Blackbirdin' and piracy o' the high seas, so they

charged Hackett and his mate and six o' the crew that was hung there, six months later. And I was hid in the dunes and watched 'em swing. Some brave, some beggin' like dogs. Bloody Jack Hackett cursin' the *padre* as wanted to confess him, though I've wondered, lad, if he wasn't tryin' to get the word from the skipper concernin' the buried gold. Bloody Jack never knew that Handy Hands had dug up the stuff and hid it where it's safe."

"Ees damn' locky theeng *por* you that my father, he come that way, honting thee cattle, no?"

"Lucky, aye. And no less lucky for him, by the same bloody token. For I led him to gold enough to buy all the cattle and horses in Mexico. And what does he do with it? Strike me blind, if he don't use it to build churches and stow grub in the bellies of the poor. A waste o' gold as had bin fought for, I calls it. And Handy Hands, as had killed men for the yellow stuff, hidin' here because the same rope as hung Cap'n Jack Hackett was waitin' for the neck o' them as served under him. Me, a damned millionaire as could have a crew o' flunkies and a yacht to ride the seven seas fer pleasure, holed up like a mad dog. . . . without even Billy Bones fer company. Ye looked fer the bird, lad?"

"*Sí.* And there ees many of thees parrot birds. Only none that seengs those pirate song and says thee Lord's Prayer and swears so nice. But I shall look some more longer."

"Get me the birdie, lad, and I'll chart ye a land course as'll take ye to gold. For when I think of how foolish old Don Ramón Rodriguez spent gold, I want of a humor to chart a course to the bulk o' the stuff, but it lays where it's laid fer years, afore ever Hackett and his crew swung at Whalebone Cove. Wasn't I the only one o' that buryin' crew left alive? It took sixteen big black men to carry the chests. And when they'd dug the hole, the skipper and me, we hacked 'em down and covered the chests down in the pit with their bleedin' black carcasses, then piled in the sand. And Billy Bones perched on a rock a-spoutin' his Lord's Prayer. And the load in Hackett's pistol that he saves to finish me is fouled with the black men's blood, and fails. And there he stands, lookin' foolish as a school boy caught with his pants ripped, not a-darin' to cross cutlass with old Handy Hands. And me a-laughin' fit to bust, he looks that damn' comical. Aye, I've cursed myself to sleep many a night because I didn't cleave him from neck to brisket and spill his guts there on the sand. But I was but a lad and tender o' heart, and I let him live. The chance never come up again. And he left me a-dyin', me as had bin his mate, there at the Whalebone Cove. Unfair, I calls it."

"*Sí, Señor* 'Andy 'Ands. I bet thees pirate business ees 'ard on thee clothes, no? So damn' moch blood always. Well, I weel be going along. Thees highjack business keeps highjacks on the jump. Jompin' jacks, no? Some day, when I get some more time to listen, I come again to hear you keel some more *hombres* till the blood ees knee high. *Adiós, Señor* 'Andy 'Ands. I shall look some more for thees parrot bird."

Alone, driving the pack train of mules along the trail, rode Don Riley Rodriguez. He had recovered his guitar, and, as he rode along, he fingered its strings and sang softly. On along the narrow, twisting trail, then into a deep cañon filled with palms and giant ferns and a swift creek tumbling down in silvery waterfalls.

Now he halted and took from his pocket a silver whistle. Its clear, shrill blast brought a myriad of echoes that caromed against the high rock walls. From up the cañon came a brief bugle call.

Don Riley Rodriguez brushed some dust from his beautiful clothes. He rolled and lit a cigarette, adjusted his huge sombrero, twisted his slim, black mustache to needle points. Then, circling the pack mules that had gone to grazing, he rode at an easy gait along the grassy trail to where a band of ragged followers were drawn up at attention.

Don Riley saluted grandly. "Behold the return of your own Don Riley, *hombrecitos!*" he said in Spanish. "Alone I highjacked the guns meant for that pig of a pig, *General* Manuel Herrera. I am king of the highjackers. Guns for every man. And by tomorrow, horses. Did I not promise these things? I tell you, *hombrecitos,* you have the great good fortune to follow a grand *caballero.* Now, take my horse and tend his needs. I myself, Don Riley, shall rub down his legs when the sponging is done. Grain him, find him the best grass. For some day, before we are too old to enjoy it, I shall ride to the doors of Chapultapec on that best damned horse in all Méjico. You, my faithful ones, my children of the wars, you shall ride behind me. And the band shall play this marching song which I am, by my own hand, composing. Now, *por Dios,* wine and grub for the old belly. Even Don Riley is subject to hunger."

VI
"Watch your Step"

Port San Angelo's lights blinked like opening eyes in the purple night. Evil eyes they were, perhaps, like the glittering eyes of beasts of prey, but, nevertheless, beautiful in a sinister, deadly sort of beauty. Lights that beckoned with siren glance at the rough sailormen coming into port with contraband. Promising the fulfillment of every lust known to mankind.

They winked yellowly as the skiffs grounded on a white beach were lapped by a sea that left a strip of phosphorous with each wave that fingered across the smooth, wet sand. Sea-going craft of every description rode at anchor. The bay mirrored the riding lights of boats that came and went on secret missions.

Out there, among the dingier tubs, poised a yacht that looked like a greyhound dressed in white, red and green lights aglow with a single lighted porthole and a dim light on the bridge. Shadowy forms paced the deck which was holystoned to spotless perfection. Waterproof tarpaulins covered the mounted guns that might telltale the fact that this trim, slender-lined yacht was not pleasure-bent.

"Blind yourself to the rotten, squalid stuff back up town, Driscoll," said Harley Hamlin. "Use the jolly old imagination a bit, y'know, and out there in the bay is beauty."

They stood, with Captain López, on a small wharf. Driscoll, Hamlin, and the army officer were side by side. Behind them stood a half dozen soldiers, alert, vigilant.

"Who owns the yacht?" asked Jim Driscoll.

Hamlin knocked the ashes from his brier pipe into the water below.

"And I thought the Irish were romantic. I point out the beauty of the water and the lights and what not, bracing myself, y'know, for a poetical outburst, and you pop out a prosaic question. Tell him the answer, Captain López. He's taken the dreamy old wind out of me."

"The yacht belongs to Don *Diablo,* otherwise known as Captain Wylie Hackett. Fastest thing afloat in the Mexican waters, *Señor* Driscoll."

"Do you reckon Hackett would be aboard?" asked Jim Driscoll.

"If he should be aboard, old man," said Hamlin, "it

would do us no good to try to board her. Before we got halfway out there, we'd meet up with a bit of bad luck. Some fast motorboat would ram us. Our engine would go dead. Or, if we used a skiff, the ruddy oarsmen would somehow capsize us. Just an accident. And we'd never reach shore. Report would be that the sharks gobbled us. Do you follow me, old chap?"

Jim Driscoll nodded. "I'm just beginning, Hamlin, to see what a tough layout I'm up against. It's a mighty well-organized game down here."

"Even better organized, Driscoll, than you imagine. Ain't that right, Captain López?"

"So well organized," came from the trim captain in his precise English, "that I would suggest we go back uptown where the lights are brighter. It is not exactly safe here in the dim light, even with the soldiers."

"Right," agreed the Britisher grimly. "I've been hanging onto two automatics until my fingers are jolly well numb."

"Yeah, we better sift back among the lights," grinned Jim Driscoll. "Hamlin, you're worth the price of admission. Hanging onto your guns and asking me to see the beauty of San Angelo bay."

"Why not? As well think of the ruddy old moon and the jolly little stars, what? Shuffling off the . . . damn it, the line of poetry has quite slipped from me. Recall it, Captain? No? It's from 'Thanatopsis' . . . or Saul's jolly old funeral march . . . or from somewhere, no doubt."

Behind the careless flippancy of Harley Hamlin lay a grimness that to Jim Driscoll was a thing that made a man wonder. Harley Hamlin, that morning, had come riding into the federal barracks at San Angelo with a letter from Don Riley Rodriguez.

"My compliments, Driscoll," he had said. "I have just

been through bankruptcy in the game I was playing. I think I know your dreary old racket, and I'm lending you the support of the old right arm, y'know. One for all and all for one, what? Providing, Driscoll, that you are accepting recruits of baser metal. In words of simplicity, old man, I'm here to join your lovely crusade against crime. I've been blackballed by the select fraternity of blacklegs. I ask no salary. I ask, in fact, nothing. All I can offer in the way of value is that I can lead you to a decent drink, a well-cooked meal, and comfortable quarters, such as they are, and my support in whatever you have in mind. I own the one and only shower bath in San Angelo. And a phonograph with a select stack of records. When sober, my Chinaman serves a palatable meal. I've a spare bedroom that you're welcome to. And all I ask, when all's said and finished, is a decent burial and a letter mailed back home, breaking the news that Harley Hamlin, importer and exporter, actively retired, has passed on."

Captain López later told Jim Driscoll that Hamlin was marked for death. In killing Raymond Quick and Pancho Gómez, the tall Englishman had signed his own death warrant. That it was merely a matter of time until Hamlin would be killed.

Jim Driscoll had taken up quarters at Hamlin's humble adobe home. The Chinese cook was excellent. Jim had been somewhat astonished when, that evening for supper, Hamlin had appeared in formal dinner clothes. Captain López, however, had taken the Britisher's formality with a grace that was typical of his people. The three, after excellent cocktails, a well-cooked dinner, and cigars, had strolled down to the wharf.

Now, as they strolled back uptown, Harley Hamlin guided them to a really decent-looking *cantina*. From a dimly lighted patio came the soft strains of a stringed orchestra. And a woman's voice, worthy of a far better setting, singing that haunting Mexican song that, translated, means to die dreaming.

The three men entered through the barroom. It was filled with a motley crowd. Hamlin spoke to the suave-mannered Mexican proprietor, who bowed a trifle mockingly, so Driscoll thought, as he escorted the three customers back through a short hallway to a heavy oak door. At a signal, the door swung open.

Jim Driscoll, Captain López, and Harley Hamlin stepped into the patio, a thing of rare old beauty. Tropical fruit trees; the strong, haunting odor of gardenias; tables; an orchestra back in the shadows; a fountain of old tile. A beautiful woman in white with a scarlet rose in her jet hair stood alone, singing.

Two of the tables were occupied by groups. At a corner table, sitting alone, was a tall, bronzed, clean-featured man in white flannels. The man, at the entrance of the three newcomers, rubbed out the coal of his cigarette and rose. He was tall, heavy-shouldered, with ash-blond hair. His teeth flashed in a smile, but his blue eyes were as hard and cold as ice.

"Ah, Hamlin. And Captain López. And do my eyes see rightly, none other than Jim Driscoll."

"Thought we'd find you here, Captain," came Hamlin's cool reply. "Driscoll, you've met Captain Wylie Hackett?"

For a tense moment Jim Driscoll and Captain Wylie Hackett stared into each other's eyes. Under his immaculate flannel jacket, Hackett's powerful shoulders flexed and bunched. Driscoll's fists were knotted, and his face was a shade pale under its sun bronze.

"Yes," said Jim Driscoll, "I've met Hackett. Don *Diablo*'s

the present title, they tell me."

"Don *Diablo,*" sneered the tall Captain Hackett, "is a name I spread among the peons. They're fond of color. I suppose, Mister Uncle Sam's spy, that I should be flattered by your interest in me. And after a fashion, it does tickle my vanity and amuse me. But get this right now, brother Driscoll . . . this is Mexico. And Port San Angelo is my particular part of Mexico. I was born near here, and this is my country. What I say here, goes. Don't stay so long that you'll wear out your welcome, Driscoll. Don't linger around until what is now so amusing to me begins to bore me, and then annoy me. I don't like to be annoyed."

"So far as I'm concerned," drawled Jim Driscoll, getting his temper under quick control, "you can start in getting annoyed whenever it pleases you."

"This is not the place," smiled López, "and this evening is hardly the moment for quarreling. The young lady's song is being rudely interrupted."

"You're not trying to threaten me, are you, *Señor Capitán* López?" sneered Hackett.

"I am merely attempting, *Señor Capitán* Hackett, to remind you of the fact that you are a gentleman, and there are ladies present."

"You flatter me, López. I've never claimed that so badly misused title of gentleman. And I was unaware of the fact that there were any ladies in San Angelo port."

Captain López stiffened. His hand dropped to his gun.

The calm, unruffled voice of Harley Hamlin was like a deluge of ice water on fire: "Don't let the skipper get your ruddy old goat, López. Seems to me this is all a bit silly. Might we not sit down and, while the jolly old weight is off our feet, partake a bit of liquid? Driscoll, old top, the young lady with the charming voice wishes to speak to you. May we sit at your table, Hackett?"

"Aren't you afraid I might slip a bit of poison in your drink, Hamlin?" Captain Hackett grinned crookedly as he waved an invitation to the three men to join him.

"I fancy you'd rather shoot me, Hackett. Poison is a rather insipid form of retribution, what?"

"You're a cool-nerved sort of chump, Hamlin. Sometimes I'm damn' close to liking you. Sit down, gentlemen."

Jim Driscoll, hat in hand, had stepped across the patio, hand outstretched to greet the black-haired *señorita* in the exquisite white *mantilla*.

"Ah, *Señor* Driscoll!" She smiled, her dark eyes alight. "Thees ees thee great pleasure once more to see you, no? In other words of good, plain old United States, Jim, how goes it?"

"Can't kick a bit, Kit. Still doing the Mexican fandangos and La Paloma, eh?"

"That's my line, Jim, and I'll stick to it. Where was it we met last? Tía Juana, Nogales, Juárez?"

"In jail in El Paso" — Jim grinned — "where you'd gone to spring some fuzzy blonde percentage girl from a thirty-day trick for rolling a dude in a Juárez joint." Jim Driscoll lifted an eyebrow. "You were with some high-powered playboy son of a millionaire Boston family. He was tight as a tick. And you were going to marry him that night."

Katherine O'Rafferty laughed. "I got cold feet, Jim. He was a decent kind of kid, even if he was the world's best rum hound. He'd showed me pictures of his family and used to read me letters from his kid sister who thought he was just about the greatest one guy that ever swung a polo stick. And imagine a boy like that dragging home a dance-hall quim whose line is Mexican stuff? Nope, Jimmy,

I just couldn't see it for dust. So the same night that you got Flossie out of jail for me, we poured Gerald into his hotel, packed up, and came as far as our jack would take us away from El Paso. I never did get a chance to thank you, Jim, for what you did for me and the Flossie kid that night. She was innocent, Jim. What I mean . . . she needed that bimbo's roll worse than he did. She'd been to the doctor's that day, and he'd given her the verdict. Spots on both lungs and six months to live, if she didn't quit the racket. She needed rest and sunshine and milk and no worry. Try and get all that hustlin' drinks in a border town.

"So we see this name of San Angelo on the map. Angelo sounds like angel. Kinda holy, see? So here we landed, flat broke, no friends, no jobs. And places like Juárez or Nogales look like Mormon church towns compared to this dump. And Lord knows, Jim, what we'd have done if a regular little guy named Don Riley Rodriguez hadn't pulled the big brother act. He landed me a job here while he gets Flossie and me a place to board with some poor, but respectable, Mexicans. So here we are. And gee, Jimmy, if it ain't askin' too much of you, drop around to the house and give the Flossie kid a chance to thank you. The darned little kid's been prayin' for you, Jimmy. Honest. She learned some prayers and gets down on her knees, Jimmy, night and mornin'. And her that never gives religion a tumble in all her days as a chorine and sister act on cheap vaudeville. And the funny angle is that she believes it all.

"Gee, Jimmy, before you blow town, let the Flossie kid thank you. She's sick, see? And . . . well, she got her little old sunshine and rest and milk just about a year too late. It won't be long now, Jimmy, till she quits all this for a new start in a new world. And, Jimmy, it'd do her good to meet you. I know she's just a dance-hall dame, the same as me, but she's on the level with her pals. And no matter what she's been or what she's done, she's a trouper. Give the kid a tumble, Jimmy. Just let her shake hands with you."

"Sure, Kit. Of course, I'll be glad to see her. And whatever I can do. . . ."

"That's the ticket, Jimmy. Now go on back to your party. I'll sing you some songs. You're a hell of a regular guy, Jim Driscoll. And bless your darned hide, I'll tell you some day, perhaps, why I didn't marry that Gerald kid from Boston. . . . Now trot back to your party. But watch that big shot they call Don *Diablo*. He's one hard customer. Hamlin's better, but not so good. I don't know the dolled-up Mex officer. Watch your step, Jimmy. I don't know your racket. Never did. But you're among thieves, and what I mean, honey, they're some tough gang. I'm off at midnight."

Kit gave his hand a squeeze and slipped back into the palms and pomegranate trees. As Jim Driscoll went back to the table where Hamlin, López, and Hackett sat, he heard Kit's voice, rattling off fluent Spanish. He caught the lilt of her laughter.

VII
"When Blood Boils Over"

Captain Wylie Hackett waved Jim to a seat.

"How about an armistice, Driscoll, for the evening? Hamlin and López favor the idea. And, God knows, I'd welcome an evening of decent companionship for a change. Enemies tomorrow, maybe, but tonight let me be your host. How does the idea strike you, Driscoll?"

Jim Driscoll's glance flitted across the three faces of his companions. Had they hatched some plot? Harley Hamlin's eyes were inscrutable. López was watching the palms that hid Kit O'Rafferty. There was, in the blue eyes of Captain Wylie Hackett, a disarming frankness, a sort of boyish appeal.

"Once, Wylie," said Jim Driscoll, "you and I were good friends. It wasn't me that broke that friendship."

"That's right, Jim." Captain Wylie Hackett got to his feet. "I had a hell of a nerve to ask it of you. The best thing I can do is bow myself out of the picture. Gentlemen, good night."

"Hold on, Hackett," said Jim. "Don't go off half-cocked. I'm takin' you up on that. I'll be glad to declare a night's armistice. God knows, the relaxation will be welcome."

"O K, Jim. Harley, you get better results from these stupid-headed waiters than I do. Order some real wine. And we'll forget what we are for a few hours. The *señorita* is going to sing again. Who is she, Jim? . . . or is that an off-side question?"

"That's for the *señorita* to say, Wylie. But she can sing and dance."

"Rather," smiled Harley Hamlin, beckoning to a waiter. "And with the face of a madonna. I'd wager she's as straight as a die, if I were the kind of mucker that lays bets on the morality of women."

"I wouldn't call the bet, Harley," laughed Hackett. "I've tried. She's straight as a die."

"Just a minute, boys," said Jim Driscoll, and his voice was hard and taut. "If this is to be a friendly pow-wow, just drop that talk . . . because I don't like it."

"Right," came Hamlin's crisp apology. "Eh, Captain Hackett?" And the Britisher's eyes were like ice.

"Right," shrugged Hackett. "Forget it. There's the song. Here comes the wine. And we'll drink to the dead pirates of

Whalebone Cove. And the gold buried there by Bloody Jack Hackett, skipper of the blackest ship that ever dropped her mud hook in Port San Angelo. To the days of wooden ships and iron men. To the days when the loser walked the plank. We're drinking wine that was old before we were born. From the cellars of a monastery in Spain. Brought to Port San Angelo by the lawless son of a pirate sire. A drinking, fighting, lawless son doomed to hear the creak of a gallows tree. Drink, men!"

Through the mind of Jim Driscoll ran the thread of stories linked with the name of Captain Wylie Hackett who had, during the war, commanded a submarine that flew no country's flag. There were hinted sinister things connected with that submarine boat that had been captured by Hackett when it put into a certain port. The story went that this port had been none other than Whalebone Cove where Wylie Hackett had put in with his yacht. The tale ran that Hackett and his lawless crew from the yacht captured the sub, killing every man aboard. From that date on the U-boat and the yacht were said to have cruised together into every sea, preying on merchant ships flying the German flag. And the flag that was raised on both yacht and captured U-boat was the Jolly Roger with its white skull and crossbones against the black background.

You could tell the tale for what it was worth, but there were documents on secret file in the archives at certain great cities of the Allied Powers, and those records made mention of the name of Captain Wylie Hackett. They cited the sinking of various German ships. And that was in black and white.

No country claimed this Captain Wylie Hackett. There was a shadow of mystery thrown across that part of the sea raider's record. But strange tales of cold-blooded fighting and stark heroism marked the name of Wylie Hackett, tales of scuttled ships, looted of their papers and log book, the defeated captain and his crew never heard of again. The sea does not give up the secrets of her dead. And if piracy were done, then the crime was lost in the turmoil of the war's chaos.

"To pirate gold!" said Harley Hamlin, a strange look of excitement in his usually steady eyes.

Jim Driscoll fingered the gold piece that had been the luck charm of Pancho Gómez. He felt his blood pulse faster through his veins. Hackett, Harley Hamlin, even López were held by the spell of that mention of pirate gold.

As the men stood up, glasses touching, there floated across the patio, with its dim lights and its haunting perfume of gardenia, a song. With a small orchestra accompanying her, Kit O'Rafferty, with her voice of plaintive, lilting sweetness, was singing. It was a song of old Mexico, a song that told of the happiness for which men cross oceans and deserts to find, and somehow do not ever find —*morir sueñando* — to die dreaming.

The four glasses clicked, followed by silence as they emptied the rare old wine down their throats, silence, save for the heart-pinching refrain of the girl in the white *mantilla*. Now another voice joined the song. A man's voice, whispering its accompaniment with guitar strings. And there in a far doorway, resplendent in black and scarlet and silver, there stood Don Riley Rodriguez, apparently oblivious to all the world save the girl in the white *mantilla* whose song he was accompanying. Don Riley then sauntered from the doorway. Kit O'Rafferty's dark eyes lighted with pleasure. And there in the mellow light, the song ended.

The men at the table were still held by the spell of the music. Don Riley handed his guitar to one of the members of the orchestra. With a sweeping gesture that belongs to no man save a true *caballero,* he tossed his huge sombrero onto the dull red tiles. At the snap of his fingers the orchestra struck up a pulse-quickening tune. The next moment Kit O'Rafferty, half Irish and the rest of her Spanish, was whirling into a dance so dear to the heart of Mexico. And dancing with her was Don Riley Rodriguez. Don Riley, true son of a Castilian Spaniard named for an Irish gentleman whose lineage had, before Don Riley's time, crossed from cobblestoned County Kerry to the red tiles of Castile.

White and black, scarlet and silver. The click of castanets. The staccato beat of boot heels and slipper heels, perfection of rhythm, grace, the fire, and the sweeping fervor of Mexico in their graceful bodies. There was at this moment no more beautiful girl in all Mexico than this Spanish-Irish *señorita,* no more dashing *caballero* than Don Riley Rodriguez, reckless, gallant, brave-hearted. Laughing at life and at death. Tears and prayers for *mañana.* Tonight belongs to tonight alone.

At the table the four men watched. Pirate gold. Rare wine. Music. Love. What more could men of adventure ask of life? What matter if they die tomorrow? Their pulses pounding, their eyes alight with strange reflections, those four men watched the dance. Names, incidents, friendships and hatreds forgotten, they sat there, breathless, fascinated.

Kit O'Rafferty and Don Riley Rodriguez circled the sombrero on the floor, there in the mellow light. Feet beat swift cadence to the swing of rapid dance music. Their eyes flashed in parrying glances. The man's eyes begging, pleading, worshipping. The dark eyes of the girl mocking and promising and rejecting.

In this dance of old Mexico, should the sombrero be kicked from the floor by the slippered foot of the *señorita,* then the owner of the sombrero knows that his plea is rejected. But should the girl pick up the sombrero and wear it, then he knows that his love is welcome. Perhaps she might even try on the sombrero, in a spirit of coquetry, then toss it aside even as his trembling arms are reaching to claim her.

"El sombrero . . . El sombrero," rippled the whispered name of the dance among the spectators.

Every one of the four men at the table knew that this was more than a dance put on to please the patrons of the *cantina.* This was a plea of love on the part of Don Riley Rodriguez. And the most beautiful girl that Port San Angelo had ever seen was dancing *El sombrero* with this gallant *caballero.*

"Look, *señores,* at the light in Don Riley's eyes," said Captain López. "And, *por Dios,* the flush of the excitement painting those ivory cheeks of the *señorita.* Would she kick the sombrero from the floor? Would she wear that magnificent silver sombrero? *Madre,* what a pair. *Santa María,* what a dance."

Jim Driscoll's eyes were strangely bright. His tongue wet his dry lips. Captain López, almost pale, followed every glance, every gesture of this girl who had so quickly captivated his heart. Captain Wylie Hackett, ruler of San Angelo, ruthless in his pursuit of love, gripped the arms of his chair till his knuckles showed like bare bone. Even the imperturbable Harley Hamlin, puffing on a pipe that had gone out, lost something of his calm as his gaze feasted on the loveliness of this dancing girl, this girl who had come from nowhere to dance in the *cantina* at San Angelo and whose laughing banter had dampened this Britisher's awkward advances.

As Kit danced, her glance sometimes slid from the hot

eyes of Don Riley. She was seeking the face of Jim Driscoll, although each of the others at the table claimed her glance as his own.

Harley Hamlin was the first to sense the approaching danger. His glance had discovered the expression on the face of Captain Wylie Hackett. Hackett was tense as a tiger about to spring. Muscles were quivering from tautness, lips bared slightly in an animal's noiseless snarl, nostrils distended, eyes as cold as ice. Hamlin's right hand slid inside his dinner jacket. His fingers wrapped about the butt of a flat automatic.

But it was Don Riley whose one slight action gave Jim Driscoll an inkling that danger threatened. Don Riley danced with the lithe grace of a past master. As he raised his arms above his head in the swinging gestures of the dance of the sombrero, Jim noticed that, without seeming to do so, the tips of Don Riley's slim fingers touched the collar of his silver and black jacket. Jim Driscoll knew that down behind that jacket, fitted into an ingenious scabbard, Don Riley always carried a slim-bladed knife. And he could throw it with a speed and accuracy that was uncanny in its perfection. Jim knew that Don Riley was making sure the knife was in its place, ready for his hand.

The dance moved more swiftly, more madly now. The climax of *El sombrero* was approaching. Jim Driscoll, suddenly alert to the danger that threatened to change beauty into tragedy, glanced furtively about. He saw the tense Hackett, saw Captain López's eyes blazing with jealousy. Then Jim's glance met that of the vigilant Harley Hamlin. One of the Englishman's brows lifted ever so slightly.

Now Jim Driscoll's eyes sought those of Kit who, from the start of that dance, must have known of the danger. Perhaps, with that feminine love for worship, she had allowed her better judgment to be bested by the thrill of the adoration of these men. There was, as Jim Driscoll well knew, a streak of the imp in Kit. But now, as the danger of it all came to sober her, she was seeking a way out. Her eyes met those of Jim. She flashed him a brief little smile as she read his silent message.

Jim Driscoll sat back. His glance transferred to Harley Hamlin, a message that somehow Kit would solve, or attempt to solve, the dilemma. Hamlin's hand still gripped his hidden automatic.

Now, Kit, with a swift movement, picked up the sombrero. But no sooner had it left the worn tiles than it spun through the air to light with uncanny accuracy on the head of Jim Driscoll.

For a moment Don Riley stood there, astonishment giving way to white-lipped anger, then chagrin. Erect, his sensitive, dark features showing the stab of humiliation, his eyes traveled from the laughing Kit to the very much astonished and bewildered Jim Driscoll. Jim took off Don Riley's sombrero and stood up with it in his hand.

"The joke's on me and you, Riley. Here's your hat, buddy."

But Don Riley made no move to take it. His eyes, hot with anger and resentment, were glittering like live coals.

"I would have said, *señor*" — his voice cut the silence like a knife blade as Don Riley spoke in his native tongue — "that Jeem Driscoll would be the last man alive so publicly to insult me in the presence of my enemies. Because of what we have been together, I cannot fight you. Otherwise, *Señor* Driscoll, I would kill you where you stand."

He bowed with bitter mockery to the girl.

"For the pleasure of the dance, *señorita,* I thank you. It may please you to know that never again will Don Riley Rodriguez annoy you with his presence. *¡Adiós!*"

He took his hat from Jim Driscoll, who stood there dumbly. And with a quick leap over the low wall of the patio, Don Riley was gone. A moment later the swift pounding of hoofs sounded his departure.

For a moment the girl, white as ivory, stood there, a stricken look in her eyes. Then, with a husky little sob, she turned and ran out of the patio.

Captain Wylie Hackett made as if to leave his chair. Harley Hamlin's voice halted him.

"Don't be an ass, Hackett. Can't you see she wants to be alone? Sit down. And Driscoll, old man, be seated and have a drink. A spot of that old pirate rum will buck us all up. You chaps take a pair of woman's eyes too damned seriously. As master of the jolly old ceremonies and one of the fair lady's several rejected suitors, I move we all calm down a bit. Much ado about nothin'. López, old warrior, you have the exact expression of a dying calf."

Jim Driscoll forced a grin. Hackett leaned back in his chair and pounded on the table.

"Rum! You're right, Hamlin. We need a lot of rum. Damn Riley for spoiling a nice, quiet evening."

"Save a couple of damns for your own self, skipper," said Hamlin. "In your own sweet way, old pirate, you were every bit as asinine as Don Riley. You've no kick coming. Perhaps, when the bally thing has had time to lose its potency, it will occur to all persons concerned that the lady and the jolly old Driscoll chum saved a messy sort of scene. And they both are now in the ruddy old throes of enjoying the proverbial reward of peacemakers. Haw!"

Hurt as he was, Jim Driscoll could not keep from smiling. Hamlin was laughing in bursts of audible merriment that started the Mexicans going who had watched the thing. Now their laughter mingled with Hamlin's. Tragedy became comedy.

Hackett's big fists pounded the table as he bellowed for rum like some old buccaneer. Captain López smiled in a sickly fashion. The members of the orchestra, taking their cue, struck up a gay tune. Hands that had sought weapons now picked up brimming glasses.

All this while, Don Riley Rodriguez, goaded by humiliation, was riding like a man gone mad. A sob choked his throat; his eyes burned with unshed tears. For in his boyish heart, he knew the bitterness of a terrible hurt. He had lost the love of a woman and the friendship of his dearest comrade. Alone, riding under the stars, Don Riley sought solitude. And his great heart was flooded with the poignant grief of a child.

VIII
"Smashing Fists"

Captain Wylie Hackett, known among the Mexicans as Don *Diablo,* was drunk. He was roaring, pounding the table, singing lusty sea songs. His was all the swaggering, rough-voiced, hard-fisted manner of some olden-day pirate. He bragged of men he had sent to their deaths. He spoke of that submarine he had commanded, of the yacht that had turned raider with her sides painted black and a Jolly Roger flying at the masthead. Of captured enemies made to walk the plank. Of hand-to-hand fights against big odds.

He taunted Jim Driscoll with open confessions of his smuggling trade. He baited poor Captain López until that hot-tempered little officer was white-lipped with futile fury. He insulted the imperturbable Harley Hamlin again and again, calling him a blackleg son of British decency. He ripped off his coat and shirt and undershirt, baring a sun-tanned torso that was a perfection of knotted muscle. Stripped to the waist, Captain Wylie Hackett drank raw rum like water. His bellowing voice challenged any man alive to meet him in combat of any kind. And across that bronzed chest ran ugly scars made by the ripping knives of men who had fought him. Perhaps Captain Wylie Hackett was not quite sane.

Jim Driscoll was taking his cue from Hamlin. The Britisher sat there, sipping watered rum, pulling on his pipe, unruffled, wary, his hand never far from the gun that snuggled under his immaculate dinner jacket. López, unused to so much liquor, was tipsy.

To Jim Driscoll, Hamlin's glance had telegraphed a message that, put into words would have said: *Sit tight. Listen. And you will learn something of what you came here to learn. Sit tight.*

So Jim Driscoll sat tight. He drank sparingly, but what little he had been forced to drink had fired his blood and dizzied his brain a little. The rum they drank was old and powerful. Jim wondered how long this party would last until it ended in a terrific fight. Back there in the shadows lurked men who were under Hackett's command. Tough men, heavily armed, ready to kill at the command of the roaring, swashbuckling buccaneer they served.

"Hackett, old pirate," said Hamlin, "don't let it slip the old mind that this is an armistice, what?"

"You'll get a cramp hanging onto that gun you pack," roared Captain Hackett. "Sure, it's an armistice. If only we had Don Riley and Tovich here, we'd have all the gang. Driscoll, how'd you like to be my guest on the island? I'll take you aboard the yacht tonight, and we'll shove off.

You'd enjoy it. I'd even guarantee that I'd bring you back safe. And you could write a report to your chief that you'd gotten all the inside dope on this racket of mine."

"I figure on getting out to your island, Hackett. But I'll not go there as your guest."

"I wouldn't discourage you for the world, Driscoll, but you haven't got a rabbit's chance of ever settin' foot on that island unless I take you. There's them that's tried. They're stowed away in Davey Jones's locker this minute. I can show you their bones when the tide is low. And I can point out the shark fins that cut the water in the wake of Captain Wylie Hackett's yacht."

"You know what fetched me down here, Hackett?"

"I know you wear a nice, shiny badge pinned to your undershirt. I suppose you're smellin' out the smugglin' trade."

"I reckon to uncover some of that sort of stuff, Hackett, before I'm done. But the man or men that I take back with me will go to the hot chair. They'll face murder charges. And I'll have enough on 'em to hang 'em or send 'em to the hot seat. It may be, Hackett, that you'll be among those present at the ceremony."

"What makes you think, Driscoll, that you'll ever leave San Angelo alive?" Hackett's slitted eyes and sneering mouth mocked Driscoll.

"I wonder, Hackett, if you're trying to scare me? With your damned pirate stuff and shark fins? When the time comes, Captain Wylie Hackett, or Don *Diablo,* or whatever you want to call yourself, I'll take a trip to your two-bit island. And I'll pick your racket apart to see what makes it click. And whoever tries to stop me, gets hurt. I've lost three men down here. And God have mercy on the skunks that killed 'em, because I'll swing the murdering blackguards or shoot 'em down where I find 'em. You've roared and bellowed around here until these Mexicans have half a notion that you're bad. You've bragged about how many men you've killed with your hands. You're a tough *hombre* from Whalebone Cove . . . a sea-going, salty son of a buccaneer."

Jim Driscoll kicked back his chair and shrugged out of his coat.

"Stand on your feet, Hackett, and we'll get this over once and for all. I'll fight you to the finish right here and now. And, Hackett, I'll kill you. You may be the bully of San Angelo port, but you look like a four-flusher to me. You always have looked yellow. Stand on your feet and fight!"

For a long moment, Captain Wylie Hackett sat there as if dazed. López and Harley Hamlin were aghast. Driscoll, who was neither big nor especially powerful of build, had challenged that blond giant whose nakedness from the waist up revealed the torso of a wrestler. Huge, bulging knots of muscle lumped his shoulders and chest and neck. Gorilla arms. A battered face like that of a professional prize fighter. There was nothing about Jim Driscoll that seemed to warrant this wild challenge. And yet Hackett was a trifle slow in accepting. The big giant got to his feet slowly, half crouching. The table was between him and Driscoll. Hamlin and López rose and stood back.

"I say" — Harley Hamlin made a desperate effort to prevent the clash — "this was to be an armistice. You're both tight as drums. Driscoll's outweighed fifty pounds."

"Keep out of this, Hamlin," said Jim Driscoll. "Hackett knows why I have to kill him."

With an ugly snarl Hackett flung aside the table. Jim met the big man's rush with a right and left that thudded into Hackett's mid-section. Hackett's swings grazed Jim's head. Then they met with a force that threw both off balance.

Hackett's big hands sought Driscoll's throat. Jim ripped in a few short hooks into the big man's wind, then slid free of the gorilla arms. With a twisting leap he was on his feet. As Hackett struggled from the floor, Jim's swift fists again pounded in under Hackett's ribs. None of Hackett's powerful punches landed squarely.

The crowd that packed against the patio walls watched in awed silence. Captain López and half a dozen of his soldiers kept the doors blocked. Harley Hamlin, a big automatic in each hand, kept any of Hackett's men from interfering.

"I'll kill the first ruddy son-of-a-bitch that becomes exuberant. Back where you belong, you damn' scum!"

"Stand toe to toe, you lousy cop!" bellowed Hackett.

"That's not the way I learned to whip big bums like you, Hackett. Here, taste this. . . ." A left followed, and a cross.

Three times Jim Driscoll's fists landed with punishing force. Hackett, too muscle-bound to box, was at a disadvantage. Jim Driscoll twisted and ducked and side-stepped and danced out of reach, only to step in, fists lashing out, then slipping away from Hackett's clumsier swings. It was simply the case of a heavyweight wrestler pitted against a light-heavy fighter skilled in the art of boxing. Jim's hands were like iron mallets as they slid like machine-made things. *Spat. Spat.* Into the big man's belly. Pistons of steel. Jim's timing was accurate; his footwork, in spite of the high-heeled boots, was beautiful. In and out. Back in under Hackett's guard again, pounding at that belly.

Hackett's face twisted with pain. His labored breathing betrayed his distress. Now Jim let Hackett rush past him. As the bigger man, just an edge off balance, whirled, Jim Driscoll swung a left that was a hallmark of perfection in the science of fighting. It caught Hackett just a trifle low.

The big man went down in a limp heap.

"Keep 'em back, Hamlin," rasped Jim Driscoll. "I won't put the boots to their bully from Wishbone Cove. I'll let him up, when he's able to get up. Then I'll knock him down again. And I'll keep on knocking him down, so I can finish this roaring pirate of Port San Angelo. I came a long way to kill him, and I'm killing him now. And he knows why. It's a reason that doesn't concern a man here. So keep out of it. Keep back . . . !"

Hackett, a little groggy, got back on his feet, on the defensive now. Jim Driscoll edged forward. His eyes, holding Hackett's bloodshot stare, were killer's eyes — relentless, devoid of mercy. He feinted, drawing Hackett's fire. As the big fists missed and Jim's left hook staggered the big man, Jim Driscoll grinned horribly.

"You knew I'd boxed in the Army and before I went in the Army, didn't you, Hackett? At San Francisco, at the Olympic Club. And you've been leery. But here, Hackett, on your own stinking dunghill, I've forced your dirty hand. And you'll take 'em where they hurt most. I'll kill you with these two fists. I'll beat you till you scream with the pain of it. Till you vomit up your insides. There'll be blood mixed with the pirate rum when it spills out of your gagging throat, Hackett. You like the sight of red blood? Well, sample this jolt."

He crouched, Hackett instinctively guarding his middle, and Jim's fist smashed with blinding force into Hackett's nose. Blood spouted as the big bully reeled backward. Now Jim ripped in a right hook that dropped Hackett.

"He's got enough, Driscoll, old battler!" called Hamlin. "Let him holler quits."

Jim Driscoll's laugh was an ugly-sounding noise that came from a twisted mouth. He stood back, his bloody fists cocked, waiting for the groggy Hackett to get up, so that he could knock him down again. Jim Driscoll's face was a mask of hate, his bloodshot eyes glittering, his lips pulled apart in a snarl. Behind him was a background of fighting Irish ancestry. Terrier fighting-stuff that knows not the meaning of the word quit. Courage, tenacity, the heart of a fighter. Harley Hamlin shuddered. Captain López furtively crossed himself. The crowd hung back, awed, perhaps a little sick.

Jim Driscoll snarled at his fallen enemy: "Stand up, Hackett! Get on your feet, you black-hearted son-of-hell, so that I can kill you. Die like a man, damn you!"

Even as Captain Wylie Hackett began to lift his groggy weight from the tiles, there came the staccato burst of rifle fire from the street. Horses tore past. Men were shouting confusedly. A woman screamed.

"Viva Herrera! *Viva* Herrera! *¡Viva la revolución!"*

And then another voice, rising above the other sounds, a voice that snapped Jim Driscoll back from the red madness that blinded him.

"Powder Reever! Let 'er bock! *¡Andale, hombrecitos!"*

"Herrera," gasped Captain López. *"¡Válgame Dios! Revolución!"*

He leaped for the door. The night was filled with the crack of rifles. Confusion was everywhere now. Forgetting the bloody Hackett, Jim Driscoll stared at the crimson stain on the white silk shirt of Don Riley who now suddenly appeared. A raw wound marred Don Riley's face.

"Let 'er buck!" yelled Jim, and ran toward Don Riley.

Hamlin, swinging his two big automatics, was at Jim's heels as they piled out of the patio with the soldiers and López.

Out there in the dusty street the fighting was a confusing

mêlée. In the dim lights shed by lamps in windows, they fought.

"Riley! Don Riley!" called Jim Driscoll.

But no reply came. For Don Riley was charging down the street with his ragged troops, down against the superior forces under General Herrera.

"This way, Driscoll. And hurry, man!" Harley Hamlin dragged Jim Driscoll into a doorway, through a house that was filled with frightened women and squealing children. Into an alleyway, then up a side street. There some saddle horses stood, their horsehair hackamore ropes held by a badly frightened Mexican.

"The old emergency mounts," explained Hamlin. "Always keep 'em handy. Had a rummy sort of hunch we'd need a saddle tonight. Up we go, old man, and down this street to flank the rebels. Herrera's a bad 'un if he gets the upper hand. Don Riley'll be in the next street. With the López chap by his side. Friends today, tomorrow enemies. A kiss on the rosy cheek or a knife in the jolly old back. Gad, Jim, you trimmed Hackett! You've a left that would take you . . . look out!"

They were almost run down by a compact gang that rode pell-mell from an alleyway. Jim and Hamlin swung aside just in time. Ten or twelve riders rode by, bunched to form a wedge.

"That," smiled Hamlin thinly, "is none other than Captain Wylie Hackett being taken to the safety of his yacht. He's in need of some patching, what? Let's go, eh?"

There was a carbine in the saddle boot. A double-rowed cartridge belt, every loop filled, hung across the saddle horn. Stirrup to stirrup, Hamlin and Jim Driscoll charged the end of the street where the rebels under Herrera had halted. And in behind Hamlin and Jim there rode a yelling, taunting troop of riders.

"Some of the local chaps," grinned Hamlin, "that work for me. They're a rough lot, but hardy. They're comin' along just for the ruddy old buggy ride, y'know. At 'em, men! Hit 'em hard."

The next moment Jim Driscoll was in the thick of it, swallowed in the mêlée of fighting. Then something struck him from behind, and he slid from the saddle, unconscious. Harley Hamlin grabbed his limp form and dropped it across his saddle. Harley Hamlin's right hand swung to the left, its big automatic spitting. One of his men reeled drunkenly in the saddle and pitched sideways to the ground.

"Had my eyes on you for some time, you dirty blighter!" he gritted. "One of Hackett's bright lads, eh? Well, you're paid off."

Hamlin, riding hard down the street, turned to the man who rode beside him. They pulled rein.

"Take Driscoll to my house, Joe. That rat of a Jones rapped him with a rifle barrel from behind. I got Jones. See that Driscoll gets a doctor's care. Sorry to deprive you of the old ruckus going on downtown."

"That's O K wit' me, boss. Dere'll come other chances ta do battle wit' dese boids. Does dis guy need a doc or a jolt uh hooch? He looks kinda soused."

"He just finished whippin' our old chum, Hackett, and what a neat bit of work it was. If the chap looks beefy, he's merely stopped a few of brother Hackett's swings."

"Honest, boss?"

"That's the gospel, Joe."

"Criminy," breathed Joe, starting away. "Criminy, and I missed de bout."

Joe's hands had found Jim's badge. A queer look crossed his battered-looking face.

"Imagine dis," he muttered, as he carried the unconscious Jim Driscoll into Hamlin's house. "Me, Joe de Gun, playin' noise-goil to a dick! And dey say de trut' ain't stranger dan fiction! Criminy!"

IX
"Sea Chase"

The street fighting was growing more furious each minute. Herrera's men were well-armed and well-mounted, far better equipped than the ragged warriors under Don Riley. But Herrera's men lacked that loyalty to their leader which now carried Don Riley's men into battle. Harley Hamlin and a handful of rough-looking men, engaged in the nefarious trade of gunrunning and whiskey running, took a stand behind a crude barricade hastily thrown up. They were equipped with a Lewis gun and Winchesters, a profane, flippant, hard-bitten crew. Motley of garb and race, Hamlin in his now soiled dinner jacket and white linen made an odd-looking leader for his derelict crew.

"Hold everything, lads, till we can pick the enemy from the jolly old chums. There goes López on a trot with his 'dobe soldiers. Give the old constabulary a cheer, mates. And don't open up the fireworks until Tovich and his rats show up. Dutch Schwartz will give us the tip-off."

The shrill blast of Don Riley's whistle. The rattle of rifle fire. The ribald cheering of Hamlin's ruffians. Horses carrying grim-lipped riders. It looked like Don Riley's men had Herrera's forces on the run. Herrera, who had planned a surprise attack, had been checked by the sudden appearance of Don Riley's rag-tag army. Now the wily General Herrera was retreating.

There came presently another armed force of mounted men. Tovich, his shoulder tightly bandaged, half drunk on vodka, riding like a madman, voicing his barbaric Cossack yell, led his band. A lone man on horseback raced along the side street. His face was a smear of blood, and he swayed drunkenly in the saddle.

"Schwartz!" called Hamlin. "This way, old lad! Someone lend Dutch a hand, he's hurt."

"Tovich . . . !" Schwartz's voice came thickly through bloody froth. "The black-muzzled bastard got me, Hamlin. . . . because I'd slipped word to Don Riley about this attack. Tovich and Herrera double-crossin' Hackett. I run into Don Riley alone. He wasn't coming at first . . . said Jim Driscoll had insulted him. Then I told him Tovich was after Driscoll and the dame that dances at Las Palmas *cantina*. So he gathered his men and came on. Tovich tricked me. Shot me in the back. Tell old Jim Driscoll that I never . . . deserted him. I was . . . just playin' my cards, Hamlin . . . just playin' . . . my . . . hand . . . out."

Harley Hamlin laid Dutch Schwartz gently down behind the barricade.

"A brave lad just died, boys. One of the bravest. Even if he was a cop. He wanted to get Tovich. But the poor old chap was out-foxed. So it's up to us to carry on. Here comes the black-bearded son-of-a-bitch. Hold it, lads. Hold it till . . . slip 'em the news, lads!"

The Lewis gun stuttered. The bullets flew high, too high to do much damage. The man behind the spitting gun swore softly. He'd get the Tovich mob this time or . . . hell! . . . jammed gun . . . O K now . . . but too late. Tovich and his men had swept up a side street.

"Come back and fight, ye scum!" roared the gunner.

Then Don Riley's men cut off the Tovich gang. There

was a furious few minutes of hand-to-hand fighting. Then Tovich whirled and ran, his men with him, to that end of the main street where Herrera was rallying his confused troops.

Tovich threw his men into the doorways along the street. He barked some short commands to them. He called something to Herrera, then rode on through the confusion, five picked men behind him.

Don Riley jumped his horse over a low wall and into an alleyway. "Powder Reever!" he yelled. "Let 'er bock! Thees time, Toveech, I shall take thee 'ell of a pleasure een. . . ."

"Riley!" called a man who staggered from an open doorway. "Hey, you boneheaded, chili-garglin' son!"

"Jeem! You are hurt?"

"Hell, no. Dizzy. Which way?"

"Jomp on behin'!"

Don Riley pulled Jim up beside him. Joe the Gun came running from the house Jim had just left.

"Hey, ya big stiff, come back. Youse is hit. Come back!"

"See you later, New Joisy!" called Jim. "Where we bound for, Riley? Where's the bulk of the scrapping?"

"The bolk of thees fightin', Jeem, ees goin' to be at a house down thee street where thees *señorita* who loves you . . . she leeves. Forgeeve me, my frien', for getting so damn' hot een thee bean. She loves you. That ees planty enough *por* me. I shall geeve to you a gran' weddeeng present."

"You loco chump." Jim poked him in the ribs. "Kit don't love me any more than I love her."

"No? We see about that, boddy. Get ready thee gons, my frien'. We are about to get eento thee 'ell of a tangle weeth Toveech."

Don Riley's horse, carrying its double burden, raced for a squat adobe at the far end of the dark street. A yellow light showed in the window.

"Thees horse, Jeem, ees one I borrow. My best horse ees hid. I borrow thees one from somebody. Ees not so fast, but not so damn' slow, neither. Here we are! *¡Andale!* Toveech ees not yet get here. *Bueno.*"

Quitting the horse, they rapped on the door.

From within came a faint: "*¿Quién es?*"

"Don Riley!"

A bolt slid back. The door opened. Jim and Don Riley saw a slim, pale, sick-looking girl in a faded pink kimono, an automatic in her hand. Her gray eyes lighted with joy.

"Gee, I'm glad you came, Don Riley. I heard all the shootin', and I've been worried about Kit. When she didn't show up, I got scared. The Kitten's all right, ain't she?"

"You mean she's not here?" asked Jim. "She didn't come home about two hours ago?"

"No. A guy who works on Hackett's boat come by about an hour ago to tell me Kit's gonna be workin' late. The guy says Hackett's throwin' a party and is payin' Kit big dough ta sing."

"Thees guy who say that," said Don Riley tensely, "ees he a red-haired one weeth a red mustache an' thee one eye?"

"That's the bozo. Listen, nothin's happened to Kit, has it?"

"Ees like I am so damn' afraid," groaned Don Riley. "That Captain Hackett has that red one steal her. She ees by now on that yacht. Per'aps already on thee way to that island. *Santa María*. May thee Mother of God keep her safe unteel . . . com', Jeem! *¡Andale! Por Dios,* let us be een time, my frien'."

A Mexican woman had paddled into the room on sandaled feet. To her Don Riley talked in rapid Spanish.

Then he spoke again in English. "And do not worry, *Señorita* Flossie. Jeem Driscoll ees thee best damn' soldier from thee *gringo* war. We shall make the gran' rescue. Do not worry. *¡Adiós!*"

"You're Jim Driscoll?" As the sick girl spoke, she took one of Jim's hands in her two frail ones. Before he could stop her, she was kissing one of his grim, blood-smeared hands.

"Here, little lady, don't do that. You just keep the old light burning, and we'll have Kit back safe."

From an adjoining room came a high-pitched voice reciting the Lord's prayer.

". . . *Amen*. Handy Hands and the bos'un's mate! And steer a straight course fer the masthead atop the shiprock. Ten paces east by nor'east. To the white rock . . . pipe down, ye sons-o'-bitches!"

"*¡Madre!*" gasped Don Riley. "Where did you get thees parrot bird?"

"A drunken gob give it to Kit."

"Guard well thees bird. Cover thee cage so he cannot make thee talk. *Válgame Dios,* hide thees parrot bird teel we come back once more. *Adiós*. We go . . . here comes Toveech! She's thee fight, Jeem!"

Jim and Don Riley leaped outside, slamming the door behind them.

"Lock it, girl!" snapped Jim, jerking his six-shooter.

As the door bolt clicked, the two partners crouched in the outer darkness. Tovich and his men came with a rush. Don Riley's gun roared, and a man tumbled out of his saddle. Jim Driscoll was shooting now. But the light was too dim to make for accuracy.

Two, then another of the men, were knocked from their saddles by the bullets of Jim and Don Riley. The remaining riders whirled and raced for safety.

"Cowards!" yelled Don Riley, grabbing a horse by the dangling bridle reins. "Coyotes! *Andale,* Jeem! Le's go!"

Jim vaulted into an empty saddle. Together they spurred for the wharf. Tovich had gotten away. They saw his fleeing horse some distance ahead. Tovich and his two remaining men were heading for the bay.

Even as Don Riley and Jim pulled up their sweating horses, the *chug-chug* of a motorboat mocked them from out on the water. It was spotted by the riding lights of boats at anchor out there.

"Queeck, *por Dios!*" panted Don Riley, leaping like a cat from the wharf into a motorboat that was just leaving the float.

Jim was right behind Don Riley. The two men in the boat jerked guns, then decided better of the notion as the guns of Jim and Don Riley were pointed at their bellies.

"Take us out to thee yacht of Captain Hackett" gritted Don Riley, "or you weel be two corpse' een one damn' second. *¡Pronto!*"

"No tricks," added Jim.

The boat sped across the smooth surface of the bay. It was almost in the frothy wake of the motorboat carrying Tovich.

"What the hell you guys celebratin', anyhow?" growled the man at the wheel. "First One-Eyed Red shows up with a dame. Then comes Hackett, lookin' like somethin' the pups had bin fightin' over, then that lousy Tovich. Now you show up, Rodriguez, with a cowboy that was pointed out to us guys as a gover'ment dick. What the hell's goin' on?"

"For many weeks, Greasy," said Don Riley softly, "I 'ave resist thee temptation to bomp you off. One more damn' leetle question out of you and pop goes thee weasels. Tell thees *hombre* een English-American, Jeem, w'at I'm try' to put over against heem."

"I don't need no interpreter, Don Riley. You got the bulge. It's your party. And if it turns out to be your funeral, I'll send posies. Hard over there, you blasted, lousy bums!" The man cursed the lightless craft that grazed the side of their motorboat.

"The old blockade, see," gritted the hard-faced pilot of the speeding commandeered motorboat. "One of Hackett's dummies. Dead eyes, me and Bill calls 'em. If this is a high-jackin' graft, count me and Bill in, Don Riley. Business is lousy, see. Hackett's put the old boycott on us. Me 'n' Bill is always in the humor ta pick up an odd piece of change. We'll go through, Rodriguez, for a hundred apiece."

"I'll make eet five hondred apiece," purred Don Riley, "eef you stay weeth me and my frien', Jeem. We are out to get Hackett and thees One-Eye Red and thees Toveech. Five hondred apiece, Greasy."

"You ain't took over much of a contract, have ya, mister? You think we kin take anything above a plugged nickel off that yacht?"

"Then gimme that wheel," snapped Jim, "and jump overboard. You either go the limit or walk back from here, get me? *Pronto,* buddy, want the game, or don't you?"

"Wit' a gun lookin' me over, brother, where's my choice? Me and Bill goes on through from here. Suicide club. Watch the boat ta sta'board, there. She's . . . cripes!"

A small boat without lights had cut loose with a couple of guns. Jim and Don Riley returned the fire, just as the man at the wheel with a gritted curse rammed the lighter craft, upsetting it.

"The rats needed bathin', eh, Bill?"

Bill gave back no reply. He was standing there with a

rifle, his eyes staring across the water, watching ahead. A fog, thick as pea soup, was rolling in from the ocean. In a short time its gray shroud would cover the bay. The motorboat cut the water like a knife. Behind, the water was churned white.

Now Bill grunted and pointed ahead. Where the yacht had been, there remained only the empty water. The boat carrying Tovich was milling about in crazy circles. The Russian's voice could be heard cursing horribly. Captain Wylie Hackett's yacht had lifted anchor and shoved off.

"*Madre de Dios,* Jeem!" groaned Don Riley. "We are come too late!"

"Listen, feller," said Jim Driscoll to the pilot of the motorboat. "Do you know the course that we'd take to reach Hackett's island?"

"I bin that far along in navigation, doc," said the fellow jeeringly, "and I could make the island. Only I'd need a boat twice this size. This is a motorboat, brother, not no ocean-goin' craft."

"No? Well, she'll be converted tonight. Point her nose out to sea, feller, and give 'er the gun."

"Cripes, guy, we'll be swamped first time we hit a big breaker. This ain't no sea-goin' boat."

"She's going to sea tonight," said Jim grimly. "With you or without you. If you don't feel game, give me that wheel and jump overboard. And take your pardner along when you jump. My friend Riley and I are craving an ocean voyage. Where the hell's your compass? Riley, show the two gents to the rail and push 'em over."

"Not me, sir," said Bill quietly. "I got a half interest in this tub. Where she goes, I goes. And if Greasy ain't got the guts to handle the wheel, lemme take it. I helped build this baby, and I'll go down in 'er."

"Bill," said Jim Driscoll warmly, "you're regular. You won't lose much, if we pull this off right. If we don't win, we lose. But if we can land on Hackett's island, you'll be damn' well paid. Let's go. What do you say now, Greasy?"

"I got only one life ta slough off, mates. It belongs ta me, see. Make it one grand, and I'll lay it down fer my country. Who bids one grand? One thousand simoleons?"

"The price Don Riley quoted was five hundred," said Jim Driscoll flatly. "Take it or jump overboard."

"I left me water wings home, see," grinned Greasy. "Five hundred smackers she is. Lay 'er on the line, buddy."

"Take us to the island and you'll get it. Now shut up. And swing this canoe over across to where Tovich is. I want a word or two with that dude. Bill, keep that rifle pulled down on the other boat. Riley, old pard, we're out for an evening's sport. Kind of deep-sea hunting. We better take Tovich along, no?"

"That ees thee damn' swell, elegant idea, Jeem. And when we get out to where thees sharks leeve, poosh heem overboard."

They overhauled the other boat. Tovich was frothing with rage as the boats scraped sides. Jim Driscoll had found a coil of rope. Fashioning a loop as they came up on the other boat, Jim neatly roped the Russian. "Pull hard to the left, Greasy. I've done roped us a maverick!" The next moment Tovich, on the end of the makeshift lariat, was sputtering and floundering in the water. Jim and Bill hauled him in over the side.

"You seemed like you wanted to get aboard Hackett's yacht, Tovich. We'll ferry you out there. No charge."

Jim's gun poked the Russian's ribs. Don Riley disarmed the sputtering, half-drowned Tovich. Bill, with a phlegmatic calm, was sending bullets at the other boat that now turned tail and raced back for shore. Tovich was cursing in broken English. Don Riley's knife tickled his throat.

"Now, peeg, hush thee mouth. No noise. Because we mus' behave een thee presence of thee United States law."

"Relax, Tovich," grinned Jim. "You'll get high blood pressure. I want you alive for the hanging party."

Tovich nursed his wounded shoulder and swore into his tangled black beard.

"Sometheeng," said Don Riley, speaking into Jim's ear in a barely audible undertone, "ees tell me that trouble ees come' at Hackett island."

"I didn't reckon we were going to a Sunday school picnic, Riley."

"I do not mean about us. Thees parrot bird shows up. That ees very fonny. After fifty years, thees bird that belong to 'Andy 'Ands ees get found. Toveech and Herrera ees double-cross Hackett. Thees One-Eye Red ees hate Hackett. I would not be surprise', Jeem, eef One-Eye Red and thees Toveech make thee mutiny amongst thees yacht gang. But Captain Hackett has always got theem scare' too bad. He ees keel theem."

"The last I saw of Hackett, Riley, he couldn't hurt anybody."

Briefly Jim related the fist fight with Hackett. Don Riley whistled noiselessly. "When thee leader of the wolfs pack ees get hurt, thee other wolfs, they keel heem . . . and eef thees parrot bird has mak' thee talk, then ees jus' too bad."

"What the devil has a parrot got to do with mutiny, Riley?"

"Thees parrot bird ees belong to 'Andy 'Ands, the 'ermit of the Sangre de Cristo. Captain Bloody Jack Hackett, thee pirate, ees take thees bird when he leave 'Andy 'Ands to die at Whalebone Cove. And when he bury thees gold, he tell thees parrot how to find heem. He teach thees bird to learn what he say. You hear that parrot bird say about thee masthead on thee shiprock, no? Ten paces east by nor'east to thee white rock. That parrot bird ees know. But eef thee bird 'as talk to somebody, then that somebody go there an' fin' thee gol'."

"You think there's buried treasure around here, then?"

Don Riley nodded and smiled. "Some day I tell you about thees 'Andy 'Ands. . . .about thee gol' at Whalebone Cove. Some day, Jeem, eef we do not die before then. *Caramba,* the waves, they get beeg, no?"

X
"Pirate's Death"

No further time for talk. The sea tossed the light craft like a cork. The fog poured down until all about them it was black. But Greasy held the motorboat to a steady course. Jim felt a little sick, and Tovich looked greenish in the light of the ship's lantern Bill had lit.

"She's a boat," said Bill proudly. "What I mean, mates, she's a boat. I built 'er. Lissen to that engine. Gimme the wheel, Greasy."

"Bill's a skipper," grinned Greasy. "And how! This ain't his first trip outta San Angelo bay in this boat."

"Not by fifty times," said Bill, munching on a huge wad of tobacco. "And on some of the dirtiest nights ever made."

"This one's dirty enough for me." Jim forced a grin. "I hope to gosh I'm not getting seasick."

Don Riley chuckled. Tovich was moaning a little, there at the aft end of the tossing boat. Don Riley crouched beside Bill, eyes on the compass. Greasy lit a foul-smelling pipe. From a locker they'd dragged oilskins and tarpaulin jackets. In the same locker were stowed half a dozen rifles and boxes of ammunition.

On through the black fog. Somewhere a fog horn boomed. Its sound was soon lost in the distance. Then the muffled clang of a bell buoy.

Bill swung the little boat hard to port and grunted something into Don Riley's ear. Don Riley doused the ship's lantern. Save for the hidden light above the compass, the little motorboat now showed no light. The boom of a nearby surf drowned the noise of the motor.

Against the dense fog loomed the black bulk of Hackett's yacht. It was spotted with round yellow lights, where the lighted portholes showed. With a swift motion, Bill cut off the motor. In silence they drifted into that eerie curtain of fog between the yacht and the pounding surf to starboard.

"Sweet work," whispered Greasy. "Bill's a pilot, and how."

"Shut up," gritted Jim.

From aboard the yacht came a jumble of sounds. Drunken singing, a chorus of bellowing voices. Cursing. A pistol shot that silenced the chorused song.

"Pipe down, you buckos. There'll be heads cracked in a holy second. We ain't got a month ta get this over. Drop the yawl over the side, and we'll go ashore fer the stuff. Easy on that line, ya swab! Dago, send up a rocket so's the boys'll know."

"Ees like I say, Jeem," whispered Don Riley, his knife point against the thick throat of Tovich. "Ees mutiny. Let thee yawl go ashore. Then we board thee yacht. And eef you know thee prayers, Jeem, say theem. Ees look damn' bad, I tell you. Toveech, you lousy bom, one sound from you and thee neck gets cut open. *¿Sabe?*"

The motorboat drifted close to the side of the yacht. Bill, at the wheel, whispered into Don Riley's ear. Don Riley nodded. Jim took advantage of the moment to stuff a gag in the mouth of Tovich and bind the Russian hand and foot. The rude gag, donated by Greasy, was a wad of oily waste.

Davits creaked, and oars in the oarlocks. A rocket flared, red against the black sky. The splash of oars sounded. The yawl was pulling shoreward in the fog-filled silence.

Then the motorboat softly bumped the side of the yacht, and Greasy was hanging grimly to a lowered rope ladder that came down from the yacht's deck. Luck. Pure luck, that ladder hanging there where the drunken crew had neglected to haul it back up after the cursing One-Eyed Red had gone down it into the yawl.

Jim Driscoll was climbing the ladder even as the nimble Greasy tied the boat's painter fast to the dangling rope of a davit. Behind Jim came Don Riley. They were on deck now. A man lurched up out of a lighted hatchway. Don Riley's gun barrel silenced the cry about to burst from his open mouth. Then, from the forward end of the yacht, came a woman's sobbing followed by a man's voice, strained and husky and choked with anger.

"No use weepin', girl. Your friend, Driscoll, messed up the deal, that's all. Take the bad with the good breaks."

Jim Driscoll ran forward, Don Riley at his heels. Two men loomed out of the darkness. Don Riley's knife slithered across a ten-foot distance, and Jim's gun barked once. The next moment they burst into the lighted cabin where Kit and Captain Hackett lay bound hand and foot on bunks.

"Speak of the devil," grinned Hackett, "and here he pops up. Cut us loose, Driscoll. And lend a hand. My God, man, I'll give you all the damned gold, all . . . thanks, Driscoll."

Jim's jackknife had freed Hackett's ropes. The big captain, battered and half-naked, blood-spattered, flexed his cramped muscles.

Kit was in Don Riley's arms, laughing and sobbing brokenly.

"Driscoll, I never went back on my given word to any man. If you have any way of getting me to the island, and if I'm alive when I get done with the job there ahead of me, I'll give myself up to your law and hang from your damned gallows. I'll give you gold. Gold enough to make us all millionaires. Only get me to the island before it's too late."

"I don't want your gold, Hackett. All I want is the chance to kill you as you killed Dave King and Tex Edwards and Bud Fallen, the boys I sent down here to get a line on your opium trade. That's where your dirty gold comes from, Hackett. From the hop dealers. From the poor devils that would sell their souls for a pipe of opium, or a sniff of your damned cocaine. All your big talk of pirate gold was to cover your drug traffic. What's on your island that needs your immediate presence? What reason can you give me for not killing you, here and now?"

"Take me to the island, Driscoll, and I'll show you. King and Tex Edwards and Bud Fallen were killed at Port San Angelo, as far as I know. I never saw 'em. Pancho Gómez or Ray Quick would know what happened to 'em, perhaps. They came by the way of the Sangre de Cristo. They were warned by the old hermit to turn back. He's there to scare away travelers. They crosses the desert at their own risk . . . look out behind you, Driscoll!"

Jim Driscoll whirled. At that instant Hackett's big fist crashed against his jaw. Before Jim or Don Riley could move, Hackett had leaped out the door and was gone, a faint splash as he dove over the rail. Then the fog hid him as he swam with powerful strokes for the island.

Hackett's blow had floored Jim. He got up, grinning crookedly, rubbing his jaw.

"Well, Riley, the big son-of-a-bitch sure put over a fast one. If the sharks don't get him, he'll make the island."

"And when he mak' thees island, then he most fight planty more weeth that One-Eye Red and thees other *hombres*. Jeem, you stay here on thees yacht, you and thee *señorita*. I, Don Riley Rodriguez, go to fight side by side weeth that beeg son-of-a-gon. He ees one against so many. He does not even have thee knife. Ees game, that Captain Wylie Hackett."

"What's he want there on the island, Riley?"

"That, my frien', ees sometheeng I do not know. Only eet ees not thee gol' he goes for. I go now."

"Not alone, you don't," said Kit. "Jim, just when I fall for this darned Don Quixote, he takes a powder on me and fades out. Where you go, Riley, there also goes Katherine Mavourneen O'Rafferty. And we stick together until further orders. Jim, you've got some wrong notions about Hackett. Give the guy a chance. You know why he's swimmin' for land right now? No, you don't. And Riley doesn't. But I do. Because I'm a woman, and I know that only love can make a guy do what that big bimbo is doin' now. There's a dame on that island, and Hackett's goin' to fight for her. And when you think he's in the hop-runnin' racket, you're wetter than his pants are this minute, Jimmy boy. Give the guy a break. He's white. Look at this."

Kit showed Jim and Don Riley a tiny vial filled with colorless liquid.

"He slips me this when he thinks it's curtains for him and me . . . when this one-eyed, red-headed yegg is makin' his big noise. It's his last little bet, see. His hole card. And he slips it to me. And he does it knowin' that this one-eyed yegg is goin' to torture him slow till he croaks. Listen, Jimmy, that big boy does things in a big way. He's a loud-mouthed, rum-guzzlin', ten-minute egg, but somewhere inside him he's got a heart. A soft spot, see? It wasn't him that pulled this shanghai gag on me. It was that one-eyed guy. Say, he's been white to me and to Flossie. A gentleman. Gee, I can't waste time tellin' you boys that Hackett's regular. He's there in the water, swimmin' for shore to fight them other highbinders with nothin' but his bare hands. Give him a break, Jimmy. Let's go!"

"Let's go, then." Jim grinned widely. "And I hope you're right, Kit."

Together the two men and Kit scrambled down the ladder and into the boat where Greasy and Bill were waiting.

"Got that five hundred on ya, chief?" asked Greasy.

"I'll have it when we get back from the island. You and Bill get this engine started, then pile up the ladder onto the yacht. Don't let anybody on board. And while you're waitin' for us to come back, take a look around. Disarm any men you find and lock 'em up. Start the motor, Bill."

"Listen, guy, you can't ever land wit'out crackin' up on the rocks," protested Greasy.

"Then that's where we all lose," said Jim grimly. "Get this thing in gear."

"Your funeral, feller," sighed Bill.

The motor came alive with a snort. Bill and Greasy swarmed up the rope ladder. Jim spun the wheel, and the boat slid across the black water.

"We're in the lap of the gods now," he gritted.

"Point to thee right, Jeem. I 'ave a knowledge of thees island. Always there ees thee light at thee white cove. Hah! There, straight ahead! There shows thee light. Hold up,

Jeem. Reverse the . . . *bueno!*"

Don Riley threw a rope to the swimming Hackett whose head showed like a black ball on the water. They had almost run him down.

"Grab it, Hackett. God knows why, but we're for you," called Jim.

Hackett, dripping wet, pulled himself over the side of the motorboat.

"Sorry about that lousy trick, Driscoll. But I had to get ashore. . . . two women there at the house. My mother, Driscoll, and my wife. Now, dammit, do you savvy?"

"Your mother. . . . your wife?"

"You heard me."

Hackett pushed Jim aside and took the wheel. He swung hard to port and barely grazed a big rock.

"Phony light," he explained. "Have to smell your way in. The light's there to throw these wise pilots onto the rocks."

A few moments later Hackett grounded the motorboat on smooth sand. The yawl from the yacht was beached almost within arm's reach of where they landed. It was empty of men with no guard there to watch it.

Jim jerked open the locker and handed out guns to Hackett and Don Riley.

"Better hide somewhere, Kit."

"You boys go ahead. Kit will look after herself. Good luck. And hurry!"

The three men were now running up a steep pathway toward the big, black shadow of a house, built after the fashion of old feudal castles, turrets nosing bluntly into the black sky. A shot ripped the night. The next moment the three men were in a courtyard, shooting at moving forms that ran confusedly about. An open doorway, lighted inside. A hallway that was hung with rare old tapestries. Into a room where a dozen evil-looking ruffians were pounding at a large steel safe with crowbars, axes, and sledge-hammers.

The next instant Hackett leaped forward. His rifle thrown aside, his big hands gripped the throat of a villainous-looking one-eyed man with fiery red hair. The one-eyed mate of the mutinous crew was no mean antagonist. Snarling, biting, gouging, he closed with Hackett. Almost a match in weight and height, the red-haired mate with a curved-blade dirk, Hackett with his bare hands, they fought like two beasts. The drunken crew backed away under the guns of Jim Driscoll and Don Riley.

There was the scuffle of feet as the two men fought, and their labored breathing. Jim Driscoll, with a sudden shock, realized that Hackett was using tactics that, if he had chosen to use them in their fist fight, would have beaten Jim at the start. The one-eyed mate was trying to twist the curved dirk into Hackett's back, while Hackett, his lips pulled apart in a ghastly grin, gripped the one-eyed mate's thick wrist.

"The tough bucko mate, eh?"

Hackett crouched, threw his weight to one side. There was a sickening crack of breaking bone. As the one-eyed mate screamed in agony, Hackett's fist crashed into the man's face. One-Eyed Red slumped to the floor, his head twisted sideways.

Before Don Riley or Jim could move, that big skipper of the mysterious yacht was among his crew, smashing right and left. The crunch of his huge fists was horrible. His booming roar filled the room. The cowed men, a rough-looking lot of sailors, fell like tenpins under the terrific onslaught.

"¡Madre de Dios, mira!"

Don Riley pointed to the sun-baked torso of the berserk Hackett. There, plunged hilt deep in the blond giant's back, was the dirk. Hackett's back streamed blood. But still he fought on alone, smashing into the sullen crew that gave way before him.

Roaring, smashing, cracking heads, Hackett beat the mutineers into submission, until they howled and begged for mercy — even as his pirate sire before him had fought, there at Whalebone Cove, back to back with Handy Hands, when the sand puddled red, and the groans of dying men were blotted out in the crash of cutlass blades.

Dawn, fog-drenched, gray as death itself, was paling the night. There came the sound of the booming surf on black cliffs. And here in the main room of this big castle, Captain Wylie Hackett, son of Bloody Jack Hackett, buccaneer, fought down his faithless crew with fists that were broken and red with blood.

When he could not longer stand, he dropped on sagging knees to the floor, crawling toward the dead body of the one-eyed mate. Even as his big hands gripped the mate's broken neck, he was slipping away.

Don Riley held the crew under his gun muzzle. Jim bent over Hackett. He pulled the dirk from the big man's back. Hackett's eyes, bloodshot, glazed with approaching death, focused for a moment. His bruised mouth smiled twistedly.

"In my pocket, Driscoll, is the key to the tower room. There you will find the woman I stole from you. Forced her to marry me. But as God is my judge, a wife in name only. . . . because, you see, Driscoll, I loved her. I thought in time she'd love me. But it was always you . . . understand? . . . that she loved. God, how I hated you. I still hate you, because the only woman I ever loved will belong to you, now. The only woman that I ever treated decently. Except that Kit girl. She never gave me a chance to . . . get me a drink of rum, Driscoll. I'm about to pull out for a new land. I'm shovin' off. And I'll clear port without any papers. Rum, damn your eyes!"

Jim brought a bottle of rum and a glass. Hackett smashed the glass and drank deeply from the bottle.

"You think you're a man, Driscoll. But you was never the man that Captain Wylie Hackett was. With a woman in every port from Shanghai to Cape Town and from Bombay to Galveston. I've made better men than you walk the plank off that yacht anchored out yonder. I don't know why I didn't kill you when I fought you, Driscoll, the same as I killed this red-headed swab just now. I could kill ten like you. But I let you live. I fought your way and let you beat me. And I'm damned if I can tell you why. But when you unlock the door to that tower room, you'll find two women. One is the woman you'll marry. The other is my old mother. And Driscoll, if you harm that old lady, I'll come back from hell to get you. Back . . . from hell!"

Captain Wylie Hackett's voice rattled into silence. Jim Driscoll got to his feet.

"He's dead, Riley. Keep an eye on this gang."

He held a large key in his hand.

"A Yaqui gave me a message from the girl I had hoped to marry until she ran off with Wylie Hackett, owner of the Hachita Rancho. The Yaqui told me she was a prisoner here. So I came, buddy, to kill Hackett and take her back. Wylie Hackett is dead. I'm going to unlock that door."

"May you fin' love and happiness, my frien', when thee key turns een thee lock."

XI
"Mightier than Gold"

The huge key grated in the lock. Jim Driscoll pushed open the massive, brass-studded, oak door. There, inside a long, elegantly furnished room, stood a tall, copper-haired girl in black. In her hand was a jeweled dagger. With a gasping, soundless little cry, she dropped the dagger. Pale as aged ivory, magnificent, the firelight from the huge old Spanish fireplace making her hair into bronze, stood the girl.

"Jim . . . you came, didn't you, Jim? I was just going to do something terrible. You see, Jim, the only friend I had, the only consoling voice in my world has just died. Wylie Hackett's mother, Jim. A saintly woman whose burdens were many. Her poor little mind gone, she lived on in a dream world. A world that held nothing but beauty and kindness and love. Victim of a foolish love, wife of a pirate, and mother of Wylie Hackett, she paid her price of suffering. But it was that poor, dear, old lady, Jim, who kept me from killing myself. Her prayers, her companionship, her sweetness kept courage and hope in me. Her prayers and mine, Jim, are answered."

There was something in the quietness of the girl's voice that told Jim Driscoll more than any words could tell him, the story of her terrible suffering. When he had held her a long time in his arms, she took his hand and led him to the canopied bed where the little old lady who was Wylie Hackett's mother lay asleep in death. A kindly smile, that might have belonged to some saint, had smoothed the gentle lips.

"I don't think she ever suspected, Jim, that her son was not a good man. With her he was as kindly and thoughtful as ever a man could be. Wylie Hackett worshipped her as few men ever adored a mother.

"When he kidnapped me and brought me here, I saw nothing ahead but horror. But when that old lady took me as a daughter, Wylie dared not touch me. And so I've lived here in this room, companion to her, all these many months."

"Barbara," said Jim gently, "Wylie Hackett is dead. We're going to leave here now. Later, when you've rested some and things shape up all right, we'll bury Hackett's mother alongside Hackett. We'd better go now."

As Jim led her from the room, Kit stood waiting in the hallway.

"I thought I'd better sort of trail along, Jimmy. And while you and Riley are mopping up and so on, us gentler sex will powder our noses and get acquainted. Riley slipped me the news, and, while I don't know your name right now, miss, it ain't hard for even a dumb cluck like me to know that I'm just about to kiss the future Missus Jim Driscoll. And take it from Kit O'Rafferty, you're both gettin' a great break. Honey, let's go into some nice quiet room and weep. I'm just dyin' for a grand weep. Jim, Riley wants you."

Jim grinned and left them there, their arms about one another's shoulders. He found Don Riley sitting in an old Spanish chair, strumming a guitar, singing some Mexican song. The crew of the erstwhile pirate yacht stood with their faces to the wall, hands lifted.

"Thee first one that moves," explained Don Riley, nodding toward an array of evil-looking knives that had once been wall decorations, "gets thee knife een thee back. By thee way, Jeem, I am afraid that *muy maldito* Toveech has escape'. He got loose from thee ropes, and he ron away."

"Where did he run to, Riley?"

Don Riley shrugged. "Always that Tovich ees thee damn'

fool. He ron away een thee boat. Thee boat she hit thee rocks and bost all to 'ell. The sharks weel get thee belly-ache. Listen, my frien', to thees song wheech I am mak' op to seeng to my Katrina. Ees a swell song, I tell you."

"Save it, Riley. How do you know Tovich made that break?"

"My Katrina . . . how you call heem? . . . Keet, she ees watch'. Ees smart, that *señorita* who ees to be thee *Señora* Rodriguez. She see thee whole theeng. Now we mus' pay that Greasy an' that Beel for thee boat, no? And w'at thee 'ell we use *por* money? I jus' open thee safe, and w'at you theenk? . . . she's empty. And, instead of thee money ees thee note from that Captain Hackett. The note say that many years ago he have thee parrot bird and thee parrot bird talk about thee buried treasure. Thees gol' ees een a cave where nobody can go excep' when thee tide she's most low. And me, I now theenk them pirates ees not so smart, because thees letter of Captain Hackett ees say that thee tides ees carry away thee chests of gol'. Only a small amount ees left. And that ees already spent. And thee rest ees there where thee shark fishes sweem."

"What about the gold Hackett promised us if we fetched him here?"

"What ees the name of that long sausage that ees look like the beeg hot dogs?"

"Baloney?"

"*Sí,* my frien'. Baloneys. No less. Would you not peddle thee baloneys, Jeem, eef you weesh to fight *por* your mother?"

"Well," said Jim, "I reckon we can scrape up enough to pay off Greasy and Bill. Raymond Quick, Pancho Gómez, Tovich, and Hackett have passed on. Two governments will be grateful for their passing to the tune of a tidy sum."

Don Riley smiled. "*Sí,* my frien'. There ees also thee reward on Harley Hamlin and Riley Rodriguez. Then you 'ave clean up the whole damn' works, Jeem. There weel be enough to pay off thees Greasy and Beel. Also enough to buy for Jeem Driscoll thee wedding suit, no?"

"Hamlin's played fair with me, Riley. And, as for you, I'd quit my job rather than connect you with this smuggling racket."

"Thank you, my frien'. But I do not deny thee fac' that Don Riley Rodriguez ees thee bes' damn highjack' een Méjico. But not *por* thees opium. I highjack the gons and bullets off these others *hombres.* I geeve thees gons and bullets to my *hombrecitos.* I lead them eento thee fight. And then, when I mus' leave thee fight to come to thee Hackett island, thee *Señor* Harley Hamlin ees carry on. By now, there ees no more *revolución.* And *mañana* thees grand oncle of mine ees make me thee colonel. I shall ride down thee street to thee palace of Chapultepec. Behin' me comes my gran' army, eencluding the soldiers of Captain López. Ees not soch a bad guy, that López. Only ees get thee high hats, and now hee weel be the lieutenant colonel under Don Riley. And I weel speak to thees oncle of mine about my frien', Harley Hamlin, who weel mak' thee 'ell of a swell, elegant army officer *por* Méjico. W'at you going to do, Jeem?"

"I'm going back to ranching, Riley. I took this job for a reason, and now my work here is done. I'm all washed up and ready to go home."

"Now that I 'ave got back to be good frien' weeth my oncle," said Don Riley, "that ees mean that I also and likewise get back the Rodriguez Rancho. Ees damn' good rancho. One hondred thousand acres. Planty cattle, planty horses, planty grass and water. Me, I am a soldier and too busy to look after thees rancho. I make you my half partner.

Do not make no arguments about thees, Jeem."

"I'll buy in with you, Riley, and be glad to."

"Buy een? Your money ees no good here. You are my frien'. *Bueno.* Ees all settle'. But before we go to thee City of Méjico, there ees one more theeng to do. I 'ave one more promise to keep. And you, my frien', you shall also come weeth me. We got to take thees parrot bird to 'Andy 'Ands, the 'ermit of the Sangre de Cristo."

"I don't quite get the idea, Riley, but I'll . . . God!"

A low rumble. A sickening rolling of the floor under them.

"Earthquake!" cried Jim.

They ran for the room where Kit and Barbara had gone. Even as the rock walls crashed around them, they dragged the women to safety. Hackett's crew was already scattered but not toward the shore of the island.

Jim and Don Riley were able to lift the girls into the yawl the mutineers had used. Jim worked in frantic haste over the motor. The sea was running in huge oily swells and behind them the crash of the stone castle was like a cannonade. The little boat was whirled and tossed about madly. The group in the yawl pulled in frantic terror for the yacht.

A sullen rumble. A wave that tossed the yawl like a cork. Then a deadly, ominous calm broken by a guttural rumble.

"Look!" gasped Jim. *"Look back! The island! It's gone!"*

An awed silence gripped the four. There in the gray light of dawn, fog-drenched, eerie, there remained nothing of the tiny island. It had gone, taking down into the sea its pirate lore, its dead mistress, its half-mad owner's dead body and the mutineers. The mighty hand of God had, in an instant, wiped out that which He chose to destroy.

In silence, they made the yacht. Greasy and Bill, badly frightened, helped them aboard. Although they waited for two hours, searching the deep green surface of the morning sea, they found no trace of any of the mutineers.

Hackett's island was no more. From his pocket Jim Driscoll took the gold piece that had come from the neck thong of Pancho Gómez. He tossed it overboard with a quick movement.

"W'at you trow away, Jeem?"

"I threw away a luck piece, Riley. A gold coin from your Whalebone Cove. I threw away the temptation to forget better things to hunt for other coins like it."

"I theenk I onderstand, Jeem."

They stood on the deck of the yacht, leaning across the rail as Greasy and Bill got the craft under way. Two men and two women and love that had endured its dangers.

Men still hunt for treasure at Whalebone Cove. Prospectors and travelers still stop at the deserted rock hut at the Sangre de Cristo. And those who have the temerity to look around will find the grave of the hermit who once dwelt there.

Near Mexico City is a ranch. There live Jim Driscoll and his wife. You'll find Harley Hamlin, grave, courteous, white of hair, at a modest home in the city, with his pipe and his spot of Scotch and his books. Whenever Colonel Riley Rodriguez can spare the time, he and Hamlin ride out to the Rodriguez Rancho.

And there, sometimes, grouped around an old Spanish fireplace, you will find them all. There also is a slender girl with gray eyes and ash-blonde hair who sits always beside Harley Hamlin. And when Don Riley has put aside his guitar, this blonde-haired girl, who has become Mrs. Harley Hamlin, will bring out an aged, decrepit-looking green parrot who recites the Lord's Prayer and swears like a pirate.

When the ladies have retired and the three men sit there in the candlelight, while Billy Bones chants off the location of pirate gold, the men talk on into the night of treasure hunts, and always, before they finish their last glass of wine, Don Riley will sing to the soft strumming of his guitar.

His song is as old as Mexico. It tells of the love of a man for a maid. And when three glasses are lifted in a good night toast, it is to love, not to gold, that they drink.

"To thee love of a woman. To thee dreams of adventure. To thee *compadres* by a fireside. *¡Señores. . . . salud!*"

The Secret of Crutcher's Cabin

"I know," Walt Coburn wrote in his autobiography, "that somewhere along the trail the *Señor Dios* laid a hand on my shoulder and shaped my destiny. Such is my belief and will continue to be until I follow the ghost rider on the pale horse on my last circle into the Shadow Hills." Often what happens in a Western story by Walt Coburn has about it quite this same sense of destiny in which the *Señor Dios* has His rôle to play. "The Secret of Crutcher's Cabin" was first published in Street & Smith's *Western Story Magazine* (9/20/24). It was subsequently reprinted, a decade later, in another Street & Smith magazine, *Western Winners* (3/35), under the title "Crutcher's Cabin." This marks its first appearance in book form.

I
"Coyote's Passing"

"Looks like we'd done caught Coyote Crutcher with the goods this time, Ross."

Rawhide Dan Taylor, wagon boss of the T Down outfit, handed over his field glasses to Ross Burnett, his employer.

Burnett's tanned face hardened into stern lines as he focused the glasses on the little scene in the valley below. Slow to anger, generous to a fault, the big-framed, gray-eyed cowman never ceased to be a puzzle to his quick-tempered foreman.

Rawhide watched the big man closely now, waiting for some sign of anger to flare up in his employer's eyes.

"Mebbeso Crutcher's butcherin' one of his own critters, Rawhide. Don't go to condemnin' the feller till we know fer shore."

"Coyote Crutcher butcherin' his own beef? Don't make me laugh, Ross. A bite of his own meat'd p'izen him."

"But he's got his kid with him, Rawhide. Don't look like a man'd drag along a twelve-year-old kid if he was plannin' on stealin' beef."

"But you gotta figger that Coyote Crutcher ain't a *man,* Ross. He's a two-legged coyote, too yaller to be plumb bad, too ornery to be honest. As fer his whelp of a kid, the little varmint is as ornery as his old man. He'll be worse than his dad when he gits growed, a heap worse because he's half Injun. Mind what I say, Ross, if Pete Crutcher ever grows up, he'll be a plumb bad 'un. It's in the blood." Rawhide Dan shifted impatiently in his saddle. "Do we ride down and grab this beef-butcherin' coyote er do we set here augerin' till he's got away on us?"

"We'll ride down and pow-wow with the gent, Rawhide," said Ross. "Mebbeso I kin kinda throw a scare into him, and he'll turn honest."

With a snort of disgust, Rawhide swung his horse down the steep slope. Ross Burnett followed more slowly, with a very thoughtful look in his gray eyes.

Down in the valley, at the edge of a clearing, Coyote Crutcher rolled back the sleeves of his tattered, flannel shirt and reached for a skinning knife. Tall, rawboned, his sand-colored hair and beard matted and untrimmed, his shifty green eyes darting here and there, the man well merited the title of Coyote. Even his most casual movements seemed furtive. His eyes and features bore traces of both fear and cruelty. Behind the thin lips that lifted in an occasional, meaningless grin were ugly fangs, discolored with tobacco.

"Keep yore eyes peeled, Pete," he snarled out at the undersized, ragged boy who stood nearby. "If I git cotched, I'll whup yuh till yuh can't stand. I'll git the brand cut outta the hide and the ears cut offen this critter, soon as he quits kickin'. Don't stand there gawkin' at me thataway er I'll knock yuh in the head!" He swung a vicious, open-handed blow that caught the boy in the mouth, sending him reeling.

Little Pete got to his feet with the agility of a cat and was out of reach before a second blow landed. A trickle of blood came from the boy's mouth, but there were no tears in the dark eyes as he faced the man. Pale beneath his tan, his eyes narrowed to thin black slits, he backed slowly away.

"Some day, when I'm bigger, I reckon I'll kill you, Pap," he whispered hoarsely.

The man's lips spread in a snarl. "That sounds like yuh bin listenin' to Tug Moran. Him and that Injun mother uh yourn has been loadin' yuh with killin' idees, eh? Git up on that knoll yonder and keep watch, yuh brat!"

Pete turned to obey, then ducked into the brush like a rabbit.

"Look out, Pap! Run!" he called shrilly.

Coyote Crutcher's hand darted to the .45 in the waistband of his overalls.

"I wouldn't go makin' no gun play, if I was you, Crutcher," called Ross Burnett as he and his foreman rode into the clearing. The cowman made no move to draw his gun as he looked down at the cattle thief. Rawhide Dan, however, was more cautious. He pinched out the coal of his cigarette, and his right hand dropped to the black butt of the six-shooter in his chaps pocket.

"We got you dead to rights, Crutcher," Ross went on. "But if you'll promise. . . ."

Coyote Crutcher's gun roared, its bullet tearing through the cattleman's shoulder. Then there was a flash of fire and a puff of white smoke from the region of Rawhide's hip. Coyote Crutcher fell face forward across the beef, his second shot going wild.

"Hurt bad, Ross?" called the wagon boss, white with anger and excitement.

"Jest a scratch, Rawhide. You killed him?"

"I'd tell a man I did! The sneakin', yaller-hearted coyote. He's killed his last beef. I should've. . . ."

The whine of a bullet cut short his speech. He whirled his horse to ride straight at the spot in the buckbrush from where a white cloud of powder smoke was thinning. A moment and he was back in the clearing. He was on foot now, and his left hand grasped the collar of little Pete's shirt.

The boy, kicking and fighting like a wildcat, tried in vain to grab the long-barreled six-shooter that Rawhide was holding at arm's length.

"Hand me that gunny sack yonder, Ross," called Rawhide grimly to Burnett, who had dismounted and was bending over the body of Crutcher.

Despite the pain in his shoulder and the seriousness of the situation, Ross smiled as he looked at the boy. Then he handed over a burlap sack that lay on the ground.

Rawhide, after a moment's struggle, succeeded in shoving the kicking, twisting, little form in the sack and closing it so that only Pete's head was visible.

"I told you the little devil was bad medicine, Ross. He was in the brush and cut loose with that long-barreled ol' cannon. It wasn't his fault that he didn't kill one of us. He'd orter be thankin' us fer killin' that no-account dad o' his'n."

"Pap's dead?" Pete spoke for the first time.

"Deader'n a rock," answered Rawhide grimly.

"Then I won't have tuh kill him. I was afeerd I'd have to, some day. I ain't holdin' it ag'in' you fer downin' Pap."

"You ain't?" growled out the astonished Rawhide. "Then what in tarnation did you shoot fer?"

"I . . . I kinda aimed fer tuh skeer you off, I reckon. I done heerd Pap and Tug Moran 'low as it'd be a stretch in the pen if ever we was cotched a-butcherin'. A stretch in Deer Lodge'd jest about kill a li'l kid like me, mister. Couldn't you kinda knock me in the head er drown me er sumthin'? I won't be holdin' it ag'in' you, honest."

Ross Burnett, busy with the bandage that he and Rawhide were wrapping about the cowman's wounded shoulder, looked curiously at the little face that showed above the burlap sack. Undernourished, pinched, there was an uncanny mixture of childishness and wisdom in the dark eyes that met Burnett's without flinching.

"You want us to knock you on the head, son? Why?"

"Deer Lodge'd kill me slow-like. Tug Moran says Injuns and 'breeds dies off like flies inside there. And I'm a 'breed. If you was to hit me right hard on the head with yur gun, I'd never know what hit me. I ain't skeered. And you'd ortn't to mind. I'm jest a onery ol' 'breed kid."

"Turn the kid loose, Rawhide." Ross Burnett's voice sounded husky.

Rawhide obeyed in silence.

"Git your pony and hit the trail for home, son," ordered Ross.

"You mean I ain't goin' to the pen?"

"Nope. Go on home to your mother. She'll be needin' you now that your dad's gone."

"She'll go back to the squaw camps on the reservation," the boy said, seeming to be musing aloud. "And I'll have to go live with them blanket Injuns er stay with Tug Moran, Pap's pardner. I don't like Injuns, and Tug'd beat me like Pap done. If it's the same to you, mister, I'll jest quit the country. I'm shore obliged tuh you gents fer lettin' me go." He held out a small hand toward Ross.

Ross shook hands gravely with the boy, vainly watching for tears or some sign of weakening in the pinched little face.

Pete, clawing at the saddle strings, managed to mount the horse Coyote Crutcher had ridden.

"Game little devil," grunted Rawhide. "Might have the makin's of a man in him. But he'll never git the chance tuh show it."

"Dunno about that," said Ross, grinning. The cowman turned to Pete. "I done changed my mind about lettin' you go, boy."

Pete winced as if struck. "You was jest kinda pokin' fun at me? You're a-sendin' me to Deer Lodge?" His voice almost broke.

"No, boy. I'm takin' you home with me. I'm goin' to see what a decent home and good treatment will do toward makin' a man outta you."

"Tarnation, Ross!" gasped out Rawhide. "Your wife'll jest nacherally raise Cain with us, comin' home with Coyote Crutcher's kid. You know she don't like tuh have Dixie playin' with 'breed kids."

"We killed the boy's father, Rawhide. He didn't amount to much, but he was the kid's dad, jest the same. We can't let the young 'un go wanderin' around the country, starvin' like a wind-bellied calf. The boy's goin' to have his chance."

"You mean you're takin' me to the T Down, mister?" asked Pete dazedly. "I don't reckon you're meanin' that. I'm Coyote Crutcher's brat and a half-breed Injun. I ain't your kind. Tug Moran says so, and I reckon he's plumb right, him and Mister Rawhide."

Ross shook his head, smiling. "Get some uh the boys to help you with Crutcher, Rawhide. I'm takin' the kid to the ranch. I'll get word to the sheriff about the killin'."

If they'd only killed the brat, I'd feel easier, mused Tug Moran, hidden in the brush, his lean-jawed, sinister face hardening. *That kid's no fool. He's liable to talk, and, if he does, it means trouble. I always told Coyote he was lettin' that kid see too much of what went on.*

Moran waited until Rawhide was out of sight and there was no one to see, then he rode down to where the body of Coyote Crutcher lay. With a faint smile playing about his thin lips, Moran searched the clothes of the dead man. Tobacco, cigarette papers, and various odds and ends came to light.

"You have it on you somewheres, blast you!" muttered the searcher. He turned his attention to the dead man's boots. Slitting the boot leg with his pocketknife, Moran's long fingers worked methodically as they probed for something. Then, with a grunt of satisfaction, he brought forth a flat package wrapped in oiled silk. Unwrapping the silk, Moran's eyes swept the legal-looking document and the other papers that it held. Then he carefully rewrapped them, placed them in his coat pocket, and without so much as a glance at the dead man mounted and rode away, smiling to himself in a satisfied manner.

II
"Jim Rutledge"

There had been a time when no boundary line marked the T Down range from the Circle Bar. What need of boundaries between men like Ross Burnett and Jim Rutledge? They ran their cattle together, their cowpunchers were friendly, and the bond of friendship between the two cowmen became a byword in the cow country.

"As clost as Ross and Jim," men said when they wished to make clear to one another a strength of unity. And when Ross Burnett married the little tenderfoot girl that taught school at Alkali, folks wondered what Jim would think and do. Jim had been best man at the wedding, then hastened on to Chicago with a trainload of beef cattle.

It was a month before Jim Rutledge returned. With him came a big, bluff-mannered man whom Jim introduced as Charlie Kilraine, his new partner in the Circle Bar outfit. And that night, in the little cabin that served as Ross Burnett's office, Burnett and Rutledge decided on Box Elder Creek as the line between the two outfits.

"I ain't the sort that hollers when he's hurt, Ross," Jim had told his old friend as the two sat and smoked far into the night. "But I ain't goin' to see you git any the worst of it. Kilraine may be on the square. We won't condemn the man till we know. I was drinkin' some the night in Chicago when I loses half my ranch to him. Mebbeso them cards wasn't jest right."

"We got enough money to buy him out, Jim."

"He won't sell. Says he's set his heart on ranchin'. He's aimin' to bring his wife and kid out."

"Hmm," Ross had mused aloud, then had cursed softly to himself.

"There's somethin' more I want you to know, Ross," Jim had said, breaking an awkward silence.

"Yeah? Git it off your chest, pardner," Ross had said.

"I . . . I done got married back in Chicago."

Ross had gasped. "Married?"

"Uhn-huh. Dancer in a cabaret. She's a friend uh Kilraine's. Ross, I jest nacherally played the devil on that trip East. Oh, she's a nice enough gal, but not our sort, Ross. She's more Kilraine's kind. She acted all right for a while, then she got mad at me and walked out."

"Jim, it's kinda my fault, your gettin' into this mess. I'm goin' tuh see it through with you."

"No, Ross. It's my game. I'm playin' it lone-handed. Me 'n' you is the same old friends, Ross. But from now on Box Elder marks the boundary between the ranches. Mebbeso, some day, this Kilraine'll sell out to me, and we'll go back to the old way of doin' things. But until he does, I'm playin' a lone hand, savvy?"

As months went by, things adjusted themselves somewhat. Kilraine seemed decent enough and in his loud-voiced, bluff manner, that passed with many for good fellowship, made friends with the cowmen. Jim Rutledge, except for the fact that he made frequent visits to Tug Moran's saloon at Moran's Crossing on the Missouri River, went about his work in much the same manner as before. Ross Burnett watched and shook his head. Only too well he knew the futility of attempting to interfere with Jim's solitary trips to Moran's Crossing. Jim was a hard man to talk to at times.

Then one night Jim rode over to the T Down and showed Ross a letter that had come in the mail.

"She's comin' out here, Ross," he told his partner. "There's a baby now. Mebbeso it'll kinda make things turn out all right. I'm quittin' the booze, Ross. And I aim to do my best for her and the kid. I know it's askin' a heap, Ross, but, if you and the missus'd bring the baby and come over sometime, I'd shore. . . ."

"Come over? I'd tell a man we're comin' over, Jim. Your wife'll be company fer Betty, and the kids'll play together. Dog-gone, Jim, ain't it fine? Both of us ol' rannyhans married and havin' kids. What's yours? Boy er girl?" Ross Burnett was as happy as a schoolboy.

"A boy, Ross. We'll learn 'em to ride and rope, and they kin go off to school somewheres and. . . ."

"And when they grow up, mebbeso they'll git married, Jim! Dog-gone! Beats all get-out how things happen, don't it? When's the wife comin', Jim?"

"She's due to be in Lewistown in three days. I'm leavin' tonight to meet her. We'll come home by way uh Moran's Crossin'. That's the only place we'll be able to ford the river."

"Good. What does Kilraine say, Jim?"

Jim Rutledge laughed wholeheartedly. "I'm buyin' Kilraine out, lock, stock, and barrel. It's takin' about all I got in the bank, but it's worth it, Ross. We're closin' the deal at Moran's tonight. Cash deal. Ross, ol'-timer, that boundary line's about to be wiped off the map."

Jim Rutledge rode away from the T Down Ranch with a song on his lips, and from the lighted doorway of the cabin Ross watched him go. It was the last time Ross Burnett saw his old partner. On the day Jim was scheduled to bring home his wife, word came to the T Down that Jim Rutledge had been drowned crossing the Missouri. Kilraine, Coyote Crutcher, and Tug Moran, waiting at Moran's place on the other side of the river, had seen Jim's horse quit in the middle of the river. They had gone out with a rowboat, but could find no trace of the cattleman or his horse. The swift-flowing, muddy water had sucked them under.

Kilraine seemed cut up about it. He seemed overcome with emotion each time he told of the drowning.

"Jim must have had the money on him to buy my share of the place," he told Ross, his voice breaking. "I loved him like a brother, Burnett."

For many days Ross Burnett and his cowpunchers dragged the river with grappling hooks and patrolled the bank, but no trace of Jim Rutledge or his horse was ever found. With mental reservations, Ross accepted the story of Jim's drowning as it was told by the three witnesses.

Jim Rutledge's wife seemed to have vanished. A woman and a child had arrived in Lewistown. She had registered at the hotel as Mrs. Rutledge. That night she had loaded her baggage on a buckboard and driven away with a stranger, taking the child with her. No one had paid much attention to her. The road from Lewistown to the Missouri River was long and seldom traveled. A T Down 'puncher had found what appeared to be the wreck of a buckboard at the base of a cliff in the badlands. That was all.

Months passed and all save a few forgot Jim Rutledge and the manner of his going. Kilraine made a trip East upon receipt of a telegram saying that his wife was dying. Weeks later he returned with a small boy, his son, so he said.

With the passing years came gradual changes. Always tolerant, Ross Burnett forced himself to put aside his suspicion of Kilraine and accept the man at his face value. Kilraine became a frequent visitor at the T Down Ranch. Often he brought Roger, his son, a rapidly growing, big-boned boy who gave promise of being fully as big a man physically as his burly father.

Mrs. Burnett shared her husband's feelings and allowed

her daughter, Dixie, to play with Kilraine's youngster. Sometimes, as Ross watched the children playing, a wistful look would come into the cattleman's eyes.

"If only that boy was Jim Rutledge's son," he would tell his wife. "I'd feel a heap better about it. Jim's boy would be a few years younger than Roger. He'd be about Dixie's age. Roger's kinda old for Dixie. Sometimes I'm scared he'll hurt her, he's so kinda rough. He's mean to animals, Betty. I've had to call him down two, three times lately about the way he treated the dogs and cats around the place. He's like his father that way. Kilraine treats his stock bad."

Quite in contrast to the attitude of Ross Burnett and his wife was the viewpoint of Charlie Kilraine. The sight of the two children playing together was apt to conjure up the vision of a future that would be the fulfillment of his fondest dreams. If Roger Kilraine married Dixie Burnett, it meant the affiliation of two of the biggest cow outfits in the state, the wiping out of the Box Elder Creek boundary, and Roger would be the heir to the T Down and Circle Bar Ranches. Sometimes, like a black cloud crossing a blue sky, would come the memory of Jim Rutledge to mar this vision of wealth and power to be bestowed upon his son. Did Ross Burnett believe the story of Jim's drowning? Would Coyote Crutcher or Tug Moran ever weaken and give out the true story of the cowman's fate and the disappearance of his wife and son? As long as Crutcher and Moran lived, Charlie Kilraine's position was in danger. If only he were rid of those two men. . . .

III
"Little Pete Finds a Home"

Mrs. Burnett was on the verandah of the big log house talking to Kilraine, who had come to spend the evening.

"H'lo, Betty. Howdy, Kilraine," called Ross as he and little Pete drew rein. He swung to the ground and handed the boy his bridle reins. "Take the horses around to the barn, Pete. You'll find empty stalls. Then come on back to the house."

Pete flushed as he met the gaze of the cowman's wife. Glad of an excuse to be gone, he started for the barn.

"Ross! You're hurt!" cried his wife as he stepped forward on the verandah.

"Just a scratch, Betty. It'll be all right in a day or so."

"Something's happened, Ross. I can see it in your eyes. How did you get hurt and who is the queer-looking little boy you brought home?"

"We jumped Coyote Crutcher while he was killing a T Down steer. Crutcher opened up with his Forty-Five, and Rawhide killed him. I brought the kid home with me."

"Crutcher's dead?" Kilraine's voice sounded strained. "Did he die instantly?"

"He never knew what hit him. What's the matter, Kilraine? You look plumb white."

"It's . . . it's one of my heart attacks, Burnett. I'll be all right in a minute."

"Reckon we can dig up some clothes for the kid, Betty? We'll clean him up outside and then begin on his inside. And unless I'm a poor judge of humans, it'll be as easy to save his soul as it is to clean his body. He's like a little animal now. Half scared to death but game as they make 'em. It'll be fun watching him grow up."

"Surely you don't mean to adopt the child, Ross? He's part Indian, isn't he?"

"His mother's a squaw, Betty. We're not really adoptin' the kid. Jest takin' care uh him like he was a motherless calf. He's half-starved, and he's been beaten till he's black and blue all over. Please be kind to the poor little fellow, Betty."

"Of course, I will, Ross. But aren't you afraid a boy like that will be a bad influence for Dixie?"

"That's what I was thinking, Burnett. A dirty little 'breed kid, that's all he is, and with Coyote Crutcher's blood. . . ."

The scream of a child cut short Kilraine's speech. The next instant Dixie burst into view, running from the direction of the barn.

"Come quick, Daddy!" she called in a frightened little voice. "There's a strange little boy in the barn, and he's killing Roger!"

Ross was on his feet in an instant and headed for the barn. Kilraine followed at top speed.

Ross rounded the corner of the barn and halted. Then he stooped over and separated the kicking, twisting bodies that threshed around in the thick dust. With difficulty he succeeded in prying loose little Pete.

Roger Kilraine, taller by twelve inches and heavier by many pounds, ran to his father. Sobbing and choking from the dust that filled his mouth, he was the picture of abject terror.

Ross released his grip on little Pete's collar. Pete, his fists clenched into knots, his dark eyes blazing, made no sound. Panting and defiant, he faced Ross. Dixie had come up with her mother and peered at the strange boy from behind her mother's skirts.

"What's the row, Pete?" asked Ross.

"He jumped on me for nothing!" sobbed Roger. "Got me from behind, too! I was playin' with that hound pup yonder, and minding my own business."

"How about it, Pete?" asked Ross sternly.

"I reckon he's lyin', mister. Ask her," he said, pointing to Dixie who promptly ducked behind her mother.

"Tell us about it, honey," said Ross.

"Roger was playin' that the pup was a wild bull. He roped him and was tying him up when that ragged little boy jumped on him. Then I got awful scared and ran."

"Jumped on Roger from behind, eh?" said Kilraine sneeringly.

"She ran afore she seen me give him his fair chanct," panted Pete. "I let him up after I'd tuk the pup off him. He had his fair chanct."

"You're lyin'!" sobbed Roger. "You're a lyin' 'breed!"

Ross caught Pete's collar just in time to prevent a renewal of the battle.

"Of course, the brat's lying, Burnett," growled out Kilraine.

"I reckon not," drawled a man's voice, and Rawhide Dan stepped out of the barn. "I happened to see the whole fracas from the start."

"Then why didn't you stop the fight?" said Kilraine.

"Because that overgrown son uh yourn had a beatin' comin' to him, Kilraine," replied Rawhide, his voice hot with anger. "Your kid was torturin' the pup. Pete jumped him and set the pup loose. Then he gives that big bully the squarest, neatest workin' over that he'll ever git. Shake, Pete, I'm for you, Injun er no Injun." And, he held out a hand, and little Pete took it solemnly. Ross grinned appreciatively.

"Looks like you and Roger was in the wrong, Kilraine," Ross said quietly.

"You mean that . . . ?"

"I mean that from now on, Pete's one uh my family, and he'll be treated as such, savvy?" He turned to his wife. "Take the boy to the house, will you, Betty? He needs a bath and clean clothes worse than ever now. Pete, this is Missus Burnett, and the little girl is Dixie."

"Howdy, ma'am," said Pete embarrassedly as he held out a timid hand, grimy and stained.

Mrs. Burnett looked down at the boy. Tears came into her eyes as she read with woman's intuition the wistful hunger for affection that lay hidden in Pete's dark eyes. With a muffled cry she stooped and gathered the tattered little figure in her arms.

For a moment the boy struggled feebly. Then, with a great sob that seemed wrenched from him by force, he buried his head against her shoulder and cried as if his heart would break. Nor did he resist when she carried him in her arms to the house, for, after all, he was but a boy of twelve and this strange miracle that had broken down the barrier of his reserve was a thing called mother love.

Rawhide blew his nose violently, made some mumbled remark about the sun being in his eyes, and beat a retreat to the barn. Ross, swallowing hard, forgetful of the presence of the Kilraines, followed his wife to the house, Dixie clinging to his hand.

"Looks like we weren't so badly wanted around here, Son," said Kilraine as he led the way to their horses.

For some time father and son rode in silence. Kilraine seemed out of sorts and cursed softly under his breath as he rode.

"How did it happen you let that little Injun lick you?" he growled out at last.

Roger, who had inherited all his father's arrogance and

was, in a way, shrewd beyond his years, looked insolently into his father's eyes. "For the same reason that you let a tinhorn gambler like Tug Moran tell you what's what," he replied, his bruised lips spreading in a sneer that was ludicrously like that of his father's.

"Me take water from Moran? Nonsense. You're itching for a good hiding, and a few more wisecracks like that out of you and you'll get it. A kid your size, lettin' a half-starved 'breed brat whip you? I'm going to take you over there some day again. When I do, you thrash that Injun within an inch of his life, understand?"

They had rounded a rimrock, and Kilraine jerked his horse to a halt as a rider appeared in the trail ahead as if by magic.

"You seem to be kinda on the prod, Charlie," called Tug Moran. "I could hear your musical voice half a mile away. Has the son forgot his Sunday manners while he was visitin' the T Down?"

"What are you doin' here, Moran?" growled out Kilraine, eyeing the other suspiciously.

"Send that cub uh yourn on ahead, and I'll tell yuh."

"Hit the trail, Roger. And don't stop till you get home." Kilraine seemed nervous and upset.

"Coyote's done cashed in his chips, Charlie," Moran said, leering into the other man's face.

"Good riddance. He croaked without squealin', didn't he?"

"He shore did. And to save yuh the trouble uh searchin' his shack for any . . . ah . . . papers, Charlie. . . ." Moran's left hand brought forth the package wrapped in oiled silk that he had found in Crutcher's boot.

"Blast you, Moran!" Kilraine's gun slipped into view.

Moran, still with a twisted sneer on his lips, grabbed Kilraine's gun hand just above the wrist. His grip tightened, and Kilraine dropped his gun with a cry of pain.

"Yuh'd orter know better than to try that on Tug Moran, Charlie." Moran shoved the papers back in his pocket. "There's an old saying, Charlie, that if a man wants a thing done right, he'd better 'tend to it hisself. Yuh made a mistake by hirin' me and Coyote to do yur dirty work. I knowed Rutledge had papers on him that night, but Coyote beat me to it. Coyote's bin comin' to yuh for money every now and then. I knowed it because I'd win it off him at the Crossing. Coyote was a piker. I'm goin' to bleed you white, Mister Charlie Kilraine, and yuh'll stand for it, too. Coyote was scared of yuh, but I'm not, savvy? I know yur breed, and the yaller streak is a foot wide up yur back. I'll be needin' a thousand dollars about next week. Have it ready, Charlie."

"But that's an. . . ."

"Bring that dough to the Crossing next week, Charlie," warned Moran. "Bring it, or I'll have Crutcher's squaw tell what she knows."

"I'll do it, Moran, I'll do it. I'll bring the money to. . . ."

"Good," Moran interrupted. "Now about Coyote's kid. You was at his ranch when Burnett brought the brat in. What's Burnett goin' to do with the kid? Put him through the third degree?"

"Nothing like that," snarled out Kilraine disgustedly. "He's takin' the kid to raise as his own. Can yuh beat that?"

Moran whistled soundlessly. Then he smiled softly to himself as if he thoroughly enjoyed the situation.

"Hmm, well, I'll be hanged. Burnett's adoptin' little Pete, eh? Lemme see. Yeah. That'll be playin' into my hand strong. Shore will. Uhn-huh. Say, Charlie, suppose the kid makes good, and Burnett gets to thinkin' a heap uh him. That'll kinda knock yur plans some regardin' marryin' off yur Roger to Burnett's gal, eh?"

"Bah! . . . Burnett let his kid marry a 'breed? I reckon not." Kilraine laughed, but there was a false note to the laughter. "How much would it be worth to yuh to get that kid outta the way, Moran?"

"Kill the kid?"

"Use yuh own judgment about that. How much?"

"I'll tell yuh later, Charlie," said Moran. They had come to where the trail forked, and pulled their horses to a walk.

"I'll make it worth your while, Moran. Better take what you can get outta me. Because if you don't want the job, I might take your advice and turn the trick myself."

"Oh, no, yuh won't, Charlie. Because if yuh do, I'll have yuh jest where I want yuh. And I'll squeeze yuh loose from every dollar yuh own. Lay off that kid, get me?" Moran's eyes narrowed to slits.

"Well, get busy on it, then."

"We'll see, Charlie. I'm goin' over to break the news about the Coyote to his squaw now."

"Does the squaw know about the papers?" asked Kilraine anxiously.

"That's what I aim to find out." There was an ugly look in Moran's eyes as he spurred his horse onto a dim trail and left Kilraine sitting in his saddle, watching him out of sight.

IV
"Pete Makes a Night Ride"

Little Pete was learning to laugh. Scrubbed until his tanned cheeks glowed, clad in makeshift garments, he sat on a stool in the bathroom while Rawhide Dan cut his hair. Dixie, her eyes bright with excitement, sat nearby, watching the tonsorial transformation.

Ross Burnett and his wife, seated in the living room, heard the odd little laugh and exchanged a quick glance.

"You ain't sorry I brought the little feller home, Betty?"

"Sorry? I'm glad, Ross. Such an odd mixture of old man and child in him. He told me he'd never been kissed or loved in his life. Yet he has a mother. I can't understand a woman who does not mother her young. Are Indians that way?"

"Search me, Betty. I've seen Crutcher's squaw several times. She's an ugly-looking, fat, old hag. Always drunk. They live in a shack down in the badlands near Moran's Crossing."

"What a terrible heritage for the child! What surroundings! I hope Peter will not inherit the traits of his parents, Ross. We'll have to watch him closely."

"The boy'll have his chance, Betty. If he makes good, he'll have a home. And I'm sure he'll come out all right, no matter what his parents were."

Rawhide, leading the two children, appeared in the doorway. "Pete shore has changed, eh, Missus Ross?" said the foreman. "He's a right, smart-lookin' young 'un when he's fixed up. He's learnin' manners, too. Ain't you, Pete?"

"Yes, sir," mumbled Pete shyly.

"Hear him? He's got brains, I'd tell a man. Now ask Ross about goin' home, Pete."

"I . . . I jest wanted to ride over to tell Maw about stayin' here, Mister Ross," Pete began. "She'll be kinda worryin' about what's become uh me, I reckon. She was allers afeered somethin' 'ud happen to me. I heered her and Pap a-sayin' that, to some folks, I was worth a heap more dead than I was alive. Onct when her and Pap was drunk and fightin', I pulled out and hid in the brush. Her and Pap took on scan'lous about it. I'll be back afore mornin' so's I kin help with the chores. And if you don't keer, I'll bring Scrub with me."

Ross looked at Rawhide, and the foreman nodded his head.

"You can go, uh course, Pete. But hadn't you better wait till tomorrow?"

"I'd rather go this evenin', if I could. Scrub'll be hungry as a wolf. Maw never feeds him."

"Who's Scrub?" asked Ross curiously.

"Scrub's my hound pup. He . . . he don't eat much, Mister Ross. I kin kill rabbits fer him, if you'll lemme have my gun back."

Ross gasped. "Dog? And you'll kill rabbits with that old cannon Rawhide took away from you? Ever kill any rabbits with it, Pete?"

"Yeah . . . yes, sir. Heaps. Pap 'lowed I was right handy fer a kid when it come to shootin'. I'll be goin' now to tell Maw good bye. She'll want to pull out fer the squaw camps, come mornin'." He started uncertainly for the door, then halted. "I plumb enjoyed the supper, ma'am," he gravely told Mrs. Burnett.

"I'm glad of that, Pete. Rawhide will fix you up a bunk in his cabin when you get back."

Pete grinned his thanks. Somehow he understood Rawhide, and the foreman treated him like a man. It was flattering, indeed, to be allowed to bunk with the wagon boss. He gained the door and turned.

"So long," he said stiffly.

"So long, Pete. See you in the mornin'," returned Ross soberly, a twinkle in his eyes.

"Don't forget to come back home," said Mrs. Burnett.

Dixie's curly head showed for a moment as she peeked from behind her mother's chair to flash Pete a smile.

"So long, girl," mumbled the boy, then he turned quickly and beat a retreat.

Rawhide helped him saddle a horse, lifted him to the saddle, and watched him ride from sight along the trail that led to Moran's Crossing and the shack that Coyote Crutcher had called home.

"Reckon you'd better foller the kid, Rawhide?" Ross had come from the house and now stood in the barn door beside his foreman.

"Jest what I was thinkin', Ross. There's queer things happen at Moran's Crossing. Danged queer. The kid's seen a heap that he won't talk about because he's scared uh Moran. Today, when me 'n' the boys got back to where Crutcher was layin', some gent had gone through his clothes, huntin' somethin'. Whatever it was that they was huntin', they found it in Crutcher's left boot."

"Hmm . . . how d'you know they found anything, Rawhide?"

"Crutcher's left boot was ripped open. If they hadn't found it in that left boot, they'd 'a' cut open the right 'un, wouldn't they?"

"Sounds reasonable. It couldn't uh bin money that they was huntin'. Crutcher never saved a cent. It must've bin papers uh some kind. And the papers might have something to do with pore ol' Jim Rutledge, eh?"

"That's my idea of it, Ross. Me 'n' you both know that Jim never drowned without bein' shoved under. When he died, he was packin' either a bunch uh money er the deed to the Circle Bar Ranch."

"I believe you're right, Rawhide. But Pete couldn't know nothin' about that. He was a baby yet when Jim was murdered."

"No, but the kid's seen a heap uh orneriness come off at

the Crossing, bet on that. And if Moran figgered the kid 'ud squeal, he'd cut his throat in a second. I'm follerin' Pete tonight, Ross. Mebbeso, I'll learn somethin'. What d'you reckon the little devil asked fer, when we went to the barn?"

"Hard tuh say," mused Ross.

"He wanted that long-barreled ol' cannon I took away from him."

"And I reckon you give it to him."

"I shore did, Ross. Mebbeso I done wrong by lettin' a kid like him have the gun, but somehow he's like a man in some ways. If he's man enough to make that forty-mile night ride, I reckon he's able to pack a gun."

Rawhide had finished saddling his horse. He spun the cylinder of his .45 and shoved the weapon back in his chaps pocket, then swung into the saddle. A careless farewell and he was gone.

V
"Coyote Crutcher's Cabin"

Hidden in a scrub pine thicket in a cañon so deep that it saw the sunlight only for a brief time during the middle of the day, the cabin of Coyote Crutcher squatted in a solitary furtiveness. Far from the traveled trails, shunned as a thing unclean even by outlaws, the wooden latch that held the sagging door had been lifted by few men save Coyote Crutcher himself. Squalid, primitive, uncared for, the buckbrush and red willow thickets choked the tiny clearing until the maze of brush threatened to cover completely the sagging log walls.

The cabin was plunged into darkness. In front of the threshold the dying embers of a campfire turned slowly to ashes. Beside the fire, her head covered by a dirty red blanket, her thick frame swaying to and fro, squatted the woman who was known as Coyote Crutcher's squaw. From beneath the blanket came an animal-like wailing sound that rose and fell and died away and rose again to a higher pitch to be taken up by the half-grown hound that slunk in the shadow. Then the howling of coyotes took up the cry and carried it into the echoing walls of the cañon.

Tug Moran, riding down the steep trail, heard the cry and with an involuntary shudder reached for his gun. He thought: *Somebody's told the old hag that Coyote's dead, and she's puttin' on a wake fer him, Injun style*. He spurred down the trail and swung to the ground beside the cabin. The squaw paid no heed.

"Shut up, yuh blattin' old hag!" Moran accompanied the command with a vicious kick that sent her sprawling into the coals.

Slapping out the hot ashes from her calico dress and moaning faintly, the squaw struggled to her feet.

"Go on into the cabin and light the lantern." Moran gave her a shove, and she obeyed in silence.

Inside, she struck a match and lit a smoke-grimed lantern that threw flickering shadows into the corners of the littered cabin. Moran picked up a whiskey bottle that stood on the table, cursed shortly when he saw it was empty, and hurled it across the cabin where it shattered against a log wall. The squaw turned on him, her yellow fangs bared in a snarl, her beady eyes snapping. The lantern rays caught the bright blade of a skinning knife.

"Put that knife up or I'll shoot yuh," growled out Moran. He took a flask from his pocket, gulped down a drink, then passed it to her. "Kill it, Venus," he said.

A grimy, pudgy hand grasped the bottle and tipped it up. When she had emptied the bottle, she tossed it aside, passed the back of her hand across her lips, and spoke.

"Good whiskey. Pete? You see him?"

"Pete's safe enough. A danged sight safer than he'd be with you. What d'yuh aim to do, now that Crutcher's dead?"

"I go across Milk River to the lodges of my people. I take Pete."

"Yuh'll take nobody. Get that through yur skull. Pete stays where he is. Yuh know something about Jim Rutledge and his wife and kid. Are yuh goin' to talk?"

The squaw made no answer, but a crafty gleam came into her beady eyes. "Mebbe. I get planty whiskey, no talk. My ol' man have some paper in his boot. Mebbeso you find 'em?"

With a short laugh Moran tossed the oiled-silk package on the table.

The squaw lurched forward to grab it, and Moran's fist caught her squarely in the face. He laughed as the squaw fell among a litter of pots and pans and struggled to regain her feet.

"Yuh know what them papers mean, eh? Well, yuh'll wish to heaven yuh didn't afore I'm finished with yuh. Yuh know too damned much."

The squaw, half understanding what the white man was saying, but with her eyes on the package that still lay on the table, edged closer. "You got 'nother bottle, Moran?" she whined cunningly as she wiped her cut lips. She was almost within striking distance now, and her right hand closed over the handle of her skinning knife. Then, with a movement that was startlingly swift for one of her bulk, she sprang. The knife swept downward like a streak of shining flame and sank into Moran's shoulder.

A muttered curse. The muffled roar of Moran's

close-pressed .45. With a look of stupid surprise on her face, the squaw sank to the floor, upsetting the table and dragging its litter of dishes, food, and the oiled-silk package over beside her.

A sharp cry from the doorway brought Moran about with a jerk. White-lipped with fear and startled surprise, little Pete stood frozen in his tracks, the long-barreled .45 in his right hand, its wavering muzzle covering Moran.

"You . . . you killed her!" he whispered hoarsely. Sick with fear of this man who stood facing him, Pete's face worked convulsively as he fought back the desire to run.

"Drop that gun, yuh dirty little 'breed!" Moran took a step forward, his narrowed eyes fixing Pete's gaze and gripping it as if hypnotizing him. Another step brought him within five feet of the boy who stood, paralyzed by fear.

"Don't!" shrieked Pete, recoiling, but still holding the gun. "Don't come closer!"

"Drop it!" barked Moran. "I'll wring yur neck, yuh. . . ."

A flash of fire and the roar of the long-barreled gun crashed and echoed deafeningly in the tiny cabin.

Stiff with horror, Pete saw Tug Moran spin half around and fall face downward on the dirt floor. Then Pete dropped his gun and ducked out into the brush where he fought his way into the thicket, burrowing like an animal until he could go no farther.

Back in the cabin, Moran, his face pale and drawn, crawled along the floor, pawing through the litter until his groping hands closed on the oiled-silk package. Dizzy with pain and faintness, he glanced about the cabin. Pete's bullet had smashed his collar bone, and the pain was racking his body. His pain-seared eyes fell on a wide-mouthed earthenware whiskey jug. Fighting off the dizziness that was making his senses reel, he thrust the package into the jug and rolled the jug into a corner of the cabin. Then he lurched toward the water pail near the door. Within reach of it he fell, to lay still.

Outside in the dark, a brindle hound pup, sniffing and whining softly, crawled through the brush until he found Pete. The boy's arms went around the dog's neck, and the pup licked the little, drawn face.

Rawhide Dan, the echo of the shot still ringing in his ears, rode recklessly down the treacherous trail and with drawn gun stepped into the cabin, peering into the uncertain light thrown by the lantern that hung from a peg on the wall. A film of smoke hung in the dead air, and the acrid smell of burned powder stung the cowpuncher's nostrils. A quick examination showed that Moran still lived. The glazed eyes and horribly gaping mouth of the squaw told him she was dead.

"Pete! Oh, Pete!" he called loudly. Then, when he received no answer, he stepped outside to repeat the call.

But Pete, with the instinct of some hunted animal, made no answer. It was the growling of the dog that led Rawhide to the boy's hiding place.

"I killed him, Mister Rawhide," Pete muttered over and over. "I done killed Tug Moran, and they'll hang me."

"Not as long as I'm alive, they won't, Pete. It's all right, boy. Anyhow, Moran ain't dead yet. He's tough enough to live, worse luck."

Pete was sent back to the ranch after Rawhide had succeeded in placating the boy's fear. Left alone with Moran, the T Down wagon boss managed to bandage the two wounds and bring the man back to consciousness.

Moran, looking into the cowpuncher's eyes, sneered openly. "I'm done fer?" he asked.

"Wouldn't be surprised, Moran. Got anything to say afore you cash in your chips?"

"Not by a damn' sight, mister," snarled out Moran. "I ain't the squealin' kind."

"I want that deed to the Circle Bar Ranch, Moran. I'm sure it was you who took it off Crutcher. Where is it?"

Moran's pain-streaked eyes narrowed. "I don't know what yuh're talkin' about," he answered, then closed his eyes.

It was noon the next day when the doctor and coroner arrived. Meanwhile, Rawhide's systematic search had netted him nothing. Moran, gaining strength and assured of the fact that he would live, sneered and cursed the searcher. Finally Rawhide gave it up in despair. Moran's glance flitted to the earthenware jug in the corner, then away from it, to meet Rawhide's gaze.

"As a detective, you make a good cowhand, pardner," he said, grinning.

VI
"The Trial"

A hush fell over the close-packed, jostling crowd that filled the courtroom to overflowing capacity. More than one hand reached hipward to shift forward a .45 as the sheriff and two deputies pushed through the door with their prisoner.

Tug Moran, his manacled hands held against his chest, swept the sea of faces with a sneering glance. The prisoner's eyes narrowed ever so slightly as they met the glance of Charlie Kilraine, who stood near the rear door surrounded by Circle Bar cowpunchers.

Kilraine's left eyelid dropped, then lifted. Moran smiled, and his head moved in an almost imperceptible nod. Then the sheriff motioned the prisoner to a seat. The judge entered the courtroom and took his place on the raised platform. A bailiff rapped for order. The case of The People versus Tug Moran was on.

For weeks the cow country had eagerly looked forward to seeing Moran tried for the murder of Coyote Crutcher's squaw. A hundred rumors had it that Moran would never be brought to trial. It was broadly hinted that Kilraine was Moran's friend and would do all in his power to free the murderer. The stranger who had taken over the saloon at Moran's Crossing had been seen at the Circle Bar Ranch. Rawhide Dan had seen Kilraine at the Crossing several times during the past few weeks since the arrest of Moran.

Beside Moran sat his attorney, a cold-eyed man with a brown Vandyke beard who chewed nervously on a cold cigar. In the attorney's briefcase, carefully concealed among the papers, were two large-calibered automatics. Two other automatics reposed in shoulder holsters under the lawyer's close-buttoned frock coat. A stranger to the cow country was this cold-eyed, carefully groomed gentleman, but in Chicago, where he had come from in response to Kilraine's telegram, this suave stranger was known as The Parson. A man of many aliases was The Parson. The underworld knew him to be as quick on the trigger as he was smooth of speech and polished of manner, a con man, gambler, and a killer. And it was The Parson who was now defending Tug Moran. He pulled the briefcase closer and bent toward Moran.

"Charlie has the horses ready outside," he whispered. "We exit by the window at my back. Charlie and the boys will take care of the crowd. How's your pulse, pal?"

"I ain't scared, if that's what yuh're drivin' at," answered Moran sneeringly. "I'm namin' two bullets . . . one fer Ross Burnett and one fer Rawhide Dan. I'll git the kid later, blast his little hide."

"You'll get nobody, pal," said The Parson coldly. "No killing goes, get me? I'm hired to get you free, not to help you carry on a feud. Try any promiscuous killing, and I'll drop you in your tracks. Come back tomorrow to do your slaughtering, if you feel the urge, but you're not killing anybody today, brother. I'm not keen about having any unnecessary fireworks. I'm going back to Chi with a whole hide. Remember, no grudge killing, or I plug you, friend."

"Scared uh these gents?"

"No, Moran, just discreet. And don't make any more comical cracks about me being scared, you son-of-a-bitch. I've stood enough of your bulldozing boasting. Only for Kilraine, I'd never be here. I owe Charlie a debt, and I'm paying it."

"Yuh're gettin' damned well paid fer it," said the prisoner.

The Parson shrugged and patted his breast pocket. "Fairly well paid, pal, but not well enough to mix up in any Montana gun war. Bear that in mind and follow instructions. Otherwise, I quit you right here." He made as if to rise.

"All right, all right," agreed Moran. "I'll go gunnin' fer them fellers later. Open up yur jackpot, and I back yur play."

The Parson's gaze traveled the length of the room and met the questioning look in the eyes of Charlie Kilraine. Then the pseudo-attorney deliberately shifted the cigar from the left side of his mouth to the right side. Kilraine smiled slightly and turned to the cowpuncher at his elbow.

"Tug's agreed to run for it without shooting," he whispered in a relieved tone.

The entrance of Ross Burnett and several T Down men drew all eyes toward them. Then Rawhide Dan appeared in the doorway with little Pete.

The judge rapped for silence. "Court's open. Mister Prosecutor, call the first witness."

"Peter Crutcher!" called the prosecuting attorney.

White-faced, but with a heroic attempt to appear unafraid, Pete ascended to the witness chair.

The window behind The Parson and Moran was pushed slowly open from the outside, but nobody save these two men paid any heed to the telltale squeak of the warped window casing.

"Tell us your name, young man," commenced the prosecutor.

"Peter. Peter Crutcher, sir," replied the boy in a voice that trembled a bit. "I'm Coyote Crutcher's kid."

The Parson leaned forward across the table, his cold eyes sweeping the room. Even the sheriff and his deputies were watching Pete. The Parson slipped the two automatics from the briefcase into Moran's manacled hands, then his well-kept hands sped to his coat and came out, holding two guns. One of the guns thudded against the averted head of the sheriff, and the officer went limp. At the same moment a well-timed shot from the rear of the courtroom turned the eyes of every man that way.

The Parson shoved Moran in the ribs with his gun. "Quick, you fool!" he commanded.

A leap and Moran was at the window. A leg swung over the casing. A shove from The Parson and he disappeared from view. The Parson, with a cat-like leap, cleared the casing and landed beside Moran outside.

Shouts, trampling feet, and loud cursing sounded from within the courtroom. In a well-disguised effort to crowd through the narrow doorway, the Circle Bar men barred the exit. The windows were blocked in a similar manner. It was several minutes before Ross Burnett and Rawhide could fight their way through the mob and get outside. It was too late. Tug Moran and The Parson were nowhere in sight.

Kilraine, with a well-feigned attempt at appearing excited, was cursing and shouting orders to his men. "After 'em, boys!" he yelled. "A thousand dollars to the man that gets 'em, dead or alive!"

Ross Burnett, now mounted, heard the shouted order and cursed feelingly as he spurred his horse to a run. Rawhide, however, could not withhold his anger. He spurred his horse into Kilraine's so forcibly that the rancher was forced to grip the saddle horn to keep his seat.

"You was back uh that job, you black-hearted polecat," growled the irate Rawhide. "If there's any fight in you, go fer that gun uh yourn." Rawhide's left hand swung hard against Kilraine's mouth.

A Circle Bar rider pushed his way alongside Rawhide, and a .45 poked the T Down boss in the ribs. Like a flash, Rawhide whirled in his saddle, his gun spitting flame. The Circle Bar man dropped his gun with a yell of pain and grabbed frantically at the hole in his shoulder where Rawhide's bullet had smashed through.

"Pull your gun, Kilraine, and show your speed, you low-lived skunk!" shouted Rawhide.

Kilraine, reading the danger light in the cowpuncher's eyes, let go his gun. "I've got too much at stake to go shootin' men," he snarled. "I got to think uh my son."

"You do, eh?" shouted Rawhide as he again ran his horse into Kilraine's. "Hold the crowd off, Ross, while I whip this polecat outta town!"

Ross, knowing full well the futility of trying to stop Rawhide, swung on two Circle Bar men who now rode up. "Stand back, damn you!" he told them. "I'm backin' Rawhide, and it ain't healthy to butt in. Go to him, boy."

Rawhide had shoved his gun in his chaps. A deft move and he had grabbed Kilraine's .45 and tossed it into the street. Now he slipped his lariat free and with doubled rope fell in behind Kilraine's horse. Again and again the rope descended on Kilraine's bent back as the rancher fled. Shouted advice and ribald laughter came from the onlookers. The T Down men paused in their fighting to cheer on their boss. Circle Bar men, seeing their employer thus in full flight, being whipped out of town, gave up disgustedly. Some of them rode out of town; others sought out Ross to offer their services.

"We ain't hirin' out to no yaller coyote like that Kilraine," one of them told the T Down owner. "We're comin' to the T Down outfit, if we have to work fer nothin'. Come on, boys, let's have a drink to take the taste uh the Circle Bar outta our mouths."

From the doorway of the courthouse the sheriff, rubbing the rapidly swelling lump on his head, saw what had threatened to be a bloody fight turned into a farce. Behind the sheriff stood the judge, and clinging to the judge's hand was little Pete.

The boy's face was flushed with excitement, and his dark eyes glowed like twin coals. "Mister Rawhide's shore one go-getter, ain't he, jedge?" he shouted excitedly.

Ross rode over to the courthouse and, swinging to the ground, took Pete's hand.

"Hang me fer a dumb fool, Ross," began the sheriff, "I. . . ."

"It wasn't your fault, Sheriff," Ross said ruefully. "It come so danged sudden-like. Who'd've thought that dude law sharp was in on a deal like that. He looked like a preacher in that long coat uh his'n. Why, only yesterday he was sayin' how he hated tuh be defendin' such a man as Moran. Said he was aimin' tuh have Tug plead guilty because he didn't want to defend a man that was so plainly a low-down murderer. He shore took me in, that feller did."

"Me, too," agreed the sheriff. "Shucks! He talked somethin' scan'lous to Moran in jail. I heered him. Looks like we'd bin played fer fools. I'm takin' the trail right now, and I'm stayin' on it till I git Moran and that law gent."

The sheriff had little difficulty in locating The Parson. A two hours' ride brought him and his posse to a cut coulée where the trail narrowed. At the foot of the trail lay The Parson, shot in the back. The pockets of his clothes were turned inside out and beside his stiffened body lay the handcuffs that had once held Tug Moran. The handcuffs had been severed with a hacksaw blade. To the handcuffs was fastened a note.

So long. I got my South American stake. Some day I'm comin' back, and, when I do, some folks will shore wish they'd died afore I got here. If Rawhide had looked in the big jug in the corner of Crutcher's cabin, he might've found sumthin'. He'd've bin surprised at what it was. Ten years from today I'm comin' back.

The note was unsigned, but at the bottom of the soiled paper was a list of names. Beside each of the first three was a cross. Beside the last was a question mark. Pete Crutcher, Ross Burnett, and Rawhide Dan were the first three. The last name was that of Charlie Kilraine.

VII
"Roger Plays Some Poker"

The cluster of buildings was dwarfed by the towering cottonwoods. There were numerous corrals and a long hitch rack where half a dozen horses stood with dropped reins or tied with hackamore ropes. The squeak of a fiddle was heard and the coarse laughter of half-drunken men. This was Moran's Crossing, where life was held no dearer than the price of a barrel of smuggled whiskey.

In the card room back of the saloon, Roger Kilraine, ten years older than the day Pete whipped him, his thick features flushed from too much whiskey, shoved a stack of poker chips to the center of the table and called for one card to fill a flush.

"Shooting the works, Roger?" asked a thin-faced man who wore a green eyeshade.

"Looks that way, don't it?" growled out the youth. "Got the nerve to call it?"

The gambler smiled thinly and shoved out a stack of chips equal in size and color to those of the rancher's son. "Regular chip off the old block, aren't you, kid?" he said as he dealt the card.

Roger flipped the card face up on the table, then pushed back his chair with a curse. "Your two pair beat me, Spider. Buy a drink. I'll get revenge after supper."

Spider Parks slipped off his eyeshade and followed Roger into the barroom where a group of men stood drinking.

"When are you going to take up your I.O.U.s, Roger?" he asked in a low tone as the two took their places at the end of the bar.

"As soon as the old man loosens up with some jack, Spider. You should worry about a few hundred bucks when it's Charlie Kilraine's son and heir that puts his John Henry on the dotted line."

"Fifteen hundred bucks is always welcome, kid. I have to pay for a new lot of hooch next week, and I can't pay with I.O.U.s, even if they are signed by Kilraine's son. I'm putting you on the Injun list till you kick through with some kale, sonny."

"You mean my credit's no good in this dump?" shouted Roger in a tone so loud that the other men at the bar turned about.

"Words to that effect, Roger. Come in again when you have something besides a fountain pen in your pocket."

"Why, you insulting tinhorn sport, I'll tear you. . . ."

The gambler ducked the youth's clumsy blow and with a deft shove upset the bulky Roger. A swift kick and the boy's drawn automatic spun across the room, to lodge at the feet of a bearded stranger who stood in the doorway, his hand on the gun at his hip.

"Another gun play like that and I'm liable to muss you up, sonny," warned the gambler. He turned to the bartender.

"Give the boys a drink," he said, grinning. "And put it on Roger Kilraine's tab."

The bearded man, his eyes glinting oddly, stepped inside. The gambler eyed him searchingly.

"Step up to the mahogany, stranger," invited Spider, and he made room at the bar for the newcomer.

The bearded man stooped, picked up Roger's automatic, and with the gun in his hand stepped to the bar.

Roger, again on his feet, his face hot with resentment, opened his mouth to reply, but Spider Parks silenced the youth with a meaningful look.

"Step up and take your poison, Roger," he said in a level

tone that was effective. "Don't let anybody say Charlie Kilraine's son can't lose like a man."

Roger, a surly look in his close-set eyes, stepped to the bar. Spider, deliberately turning his back on the sullen youth, looked squarely into the eyes of the bearded stranger.

"Long time no see you," he said in a tone so low that only the bearded man heard.

"Ten years, Spider," said the other, smiling thinly. "Let's go into the back room where we kin talk."

They downed their drinks and stepped into the card room. The gambler locked the door and drew a chair up to the table.

"You've got a lot of nerve to show up in this country, Moran," he said as he rolled a cigarette.

Tug Moran ran his hand across the heavy beard and laughed. "Yuh bin the only one that recognized me so far, Spider. I reckon yuh know why I come back. Now here's the idee. Either yuh're a-goin' to keep yur mouth shut about me bein' back, and, when I want yuh, yur to lend me a hand, or else yur name goes down on the list with the others. Which'll it be, Spider?"

For a long moment Spider Parks gazed into the glittering eyes of Moran. Cold, calculating, merciless, those eyes. Then the gambler's glance dropped to the small Derringer in Moran's hand.

"Is that the gat you used to kill The Parson?" he asked quietly.

"The same, Spider. It's still in good workin' order. Yuh're keepin' me waitin'."

"I'm no fool, Moran," said Parks coldly. "I know when to lay down a pair of deuces. Let's have a look at your hole card."

"That beefy, red-faced kid out in the saloon is Kilraine's

young 'un?" asked Moran, smiling oddly.

"The same. Just out of college. He's a Kilraine all over. You saw his speed. A cheap sport, like his old man."

Moran nodded. "Charlie's prosperous?"

"Wealthiest gent in the county."

"That's good. I need money. How does he git along with Burnett?"

"Burnett puts up with him. Box Elder Creek still divides their ranges. Roger's soft on Burnett's girl, but it looks to me like Pete Crutcher has the inside track."

"Pete's made good with Burnett?"

"Made good? I hope to tell you that kid's made good. Runs the ranch for Burnett. Best rider and roper in the country . . . fights like a bear cat, and savvies cows. Burnett's as fond of Pete as he would be of his own son."

"Good," grunted Moran. "I reckon Pete and Kilraine's kid don't lose no love on each other?"

"Pete's whipped Roger a time or two. I heard Rawhide tellin' about it. Roger spread the story at college that Pete was a 'breed and his old man a cow thief. It took half the college to drag Pete off young Kilraine."

"Fine. I wonder if Ross Burnett still keeps his roll in that safe at the T Down Ranch? He got stung onct when a bank failed and swore he'd always do his own bankin' from then on. Does he still do it?"

"Yeah. And a fat little stake it is, too. You aren't aiming to crack that safe, are you, Moran?"

"Nothin' like that. I'm wonderin' if Pete knows the combination."

"I suppose so. Ross gives him the run of everything."

"Then we're settin' pretty, Spider," chuckled Moran. "Keep young Kilraine here till he gits drunk. I'm cookin' up a game that'll be worth half a million to us. And I'll have

Burnett and Kilraine both howlin' like stuck pigs afore I finish with 'em."

"Why do you hate Kilraine so bad?" asked Spider.

"Why? Because he tried to double-cross me, that's why. I had some papers on me when I killed that squaw. I cached them papers. Kilraine hires The Parson to help me make a getaway. Then The Parson tried to get holt uh the papers fer Charlie. We're ridin' along the trail, savvy? The Parson shoves a gun in my belly and takes away the two guns he gives me in the courtroom. I'm still handcuffed, and he figgers he has me foul. I promises to lead him to the papers. He's ridin' ahead, leadin' my horse." Moran grinned evilly and lit a cigarette.

"Yeah?" prompted Spider.

"He don't know that I'm packin' a Derringer in my vest pocket, savvy? A little Forty-Four Derringer that shoots wicked at, say, fifteen feet. He'd orter uh searched me closter. It shore pays to be careful about details thataway, Spider." He relit his cigarette and leered into the gambler's face. "The Parson made one bad mistake when he tried to double-cross me, Spider. I hope yuh're wise enough to let it be a lesson to yuh."

Spider Parks nodded, but there was no trace of fear in his expression. "Let's have your plan, Moran," he said softly.

"I tell no man my plans, pardner. It's sometimes bad luck. Yuhr job is to carry out orders. The first order is to get this Kilraine cub into a poker game. Between us we take him in for a big tally."

"We'd have to take his notes for the dough," protested Spider.

"And that's jest what I want. Roger Kilraine's I.O.U. for five thousand bucks is worth twice that much money to me."

"I don't get you, Moran."

"I don't aim that yuh should, Spider," said Moran. "Now let's get ready to throw the hooks into the kid."

Roger Kilraine stood at the corner of the bar, sulking by himself and drinking one whiskey after another. Spider approached the youth with outstretched hand.

"I acted a bit hasty, Roger," the gambler said by way of apology. "I must have had a few drinks too many. Your credit's good for a million. No hard feelings, I hope."

Roger, swelling visibly with self-importance, accepted the outstretched hand with a patronizing air.

"Thought you'd see where you'd acted the fool, Spider," he said. "A Kilraine makes a good friend or a bad enemy, eh?"

"Exactly," answered Spider, and there was a hint of real humor in his cold eyes.

Half an hour later and the poker game was in full swing. It was not yet midnight when Tug Moran quit the game. In Moran's pocket lay Roger Kilraine's note for five thousand dollars. Roger, bleary-eyed from drink and swaying dizzily in his chair, laughed foolishly and ordered another drink.

"Yuh shore are a game loser, Kilraine," said Moran, winking covertly at the yawning Spider.

"Game? That's me all over, old trapper. You'll have to wait a while for the money. Old man's kinda sore at me for spendin' so much. See? Oh, I know how to lose, all right, brother. You can depend on that."

"Yeah," was Tug Moran's cryptic reply as he poured his drink on the floor and started for bed. "Yeah, yuh shore do, kid. Yuhr daddy orter be proud uh yuh."

VIII
"Spider Plays Solitaire"

The baying of a hound shattered the silence of the autumn night. Other dogs took up the cry, and for some minutes the T Down Ranch was a bedlam of noise. Ross Burnett slipped on a pair of trousers, cursed feelingly as he stumbled over a chair in the dark, and, armed with a sawed-off shotgun, stepped outside and flattened himself against the deep-shadowed wall of the house.

A shadowy figure slipped along the opposite side of the house, half-crouched, a .45 held ready. This figure moved with the lithe silence of an animal. A second and he stood beside Ross Burnett.

Ross whirled with a low curse, the barrel of the shotgun poking the newcomer in the ribs.

"Easy, Dad," whispered the other.

"Pete!" gasped out the cattleman.

Pete Crutcher grinned. "Didn't aim to scare you, Dad Ross."

"Hmm, you might've let a man know you was comin'. Dang good thing I ain't got a weak heart. You're as quiet on your feet as an Injun."

"Why not? My mother was a Sioux." Pete's tone was bitter.

"What d'you reckon got into them hounds, Pete?" Ross changed the subject.

"Search me. Reckon it must have been a coyote that started 'em howling."

"Yeah. Reckon we might as well go back to bed, Pete."

"Reckon so."

Neither man, however, made a move to go. Pete laughed shortly. "Thinkin' the same thing I am?" he asked.

"Wouldn't be surprised but what I am, Pete."

"The ten years are up. Do you think Moran'd be fool enough to come back?"

"Dunno, Pete. He'd come in the night, I reckon. He's ornery thataway. Looks like it was a false alarm though, this time. Them danged dogs is always barkin' at somethin'. Good night, Pete." Ross shivered with the chill of the night air and stepped back into the house.

Pete, less easily satisfied, made a tour of the corrals and outhouses before he went back to his room. The search revealed nothing unusual, and in a short time he was again sound asleep.

In the deep shadow behind the log building that served as office and commissary, Tug Moran gripped the arm of his companion in a meaning pressure. "All set, Spider," he whispered. "They done gone back to the blankets. Let's go. Damn them dogs."

Moran led the way to the office door. Spider produced several keys and at last found one that opened the lock. Together the two men slipped inside the office. A moment of black silence, then Moran's pocket flashlight cut a hole in the darkness, and his voice hissed like the warning of a snake.

"Yonder's the safe, Spider. Get busy."

Spider slipped the gloves from his hands and crouched beside the safe. His sensitive fingers twirled the knob of the combination. As the tumblers clicked, he jotted down numbers on a bit of paper. To Moran, who crouched beside the door, a cocked gun in his hand, it seemed hours. In reality it was a scant ten minutes before the door of the safe swung open.

"Regular cracker box," said Spider. "Kid could open it. Look at the stacks of greenbacks."

“Never mind the money,” snarled out Moran. “Swing that door shut and test out that combination.”

Spider did as he was bid. Reading the numbers on the paper, he again opened the safe. Moran commanded him curtly to close it again. Then the pair left as silently as they had come. The contents of the safe had not been touched. There was not a single clue to show they had been there.

Presently the two were in the saddle, riding at a stiff trot toward Moran’s Crossing. In Moran’s pocket, together with Roger Kilraine’s I.O.U., was the slip of paper on which was plainly written the combination of Ross Burnett’s safe.

It was almost daylight when they reached the Crossing. At the end of the bar stood Roger Kilraine, half drunk and scowling.

“I got your note, Spider. What’s up?” he growled out in a surly tone.

“Smith, here,” said Spider, as he indicated Moran, “is leaving the country. He wants to collect that I.O.U. of yours, Roger.”

“But it was only two nights ago that he won the money from me!” protested young Kilraine.

“I wasn’t takin’ yuhr note fer more’n a year, kid,” said Moran sneeringly. “*Men* pay their gambling debts, even if they have to steal the money to do it.” He looked at Roger contemptuously.

“I’ll pay my debts of honor, mister,” said Roger, flushing hotly. “I don’t know how I’ll dig up the coin, but I’ll do it. I’d like to get my mitts on about ten thousand bucks.”

“Yeah?” queried Moran. Spider had slipped into the back room, and Moran was left alone with young Kilraine. The older man eyed the youth with a speculative gaze.

“I wonder just how game you are, Kilraine,” he said musingly.

"Game as they make 'em, stranger," boasted Roger.

"Hmm, supposin' I was to show yuh how to raise twenty thousand dollars and at the same time git even with a man you hate?"

"What do you mean?" Roger tensed as he met Moran's piercing gaze.

"If twenty thousand dollars was to disappear outta Ross Burnett's safe mysterious-like, who would be the gent under suspicion?"

"Pete Crutcher is the only one, except Burnett himself, who knows the combination," said Roger slowly.

"And Pete Crutcher is the son uh Coyote Crutcher, the lowest-down thief that ever hit Montana," reminded Moran.

"But I. . . ."

"If that money disappeared outta the safe and there was no sign to show any outsider opened it, Pete Crutcher would be pointed out as the gent that done it, wouldn't he?"

"I suppose so. But. . . ."

"Good! Pete Crutcher's kinda high-strung and touchy, ain't he? Mighty touchy about bein' Coyote's son. Even if Ross Burnett was to swear he thought Pete was innocent, still it would hit Pete hard because he'd think Ross *did* think him a thief and was lyin' about it."

"It would knock Pete Crutcher for a row of ash cans," said Roger. "Oh, boy! I'll say it would. He's as sensitive as a woman about his parents. I'd give my favorite eye to see him crawling off like the coyote's whelp he is!"

"If you had the combination uh that safe, Kilraine, you'd git plenty uh chances to open it when nobody was around. The T Down outfit are shippin' a trainload uh beef tomorrow. That means that Pete Crutcher and Ross Burnett will be in town to help load. You might ride over to call on the girl, savvy? Get her into the office, somehow, then cook up an excuse to be left in there alone fer a few minutes. It's as easy as shootin' fish. Burnett carries fifty thousand bucks er more in that safe. Are yuh game, Kilraine?"

Roger's face grew pale beneath his sunburn. His pudgy hands shook as he twisted a cigarette into shape and lit it.

"Have a drink," suggested Moran, and the two filled their glasses from the bar bottle. Moran slipped a bit of paper across the bar. It was the paper on which Spider had jotted down the combination of Burnett's safe.

"What's this?" asked Roger as he picked it up.

"The combination. Want the job?"

Roger pocketed the paper, downed his drink, and held out his hand. "You're on!" he whispered hoarsely. "I'll do it!"

Moran watched young Kilraine mount his horse and ride away. There was a triumphant smile on the outlaw's face as he watched the youth out of sight. Then he turned and entered the card room.

Spider looked up from his game of solitaire, a twisted smile on his lips. "How did the game of cat and monkey pan out, Moran?" he asked.

"Cat and monkey?" asked Moran, scowling.

"Old fable written by a wise guy named Æsop. About some chestnuts in the fire. I'd tell you the yarn if I thought you'd appreciate it."

Moran snorted and lit a cigarette. "Kilraine's payin' off his I.O.U. tomorrow night," he said impressively.

Spider nodded absently as he continued his game. "Æsop wasn't playing any cinch," he mused half aloud. "If that cat was to squeal real loud when he burned a paw, the owner of the chestnuts might show up. And then there'd be merry hell to pay. Ever beat this Chinese solitaire, Moran?"

Moran scowled down at the card player, growled some

inarticulate reply, then swaggered out. A few minutes later he crawled into the bed hidden in the brush.

Back in the card room, Spider Parks played on. Sometimes he smiled a thin, twisted smile, and his eyes narrowed dangerously. Twice he made mistakes in his playing. Perhaps his vision was impaired by the memory of a man lying in a cut coulée, a .44 bullet between his shoulder blades. Perhaps his memory drifted back to those days in Chicago when The Parson and Spider Parks sold papers and picked pockets together and turned over their earnings to a drunken father. A cleaner, saner environment might have made great men of those two brothers who became The Parson and Spider Parks.

Parks finished his game, stacked the cards neatly, and tossed aside the cold butt of a cigarette. Then he sauntered outside to watch the sunrise.

IX
"A Bad Heritage"

"You are sure that the money was in the safe when we left for town, Pete?" Ross Burnett frowned at the stacks of bank notes on the desk.

"Sure of it," replied Pete grimly. The boy looked a shade pale under his tan, and his features were strained and drawn.

"Queer. Danged queer, Pete. Twenty thousand dollars is gone. Somebody took it. The stuff couldn't evaporate. Does the safe look as if it had been tampered with?"

Pete shook his head wearily. "Not a sign to show it had been touched. Nobody knows the combination of that safe except you and me. Daddy Ross, it looks like Pete Crutcher has inherited the thieving tendencies of his father."

"What darn foolishness, Son! What's puttin' those ideas into your head?" Ross Burnett's voice was husky with emotion.

"Once or twice at school I walked in my sleep," said Pete thoughtfully. "Perhaps I did one of those sleep-walking performances last night, stole that money while I was asleep, and hid it."

"You talk like an idiot, Pete."

"What other explanation can account for that stolen money? All my life I've watched myself, waiting for some sign of bad blood to show up in me. Long ago I made up my mind that the first trace of Coyote Crutcher that cropped out in me would be the last, so far as anyone should ever know. I determined that I'd either kill myself or go away where nobody knew me. I've read every book on heredity that I could find, studied myself closely, and waited for myself to revert to type. And that's exactly what I've done. Because I stole while I was asleep does not alter the fact that I stole. Unconsciously I'm a low-down thief. I'll be hitting the trail in the morning."

"Pete, if I didn't know you never touched licker, I'd say you was drunk!" Ross Burnett laid an arm across the youth's shoulder. "We're goin' to forgit about that money. That sleep-walkin' theory sounds like kid talk to me. Danged nonsense. Throw them heredity books in the fire, give yourself a chance, and quit worryin' your head about bein' a thief. If you wasn't so darned big and husky, I'd thrash you within an inch uh your life."

Pete shook his head slowly. "No, I've made up my mind. I'm pulling out in the morning."

"And break the hearts uh the two women in the house yonder? Betty loves you like you was her son. As for Dixie, well, boy, I ain't blind. I've seen that look in her eyes and in yours, Pete, that means just one thing. Love. Fer months she's bin waitin' fer you to tell her you loved her. Quit bein' a fool and ask her to marry you."

"No, Dad. I'm Coyote Crutcher's son. I'm a half-breed Indian. I'm a thief. Do you think I'd take the chance of marrying Dixie and having children? Never. Can't you see what a crime it would be? What a contemptible, dastardly trick I'd be playing her? Crutcher blood is tainted. Nothing you can say will keep me from leaving. Better to go now before my love for Dixie deadens my sense of right and wrong. I'm only human, and I can't fight against that love always."

"What will they think when you leave so sudden, Pete?" protested Ross. The cattleman seemed to have suddenly grown old, and there was a beaten look in his keen eyes. He could not help but see the wisdom of Pete's decision.

"They aren't to know the truth, of course," came Pete's reply to the question. "We'll tell them I'm going on a business trip. Then, when I don't return, you can make whatever excuse seems best."

"You don't mean to . . . ?"

"To kill myself? No, Dad, I'm not that cowardly. There have been times when I wanted to, though. No, I'll go to some distant country and try to live straight. If I fall down on the job, I'll be so far away that the disgrace of it won't reflect on you."

"It will be hard on all of us, Son. We're mighty proud uh you. I wish there was some other way out of it. I don't think fer a second that it was you that took that money. And, by Harry, I'm goin' to find out who *did* take it. I'm goin' to question Dixie and Betty about who has bin around here. They. . . ."

"Don't, Dad. They might connect it with my going away.

I . . . I'd hate to have them suspect me of being a thief. And no matter how much they care for me, there would be suspicion if they knew that somebody had taken twenty thousand dollars out of the safe. There is that haunting suspicion in *your* mind. Perhaps you don't realize it's there, but it is. It *has* to be, that's all. No one but you and I know the combination of that safe. You didn't take it, that's certain. Then it must have been I. That's cold logic, Dad. I'm going to see that every cent of that money is paid back to you. But don't, if you care for me, mention the theft to Mother Betty, or Dixie. Promise me that, won't you?"

"I promise, Pete."

It was a strange parting the following morning when Pete left. In spite of his effort to appear casual, an odd restraint crept into his manner.

"You're sure there's nothing wrong, Peter?" asked Dixie as she handed him the hackamore rope of his pack horse. "You look so serious."

"Perhaps I ate too many flapjacks at breakfast," replied Pete with an heroic attempt at being jocular. "And a bellyache is more serious than some folks think. I thought, when I ate those last two, that I was going over my limit."

Avoiding the girl's eyes, he busied himself with the lacing string of his chaps.

Mrs. Burnett stepped alongside Pete's horse, and the youth leaned over. His arms went around her, and for a moment he held her close. This handsome, gray-haired woman had been more than a mother to him in these past years. There was a mist in the boy's eyes as he let her go.

Dixie watched them, a soft smile playing about her lips. She thought of the day so long ago when Pete had come to the ranch, a ragged, half-starved boy. Pete met her glance, and they both flushed.

"Ain't you goin' to kiss Dixie good bye?" asked Ross sagely. He grinned as Pete spurred his horse forward, reached over, and gathered the girl in his arms. Their lips met in a kiss, and an unspoken message of love was conveyed with the touching of their lips. Dixie's arms went about Pete's neck, and she held him close. Then he set her gently down, and picked up his bridle reins.

Ross rode with him to the fork in the trail. There the two men halted. Neither had spoken since they had left the ranch.

"Which trail, Son?" asked Ross.

"The one that leads past Coyote Crutcher's shack to Moran's Crossing."

Pete's tone caused Ross to glance searchingly into the boy's face.

"I saw a man ride that trail the other day," Pete answered the cowman's unspoken question. "The man sat his horse like Tug Moran. Remember that heavy way he had of standing in his stirrups?"

"Suppose it was Moran?"

"I'll shoot straighter this time. That man's a snake, Dad. As long as he's living, I'm afraid for you and the women at the ranch. Tug Moran will strike at the vital spot, and not directly at you. He'll harm Mother Betty or Dixie. I'm sure it was Moran that I saw. And if I cross his trail again, I'll tromp him out like the snake he is."

"Pete!"

"Yes?"

"Does it strike you as bein' kinda odd about that money bein' stole about the time Moran drifts back to this range?"

"I thought of that. But Moran's not clever enough to get into that safe."

"No, don't reckon he is. But I'm layin' a heavy bet that he knows who did take it. I'm sendin' word to Rawhide to turn over the roundup to one uh the boys and come on in to the ranch. Me 'n' him is goin' to get to the bottom uh this, regardless. Charlie Kilraine may have an iron in that same fire. Me and Rawhide has never quit hopin' that some day we'd learn how Jim Rutledge died. Kilraine knows, dang him, and so does Tug Moran. Kilraine's dead scared uh Moran. Why? Because Moran knows too much, that's why. I'd give a heap to know what it was that Moran took off Coyote Crutcher's dead body. Pete, give me your word that you won't quit the country till we've got Moran behind bars. I got a reason fer askin'. Good reason." He was scanning Pete's features as if seeing them for the first time. "Promise, Son?" he asked eagerly.

"I promise. I'll stay at the old shack in the cañon."

Ross Burnett gripped the boy's hand. "So long, Son," he said huskily. "So long and good luck."

They gripped hands, then parted. Pete, leading his pack horse loaded with bed and provisions, swung into the trail that led to Coyote Crutcher's cabin.

Hidden among the pines on a hillside not five hundred yards from the fork in the trail, Tug Moran squatted on his haunches, a Winchester across his knees. He raised the gun and drew a bead on Ross Burnett, then swung the gun to cover Pete.

Two shots'd do it, he thought, an insane light in his eyes. *But I want 'em to suffer a while. It worked. It worked out jest as I figgered. Pete's pulled out. Burnett's takin' it hard, too, blast his hide. And now I'll have another nice job fer Roger Kilraine.* He laughed to himself and mounted his horse. Taking a short cut, he rode at a stiff trot toward the crossing.

Pete, riding down the trail that was all but impassable with underbrush, approached the cabin at the bottom of the cañon. Suddenly, without warning, his horse nickered. From a clump of scrub pine beyond the cabin came the answering nicker of another horse. Pete slipped to the ground, his gun ready for action. On foot he worked his way toward the cabin. Two minutes later he stood in a clump of buckbrush that commanded a view of the entrance to the shack. He started and frowned in a puzzled manner. There was no mistaking that man who leaned idly in the doorway, blowing twin clouds of cigarette smoke through his nostrils. It was Spider Parks, the gambler who ran the saloon at Moran's Crossing.

Parks pinched out the butt of his cigarette and brushed a bit of ash from his well-tailored coat. "Come out of the brush, Crutcher," he called quietly. "You're among friends. If I was gunning for you, I'd have potted you as you came down the trail."

X
"Blank Cartridges?"

Roger Kilraine, half drunk as usual, leaned against the bar. He greeted Moran as that gentleman entered. "Well?" he asked. "What news?"

"Where's Spider?" growled out Moran in answer when he saw that young Kilraine was alone in the place.

"Gone to meet a whiskey runner. He left me in charge. Find out anything at the T Down?"

"Pete Crutcher's quit the place," grinned Moran. "Jest as I said he would. Which way did Spider go?"

"Search me. He turned over the joint to me and drifted."

Moran gave Roger a look that was heavy with suspicion. "Do you know what my name is, Kilraine?" he asked with as nonchalant a manner as he could assume.

"Sure . . . Smith. Or at least that's the name you gave the night I met you." Roger, a half-filled glass of whiskey in his hand, smiled frankly into Moran's eyes. To himself he was proud of how readily he could deceive the man of whom his father had always been so afraid.

Moran seemed satisfied. "I hope that you and Spider ain't fools enough to think you kin double-cross me and win anything," he said meaningly as he stared at the boy.

"Double-cross you? Why should we, Smith?"

"*¿Quién sabe?* It's bin done before by gents I've knowed. Yeah. Spider's clever. Almost too clever to live to be very old." Moran smiled to himself as he poured a drink and downed it. "Now, Kilraine," he said, "I got a proposition that orter tickle yuh to death. Come on into the back room where we kin talk without bein' interrupted. Mebbeso Spider gits in on this, mebbe he don't. Right now, it's between me and you."

"Money?" asked Roger.

"Better than that fer you, young 'un. How'd yuh like to marry Burnett's gal?"

"Don't kid me, Smith."

"I'm not joshin'. Not fer a minute. That ain't my line."

"Dixie'd never fall for me," replied Roger, his beefy face dropping into sad lines that brought a smile to Moran's lips.

"No? I ain't so sure of that. Suppose, some day when she goes ridin' with yuh, that a masked gent stuck yuh both up. If yuh was to shoot this gent er fight him off, she'd think a heap uh yuh, wouldn't she?"

"Perhaps," said Roger doubtfully.

"Well, then, let this gent capture her and hide out. Yuh

could pull a rescue after a day er two, and then she'd marry yuh shore. She'd be safe as she was in a church while she was in the hands uh the hold-up gent, which'd be me. How about it?"

"Worth trying," agreed Roger. "But what would you get out of it?"

Moran smiled. "Ross Burnett's son-in-law would be purty well hooked up financially. Charlie Kilraine'd slip his son a nice piece uh change if he married Burnett's gal. I kin wait a few months fer my cut uh the dough. I'd trust yuh. I don't want a cent till the deal goes through. Yuh'll pull yur rescue before he gits the chanct. Yuh'll shoot me, savvy?"

"Shoot you?"

"With blank cartridges, see?" Moran laughed knowingly.

The fertile brain of the outlaw had given birth to a scheme that was as daring as it was ingenious. For ten years he had been a hunted man with a price on his head, never daring to mingle with his fellow men, always avoiding the groping fingers of the long arm of the law, dodging, hiding, running. He had drifted halfway around the world in the past ten years and had learned that it is, indeed, a hard matter to find a hiding place free from the prying eyes of keen-witted secret service men. But if the death of Tug Moran could be established, he would be free to go to some distant country and enjoy the fruits of what money he could get out of Roger Kilraine. A year of blackmailing would secure him a sufficient sum from young Kilraine to fix him comfortably. Then? His hand slipped inside his coat to caress a package wrapped in oiled silk, and he smiled into the flushed face of Roger Kilraine.

"Well, Kilraine, what d'yuh say?" he asked.

"I'll try anything once," replied Roger, a gleam of anticipation lighting up his face as he dwelt upon a future in which Dixie Burnett figured as his wife.

"Not nary a word to Spider about this," warned Moran.

"Not a word, I promise you."

For more than an hour they sat at the card table, perfecting their plan of campaign. At last Roger rose, and together the two sauntered into the barroom. Moran smiled evilly as he perceived that Spider Parks had not yet returned.

"I'll take a bottle of Spider's best hooch with me," said the youth.

Moran shook his head. "Yuh're stayin' sober, kid. Cold sober er the deal's off. D'yuh reckon that gal's goin' ridin' with yuh if yur smellin' like a distillery? Not by a damn' sight. Yuh're on the water wagon fer a spell, savvy?"

"All right," agreed Roger.

"Mind yuh git blank ca'tridges fer that gun uh yuhrn," Moran cautioned him.

Roger nodded. "Tomorrow night, eh?"

"Tomorrow night at Coyote Crutcher's cabin. Yuh and the gal go ridin' in the afternoon. I stick yuh both up and leave yuh hog-tied, but not so tight but what yuh kin git loose. Yuh foller me 'n' the gal. Come dark, yuh locate me at the cabin and play hero. So long."

Roger was in a jubilant mood as he rode homeward. He had gone but a few miles when he detected the approach of riders. Some instinct told him to dodge into the brush. Curiously he watched the three men ride single file along the trail toward him.

Dad! he thought as he crouched lower in the brush. *Dad and his two gunmen. Now why the devil is he riding to Moran's Crossing? Hunting me? I think not. He thinks I'm on the roundup.*

Charlie Kilraine, riding between the two paid gunmen

who acted as his bodyguard, was almost abreast of Roger's hiding place now. "Better go slow, boys," Kilraine said in a low tone. "If that was Moran that you saw yesterday, he'll be on the lookout. We're dealing with a sure-enough wolf and don't forget it. Shoot first and ask questions afterward." Kilraine was toying with his gun, peering about him.

They rode on, and Roger was again left alone. The youth promptly mounted and rode at a swift pace toward home.

Supposin' the old man and his men kill Moran? he mused. He paled as a sudden thought hit home with the force of a blow. *Why not?* he wondered. *Moran's a crook. He's going to try and bleed me out of a lot of jack, if he can. I'll do it! Blank cartridges? I think not. If Dad and his gunmen don't get you, I will, Moran.*

XI
"Spider Tells a Story"

Pete, nonplused at seeing Spider Parks standing in the doorway of Coyote Crutcher's cabin, hesitated for a moment, then stepped into the open, his .45 covering the gambler.

"I'm alone, Crutcher," said Spider. "And I'm not looking for trouble. My mission is a friendly one. You and I have something to talk over, young man."

"Yes?" Pete's tone was cold, and he did not lower his gun.

"Yes. Suppose we step inside?"

Pete, suspecting a trap of some kind, followed the other man into the cabin. A hasty glance told him that the cabin was empty. He closed the sagging door and took a position where he was out of range of anyone who might be tempted to shoot through the window.

"You expected to find somebody in here?" asked Spider.

Pete nodded, watching the gambler closely.

"Moran?" asked the other as he lit a fresh cigarette.

"Perhaps. And let me tell you this much, pardner. If he's aiming to bushwhack me, you'll pay for it. This gun works on a hair trigger, and I'll live long enough to pull it." The muzzle of his gun never wavered from Spider's chest.

"Don't blame you for being cagey, Crutcher. But we're wasting time, and time is worth a lot to me. I'm here to double-cross Tug Moran."

Pete gasped. "Why are *you* double-crossing Moran?"

"Personal reasons, Crutcher. That's beside the question. Some money was taken from Burnett's safe, was it not?"

"Yes. But I don't see how you knew it."

Spider ignored the implied question. "You're quitting the country because of that?"

"Partly," admitted Pete.

"Don't make a fool mistake like that, Crutcher. Ross Burnett needs you now more than he ever did. If you drift, you'll be playing into Moran's hands. Understand?"

Pete looked squarely into the gambler's eyes. He read something in their cold blue depths that caused him slowly to sheathe his gun. "I think you're playing it straight, Parks. I wish you'd tell me what you know about that theft."

"I may when the time comes, Crutcher. Not now. I played a hunch that you'd come this way. It was a good hunch. If my luck holds out, you may be able to help me solve a mystery."

"I don't savvy."

Spider's hand went inside his coat pocket and came out, holding a package wrapped in a bit of flannel. The gambler's fingers trembled a bit as he undid the flannel and handed Pete a tiny photograph in a silver frame. It was the picture of a girl, fair-haired and delicate-featured, but even the poor photography of the cheap little picture could not hide the sad look in the large eyes or the weary droop at the corners of the girl's mouth. Pete gazed at it curiously, then looked up to see Spider staring breathlessly at him.

"Ever see this picture before?" he asked, and his voice was husky and unnatural.

Pete shook his head. "Not that I remember," he replied, startled at the odd tenseness of the gambler's features.

"I found it one day under that bunk in the corner. It had no doubt been lost by either Coyote Crutcher or his . . . ah . . . wife."

"Well?" asked Pete. "You say my father or his squaw lost this. What of it?"

"It is the picture of the only girl I ever loved," replied Spider in a tone so quiet that it startled Pete more than if the man had shouted. He waited for the gambler to go on.

"She married a man named Jim Rutledge," Spider continued after a moment. "Because Rutledge was clean and honest and everything that I was not. She loved him, Crutcher, don't forget it for a second. And she was good enough to deserve the love of any man. It was Charlie Kilraine with his crooked cards and clever lying that separated them. Charlie told her that Rutledge loved a girl out West and was on a big spree in Chicago to forget. He told her that Rutledge only married her to spite this Western girl. Like a fool, I helped Charlie with his lying and got Mary to quit Rutledge. I was fool enough to think she'd marry me, after Rutledge went back home."

Spider paused in his speech to stare frowningly into space. After a few moments of silence, he went on with his story.

"It was I that persuaded her to go to Montana to see

Rutledge. She still loved him, and there was a kid . . . Jim Rutledge's kid. I told her how I'd helped Charlie Kilraine lie to her, and she was big enough to understand and forgive me. I put her on the train that day in Chicago, kissed her good bye, and went back uptown to get drunk for the first time in my life."

Had the light in the cabin been brighter, Pete might have seen tears well in the cold eyes of the gambler.

"Years passed, and no word came from her. I had expected none. I had no right to expect a letter, understand? Then came word that there was a job here for The Parson. It was Charlie Kilraine who had sent for him . . . Charlie Kilraine who had been one of the gang back in Chi. The Parson came, and I came with him. I wanted to see the woman I still loved . . . see her from a distance, then go back home. But I did not see her, Crutcher. I did not see her because she was dead. And Jim Rutledge was also dead." Spider's voice died in a husky whisper, then rose again. "You've heard the story of their disappearance, Crutcher. Not a trace of Rutledge or his wife or his baby was ever found. Kilraine, the fool, staked me to the Crossing after Moran killed The Parson, thinking to keep me from investigating. I let him believe he had accomplished his purpose. But across the bar, when they've been filled with liquor, men will let their tongues wag, Crutcher. Bit by bit, I picked up threads of that mystery and weaved them together. While I have no actual proof, I learned that Jim Rutledge had been murdered at the Crossing by Coyote Crutcher and Tug Moran. Then they met his wife at Lewistown, lured her to Coyote's cabin, and murdered her and the baby boy. I found their graves not a hundred yards from here, hidden in the brush. Coyote Crutcher did that job alone, and the squaw helped bury them. Coyote made her help him. You were a baby then, about the age of the baby they buried. I guess your mother felt some pangs of remorse, because I found traces of wilted flowers on the baby's grave. It was those flowers that caused me to dig around until I found the skeletons in their unmarked graves. That same day I found Mary's picture under that bunk."

Pete, sick at heart, had listened in silence throughout the tale. "You're sure of the facts, Parks?" he asked finally.

"Dead sure, Crutcher. Most of the story I got from Charlie Kilraine himself when the fool was drunk. He claimed Moran and Coyote Crutcher did it because they hated and feared Jim Rutledge. But I'll bet a million it was Kilraine's money that paid them for it."

"Why didn't you go to Ross Burnett and tell him what you'd found out?" asked Pete.

"Because I've been waiting for Tug Moran to return. Moran has papers that will tell much. The Parson was to get those papers. He failed, as you know. Pete Crutcher, regardless of who your parents were, you look like a real man to me. By helping bring Kilraine and Moran to justice, you could help erase the crimes of your parents. Will you help me?"

Pete held out his hand, and, as Spider gripped it, they held each other's gaze. A look of complete understanding passed between them, and in that instant a bond of friendship was cemented.

"I wanted you to know the story, Crutcher," Spider went on, "because Moran may kill me before I can finish my job. He's mighty suspicious of me. He's a gunfighter, and I'm not. I never was fast with a gat. So if I'm croaked, you can carry on."

"Any plan in mind?"

"Moran's planning something, I don't know what. He'll

use Roger Kilraine as a tool. Suppose you pitch camp near here and lay low. I'll watch my end from the Crossing. When Moran spreads his cards, we'll lay out a mittful of aces and cop the jackpot. Something's about the happen. We won't have long to wait."

Once more they shook hands, and Spider rode swiftly toward the Crossing.

Pete took a dim trail that led him to a remote spot up the cañon. Here he pitched camp and prepared to await whatever might turn up. As he unloaded his pack horse, he went over in his mind the odd story of Spider Parks. Suddenly it occurred to him that Parks had not cleared up the mystery of the twenty thousand dollars that had been stolen from Ross Burnett's safe. Still, the fact remained that the gambler knew of the theft. That proved conclusively that he had either taken that money himself or knew who did take it, because at the T Down Ranch Ross and Pete himself were the only ones who knew the money was missing. This knowledge seemed to lift a weight from Pete's shoulders, and he whistled a bit as he cooked supper.,

I'm not a thief, Dad Ross, he mused. *I'm not a thief. And it looks like we're going to uncover a lot of well-covered trail, if things go right.*

He broke off in his musing to stare into the flickering blaze of his campfire. Into his mind came the picture of a fat, old squaw, her gait uncertain from too much liquor, picking wild roses along the creek.

Leaving his food in the Dutch oven, he set out. A few minutes of crawling through the brush and he was in the little clearing. A quick glance around told him that Spider had dug up the graves, then reburied the skeletons. A bunch of freshly picked wild roses lay at one end of the larger grave. There were remnants of similar bunches of wild flowers, dried and withered. Spider had placed those flowers there. Never a day had passed that the gambler did not visit the lonely grave. These pitiful signs of the man's devotion awed Pete. With uncovered head he stood beside the grave.

Pete passed on to the smaller mound and sat down on a log. Staring with unseeing eyes at the ground, he was lost in memory. Again he was the half-starved, abused little boy whose only friend was a hound pup that shared many of his whippings. Some object on the ground attracted his attention, and he stooped to pick it up. It was a tiny moccasin, warped by the weather, the once bright beads tarnished with age. Even the sole of the moccasin was beaded. Peter frowned. His mother had never made moccasins like that for him that he could remember. His had never had a single bead on them. Then to whom could this moccasin belong? Had Coyote Crutcher's squaw beaded them for the dead baby of the white girl? He could not picture her doing such an act of kindness. Yet she had put flowers on the little grave, after the manner of white people. Pete, a puzzled frown knitting his brows, placed the little moccasin in his pocket and walked slowly toward camp.

His fire had almost died out, so he threw on fresh wood and sat down. Apparently he had forgotten about supper, for he sat staring into the fire in moody silence, the moccasin in his hand. The stars came out, and the moon rose above the ragged rim of the cañon, but he paid no heed. Only when the chill of the night penetrated to his marrow did he stir from his position beside the fire. His food untouched, he unrolled his bed and retired for the night.

XII
"Moran Goes into Action"

Ten years of being hunted had made Tug Moran more than cautious. He suspected everyone and made his plans accordingly. The absence of Spider Parks could mean only one thing. Spider was double-crossing him. Moran rose from the table and, letting himself out by the rear door, slipped into the brush. No man knew this section better than Moran. Every inch of the ground was familiar. Moving swiftly, he made a hasty reconnoiter that finally led him to a high cutbank a hundred yards above the ford. Unsheathing a pair of binoculars, he swept the opposite bank of the river, combing every brush patch and clearing with the glasses. At last he gave a grunt of satisfaction. Back from the river, three men had ridden into a small open space among the cottonwoods.

"Kilraine," muttered the watcher. "Charlie Kilraine! So *that's* Spider's game, eh? And Kilraine's brung his killers along to do the slaughterin'."

He saw Kilraine dismount, and the other two ride into the brush toward the ford. He waited no longer. He started for the saloon at a run, grinning evilly. A few moments and he was in a shed back of the saloon. Presently he emerged from the shed, dragging two huge bear traps. One of them he placed in front of the rear entrance, spreading its steel jaws and chaining it to a steel hasp in the log wall. The second trap was set in the trail by the front entrance and chained in a similar manner.

Minutes dragged. The long shadows cast by the setting sun faded, and the first gray of twilight settled over the river bottom. Moran frowned impatiently and caressed his gun. Had they seen him? Hardly. But why didn't they come? Where was Spider? He wanted to smoke, but dared not take a chance on lighting a cigarette for fear it might lead to detection. Suddenly he stiffened. A rider was approaching from the ford.

He's bin givin' the other 'un time to circle to the rear uh the cabin, thought Moran. He could see the shadowy form of the other man now, cautiously approaching from the rear. The man was on foot, and his movements were furtive.

The rider halted boldly at the hitch rack and swung to the ground. With the well-assumed carelessness of a cowpuncher in search of liquid refreshment, he sauntered along the dusty path toward the open door. But Moran took note that the man's hand never strayed far from his hip.

The other man was within a few feet of the door at the rear. A moment and he would step into the trap.

The man who had left his horse at the hitch rack was within three feet of the entrance now. He took a step forward. There was a cloud of dust as the great jaws of the bear trap clamped on his leg — an agonized cry as the man was thrown off his balance. The gun in his right hand roared as he fired at some fancied movement inside the saloon.

The man approaching the rear of the cabin sprang forward. Then he, too, fell, and his sharp cry of mingled fear and pain blended with the cry of his companion.

"Come out in the open and fight like a man, Moran!" the man at the front entrance called. "Come out unless yuh're the low-down polecat that they claim yuh are!"

Moran's bearded lips curled back in a snarl as he took deliberate aim from his ambush. A loud report, a puff of white smoke, and the man in the trap shuddered convulsively, then lay still. His stiffening finger pressed the trigger of his gun, and the lead slug tore through the dirt to lodge in the log wall.

Reloading, Tug Moran stepped into the open and crossed to where the man lay. He kicked the inert body contemptuously and stepped across it into the barroom. He poured himself a stiff drink, then sauntered leisurely to the rear of the building, his .45 held carelessly in his hand. Standing in the doorway of the rear entrance, he looked sneeringly down at the moaning wretch in the trap.

"How d'yuh like it out West as fur as yuh bin?" he said, laughing.

"Take this thing off my leg!" begged the man. "For Christ's sake, have mercy on a man! It's killing me!" He crawled to within a foot of Moran, begging piteously.

"Shut up, yuh howlin' weaklin'," snarled out Moran, and his high-heeled boot caught the man full in the face. It was a vicious kick that smashed the man's lips into a bruised pulp. The man covered his face with his hands, moaning and begging.

"A fine gunman yuh are!" sneered Moran. "Quit blubberin'. If yuh come clean, I'll let yuh go, mebby. Where's Spider Parks?"

"I don't know! So help me, Moran, I don't! He ain't with us!"

"Where's Kilraine?"

"Charlie's across the river, waitin' fer the signal." The man was suffering agonies as the jaws of the trap bit deeper into the bone.

"Signal, eh? You was to give him the signal when you'd done fer me, eh?"

"Yes," moaned the man feebly. "Take this devilish thing off me, and I'll do anything you say, Moran."

"What was the signal?" barked out Moran. "Tell me the signal, and I'll put yuh outta yuhr pain."

"Three shots in quick succession," groaned the man.

"He was to come when he got the signal."

Moran pointed his gun in the air and fired three times. Then, grinning down at the groaning man, he carefully reloaded.

"Yuh said yuh'd turn me loose," the man pleaded piteously.

"I said I'd put yuh outta yuhr misery, and I'll do it, pardner," said Moran, grinning evilly. And the barrel of his .45 thudded against the unprotected skull of the man in the trap. The man went limp, a huddled, dusty figure. Moran shrugged and, sheathing his gun, rolled a cigarette. Then, still moving unhurriedly, he swaggered to the front of the saloon and went outside. Without removing the cigarette from his lips, he dragged the dead man, trap and all, into the saloon and deposited the body in a corner. It was growing a bit dark inside the saloon, and Moran lit the big kerosene lamp at the end of the bar. Then he again stepped outside to wait for the coming of Charlie Kilraine.

He had not long to wait. Kilraine, his horse traveling at a stiff gait, drew rein and swung to the ground.

"You got him, boys?" he called as he stepped into the lighted saloon. He gave a start of surprise when he saw no one in the place. Then he saw the huddled figure in the corner.

It did not occur to Charlie Kilraine that this could be one of his own men. He was smiling evilly as he crossed the room to examine the body. As he bent over the dust-covered form, his eyes widened with horror, and his heavy jaw sagged. With a frightened, choking cry he straightened.

"Well, if it ain't my old friend Charlie!" called Moran from the doorway. The outlaw's carelessly held gun was covering the cattleman.

Charlie Kilraine gulped. His bloodless lips opened, but no sound came forth.

"Yuh don't seem glad tuh see me, Charlie," Moran went on. "Yuh look like yuh was seein' a ghost. Better take a drink afore yuh choke."

Like a man in a daze, Kilraine obeyed. Tug Moran poured himself a drink.

"Success!" exclaimed the outlaw, and downed his drink. Kilraine tried to smile, but the effect was ghastly. He spilled half his liquor getting it to his mouth. Moran slipped Kilraine's gun from its holster and tossed it behind the bar.

"Now git into that back room, yuh big, yaller-hided skunk," he continued.

Staggering like a drunken man, Kilraine obeyed. Moran shoved him into a chair, then bound and gagged him.

"Now we're all set to welcome Spider," Moran said, leering down at him. "Spider, the gent that tipped yuh off that I was here. Yuh jest nacherally spoiled all my plans, bustin' down here, Kilraine. And I'm tellin' all hands you'll pay plenty fer it. Me 'n' that crooked son of yuhrn had a nice little game fixed up, but it's all off now. I'm hirin' fer a tough hand and playin' my string out, savvy? I'm killin' yuh and yuhr kid both. That is, unless yuh do as I say. I'm. . . ."

Moran quit speaking to whirl about. A man had entered the front door of the saloon and halted, glancing about as he lit a cigarette. The man was Spider Parks.

The door between the card room and the barroom was wide open. Spider caught a clear view of Kilraine and Moran. Then Moran's .45 came to full cock with an ominous click. The gambler smiled mirthlessly.

"Neatly done, Moran. But why pick on me?" he asked in an even tone that was a bit disconcerting. Moran had expected something different in the way of salutation.

"Thought yuh'd slip one over on me by squealin', didn't yuh, Spider?" Covering the gambler, Moran stepped forward until he was within a few feet of the other. "It was yuh that put Kilraine and his men on my track, Spider. I'm aimin' to make yuh pay fer it."

A relieved look came into the gambler's eyes. Moran was not aware that he had seen Pete. Some odd twist of fate had brought Kilraine here, and Moran was blaming him. He felt relieved.

"You're jumping at conclusions, Moran," he said quietly. "Think it over carefully. Why should I put Kilraine on your trail? I've had more than one chance to down you since you came here. You know that. And I'm not the kind that hires other men to do my killing. I don't know how Kilraine knew you were here. I'm not lying when I tell you that. Take it or leave it."

Tossing aside his half-smoked cigarette, Spider turned his back on Moran and stepped to the bar. It was a bold thing to do. Not one man in a thousand could have done it without being killed. But Spider, who knew men as he knew cards, was a past master at the art of bluffing and took the gambler's chance that Moran would not shoot.

The muzzle of the outlaw's gun swung to cover the man at the bar. Then the gun barrel slowly lowered. Spider, through narrowed eyelids, saw the lowering of the gun as he looked into the cracked mirror back of the bar.

"Join me in a drink, Tug?" he asked pleasantly.

Moran, a bit dazed by the sheer nerve of the gambler, shoved his gun back in its holster with a curse. "I shore will, Spider," he growled out and, stepping up to the bar, said: "Yuh win that pot. Yuh're the nerviest cuss I ever ran acrost."

He watched Spider pour the drink. The gambler's hand was as steady as a piece of machinery.

"Did Kilraine say I squealed on you, Tug?" he asked.

"Don't know as he did, Spider. But where yuh been? How come yuh to leave the saloon?"

"An affair of the heart, if you get me, Moran."

For the first time Moran noticed that Spider was wearing his best coat, a clean white shirt, and a tie. He did not know that Spider always groomed himself carefully when he made those visits to the grave of the woman he loved.

"Who'd've thunk it?" He laughed harshly. "Come to think of it, there *are* some right good-lookin' 'breed gals strung along the river. Never knowed yuh was a ladies' man, Spider." He clapped the gambler jovially on the back.

"A man gets lonesome here on the river at times," said Spider. He nodded toward the huddled form in the corner and indicated Kilraine with a careless wave of his hand. "Looks like you've been having a Fourth of July around here, Tug. Got my joint all cluttered up."

"Yeah." Moran smiled nastily.

"Is the fella in back dead?"

"Should be, less'n his head's made uh wood. I hit him hard enough. Is that door on the dugout still solid?"

"Solid as a jail door, Tug."

"Then lend a hand and we'll put all three of 'em in there. Charlie thinks a heap uh them gunmen uh his. I won't separate 'em. He'd orter enjoy that dark root cellar with two dead 'uns fer company."

Spider repressed a shudder and helped carry the two gunmen to the dugout. He did not tell Moran that the one who lay at the rear of the cabin still breathed. An hour, perhaps, and the man would regain consciousness. Then they placed Kilraine in the dugout, lit a candle, and barred the heavy door from the outside. The candle was Moran's clever idea.

"Charlie's plumb spooky about ghosts and dead bodies,"

he told Spider. "He'd orter have a plumb good time in there. There's an old friend uh his buried under the floor. He helped plant Jim there, and I whispered in his ear to remind him."

"Jim Rutledge's buried there?" asked Spider carelessly.

"Jim Rutledge," chuckled Moran. "Charlie will shore spend one peaceful night. That candle will throw shadders that'll shore make his hair curl. Charlie's spooky thataway."

Moran seemed to grow unusually thoughtful after the two had gone back in the saloon. Spider, accustomed as he was to bloodshed and brutality, was awed by the cold-blooded calm of the man. It was plain to be seen that the outlaw was turning over some plan in his mind. Spider watched him like a hawk, and the gambler's right hand was never far from the pocket where his automatic reposed.

"Spider," said Moran at last, "I could use a gent with nerve like yuh got. And yuh could drag down some easy money, too. There's two ways I kin use yuh."

"Yes?" Spider said.

"Yeah. Two ways, Spider. Dead or alive. I'll give yuh yuhr choice."

"I naturally prefer that alive job," answered Spider thinly. "Let's have the lay."

"Tomorrow afternoon I'm goin' to kidnap Ross Burnett's gal," said Moran impressively.

"Yes?" Spider seemed unmoved by this piece of news.

"When her and Roger Kilraine goes fer a ride. Roger is goin' to be tied up so's he kin escape. He'll foller us, and, when it comes dark, he'll pull a rescue, savvy?"

"Would you mind telling me just what the idea is?" asked Spider, showing signs of interest.

"Roger is rarin' to marry her, savvy?"

"I get you, Moran. Roger pays well. Go on." There was

an ominous glitter in the gambler's eyes that Moran failed to see.

"Roger follers me 'n' the girl. I let her know that I'm Tug Moran. I let her know that I'm pullin' the job single-handed. And I tie her hard and fast, gag her, and leave her in Coyote Crutcher's cabin. Then I go outside to stand guard and wait fer Roger. And there is where yuh come into the game."

"Yes?" Spider Parks was thinking rapidly. Pete Crutcher was camped near the cabin. If he could only find out where Moran kept those papers that meant conviction of Charlie Kilraine . . . if. . . .

"Yeah." Moran broke into the trend of his thoughts. "Yeah, that's where yuh earn yuhr money, Spider. With a mask over yuhr face and with my clothes on, Roger will like as not mistake yuh fer me. I come outta the cabin, savvy? Yuh be waitin' in the brush. Me 'n' yuh swap clothes, and yuh slip on the mask." Moran chuckled.

"Go on, Moran, your plan sounds great," said Spider.

"Roger rides up, shoots yuh, and rescues the gal," said Moran, laughing.

"Pleasant thought. Looks like I lose."

"Young Kilraine is supposed to have blank shells in his gun," said the outlaw.

"He's *supposed* to. But will he?"

Moran shrugged. "That's what *I* was wonderin', Spider. Roger ain't none too careful about his promises. He might take it into his head to use real ca'tridges. That's why I'm hirin' yuh to take my place."

"Ah!" Spider smiled wryly. "Another cat and monkey game. And I'm the cat. I'm frank to say I don't care for the job, Tug."

"No?" Moran's eyes were thin slits of red fire as he looked

at the gambler. As if by magic the little Derringer had appeared in Moran's hand and the gun was covering Spider. "Then I reckon I use yuh dead. Whether or not Roger Kilraine shoots blanks, there'll be a dead man when the coroner and the sheriff gits there to investigate young Kilraine's story. On the dead man will be papers to show that the dead gent is Tug Moran. One uh them papers will be the deed to the Circle Bar Ranch. That deed will send Charlie Kilraine to the pen. His buttin' in tonight give me that idee. As I said, there'll be a dead man there to take my place. I've bin thinkin' uh yuh fer that part, Spider. I'm coverin' yuh now. And I'm gettin' impatient. Want that job at the cabin?"

For the second time within the hour Spider Parks stood on the brink of the valley of death. Save for a slight narrowing of his hard eyes, he gave no sign of emotion. "I'll take the job, Moran." His voice was quiet and without a quaver.

"Good. We'll use that gunman uh Kilraine's fer the dead man. He's more my size, anyhow. And by the time the wolves finish with him, he'll pass for Tug Moran." The Derringer went back in his pocket.

Spider struggled to keep from shuddering. "Got that deed on yuh, Tug?" he asked.

"Never mind the deed, Spider. I'm takin' care uh that."

Spider laughed mirthlessly. Moran had told him enough to convince him that the outlaw and Charlie Kilraine were partners in crime. If only Moran would drop his guard for a moment, he would cover the murderer. . . . kill him, if he had to. Physically, however, the gambler was no match for the heavily muscled outlaw, and Moran was much the quicker man with a gun. Spider wished Pete Crutcher were here.

"Jest shove yuhr hands this way, Spider," commanded

Moran. The Derringer had again sprung into view, as if the outlaw had read the other man's thoughts.

Spider obeyed. Another instant and a pair of handcuffs had clamped tightly on the gambler's wrists.

"I'm takin' no chances on yuh spoilin' the game," said Moran. "I reckon the dugout's a good place fer yuh to spend the night. And keep yuhr mouth shet, savvy? Not one word about my plans to Charlie Kilraine. I'm puttin' Charlie through the third degree afore me 'n' yuh go to Crutcher's cabin tomorrow night. Charlie's yaller enough to squeal on yuh, if yuh've said anything. And if yuh have told, I'll kill yuh, savvy? And I'll kill him fer knowin' too much."

"I get you, Moran," said Spider grimly. "I'm keeping my trap shut. The dugout it is. Let's go."

XIII
"Kilraine Talks"

Perhaps it would have been more soothing to Charlie Kilraine's peace of mind if there had been no light at all in the dugout. The flickering blaze of the candle, pale and unhealthy, cast infernal, grotesque shadows on the dirt walls. On one side of him lay a dead man; beyond was the other one who muttered and groaned in half delirium as consciousness returned. And then there came the hidden rustling of curious pack rats scurrying from their holes across the damp floor. Charlie Kilraine wanted to scream from fright. Then the door opened, and Spider was ushered in.

"Sweet dreams," called Moran mockingly. "See yuh in the mornin'." The heavy door swung shut, and the bar clattered into place.

Spider built a cigarette with his manacled hands and lit it

from the candle. Kilraine eyed him suspiciously. At last, when Spider made no effort to break the silence, desire for companionship overcame Kilraine's sullen suspicion of the gambler.

"Make me a smoke, will you, Spider? Or untie my mitts so's I can get to my tobacco. Gad, what a hellish place to leave a man."

Spider nodded absently, but made no move to get the desired cigarette for his companion. Kilraine frowned. The gambler turned his attention to the half-conscious gunman. Five minutes of heartbreaking, torturous effort freed the man from the bear trap. The poor wretch ceased moaning and lapsed into unconsciousness. A pack rat scurried across the legs of the recumbent Kilraine. The big man shuddered and cried out. Spider grinned down at him.

"For Christ's sake, Spider, cut my hands loose from this rope," he pleaded.

"Later, perhaps. Not now, Charlie. Tug might not like it." Paying no heed to Kilraine, Spider picked up the stub of candle and made an inspection of the place. It was a square room, some twelve feet across and probably eight feet high. The walls and floor were of dirt, and save for some empty boxes and a whiskey keg the place was empty.

"What the devil are you hunting, Spider?"

"Don't know, Charlie, don't know. Just felt a little creepy. Nervous, I suppose, but it seemed like there was someone standing over me in the dark. Felt like a hand on my shoulder. Odd. I'm not usually given to hallucinations." He replaced the candle, then squatted opposite Kilraine.

The rancher's face looked drawn and scared.

"Regular tomb, this joint," Spider went on. "I'd. . . ." He whirled about suddenly, then shrugged. Grinning a bit shamefacedly, he again turned to Kilraine. "I'd have sworn something touched me then. Do you hear an odd noise like a whisper, Charlie?"

"No, you fool!"

"Guess it must be my nerves. I went to a spiritualist meeting once. Felt the way I do now. The guy that was running the show said I was a good subject or something. I wish it was daylight."

He smoked in silence for some time. A scampering rat passed within six inches of Kilraine's face, and he rolled over with a scream of terror. Spider leaned forward, and his hand closed over the candle.

"Now you've done it, Charlie," he growled out. "Knocked out the light, hang it." He slipped the candle stub in his pocket. "Got any matches, Charlie?"

"Moran cleaned my pockets," replied Kilraine. "Haven't you got one?"

"Not a one. I'll frisk these other two gents." Spider moved away in the darkness, but he made no attempt to hunt a match. After a time, he spoke once more. "No go, Charlie. Not a match. Hold on, here's some." He approached the spot where the candle had rested on an overturned box. The match sputtered and flared up. Kilraine breathed a sigh of relief. It was short-lived, however.

"It's gone, Charlie. The candle's gone! Look!"

Kilraine groaned. There was no trace of the candle. This was but natural considering the fact that the bit of yellow tallow rested in the gambler's pocket. Spider, playing his part well, lit match after match in a vain search for the candle. The match died out, and he spoke.

"Guess we'll spend the rest of the night in darkness, Charlie. It's all-fired queer where it went."

Kilraine mumbled some inarticulate reply. Both men fell silent. With the darkness cloaking his movements, Spider moved without a sound toward Kilraine, who had struggled to a sitting posture. Kilraine's labored breathing told the gambler where the big man sat.

Suddenly Kilraine yelled with terror.

Spider, again in his old place, spoke. "What's the matter, Charlie?"

"Some . . . something touched my cheek," he whispered. "Something cold and inhuman."

"Nonsense," scoffed Spider, but he let a husky note creep into his tone, and the effect was not lost.

"You're scared yourself, Spider."

"Ridiculous!" But the gambler's husky tone belied his reply.

"If you'll untie my hands, I'll make it worth your while, Spider." Kilraine was almost whining in his fear.

"You stand a fat chance. Moran's croaking us both."

"No?"

"Yes, I tell you. Think he'd be fool enough to turn us loose?" Spider laughed softly. "Scared to die, Charlie?"

No answer. Only Kilraine's labored breathing, the faint groaning of the unconscious man, and the pattering scamper of the huge rats. Then another sound came, indistinct, elusive, weird — the crying of a child. Then a man's voice. Or was it a man's? An odd, unearthly voice.

"Mary," it called, and repeated the cry, more faintly this time.

"Jim!" Faint, high-pitched, came the cry of a woman in mortal terror. "Jim!"

"Spider! Help me, Spider!" Charlie Kilraine's voice was hysterical in its terror. Then his voice died in a strangled gurgle. Kilraine's breath came in horrible, whistling sounds as a pair of hands slowly throttled him. Then, when consciousness was leaving him, the hands relaxed. Kilraine gasped, and his reeling senses registered the odd fact that Spider Parks, ten feet away, was lighting a cigarette with the stub of a match.

"What's all the fuss about, Charlie?" asked the gambler in a calm voice as he stepped forward, cupping the precious flame.

"I . . . I . . . somebody was choking me, Spider. And those infernal, devilish voices."

"Choking you? Voices? You're batty! Only sound I heard was you sort of gurgling. You must have swallowed your tongue in your sleep." The match went out. The blackness of the dugout was dotted by the glowing end of Spider's cigarette.

"I wonder how long we'll last before we starve to death, Charlie?"

"Starve to death? You mean Moran's leaving us here to starve?"

"Why not?" The glow of the gambler's cigarette lit his lean face with its inscrutable smile.

"I . . . I don't want to die, Spider. I'm scared!"

"Yes? What are you scared of, Charlie? We can't live forever."

"It's meeting Jim that I'm scared of, Spider! Jim and Mary and the baby!" His voice was almost pitiful in its terror.

"Jim who?"

"Jim Rutledge. And Mary, his wife. You remember Mary, Spider? You used to be soft on her yourself."

"What about 'em?" Spider's voice was calm. Too calm.

"It was me that hired Moran and Crutcher to kill 'em. God help me! Jim's buried in that corner. Tug shot him. Tug and Coyote! And then they did for Mary and the kid!"

Spider took the stub of candle from his pocket and deliberately lit it. Kilraine gasped, then turned deathly pale as he met Spider's eyes in the flickering light of the candle.

"What are you . . . Spider, you won't make . . . ?"

Spider's manacled hands seized Kilraine's and with a display of strength that was surprising threw the big man face downward on the floor. A moment and Kilraine's hands were free. Spider stepped back and kicked Kilraine to his feet. There was a terrible smile on the gambler's thin lips — a smile that made Kilraine shudder.

"You outweigh me sixty pounds, Kilraine," said Spider in a hard, toneless voice. "And I'm handcuffed. But I'm going to kill you. I never killed a man in my life, but I'm starting now. Stand on your feet and fight."

Kilraine looked down at the smaller man. Spider, slender, his hands fettered, looked pitifully weak and small. With a snarl, Kilraine squared off.

"So it was a put-up job, eh? Those voices and spooks?"

"A little ventriloquism, Charlie."

Kilraine, an animal-like snarl bursting from his lips, sprang at the smaller man, his big fists swinging like flails. The two went to the floor in a twisting, panting knot. The candle was overturned, and the two men fought in inky darkness.

Over and over on the floor, each groping desperately for the other's throat, they fought in silence. Again and again Kilraine's big fists beat into the other man's unprotected face — smashing, battering blows that thudded sickeningly. Still those long, slender fingers kept their grip. Spider's senses were reeling now. He laughed crazily, as those blows drove his head backward. Then the blows ceased, and Kilraine's hands tore at that death grip on his throat. Spider laughed again, as Kilraine's struggles became more feeble. He did not know that he laughed. He did not know anything except that he must not relax that hold on Kilraine's throat. Like a man drowning, his senses slipped from him, and he fell across the inert body of Kilraine.

Was it daylight? Spider could not tell. In the dugout it was still dark, and he had no way of knowing. Aching in every muscle, his face a bruised, battered pulp, he crept across the floor away from that huddled thing that was Charlie Kilraine.

Kilraine had paid. *Kilraine had paid.* That was as it should be. Where was that candle? Spider felt in his pockets for a match. After an eternity of groping, fumbling search with his eyes aching like balls of fire, and match after match scorching his fingers, the gambler located the candle and lit it. Its flickering light showed that the cruel steel of the handcuffs had cut into his wrists to the bone, and the swollen members were throbbing with pain.

Then the door opened and a shaft of light cut the darkness. For some moments Tug Moran stood there, taking in the scene. Then, with a muttered curse of astonishment, he crossed over to Kilraine and kicked the huddled form.

"Dead?" asked Spider, his bruised lips spreading in a ghastly grin.

"Looks thataway. What's the idea in yuhr killin' him off? I was aimin' to get a piece of money outta him." Moran's tone was sullen and angry. It was evident that the outlaw had been drinking.

"He thought I had a hand in his capture," Spider replied, thinking rapidly. "Take me out of this hole and let me wash up a bit. I'll be more useful to you after I've washed up and had a jolt of firewater."

"Come on, then." Moran led the way out and barred the door on the dugout.

"You let Kilraine loose and then killed him with yuhr hands?" asked Moran, when they had entered the empty saloon.

"Yes." Spider downed his drink.

"Well, I'll be damned. Yuhr a regular bear cat fer scrappin' when yuh put yuhr mind to it, Spider. Kilraine's no easy man to handle in a rough and tumble. Lemme git them bracelets off yuh." He unlocked the handcuffs, and Spider grinned his thanks.

"Git washed up and throw some breakfast into yuh," growled out Moran. "Me 'n' yuh is goin' fer a ride. We're goin' to Crutcher's cabin, and I'm leavin' yuh there in the brush till dark. I'll have tuh stake yuh out and gag yuh, I reckon, in self-defense. Yuh're plumb smart, Spider, but Tug Moran has brains himself."

As the two rode in silence toward the Crutcher cabin, Spider kept a sharp lookout for Pete Crutcher. Would Pete see them as they rode down the trail into the cañon? It was more than likely. But Spider's eyes combed the brush in vain. There was not a trace of the youth. They reached the cabin, and Moran nodded to Spider to dismount. Again the handcuffs were adjusted, and Moran led the way into the heavy brush thicket behind the cabin. Here they halted, and Moran bound the gambler's legs and fitted a gag into his mouth.

"You certainly don't believe in halfway measures, do you, Moran?" said Spider grimly as the outlaw adjusted the gag.

"Not with yuh, pardner," said the outlaw sneeringly. "Yuh're foxy, but I'm outfoxin' yuh, savvy? Yuh see, I went ridin' last night. I got to thinkin' about yuh callin' on the 'breed gals, and somehow I couldn't jest quite picture yuh a-girlin'. So I made a visit to the camps along the river, Spider. And I asked some questions. I learned that yuh hadn't bin to any camp. Whatever yuhr game is, yuh're playin' the loser's hand, my friend. Think it over while I'm gone." With a harsh laugh, Moran turned away.

XIV
"Pete Fights"

It was not yet daylight when Pete Crutcher awoke from his dream-troubled slumber. He seemed unusually thoughtful, and his dark eyes glowed with suppressed excitement as he prepared breakfast. Wolfing his food and gulping down mouthfuls of steaming black coffee, he made short work of breakfast. It was daylight now, and Pete walked swiftly to the cabin where he had spent his childhood. A few minutes' search bore fruit in the form of a rusty spade. With this tool he made his way to the two graves hidden in the brush.

"I hate to disturb you, little chap, but it has to be done," he muttered as he sank the shovel into the spot where the baby was buried. A few minutes of digging and the grave was open. The tiny skeleton lay in an old beer case and had been well sealed with boards and canvas. A distasteful, gruesome task, this. Pete shrugged away his qualms as he pried loose the cover of the crude coffin. He spent some time examining the musty clothing. Now and then he nodded to himself. Finally he took the little moccasin from his pocket and placed it in the coffin. Then he sealed it again, covered it with dirt, and left the place.

Half an hour later he was in the saddle, riding at a trot toward the T Down Ranch. Mrs. Burnett greeted him with surprise. After the joyous greetings were over, Pete asked where Ross was.

"He rode into town to meet Rawhide, Peter. He said he

was bringing Rawhide back with him. Dixie? She went riding with Roger Kilraine. Roger came over early this morning. Said there were some Circle Bar cattle on our side of the drift fence, and he needed help to gather them."

Pete frowned. He usually frowned when Roger Kilraine's name was mentioned."You seem excited, Peter. Has anything happened?"

"It's a secret, Mother. I'm not telling you yet. Tell me, was Jim Rutledge dark or light-complexioned?"

"Quite dark, Peter. As dark as you. Ross and I are both reminded of poor old Jim whenever we see you smile. And your eyes are the same dark brown."

Pete nodded. "I had hoped you'd say that. Well, I'll be on my way. When Dad Ross and Rawhide get here, tell them to come to Coyote Crutcher's cabin. Tomorrow will be time enough. Tell 'em I'm camped below the cabin in the cañon. They'll find it easy enough. Now don't look so alarmed. There's no danger. Nothing wrong. But I'm running down some clues, and I think we're about to clear up the mystery of Jim Rutledge's death."

"You really have found out something, Peter?"

"Enough to give me hope. Which way did Dixie and Roger ride?"

"I heard Roger say that the cattle were at the edge of the badlands, not far from Coyote Crutcher's old place."

Pete started. He recalled the words of Spider Parks. Moran intended using Roger for a tool.

"Well, Mother, have to be getting back. Tell Dad Ross and Rawhide that I'll see 'em tomorrow. And tell Dad that I've changed my mind about the heredity book. He'll understand." He kissed his foster mother warmly, waved a farewell, and was gone in a cloud of dust.

As he rode, Pete became more and more alarmed. Moran

was inhuman enough for anything. Young Kilraine was a drunken, easily led scoundrel. Dixie alone with him in the badlands and Moran hiding somewhere near! Pete clamped his jaws until the muscles ached. His horse seemed to cover the ground at a snail's pace. Mile after mile he pushed the animal to the limit of its superb strength.

He was nearing the edge of the badlands now. What was that? A rider? Pete spurred his horse to a run as he recognized Roger Kilraine. Roger, riding at a walk, was fumbling at the hogging string that bound his hands and cursing Tug Moran for having done his hold-up job in such a realistic manner.

He didn't have to tie me so confounded tight, hang him, growled the youth to himself. *And that was no love tap that he handed me when I made the bluff of putting up a fight. My jaw still aches. Blast this rope! It'll take me an hour to get it loose. But I'll make him pay when I get him at the cabin tonight. Blank shells? I'll tell a man they'll be the real thing. I'll plug him. . . .*

The clatter of hoofs caused him to whirl in his saddle. Then he went deathly pale. The rider that was coming toward him at a run was Pete Crutcher.

"Where's Dixie?" asked Pete as he jerked his horse to a halt in such a manner that he also halted young Kilraine's mount.

"I . . . I don't know, Crutcher. I haven't seen her since two hours ago. We split up to gather some cattle, and I. . . ."

"What's that rope on your hands for?"

"I was practicing a very fancy knot that. . . ."

Pete's hand grasped young Kilraine's shirt collar. Swinging to the ground, Pete jerked Roger from his saddle and spun him about.

"Talk, and talk fast, Kilraine. You'll never be closer to

death than you are now." Pete's face was white with rage. He shook the beefy Roger like a terrier, shaking a rat.

"Smith," gasped out Roger. "Smith did it. So help me, Crutcher, it was Smith. I put up a fight, but he had me foul. He took her with him."

"Who's Smith? You lying young whelp, if I can't get the truth out of you this way, I'll get it another."

Pete's knife came out. A quick slash of the keen blade and Roger Kilraine's hands were free. The knife was tossed aside, and Pete's open hand caught Roger in the mouth.

"I'm beating the truth out of you, you big bulldozing pup! You claimed at school that I didn't whip you fair. Come on! I'll kill you this time." Another slap and Roger squared off.

Despite his bulk, Roger Kilraine was active. He had been the heavyweight champion of the school. And if it came to the worst, he had his automatic in its shoulder holster. With a snarl that told of revived courage, he launched himself at Pete who was lighter by many pounds.

Pete side-stepped, tripped over a rock, and all but lost his balance. With an exultant cry Roger was on him, his big fists pounding at Pete's face. Pete, caught off his guard, went down.

The high heel of young Kilraine's boot crashed into Pete's face as he rolled over. With the agility of a cat, Pete wrapped his arms about Roger's legs. A twist and Roger was thrown to the ground. Pete was on him. In a tight embrace, they rolled over, each with one arm free to strike at the other's face. A twisting, grunting mass of legs and arms, they rolled under the feet of Pete's horse. The animal, frightened into action, lashed out with both hind feet. Pete dimly heard a sickening crack, and a terrific pain racked his left arm. The horse jumped clear and bolted a few feet, stepped on the bridle reins, and halted, whistling noisily through his nostrils.

Pete, his left arm broken between elbow and shoulder, fought on. His right hand closed about young Kilraine's throat. Then came a blinding flash of red flame, the burning sensation of hot powder stinging his eyes and forehead. Something hot stabbed his head, and he lost consciousness.

Roger Kilraine staggered to his feet, his smoking automatic in his hand. Then his eyes widened with horror as he saw the slow crimson stain that oozed across Pete's temple.

His first thought was to flee. He had killed Pete Crutcher. The law would demand justice for the killing. He ran to his horse and swung into the saddle. Spurring and quirting, he rode at breakneck speed to overtake Dixie and Moran.

Had he hesitated a minute, he would have seen Pete move his head. The steel-jacket bullet had ripped the scalp and grazed the bone above Pete's temple. He groaned feebly and opened his eyes. A wave of nausea swept over him; his head was splitting. His broken arm ached and throbbed with that numbing pain that made him sick and dizzy. Swaying like a drunken man, he got to his feet, looking about for the man who had almost killed him. But Roger was nowhere in sight. Pete gained his horse and swung into the saddle.

Berating himself for a fool, he headed his mount toward Moran's Crossing. He felt sure that this Smith would take Dixie there. Who was Smith? Moran's partner? More likely it was Moran himself. Roger had lied. There was no such man as Smith. Pete's hand dropped to the .45 at his hip. There would be no fist fighting from now on. It would be hot lead. The bitterness of failure, coupled with the fear that Dixie was in danger, alleviated the pain of his arm. No power on earth could stop him from finding the girl he loved. He was a ghastly figure as he swayed in his saddle. The blood that trickled from his head caked on his face. His right hand never left the butt of his gun.

Moran's Crossing, he thought over and over. *Nothing on earth will keep me from finding her.*

XV
"The Fight at Coyote Crutcher's"

Slowly Roger Kilraine's panicky fear diminished. A plan took shape in his brain. Why not blame Tug Moran for Pete Crutcher's death? Of course! That was it. Moran's body would be at Coyote Crutcher's cabin. It would be dark. He would, as he had planned, kill the blackmailing son-of-a-bitch. Then he could empty his gun. Dixie, in the cabin, could not tell whether he was fighting one man or a dozen. And when the sheriff and posse arrived, he would have a smooth story built up for them and the evidence there to bear out the tale. He would be acclaimed a hero. There would be none to prove that he lied. His bruised lips twisted in a smile.

His head ached, and he felt stiff and sore from the effect of Pete's blows. His nose was badly swollen, and he winced at the pain as he wiped away the blood. He did not know where to spend those long hours until dark. Why not go into Moran's Crossing? That was the idea! A few drinks would make him feel better. He could wash up, too. He'd bribe Spider into keeping silent about his visit. After he had rescued Dixie, he'd make it all right with the gambler. Close-mouthed chap, Spider. Roger urged his horse to a faster gait and took the short cut that led to the Crossing.

He was astonished to find the place empty. Not a soul in

sight. And that was all the better for Roger. He'd have a few drinks and then start. He bathed his swollen face and had another drink. The fiery liquor warmed him and had a soothing effect on his nerves. He was so engrossed in his thoughts that he but dimly heard the footsteps in the saloon. Absently he looked up as the sound of the footsteps halted in the doorway between the card room and the saloon. Expecting to see Spider, he looked up, a smile of welcome on his lips.

The smile froze. Roger's pig eyes widened with horror, for it was Pete Crutcher who stood in the doorway — Pete Crutcher, swaying like a drunken man, a ghastly smile on his lips. Pete's .45 came to full cock with an ominous click.

"Where's Dixie?" cried Pete. "Tell me quick. I'm going to kill you in a minute."

"I don't know . . . ," he began, then cowered back as he read the terrible message in Pete's bloodshot eyes. Roger Kilraine knew that he was facing death, and the sudden knowledge crumpled him. Cowering, cringing to hide from that terrible look, he fell to his knees. "For heaven's sake, Crutcher, don't kill me! I'll tell! I'll tell you the whole thing!"

Sobbing with terror, he told the whole story from the beginning, told of the theft from Burnett's safe, of the plot to capture Dixie, told it from beginning to end, his words crowding each other in his haste to get them out.

"Send me to prison, do anything you want, Crutcher, only spare my life. I'll do anything you say. I'll devote the rest of my life to making amends. You wouldn't shoot me down in cold blood, Pete. You wouldn't. Surely you won't kill me this way."

"Shut up, you yellow cur! Moran's a killer. You know that! And it's Moran you've thrown in with. And you're to meet him at the cabin at dark, eh?" Pete laughed, and Roger shuddered.

"Don't kill me, Crutcher! Don't! I. . . ."

"Dry up," growled out Pete. "I'm going to lock you up somewhere and leave you till I get back. If you've been lying, I'll kill you. There's an old dugout behind here. I remember it as a kid. Coyote and Moran locked me in there more than once. Get on your feet."

Propelled along by the barrel of Pete's gun, Roger was marched to the dugout and shoved inside. Pete was too sick and concerned with Dixie's safety to hear the groan that came from the dark interior of the dugout. He shoved Roger inside and barred the door. Then he staggered back to the card room. He took a pull at the whiskey bottle, and the stuff dulled the pain that racked his body. Then he got his horse and rode toward the cabin in the cañon. It would be terrible to wait those hours until darkness had fallen, but Pete realized the wisdom of waiting. By riding slowly he would make the cabin by dark, and then Tug Moran would pay the price — pay it with his life.

Vaguely he wondered what had become of Spider Parks. It was possible that Moran had killed the gambler. Otherwise Spider would never have allowed Moran to carry out his kidnapping plan.

The going was tortuous. Sometimes Pete fainted and would fall from the saddle. His horse would be grazing when he woke up. Then he would mount once more and ride on. It was getting to be dusk now. He muttered to himself as his horse negotiated the steep trail that led to the cabin.

Was that a light in the cabin? Why did the devilish thing move about so? Now it was gone. No, there it was, brighter and bigger now. It was the lighted doorway of the cabin.

And a man stood there — a man with a mask on his face. With a crazy laugh Pete rode straight at the man, then leaped to the ground, firing as he walked toward the man who suddenly jerked off the mask. Spider. It couldn't be! It was the effect of his wound.

Pete fired twice, his shots going wild. The man had not fired once at him. A leap and the man was on him, throwing him to the ground just as a rifle flashed in the brush and a bullet sped past his head. Vaguely, as if in a dream, Pete felt the gun wrenched from his hand, felt the weight of the man's body on top of him, heard the roar of the gun as the man fired once, twice, then ceased firing.

The man leaped to his feet now, firing again as he ran toward the brush from whence the rifle fire had come. Pete, face downward on the ground, made a last effort to rise, then fell, to lie quietly.

Spider Parks, his cold eyes blazing, dragged the twisting form of Tug Moran into the clearing. Moran made no sound. But there was a defiant look in his murderous eyes that bespoke the outlaw's challenge to death.

"You're done for, Tug," panted Spider. "I got you. You won't live fifteen minutes. You planted me with an empty gun to make me a target for Roger Kilraine, but you lost. You bet I double-crossed you, Moran, but I didn't expect the cards to fall this way. You killed The Parson. He was my brother. You killed the girl I loved and the man to whom she was married. And you killed a baby, Moran, a little innocent baby. I would hate to meet God with a record as black as yours."

Moran smiled a twisted, sneering smile. "Papers," he muttered, and thrust his hand inside the bosom of his shirt that was stained crimson. There was a look of cunning in the dying man's eyes. The hand in his bosom came forth suddenly, holding the little Derringer.

As the gun roared, Spider sprang to one side. The lead slug tore past his head. A swift kick sent the wicked little weapon spinning.

"Missed," whispered Moran, and with a curse on his lips sank back dead.

Spider's first act was to relieve Moran of that package wrapped in oiled silk. Shoving the stained package in his pocket, he ran to the cabin.

Dixie Burnett, disheveled but unharmed, was freed from the ropes that bound her, and the gag was taken from her mouth. She and Spider talked as they worked over Pete. When Pete at last opened his eyes, Dixie's arms went around him, and she held him close, murmuring love words into his ear, crying and laughing. Pete's good arm went up and around her, and he grinned contentedly.

Spider had slipped outside and was examining the papers. Men had given their lives for those papers. Spider scanned them thoughtfully.

Inside the cabin, Pete was talking to the girl. "I'm a 'breed and the son of Coyote Crutcher, but I love you, dear."

"And I love you, Peter. I'd love you if you were the son of Lucifer. I want. . . ."

Spider had entered the cabin, entered with a shout that cut short Dixie's speech.

"Listen to this, youngsters! Listen closely, too. This is a statement signed by Coyote Crutcher and his squaw. It reads . . . 'To them that it concerns . . . if me and my squaw dies, this letter goes to Ross Burnett, because Ross will see that the kid gits a fair shake. Me and Moran done fer his mammy and his pappy, Jim Rutledge. But we never killed the kid. My squaw's kid had died the night afore we brung

Jim Rutledge's wife and kid to my cabin. It's the squaw's kid that's buried near the cabin. Peter Crutcher is really Peter Rutledge. He's entitled to the whole Circle Bar Ranch because Charlie Kilraine hired me and Tug to do these killings. Pete's ornery, but he's a good kid in spots, and I aim he should get a square deal when I'm gone.' "

Spider finished reading aloud. Pete and Dixie were staring at him.

"I had a hunch there was something queer, Spider," said Pete. "I dug up the baby's grave and saw that he'd been buried with all the trimmings of an Injun burial. Beaded moccasins, buckskin dress, and the rest. And the kid's toys were in the grave with it. Injun toys that the squaw had made. I wish Dad Ross was here to. . . ."

"Speak uh the devil and he'll show up!" called a voice from the doorway, and Ross Burnett, followed by Rawhide, burst into the cabin. All was confusion for some time as explanations were made, everyone speaking at once.

"Me and Rawhide hit the trail, quick as Betty told us that you'd bin to the ranch, Pete. We found the saloon at the Crossing deserted, and was about to come on to the cabin when Rawhide opened the dugout and found them gents in there. Spider, you shore did work Charlie Kilraine over plumb scandalous. But one of Kilraine's gunmen who was in there says it was a helluva fight, with you handcuffed, Spider. Oh, he's livin' and will tell it to the law. Afore we go any further, I want to declare myself here regardin' you, Spider. We ain't a-carin' what you bin, ner who your friends was. We need a man to kinda run the commissary and take care uh the books. Name your salary and write out your own check at the end uh the month."

"I was the one that found the combination of your safe, Burnett. I opened it one night at Moran's request, and he gave the combination to young Kilraine. You don't want a man on your ranch that has pulled a trick like that."

"Spider's the real goods, Dad," said Pete. "Don't let him run away."

"I don't aim to, Pete. And when we tear down that drift fence along Box Elder Crick and combine the T Down and Circle Bar spreads, we'll put him with the fence crew fer punishment, eh, son?"

Rawhide was grinning widely. "Pete Rutledge!" he said. "Now who'd've thunk it? Still, I allers claimed he weren't no regular human, Ross. Since that day at the ranch when the ragged li'l ol' kid whupped Kilraine's cub, Pete done had me hog-tied. Mebbeso you are Pete Rutledge, but to some uh us, you're still what you always bin since that day, Pete Burnett, by golly. And if Jim Rutledge was livin', he'd agree with us. Let's git goin', folks. Pete's gotta git that wing uh his patched up. Is she a-hurtin' pow'ful bad, boy?"

"Hurting? I clean forgot the darn thing was busted, Rawhide. And look here, you old sheepherder! Don't begin tearing down that fence till I'm able to get around. I'm pulling the first staple on that line fence. I pull 'er halfway. Dad Ross jerks 'er out!"

"And me and Spider will do the pantin' and sweatin'," finished Rawhide.

Walt Coburn was born in White Sulphur Springs, Montana Territory. He was once called "King of the Pulps" by Fred Gipson and promoted by Fiction House as "The Cowboy Author". He was the son of cattleman Robert Coburn, then owner of the Circle C ranch on Beaver Creek within sight of the Little Rockies. Coburn's family eventually moved to San Diego while still operating the Circle C. Robert Coburn used to commute between Montana and California by train and he would take his youngest son with him. When Coburn got drunk one night, he had an argument with his father that led to his leaving the family. In the course of his wanderings he entered Mexico and for a brief period actually became an enlisted man in the so-called "Gringo Battalion" of Pancho Villa's army.

Following his enlistment in the U.S. Army during the Great War, Coburn began writing Western short stories. For a year and a half he wrote and wrote before selling his first story to Bob Davis, editor of *Argosy-All Story.* Coburn married and moved to Tucson because his wife suffered from a respiratory condition. In a little adobe hut behind the main house Coburn practiced his art and for almost four decades he wrote approximately 600,000 words a year. Coburn's early fiction from his Golden Age—1924–1940—is his best, including his novels, *Mavericks* (1929) and *Barb Wire* (1931), as well as many short novels published only in magazines that now are being collected for the first time. In his Western stories, as Charles M. Russell and Eugene Manlove Rhodes, two men Coburn had known and admired in life, he captured the cow country and recreated it just as it was already passing from sight.